The Curse of Chalion

Other books by Lois McMaster Bujold

LOIS McMASTER BUJOLD

The Curse of Chalion

An Imprint of HarperCollins Publishers

EOS

EOS
An Imprint of HarperCollins *Publishers*
10 East 53rd Street
New York, New York 10022-5299

Library of Congress Cataloging-in-Publication Data

Bujold, Lois McMaster.
    The curse of Chalion / Lois M. Bujold.
        p. cm.
    ISBN 0-380-97901-2 (hardcover)
    I. Title.

PS3552.U397 C87 2001
813'.54--dc21

00-046586

First Eos hardcover printing: August 2001
First Eos special printing: December 2000

Eos Trademark Reg. U.S. Pat. Off. and in Other Countries,
Marca Registrada, Hecho en U.S.A.
HarperCollins ® is a registered trademark of HarperCollins Publishers Inc.

Printed in the U.S.A.

FIRST EDITION

10 9 8 7 6 5 4 3 2 1

www.eosbooks.com

ACKNOWLEDGMENTS

The Author would like to thank Professor William D. Phillips, Jr., for History 3714, the most useful four hundred dollars and ten weeks I ever spent in school; Pat "Oh, c'mon, it'll be fun" Wrede for the letter game that first drew the proto-Cazaril, blinking and stumbling, from my back-brain into the light of day; and, I suppose, the utility companies of Minneapolis for that hot shower one cold February, where the first two items collided unexpectedly in my head to create a new world and all the people in it.

Cazaril heard the mounted
horsemen on the road before he saw
them. He glanced over his shoulder.
The well-worn track behind him curled up around a rolling rise,
what passed for a hill on these high windy plains, before dipping
again into the late-winter muck of Baocia's bony soil. At his feet a
little rill, too small and intermittent to rate a culvert or a bridge,
trickled greenly across the track from the sheep-cropped pastures
above. The thump of hooves, jangle of harness, clink of bells, creak
of gear and careless echo of voices came on at too quick a rhythm
to be some careful farmer with a team, or parsimonious pack-men
driving their mules.

The cavalcade trotted around the side of the rise riding two by
two, in full panoply of their order, some dozen men. Not bandits—
Cazaril let out his breath, and swallowed his unsettled stomach
back down. Not that he had anything to offer bandits but sport. He
trudged a little way off the track and turned to watch them pass.

The horsemen's chain shirts were silvered, glinting in the wa-
tery morning sunlight, for show, not for use. Their tabards of blue,
dyes almost matching one with another, were worked with white
in the sigil of the Lady of Spring. Their gray cloaks were thrown
back like banners in the breeze of their passing, pinned at their
shoulders with silver badges that had all the tarnish polished off
today. Soldier-brothers of ceremony, not of war; they would have
no desire to get Cazaril's stubborn bloodstains on *those* clothes.

To Cazaril's surprise, their captain held up a hand as they came near. The column crashed raggedly to a halt, the squelch and suck of the hooves trailing off in a way that would have had Cazaril's father's old horse-master bellowing grievous and entertaining insults at such a band of boys as this. Well, no matter.

"You there, old fellow," the leader called across the saddlebow of his banner-carrier at Cazaril.

Cazaril, alone on the road, barely kept his head from swiveling around to see who was being so addressed. They took him for some local farm lout, trundling to market or on some errand, and he supposed he looked the part: worn boots mud-weighted, a thick jumble of mismatched charity clothes keeping the chill southeast wind from freezing his bones. He was grateful to all the gods of the year's turning for every grubby stitch of that fabric, eh. Two weeks of beard itching his chin. Fellow indeed. The captain might with justice have chosen more scornful appellations. But . . . old?

The captain pointed down the road to where another track crossed it. "Is that the road to Valenda?"

It had been . . . Cazaril had to stop and count it in his head, and the sum dismayed him. Seventeen years since he had ridden last down this road, going off not to ceremony but to real war in the provincar of Baocia's train. Although bitter to be riding a gelding and not a finer warhorse, he'd been just as glossy-haired and young and arrogant and vain of his dress as the fine young animals up there staring down at him. *Today, I should be happy for a donkey, though I had to bend my knees to keep from trailing my toes in the mud.* Cazaril smiled back up at the soldier-brothers, fully aware of what hollowed-out purses lay gaping and disemboweled behind most of those rich facades.

They stared down their noses at him as though they could smell him from there. He was not a person they wished to impress, no lord or lady who might hand down largesse to them as they might to him; still, he would do for them to practice their aristocratic airs upon. They mistook his returning stare for admiration, perhaps, or maybe just for half-wittedness.

He bit back the temptation to steer them wrong, up into some sheep byre or wherever that deceptively broad-looking crossroad petered out. No trick to pull on the Daughter's own guardsmen on the eve of the Daughter's Day. And besides, the men who joined the holy military orders were not especially noted for their senses of humor, and he might pass them again, being bound for the same town himself. Cazaril cleared his throat, which hadn't spoken to a man since yesterday. "No, Captain. The road to Valenda has a roya's milestone." Or it had, once. "A mile or three farther on. You can't mistake it." He pulled a hand out of the warmth of the folds of his coat, and waved onward. His fingers didn't really straighten right, and he found himself waving a claw. The chill air bit his swollen joints, and he tucked his hand hastily back into its burrow of cloth.

The captain nodded at his banner-carrier, a thick-shouldered . . . fellow, who cradled his banner pole in the crook of his elbow and fumbled out his purse. He fished in it, looking no doubt for a coin of sufficiently small denomination. He had a couple brought up to the light, between his fingers, when his horse jinked. A coin—a gold royal, not a copper vaida—spurted out of his grip and spun down into the mud. He stared after it, aghast, but then controlled his features. He would not dismount in front of his fellows to grub in the muck and retrieve it. Not like the peasant he expected Cazaril to be: for consolation, he raised his chin and smiled sourly, waiting for Cazaril to dive frantically and amusingly after this unexpected windfall.

Instead, Cazaril bowed and intoned, "May the blessings of the Lady of Spring fall upon your head, young sir, in the same spirit as your bounty to a roadside vagabond, and as little begrudged."

If the young soldier-brother had had more wits about him, he might well have unraveled this mockery, and Cazaril the seeming-peasant drawn a well-earned horsewhip across his face. Little enough chance of that, judging by the brother's bull-like stare, though the captain's lips twisted in exasperation. But the captain just shook his head and gestured his column onward.

If the banner-bearer was too proud to scramble in the mud, Cazaril was much too *tired* to. He waited till the baggage train, a gaggle of servants and mules bringing up the rear, had passed before crouching painfully down and retrieving the little spark from the cold water seeping into a horse's print. The adhesions in his back pulled cruelly. *Gods. I do move like an old man.* He caught his breath and heaved to his feet, feeling a century old, feeling like road dung stuck to the boot heel of the Father of Winter as he made his way out of the world.

He polished the mud off the coin—little enough even if gold— and pulled out his own purse. Now there was an empty bladder. He dropped the thin disk of metal into the leather mouth and stared down at its lonely glint. He sighed and tucked the pouch away. Now he had a hope for bandits to steal again. Now he had a reason to fear. He reflected on his new burden, so great for its weight, as he stumped up the road in the wake of the soldier-brothers. Almost not worth it. Almost. Gold. Temptation to the weak, weariness to the wise . . . what was it to a dull-eyed bull of a soldier, embarrassed by his accidental largesse?

Cazaril gazed around the barren landscape. Not much in the way of trees or coverts, except in that distant watercourse over there, the bare branches and brambles lining it charcoal-gray in the hazy light. The only shelter anywhere in sight was an abandoned windmill on the height to his left, its roof fallen in and its vanes broken down and rotting. Still . . . just in case . . .

Cazaril swung off the road and began trudging up the hill. Hillock, compared to the mountain passes he'd traversed a week ago. The climb still stole his wind; almost, he turned back. The gusts up here were stronger, flowing over the ground, riffling the silver-gold tufts of winter's dry grasses. He nipped out of the raw air into the mill's shadowed darkness and mounted a dubious and shaking staircase winding partway up the inner wall. He peered out the shutterless window.

On the road below, a man belabored a brown horse back along the track. No soldier-brother: one of the servants, with his reins in one hand and a stout cudgel in the other. Sent back by his master to secretly shake the accidental coin back out of the hide of the roadside vagabond? He rode up around the curve, then, in a few minutes, back again. He paused at the muddy rill, turned back and forth in his saddle to peer around the empty slopes, shook his head in disgust, and spurred on to join his fellows again.

Cazaril realized he was laughing. It felt odd, unfamiliar, a shudder through his shoulders that wasn't cold or shock or gut-wringing fear. And the strange hollow absence of . . . what? Corrosive envy? Ardent desire? He didn't want to follow the soldier-brothers, didn't even want to lead them anymore. Didn't want to be them. He'd watched their parade as idly as a man watching a dumb-show in the marketplace. *Gods. I must be tired.* Hungry, too. It was still a quarter-day's walk to Valenda, where he might find a moneylender who could change his royal for more useful copper vaidas. Tonight, by the blessing of the Lady, he might sleep in an inn and not a cow byre. He could buy a hot meal. He could buy a shave, a *bath* . . .

He turned, his eyes adjusted now to the half shadows in the mill. Then he saw the body splayed out on the rubble-strewn floor.

He froze in panic, but then breathed again when he saw the body didn't. No live man could lie unmoving in that strange back-bent position. Cazaril felt no fear of dead men. Whatever had made them dead, now . . .

Despite the corpse's stillness, Cazaril scooped up a loose cobble from the floor before approaching it. A man, plump, middle-aged, judging from the gray in his neatly trimmed beard. The face under the beard was swollen and empurpled. Strangled? There were no marks showing on his throat. His clothing was sober but very fine, yet ill fitting, tight and pulled about. The brown wool gown and black sleeveless vest-cloak edged with silver-embroidered cord might be the garb of a rich merchant or minor lord with austere tastes, or of a scholar with ambition. Not a farmer or artisan, in any case. Nor soldier. The hands, mottled purple-yellow and swollen also, lacked calluses, lacked—Cazaril glanced at his own left hand, where the two missing finger ends testified to the ill-advisedness of arguing with a grappling rope—lacked damage. The man bore no ornaments at all, no chains or rings or seals to match his rich dress. Had some scavenger been here before Cazaril?

Cazaril gritted his teeth, bending for a closer look, a motion punished by the pulls and aches in his own body. Not ill fitted, and not fat—the body was unnaturally swollen, too, like the face and hands. But anyone that far gone in decay ought to have filled this dreary shelter with his stench, enough to have choked Cazaril when he'd first ducked through the broken door. No scents here but some musky perfume or incense, tallow smoke, and clay-cold sweat.

Cazaril discarded his first thought, that the poor fellow had been robbed and murdered on the road and dragged up here out of sight, as he looked over the cleared patch of hard-packed dirt floor around the man. Five candle stumps, burned to puddles, blue, red, green, black, white. Little piles of herbs and ash, all kicked about now. A dark and broken pile of feathers that resolved itself

in the shadows as a dead crow, its neck twisted. A moment's further search turned up the dead rat that went with it, its little throat
cut. Rat and Crow, sacred to the Bastard, god of all disasters out of
season: tornadoes, earthquakes, droughts, floods, miscarriages, and
murders . . . *Wanted to compel the gods, did you?* The fool had tried
to work death magic, by the look of it, and paid death magic's customary price. Alone?

Touching nothing, Cazaril levered himself to his feet and took
a turn around both the inside and the outside of the sagging mill.
No packs, no cloaks or possessions dumped in a corner. A horse or
horses had been tied up on the side opposite the road, recently by
dampness of their droppings, but they were gone now.

Cazaril sighed. This was no business of his, but it was impious
to leave a man dead and abandoned, to rot without ceremony. The
gods alone knew how long it would be till someone else found
him. He was clearly a well-to-do man, though—someone would be
looking. Not the sort to disappear tracelessly and unmissed like a
ragged vagabond. Cazaril set aside the temptation to slide back
down to the road and go off pretending he'd never seen the man.

Cazaril set off down the track leading from the back side of the
mill. There ought to be a farmhouse at the end of it, people, something. But he'd not walked more than a few minutes before he met
a man leading a donkey, loaded high with brush and wood, climbing
up around the curve. The man stopped and eyed him suspiciously.

"The Lady of Spring give you good morning, sir," said Cazaril
politely. What harm was in it, for Cazaril to *Sir* a farmer? He'd
kissed the scaly feet of lesser men by far, in the abject terrified slavery of the galleys.

The man, after an appraising look, gave him a half salute and a
mumbled, "B'yer'Lady."

"Do you live hereabouts?"

"Aye," the man said. He was middle-aged, well fed, his hooded
coat, like Cazaril's shabbier one, plain but serviceable. He walked
as though he owned the land he stood on, though probably not
much more.

"I, ah," Cazaril pointed back up the track. "I'd stepped off the
road a moment, to take shelter in that mill up there"—no need to
go into details of what he'd been sheltering from—"and I found a
dead man."

"Aye," the man said.

Cazaril hesitated, wishing he hadn't dropped his cobble. "You know about him?"

"Saw his horse tied up there, this morning."

"Oh." He might have gone on down the road after all, with no harm done. "Have you any idea who the poor fellow was?"

The farmer shrugged, and spat. "He's not from around here, is all I can say. I had our divine of the Temple up, soon as I realized what sort of bad doings had been going on there last night. She took away all the fellow's goods that would come loose, to hold till called for. His horse is in my barn. A fair trade, aye, for the wood and oil to speed him out. The divine said he daren't be left till nightfall." He gestured to the high-piled load of burnables hitched to the donkey's back, gave the halter rope a tug, and started up the track again. Cazaril fell into step beside him.

"Do you have any idea what the fellow was doing?" asked Cazaril.

"Plain enough what he was doing." The farmer snorted. "And got what he deserved for it."

"Um . . . or who he was doing it to?"

"No idea. I'll leave it to the Temple. I do wish he hadn't done it on my land. Dropping his bad luck all over . . . like to haunt the place hereafter. I'll purge him with fire and burn down that cursed wreck of a mill at the same time, aye. No good to leave it standing, it's too close to the road. Attracts"—he eyed Cazaril—"trouble."

Cazaril paced along for another moment. Finally, he asked, "You plan to burn him with his clothes on?"

The farmer studied him sideways, summing up the poverty of his garb. "*I'm* not touching anything of his. I wouldn't have taken the horse, except it's no charity to turn the poor beast loose to starve."

Cazaril said more hesitantly, "Would you mind if I took the clothes, then?"

"I'm not the one as you need to ask, aye? Deal with *him*. If you dare. I won't stop you."

"I'll . . . help you lay him out."

The farmer blinked. "Now, that would be welcome."

Cazaril judged the farmer was secretly more than pleased to leave the corpse handling to him. Perforce, Cazaril had to leave the farmer to pile up the bigger logs for the pyre, built inside the mill, though he offered a few mild suggestions how to place them to gain the best draft and be most sure of taking down what remained of the building. He helped carry in the lighter brush.

The farmer watched from a safe distance as Cazaril undressed the corpse, tugging the layered garments off over the stiffened limbs. The man was swollen further even than he'd appeared at first, his abdomen puffing out obscenely when Cazaril finally pulled his fine embroidered cotton undershirt from him. It was rather frightening. But it couldn't be contagion after all, not with this uncanny lack of smell. Cazaril wondered, if the body weren't burned by nightfall, if it was likely to explode or rupture, and if it did, what would come out of it . . . or enter into it. He bundled up the clothing, only a little stained, as quickly as he could. The shoes were too small, and he left them. He and the farmer together heaved the corpse onto the pyre.

When all was readied, Cazaril fell to his knees, shut his eyes, and chanted out the prayer for the dead. Not knowing which god had taken up the man's soul, though he could make a shrewd guess, he addressed all five of the Holy Family in turn, speaking clearly and plainly. All offerings must be one's best, even if all one had to offer was words. "Mercy from the Father and the Mother, mercy from the Sister and the Brother, Mercy from the Bastard, five times mercy, High Ones, we beseech you." Whatever sins the stranger had committed, he had surely paid. Mercy, High Ones. *Not justice, please, not justice. We would all be fools to pray for justice.*

When he'd finished, he climbed stiffly back to his feet and looked around. Thoughtfully, he collected the rat and the crow, and added their little corpses to the man's, at his head and feet.

It was Cazaril's day for the gods' own luck, it seemed. He wondered which kind it would prove to be this time.

❧ A COLUMN OF OILY SMOKE ROSE FROM THE BURNING mill as Cazaril started up the road to Valenda once more, the dead man's clothes tied into a tight bundle on his back. Though they were less filthy than the clothes he wore, he would, he thought, find a laundress and have them thoroughly cleaned before donning them. His copper vaidas were dwindling sadly in his mind's accounting, but the services of a laundress would be worth them.

He'd slept last night in a barn, shivering in the straw, his meal a half a loaf of stale bread. The remaining half had been his breakfast. It was nearly three hundred miles from the port city of Zagosur, on Ibra's mild coast, to the middle of Baocia, centralmost province of Chalion. He hadn't been able to walk the distance nearly as quickly as he'd calculated. In Zagosur, the Temple Hospital of the Mother's Mercy was dedicated to the succor of men cast up, in all the various ways they could be cast up, by the sea. The charity purse the acolytes there had given him had run thin, then out altogether, before he'd reached his goal. But only just before. One more day, he'd figured, less than a day. If he could just put one foot in front of the other for one more day, he might reach his refuge and crawl into it.

When he'd started from Ibra, his head had been full of plans for how to ask the Dowager Provincara for a place, for old times' sake, in her household. At the foot of her table. Something, anything at all so long as it was not too hard. His ambition had dwindled as he'd slogged east over the mountain passes into the cooler heights of the central plateau. Maybe her castle warder or her horse-master would grant him a place in her stables, or a place in her kitchen, and he need not intrude upon the great lady at all. If he could beg a place as a scullion, he wouldn't even have to give his real name. He doubted anyone was left in her household by now who'd know him from the charmed days when he'd served the late Provincar dy Baocia as a page.

The dream of a silent, abashed place by the kitchen fire, nameless, not bellowed at by any creature more alarming than a cook, for any task more dreadful than drawing water or carrying firewood, had drawn him onward into the last of the winter winds. The vision of rest drove him as an obsession, that and the knowledge that every stride put another yard between himself and the nightmare of the sea. He'd bemused himself for hours on the lonely road, revolving suitable new servile names for his new, anonymous self. But now, it seemed, he need not appear before the shocked eyes of her court dressed in poor men's castoffs after all. *Instead, Cazaril begs a peasant for the clothes off a corpse, and is grateful for both their favors. Is. Is. Most humbly grateful. Most humbly.*

*   *   *

❧THE TOWN OF VALENDA TUMBLED DOWN OVER ITS low hill like a rich quilt worked in red and gold, red for the tile roofs, gold for the native stone, both glowing in the sun. Cazaril blinked at the dazzle of color in his blurring eyes, the familiar hues of his homeland. The houses of Ibra were all whitewashed, too bright in their hot northern noons, bleached and blinding. This ochre sandstone was the perfect shade for a house, a town, a country—a caress upon the eyes. At the top of the hill, like a golden crown in truth, the Provincara's castle sprawled, its curtain walls seeming to waver in his vision. He stared at it, daunted, for a little, then slogged onward, his steps somehow going faster than he'd been able to push them all this long journey, despite the shaking, aching weariness of his legs.

It was past the hour for the markets, so the streets were quiet and serene as he threaded through them to the main square. At the temple gate, he approached an elderly woman who looked unlikely to try to follow and rob him, and asked his way to a moneylender. The moneylender filled his hand with a satisfying weight of copper vaidas in exchange for his tiny royal, and directed him to the laundress and the public bath. He paused on the way only long enough to buy an oil cake from a lone street vendor, and devour it.

He poured out vaidas on the laundress's counter and negotiated the loan of a pair of linen drawstring trousers and a tunic, together with a pair of straw sandals in which he might trot down the street through the now-mild afternoon to the baths. In competently red hands she carried off all his vile clothing and his filthy boots. The bath's barber trimmed his hair and beard while he sat, still, in a real chair, oh wonderful. The bath boy served him tea. And then it was back to the bath courtyard itself, to stand on the flagstones and scrub himself all over with scented soap and wait for the bath boy to sluice him down with a bucket of warm water. In joyous anticipation, Cazaril eyed the huge copper-bottomed wooden tank that was sized for six men, or women every other day, but which by the happy chance of the hour he looked to have all to himself. The brazier underneath kept the water steaming. He could soak there all afternoon, while the laundress boiled his clothing.

The bath boy climbed the stool and poured the water over his head, while Cazaril turned and sputtered under the stream. He opened his eyes to find the boy staring at him, mouth agape.

"Were you . . . were you a deserter?" the boy choked out.

Oh. His back, the ropy red mess of scars piled one across another so thickly as to leave no untouched skin between, legacy of the last flogging the Roknari galley-masters had given him. Here in the royacy of Chalion, army deserters were among the few criminals punished so savagely by that particular means. "No," said Cazaril firmly. "I'm not a deserter." Cast-off, certainly; betrayed, perhaps. But he'd never deserted a post, not even his most disastrous ones.

The boy snapped his mouth shut, dropped his wooden bucket with a clunk, and scampered out. Cazaril sighed, and made for the tank.

He'd just lowered his aching body to the chin in the heavenly heat when the bath owner stomped into the tiny tiled courtyard.

"Out!" the owner roared. "Out of there, you—!"

Cazaril recoiled in terror as the bath man seized him by the hair and dragged him bodily up out of the water. "*What?*" The man shoved his tunic and trousers and sandals at him, all in a wad, and dragged him fiercely by the arm out of the courtyard and into the front of the shop. "Here, wait, what are you doing? I can't go naked into the street!"

The bath man wheeled him around, and released him momentarily. "Get dressed, and get out. I run a respectable place here! Not for the likes of you! Go down to the whorehouse. Or better still, drown yourself in the river!"

Dazed and dripping, Cazaril fumbled the tunic over his head, yanked up the trousers, and tried to cram his feet back into the straw sandals while holding up the pants' drawstring and being shoved again toward the door. It slammed in his face as he turned, realization dawning upon him. The other crime punished by flogging near to death in the royacy of Chalion was the rape of a virgin or a boy. His face flushed hot. "But it wasn't—but I didn't—I was sold to the corsairs of Roknar—"

He stood trembling. He considered beating on the door, and insisting those within listen to his explanations. *Oh, my poor honor.* The bath man was the bath boy's father, Cazaril rather guessed.

He was laughing. And crying. Teetering on the ragged edge of . . . something that frightened him more than the outraged bath man. He gulped for breath. He had not the stamina for an argument, and even if he could get them to listen, why should they believe him? He rubbed his eyes with the soft linen of his sleeve. It had that sharp, pleasant scent left only by the track of a good hot iron. It tumbled him back to memories of life in houses, not in ditches. It seemed a thousand years ago.

Defeated, he turned and shuffled back up the street to the laundress's green-painted door again. Its bell rang as he pushed timidly back inside.

"Have you a corner where I might sit, ma'am?" he asked her, when she popped back out at the bell's summons. "I . . . finished earlier than . . ." his voice died in muffled shame.

She shrugged sturdy shoulders. "Ah, aye. Come back with me. Wait." She dived below her counter and came up with a small book, the span of Cazaril's hand and bound in plain undyed leather. "Here's your book. You're lucky I checked your pockets, or it would be a mucky mess by now, believe you me."

Startled, Cazaril picked it up. It must have lain concealed in the thick cloth of the dead man's outer cloak; he hadn't felt it when he'd bundled the garment up so hastily back in the mill. This ought to go to that divine of the Temple, with the rest of the dead man's possessions. *Well, I'm not walking it back there tonight, that's certain.* He would return it as soon as he was able.

For now, he merely said, "Thank you, ma'am," to the laundress, and followed her into a central court with a deep well, similar to her neighbor's of the bathhouse, where a fire kept a cauldron on the boil, and a quartet of young women scrubbed and splashed at the laundry tubs. She gestured him to a bench by the wall and he sat down out of range of the splashes, staring a while in a kind of disembodied bliss at the peaceful, busy scene. Time was he would have scorned to eye a troupe of red-faced peasant girls, saving his glances for the fine ladies. How had he never realized how beautiful laundresses were? Strong and laughing, moving like a dance, and kind, so kind, so kind . . .

Finally, his hand moved in reawakened curiosity to look in the book. It might bear the dead man's name, solving a mystery. He flipped it open to discover its pages covered in a thicket of handwriting, with occasional little scratchy diagrams. Entirely in a cipher.

He blinked, and bent more closely, his eye beginning to take the cipher apart almost despite his own volition. It was mirror-writing. And with a substitution-of-letters system—those could be tedious to break down. But the chance of a short word, three times repeated on the page, handed him his key. The merchant had chosen the most childish of ciphers, merely shifting each letter one position and not troubling to shuffle his pattern thereafter. Except that . . . this wasn't in the Ibran language spoken, in its various dialects, in the royacies of Ibra, Chalion, and Brajar. It was in Darthacan, spoken in the southernmost provinces of Ibra and great Darthaca beyond the mountains. And the man's handwriting was dreadful, his spelling worse, and his command of Darthacan grammar apparently almost nonexistent. This was going to be harder than Cazaril had thought. He would need paper and pen, a quiet place, time, and a good light, if he was to make head or tail of this mess. Well, it might have been worse. It might have been ciphered in bad Roknari.

It was almost certainly the man's notes on his magic experiments, however. That much Cazaril could tell. Enough to convict and hang him, if he hadn't been dead already. The punishments for practicing—no, for *attempting*—death magic were ferocious. Punishment for succeeding was generally considered redundant, as there was no case Cazaril knew of a magical assassination that had not cost the life of its caster. Whatever the link was by which the practitioner forced the Bastard to let one of his demons into the world, it always returned with two souls or none.

That being so, there should have been another corpse made somewhere in Baocia last night. . . . By its nature, death magic wasn't very popular. It did not allow substitutions or proxies in its double-edged scything. To kill was to be killed. Knife, sword, poison, cudgel, almost any other means was a better choice if one wanted to survive one's own murderous effort. But, in delusion or desperation, men still attempted it from time to time. This book must definitely be taken back to that rural divine, for her to pass along to whatever superior of the gods' Temple ended up investigating the case for the royacy. Cazaril's brow wrinkled, and he sat up, closing the frustrating volume.

The warm steam, the rhythm of the women's work and voices, and Cazaril's exhaustion tempted him to lie on his side, curled up on the bench with the book pillowed under his cheek. He would just close his eyes for a moment . . .

He woke with a start and a crick in his neck, his fingers closing around an unexpected weight of wool . . . one of the laundresses had thrown a blanket over him. An involuntary sigh of gratitude escaped his throat at this careless grace. He scrambled upright, checking the lay of the light. The courtyard was nearly all in shadow now. He must have slept for most of the afternoon. The sound waking him had been the thump of his cleaned and, to the limit they would take it, polished boots, dropped from the laundress's hand. She set the pile of Cazaril's folded clothing, fine and disreputable both, on the bench next to him.

Remembering the bath boy's reaction, Cazaril asked timorously, "Have you a room where I might dress, ma'am?" *Privately.*

She nodded cordially and led him to a modest bedroom at the back of the house, and left him. Western light poured through the little window. Cazaril sorted his clean laundry, and eyed with aversion the shabby clothes he'd been wearing for weeks. An oval mirror on a stand in the corner, the room's richest ornament, decided him.

Tentatively, with another prayer of thanks to the spirit of the departed man whose unexpected heir he had become, he donned clean cotton trews, the fine embroidered shirt, the brown wool robe—warm from the iron, though the seams were still a trifle damp—and finally the black vest-cloak that fell in a rich profusion of cloth and glint of silver to his ankles. The dead man's clothes were long enough, if loose on Cazaril's gaunt frame. He sat on the bed and pulled on his boots, their heels lopsided and their soles worn to scarcely more than the thickness of parchment. He had not seen himself in any mirror larger or better than a piece of polished steel for . . . three years? This one was glass, and tilted to show himself quite half at a time, from head to foot.

A stranger stared back at him. *Five gods, when did my beard go part-gray?* He touched its short-trimmed neatness with a trembling hand. At least his newly scissored hair had not begun to retreat from his forehead, much. If Cazaril had to guess himself merchant, lord, or scholar in this dress, he would have to say scholar; one of the more fanatic sort, hollow-eyed and a little crazed. The garments wanted chains of gold or silver, seals, a fine belt with studs or jewels, thick rings with gleaming stones, to proclaim him any rank higher. And yet the flowing lines suited him, he fancied. He stood a little straighter.

In any case, the roadside vagabond had vanished. In any case . . . here was not a man to beg a scullion's place from a castle cook.

He'd planned to buy a night's bed in an inn with the last of his vaidas and present himself to the Provincara in the morning. Uneasily, he wondered if gossip from the bath man had gotten round town very far yet. And if he would be denied entry to any safe and respectable house. . . .

Now, tonight. Go. He would climb to the castle and find out if he might claim refuge or not. *I cannot bear another night of not knowing.* Before the light failed. *Before my heart fails.*

He tucked the notebook back into the inside pocket of the black vest-cloak that had apparently concealed it before. Leaving the vagabond's clothing in a pile on the bed, he turned and strode from the room.

2

As he climbed the last slope to the main castle gate, Cazaril regretted he'd had no way to provision himself with a sword. The two guards in the green-and-black livery of the provincar of Baocia watched his unarmed approach without alarm, but also without any of the alert interest that might presage respect. Cazaril saluted the one wearing the sergeant's badge in his hat with only an austere, calculated nod. The servility he'd practiced in his mind was for some back gate, not this one, not if he expected to get any farther. At least, by the courtesy of his laundress, he'd been able to provision himself with the right names.

"Good evening, Sergeant. I am here to see the castle warder, the Ser dy Ferrej. I am Lupe dy Cazaril." Leaving the sergeant to guess, preferably wrongly, if he'd been summoned.

"On what business, sir?" the sergeant asked, polite but unimpressed.

Cazaril's shoulders straightened; he didn't know from what unused lumber room in the back of his soul the voice came, but it came out clipped and commanding nonetheless: "On his business, Sergeant."

Automatically, the sergeant saluted. "Yes, sir." His nod told off his fellow to stay sharp, and he gestured Cazaril to follow him through the open gate. "This way, sir. I'll ask if the warder will see you."

Cazaril's heart wrung as he stared around the broad cobbled

courtyard inside the castle gates. He'd worn out how much shoe leather, scampering across these stones on errands for the high household? The master of the pages had complained of bankruptcy in buskins, till the Provincara, laughing, had inquired if he would truly prefer a lazy page who would wear out the seat of his trousers instead, for if so, she could find a few to plague him with.

She still ran her household with a keen eye and a firm hand, it appeared. The liveries of the guards were in excellent condition, the cobbles of this yard were swept clean, and the small bare trees in tubs, flanking the major doorways, had flowers forced from bulbs gracing their feet, blooming bright and fair and perfectly timed for the Daughter's Day celebration tomorrow.

The guard gestured Cazaril to wait upon a bench against a wall still blessedly warm from the day's sun, while he went to the side door leading to the office quarters, and spoke to a house servant there who might, or might not, turn out the warder for this stranger. He'd not paced halfway back to his post before his comrade stuck his head around the gate to call, "The royse returns!"

The sergeant turned his head toward the servants' quarters to take up the bellow, "The royse returns! Look sharp, there!" and quickened his march.

Grooms and servants tumbled from various doors around the courtyard as a clatter of hooves and halloing voices sounded from outside the gates. First through the stone arches, with a self-supplied fanfare of unladylike but triumphant whoops, rode a pair of young women on blowing horses belly-splashed with mud.

"We win, Teidez!" the first called over her shoulder. She was dressed in a riding jacket of blue velvet, with a matching blue wool split skirt. Her hair escaped from under a girl's lace cap, somewhat askew, in ringlets neither blond nor red but a sort of glowing amber in the shaft of setting sunlight. She had a generous mouth, pale skin, and curiously heavy-lidded eyes, squeezed now with laughter. Her taller companion, a panting brunette in red, grinned and twisted in her saddle as the rest of the cavalcade followed.

An even younger gentleman, in a short scarlet jacket worked with beasts in silver thread, followed on an even more impressive horse, glossy black with silken tail bannering. He was flanked by two wooden-faced grooms, and followed by a frowning gentleman. He shared his—sister's? yes, surely—curly hair, a shade redder, and wide mouth, more pouting. "The race was over at the bottom of the hill, Iselle. You cheated."

She made an *Oh, pooh* face at her royal brother. Before the scrambling servant could position the ladies' mounting bench he was trying to bring to her, she slid from her saddle, bouncing on her booted toes.

Her dark-haired companion also preceded her groom to the dismount and handed off her reins to him, saying, "Give these poor beasts an extra walk, till they are quite cool, Deni. We have misused them terribly." Somewhat belying her words, she gave her horse a kiss on the middle of its white blaze, and, as it nudged her with practiced assurance, slipped it some treat from her pocket.

Last through the gate, a couple of minutes behind, came a red-faced older woman. "Iselle, Betriz, slow down! Mother and Daughter, you girls cannot gallop over half the hinterland of Valenda like a pair of lunatics!"

"We are slowed down. Indeed, we're stopped," the dark-haired girl pointed out logically. "We cannot outrun your tongue, good heart, no matter how we try. It is too fast for the speediest horse in Baocia."

The older woman made a moue of exasperation and waited for her groom to position her mounting bench. "Your grandmother bought you that lovely white mule, Royesse, why don't you ever ride him? It would be so much more suitable."

"And so much more sloooow," the amber-haired girl, laughing, shot back. "And anyway, poor Snowflake is all washed and braided for the procession tomorrow. The grooms would have been heartbroken if I'd taken him out and run him through the mud. They plan to keep him wrapped in sheets all night."

Wheezing, the older woman allowed her groom to help her dismount. Afoot again, she shook out her skirted legs and stretched her apparently aching back. The boy departed in a cluster of anxious servants, and the two young women, uncrushed by their waiting woman's continuing murmur of complaint, raced each other to the door to the main keep. She followed, shaking her head.

As they approached the door, a stoutish middle-aged man in severe black wool exited, and remarked to them in passing, in a voice without rancor but perfectly firm, "Betriz, if ever you gallop your horse home uphill like that again, I will take him from you.

And you can use up your *excessive* energy running after the royesse on foot."

She dropped him a swift curtsey, and a daunted murmur of, "Yes, Papa."

The amber-haired girl came instantly to attention. "Please excuse Betriz, Ser dy Ferrej. The fault was mine. Where I led, she had no choice but to follow."

His brow twitched, and he gave her a little bow. "Then you might meditate, Royesse, on what honor a captain can claim, who drags his followers into an error when he knows he will himself escape the punishment."

The amber-haired girl's wide lips twisted at this. After a long glance up under her lashes, she, too, dropped him a fraction of a curtsey, before both girls escaped further chastisement by dodging indoors. The man in black heaved a sigh. The waiting woman, laboring after them, cast him a nod of thanks.

Even without these cues, Cazaril could have identified the man as the castle warder by the clink of keys at his silver-studded belt, and the chain of office around his neck. He rose at once as the man approached him, and essayed a cursedly awkward bow, pulled short by his adhesions. "Ser dy Ferrej? My name is Lupe dy Cazaril. I beg an audience of the Dowager Provincara, if . . . if it is her pleasure." His voice faltered under the warder's frown.

"I do not know you, sir," said the warder.

"By the gods' grace, the Provincara may remember me. I was once a page, here"—he gestured around rather blindly—"in this household. When the old provincar was alive." The closest thing to a home he had left, he supposed. Cazaril was unutterably weary of being a stranger everywhere.

The gray brows rose. "I will inquire if the Provincara will see you."

"That's all I ask." All he dared ask. He sank back to his bench, and wound his fingers together, as the warder stumped back into the main keep.

After several miserable minutes of suspense, stared at sidelong by passing servants, Cazaril looked up at the warder's return. Dy Ferrej eyed him with bemusement.

"Her Grace the Provincara grants you an interview. Follow me."

His body had stiffened, sitting in the gathering chill; Cazaril stumbled a little, and cursed his stumble, as he followed the warder indoors. He scarcely needed a guide. The plan of the place came back to him, tumbling through his memory with every turning. Through this hall, across those blue-and-yellow-patterned tiles, up this stair and that one, through a whitewashed inner chamber, and then the room on the western wall she'd always favored for sitting in this time of day, with the best light for her seamstresses, or for reading. He had to duck his head a little through its low door, as he'd never had to before; it seemed the only change. *But not a change in the door.*

"Here is the man as you bade, your grace," the warder announced Cazaril neutrally, declining to either endorse or deny his claimed identity.

The Dowager Provincara was seated in a wide wooden chair, made soft for her aging bones with cushions. She wore a sober dark green gown suitable to her high-ranked widowhood, but declined a widow's cap, choosing instead to have her graying hair braided up around her head in two knots and twined with green ribbons, locked with jeweled clasps. She had a lady companion almost as old as herself seated by her side, a widow also, judging by the garb of a lay dedicat of the Temple that she wore. The companion clutched her needlework and regarded Cazaril with an untrusting frown.

Praying his body would not betray him now with some twitch or stumble, Cazaril levered himself down onto one knee before her chair and bowed his head in respectful greeting. Her clothes were scented with lavender, and a dry old-woman smell. He looked up, searching her face for some sign of recognition. If she did not know him now, then no one he would become in truth, and swiftly.

She gazed back, and bit her lip in wonder. "Five gods," she murmured softly. "It really is you. My lord dy Cazaril. I bid you welcome to my house." She held out her hand for him to kiss.

He swallowed, almost gasping, and bent his head over it. Once, it had been fine and white, the nails perfect and pearl-rubbed. Now the knuckles stood out, and the thin skin was brown-spotted, though the nails were still as well kept as when she'd been a matron in her prime. She did not, by the smallest jerk, react to the couple of tears he dropped helplessly upon its back, but her lips curved up a little. Her hand drifted from his light grasp to touch his beard and trace one of the gray streaks. "Dear me, Cazaril, have I grown that old?"

He blinked rapidly up at her. He would not, he would *not* break down weeping like an overwrought child . . . "It has been a long time, Your Grace."

"Tsk." Her hand turned, and the dry fingers tapped him on the cheek. "That was your cue to say I haven't changed a bit. Didn't I teach you how to lie to a lady better than that? I had no idea I was so remiss." With perfect composure, she retrieved her hand and nodded to her companion.

"May I make you known to my cousin, the Lady dy Hueltar. Tessa, may I present my lord the Castillar dy Cazaril."

From the corner of his eye Cazaril saw the warder, with a breath of relief, relax his guard, folding his arms and leaning against the doorframe. Still on his knee, Cazaril made a clumsy bow in the dedicat's direction.

"You are all kindness, Your Grace, but as I no longer hold Cazaril, nor its keep, nor any of my father's lands, I do not claim his title either."

"Don't be foolish, Castillar." Beneath her bantering tone, her voice sharpened. "My dear Provincar is dead these ten years, but I'll see the Bastard's demons eat the first man who dares to call me anything less than Provincara. We have what we can hold, dear boy, and never let them see you flinch or falter."

Beside her, the dedicat stiffened in disapproval of these blunt words, if not, perhaps, of the sentiment behind them. Cazaril judged it imprudent to point out that the title by right now belonged to the Provincara's daughter-in-law. Her son the present provincar and his wife likely judged it imprudent, too.

"You will always be the great lady to me, Your Grace, whom we worshipped from afar," Cazaril offered.

"Better," she approved judiciously. "Much better. I do like a man who can pull his wits about him." She waved at her warder. "Dy Ferrej, fetch the castillar a chair. One for yourself, too; you loom like a crow there."

The warder, apparently accustomed to such addresses, smiled and murmured, "Certainly, Your Grace." He pulled up a carved chair for Cazaril, with a gratifying murmur of *Will my lord be seated?*, and retrieved another for himself from the next chamber, placing it a little apart from his lady and her guest.

Cazaril scrambled up and sank down again in blessed comfort. He ventured tentatively, "Was that the royse and royesse I saw come in from riding as I arrived, Your Grace? I should not have troubled you with my intrusion, had I known you had such visitors." He would not have dared.

"Not visiting, Castillar. They are living here with me for now. Valenda is a quiet, clean town, and . . . my daughter is not entirely well. It suits her to retire here, after the too-hectic court." A weary look flickered in her eyes.

Five gods, the Lady Ista was here as well? The Dowager Royina Ista, Cazaril hastily corrected this thought. When he had first come to serve Baocia, as unformed a larva as any boy of like degree, the Provincara's youngest daughter Ista had seemed already a grown woman, though only a few years older than himself. Fortunately, even at that foolish age, he'd not been so foolish as to confide his hopeless infatuation of her to anyone else. Her high marriage soon after to Roya Ias himself—her first, his second—-had seemed her beauty's proper destiny, despite the royal couple's disparity of age. Cazaril supposed Ista's early widowhood might have been expected, though not as early as it had proved.

The Provincara brushed aside her fatigue with an impatient flash of her fingers, and followed with a, "And what of yourself? The last I heard of you, you were riding courier for the provincar of Guarida."

"That was . . . some years ago, Your Grace."

"How did you come here?" She looked him over, her brows drawing down. "Where is your sword?"

"Oh, that." His hand vaguely touched his side, where neither belt nor sword hung. "I lost it at . . . When the March dy Jironal led Roya Orico's forces up to the north coast for the winter campaign these . . . three? yes, three years ago, he made me castle warder of the fortress at Gotorget. Then dy Jironal had that unfortunate reversal . . . we held the keep nine months against the Roknari forces. The usual, you know. I swear there was not a rat left unroasted in Gotorget when the word came through that dy Jironal had made treaty again, and we were ordered to lay down our arms and march out, and turn the fortress over to our foes." He offered up a brief, unfelt smile; his left hand curled in his lap. "For my consolation, I was informed our fortress cost the Roknari prince an extra three hundred thousand royals, in the treaty tent. Plus considerably more in the field that nine-month, I calculate." *Poor consolation, for the lives we spent.* "The Roknari general claimed my father's sword; he said he was going to hang it in his tent, to remember me by. So that was the last I saw of my blade. After that . . ." Cazaril's voice, growing stronger through this reminiscence, faltered. He cleared his throat, and began again. "There was an error, some mix-up. When the list of men to be ransomed arrived, together with the chests of royals, my name had been left off it somehow. The Roknari quartermaster swore there was no mistake, because the amounts counted out evenly with the names, but . . . there was some mistake. All my officers were rescued . . . I was put in with the unransomed men, and we were all marched to Visping, to be sold to the Roknari corsair masters as galley slaves."

The Provincara drew in her breath. The warder, who had been leaning farther and farther forward in his seat during this recital, burst out, "You protested, surely!"

"Oh, five gods, yes. I protested all the way to Visping. I was still protesting as they dragged me up the gangplank and chained me to my oar. I kept protesting till we put to sea, and then I . . . learned not to." He smiled again. It felt like a clown's mask. Happily, no one seized on that weak *error*.

"I was on one ship or another for . . . for a long time." Nineteen months, eight days, he had counted it out later. At the time, he could not have told one day from the next. "And then I had the greatest piece of good fortune, for my corsair ran afoul of a fleet of the roya of Ibra, out on maneuvers. I assure you Ibra's volunteers rowed better than we did, and they soon ran us down."

Two men had been beheaded in their chains by the increasingly desperate Roknari, for deliberately—or accidentally—fouling their oars. One of them had been sitting near Cazaril, his benchmate for months. Some of the spurting blood had got in his mouth; he could still half taste it, when he made the mistake of thinking of it. He could taste it now. When the corsair was taken, the Ibrans had trailed the Roknari, some still half-alive, behind the ship on ropes made of their own guts, till the great fishes had eaten them. Some of the freed galley slaves had helped row, with a will. Cazaril could not. That last flaying had brought him within hours of being cast overboard by the Roknari galley master as broken and useless. He'd sat on the deck, muscles twitching uncontrollably, and wept.

"The good Ibrans put me ashore in Zagosur, where I fell ill for a few months. You know how it is with men when a long strain is removed of a sudden. They can grow . . . rather childish." He smiled apologetically around the room. For him, it had been collapse and fever, till his back half healed; then dysentery; then an ague. And, throughout it all, the bouts of inconsolable weeping. He'd wept when an acolyte offered him dinner. When the sun came out. When the sun went *in*. When a cat startled him. When he was led to bed. Or at any time, for no cause. "The Temple Hospital of the Mother's Mercy took me in. When I felt a little better"—when the weeping had tailed mostly off, and the acolytes had decided he was not mad, merely nervous—"they gave me a little money, and I walked here. I was three weeks on the road."

The room was dead silent.

He looked up, to see that the Provincara's lips had gone tight with anger. Terror wrenched his empty stomach. "It was the only place I could think of!" he excused himself hastily. "I'm sorry. I'm sorry."

The warder blew out his breath and sat back, staring at Cazaril. The lady companion's eyes were wide.

In a vibrating voice, the Provincara declared, "You are the Castillar dy Cazaril. They should have given you a horse. They should have given you an *escort*."

Cazaril's hands flapped in frightened denial. "No, no, my lady! It was . . . it was enough." Well, almost. He realized, after an unsteady blink, that her anger wasn't at *him*. *Oh*. His throat tightened, and the room blurred. *No, not again, not here* . . . He hurried on. "I wished to place myself in your service, lady, if you can find any use for me. I admit I . . . can't do much. Just now."

The Provincara sat back, her chin resting lightly on her hand, and studied him. After a moment, she said, "You used to play the lute very pleasantly, when you were a page."

"Uh . . ." Cazaril's crooked, callused hands tried to hide themselves in each other for a spasmodic instant. He smiled in renewed apology, and displayed them briefly on his knees. "I think not now, my lady."

She leaned forward; her gaze rested for a moment on his half-mangled left. "I see." She sat back again, pursing her lips. "I remember you read all the books in my husband's library. The master of the pages was always complaining of you for that. I told him to leave you alone. You aspired to be a poet, as I recall."

Cazaril was not sure his right hand could close around a pen, at present. "I believe Chalion was saved from a deal of bad poetry, when I went off to war."

She shrugged her shoulders. "Come, come, Castillar, you quite daunt me with your offer of service. I'm not sure poor Valenda has posts enough to occupy you. You've been a courtier—a captain—a castle warder—a courier—"

"I haven't been a courtier since before Roya Ias died, my lady. As a captain . . . I helped lose the battle of Dalus." And rotted for nearly a year in the dungeons of the royacy of Brajar, thereafter. "As a castle warder, well, we lost the siege. As a courier, I was nearly hanged as a spy. Twice." He brooded. *And three times put to the torture in violation of parley.* "Now . . . now, well, I know how to row boats. And five ways of preparing a dish of rats."

I could relish a mighty dish of rat right now, in fact.

He did not know what she read in his face, for all that her sharp old eyes probed him. Perhaps it was exhaustion, but he hoped it was hunger. He was fairly sure it was hunger, for she at last smiled crookedly.

"Then come to supper with us, Castillar, though I'm afraid my cook cannot offer you rat. They are not in season, in peaceful Valenda. I shall think on your petition."

He nodded mute thanks, not trusting his voice to not break.

❧IT BEING STILL WINTER, THE MAIN MEAL OF THE household's day had been taken at noon, formally, in the great hall. The evening supper was a lighter repast, featuring, by the Provincara's economy, the leftover breads and meats from noon, but by her pride, the very best of them, supplemented by a generous libation of her excellent wines. In the shimmering heat of the high plains summer, the procedure would be reversed; nuncheon would be light fare, and the main meal taken after nightfall, when Baocians of all degrees took to their cooler courtyards to eat by lantern light.

They sat down only eight, in an intimate chamber in a new building quite near the kitchens. The Provincara took the center of the table, and placed Cazaril on her honored right. Cazaril was daunted to find the Royesse Iselle on his other side, and the Royse Teidez across from her. He took heart again when the royse chose to while away the wait for all to be seated by flicking bread-balls at his older sister, a maneuver sternly suppressed by his grandmother. A retaliatory gleam in the royesse's eye was only sidetracked, Cazaril judged, by some timely distraction from her companion Betriz, seated across and a little down from him.

Lady Betriz smiled across the board at Cazaril in friendly curiosity, revealing an elusive dimple, and seemed about to speak, but then the servant passed among them with a basin for handwashing. The warm water was scented with verbena. Cazaril's hands shook as he dipped and wiped them on the fine linen towel, a weakness he concealed as soon as he might by hiding them in his lap. The chair directly across from him remained empty.

Cazaril nodded to it, and asked the Provincara diffidently, "Will the dowager royina be joining us, Your Grace?"

Her lips pressed closed. "Ista is not well enough tonight, unfortunately. She . . . takes most of her meals in her chamber."

Cazaril quelled a moment of unease, and resolved to ask someone else, later, exactly what troubled the royse and royesse's mother. That brief compression suggested something chronic, or lingering, or too painful to be discussed. Her long widowhood had spared Ista the further dangers of childbirth that were the bane of young women, but then there were all those frightening female disorders that overtook matrons . . . As Roya Ias's second wife, Ista had been wed in his middle age when his son and heir Orico was already full-grown. In the little time Cazaril had been at the court of Chalion, years ago, he had watched her only from a discreet distance; she'd seemed happy, the light of the roya's eye when the marriage was new. Ias had doted upon toddler Iselle and upon Teidez, a babe in the nurse's arms.

Their happiness had been darkened during the unfortunate tragedy of Lord dy Lutez's treason, which, most observers agreed, had hastened the aging roya's death by grief. Cazaril couldn't help wondering if the illness that had evidently driven Royina Ista from her stepson's court had any unfortunate political elements. But the new roya Orico had been respectful of his stepmother, and kind to his half siblings, by all reports.

Cazaril cleared his throat to cover the growling of his stomach and gave attention to the royse's superior gentleman-tutor, on the far end of the table beyond Lady Betriz. The Provincara, with a regal nod of her head, desired him to lead the prayer to the Holy Family blessing the approaching meal. Cazaril hoped it was approaching rapidly. The mystery of the empty chair was solved when the castle warder Ser dy Ferrej hurried in late, and made brief apologies all round before seating himself.

"I was caught by the divine of the Order of the Bastard," he explained as bread, meat, and dried fruit were passed.

Cazaril, hard-pressed not to fall on his food like a starving dog, made a politely inquiring noise, and took his first bite.

"The most earnestly long-winded young man," dy Ferraj expanded.

"What does he want now?" asked the Provincara. "More donations for the foundling hospital? We sent down a load last week. The castle servants are refusing to give up any more of their old clothes."

"Wet nurses," said dy Ferrej, chewing.

The Provincara snorted. "Not from *my* household!"

"No, but he wanted me to pass the word that the Temple was looking. He was hoping someone might have a female relative who would be moved to pious charity. They had another babe left at the postern last week, and he's expecting more. It's the time of year, apparently."

The Order of the Bastard, by the logic of its theology, classified unwanted births among the things-out-of-season that were the god's mandate: including bastards—naturally—and children bereft of parents untimely young. The Temple's foundling hospitals and orphanages were one of the order's main concerns. In all, Cazaril thought that a god who was supposed to command a legion of demons ought to have an easier time shaking out donations for his good works.

Cautiously, Cazaril watered his wine; a crime to treat this vintage so, but on his empty stomach it was sure to go straight to his head. The Provincara nodded approvingly at him, but then entered into an argument with her lady cousin on the same subject, emerging partially triumphant with half a glass of wine undiluted.

Ser dy Ferrej continued, "The divine had a good story, though; guess who died last night?"

"Who, Papa?" said Lady Betriz helpfully.

"Ser dy Naoza, the celebrated duelist."

It was not a name Cazaril recognized, but the Provincara sniffed. "About time. Ghastly man. *I* did not receive him, though I suppose there were fools enough who did. Did he finally underestimate a victim—I mean, opponent?"

"That's where the story gets interesting. He was apparently assassinated by death magic." No bad raconteur, dy Ferrej quaffed wine while the shocked murmur ran around the table. Cazaril froze in mid-chew.

"Is the Temple going to try to solve the mystery?" asked Royesse Iselle.

"No mystery to it, though I gather it was rather a tragedy. About a year ago, dy Naoza was jostled in the street by the only son of a provincial wool merchant, with the usual result. Well, dy Naoza claimed it for a duel, of course, but there were those on the scene who said it was bloody murder. Somehow, none of them could be found to testify when the boy's father tried to take dy Naoza to justice. There was some question about the probity of the judge, too, it was rumored."

The Provincara *tsked*. Cazaril dared to swallow, and say, "Do go on."

Encouraged, the castle warder continued, "The merchant was a widower, and the boy not just an only son, but an only child. Just about to be married, too, to turn the knife. Death magic is an ugly business, true, but I can't help having a spot of sympathy for the poor merchant. Well, rich merchant, I suppose, but in any case, far too old to train up to the degree of swordsmanship required to remove someone like dy Naoza. So he fell back on what he thought was his only recourse. Spent the next year studying the black arts—where he found all his lore is a good puzzle for the Temple, mind you—letting his business go, I was told—and then, last night, took himself off to an abandoned mill about seven miles from Valenda, and tried to call up a demon. And, by the Bastard, succeeded! *His* body was found there this morning."

The Father of Winter was the god of all deaths in good season, and of justice; but in addition to all the other disasters in his gift the Bastard was the god of executioners. And, indeed, god of a whole purseful of other dirty jobs. *It seems the merchant went to the right store for his miracle.* The notebook in Cazaril's vest suddenly seemed to weigh ten pounds; but it was only in his imagination that it felt as though it might scorch through the cloth and burst into flame.

"Well, *I* don't have any sympathy for him," said Royse Teidez. "That was cowardly!"

"Yes, but what can you expect of a merchant?" observed his tutor, from down the table. "Men of that class are not trained up in the kind of code of honor a true gentleman learns."

"But it's so sad," protested Iselle. "I mean, about the son about to be wed."

Teidez snorted. "Girls. All you can think about is getting married. But which is the greater loss to the royacy? Some money-grubbing wool-man, or a swordsman? Any duelist that skilled must be a good soldier for the roya!"

"Not in my experience," Cazaril said dryly.

"What do you mean?" Teidez promptly challenged him.

Abashed, Cazaril mumbled, "Excuse me. I spoke out of turn."

"What's the difference?" Teidez pressed.

The Provincara tapped a finger on the tablecloth and shot him an indecipherable look. "Do expand, Castillar."

Cazaril shrugged, and offered a slight, apologetic bow in the boy's direction. "The difference, Royse, is that a skilled soldier kills your enemies, but a skilled duelist kills your allies. I leave you to guess which a wise commander prefers to have in his camp."

"Oh," said Teidez. He fell silent, looking thoughtful.

There was, apparently, no rush to return the merchant's notebook to the proper authorities, and also no difficulty. Cazaril might search out the divine at the Temple of the Holy Family here in Valenda tomorrow at his leisure, and turn it over to be passed along. It would have to be decoded; some men found that sort of puzzle difficult or tedious, but Cazaril had always found it restful. He wondered if he ought, as a courtesy, to offer to decipher it. He touched his soft wool robe, and was glad he'd prayed for the man at his hurried burning.

Betriz, her dark brows crimping, asked, "Who was the judge, Papa?"

Dy Ferrej hesitated a moment, then shrugged. "The Honorable Vrese."

"Ah," said the Provincara. "Him." Her nose twitched, as though she'd sniffed a bad smell.

"Did the duelist threaten him, then?" asked Royesse Iselle. "Shouldn't he—couldn't he have called for help, or had dy Naoza arrested?"

"I doubt that even dy Naoza was foolish enough to threaten a justiciar of the province," said dy Ferrej. "Though it was probable he intimidated the witnesses. Vrese was, hm, likely handled by more peaceful means." He popped a fragment of bread into his mouth and rubbed his thumb and forefinger together, miming a man warming a coin.

"If the judge had done his job honestly and bravely, the merchant would never have been driven to use death magic," said Iselle slowly. "Two men are dead and damned, where it might have only been one . . . and even if he'd been executed, dy Naoza might have had time to clean his soul before facing the gods. If this is known, why is the man still a judge? Grandmama, can't you do something about it?"

The Provincara pressed her lips together. "The appointment of provincial justiciars is not within my gift, dear one. Nor their removal. Or their department would be rather more orderly run, I assure you." She took a sip of her wine and added to her granddaughter's frowning look, "I have great privilege in Baocia, child. I do not have great powers."

Iselle glanced at Teidez, and at Cazaril, before echoing her brother's question, in a voice gone serious: "What's the difference?"

"One is the right to rule—and the duty to protect! T' other is the right to receive protection," replied the Provincara. "There is alas more difference between a provincar and a provincara than just the one letter."

Teidez smirked. "Oh, like the difference between a royse and a royesse?"

Iselle turned on him and raised her brows. "Oh? And how do you propose to remove the corrupt judge—privileged boy?"

"That's enough, you two," said the Provincara sternly, in a voice that was pure grandmother. Cazaril hid a smile. *Within* these walls, she ruled, right enough, by an older code than Chalion's. Hers was a sufficient little state.

The conversation turned to less lurid matters as the servants brought cakes, cheese, and a wine from Brajar. Cazaril had, surreptitiously he hoped, stuffed himself. If he didn't stop soon, he would make himself sick. But the golden dessert wine almost sent him into tears at the table; that one, he drank unwatered, though he managed to limit himself to one glass.

At the end of the meal prayers were offered again, and Royse Teidez was dragged off by his tutor for studies. Iselle and Betriz were sent to do needlework. They departed at a gallop, followed at a more sedate pace by dy Ferrej.

"Will they actually sit still for needlework?" Cazaril asked the Provincara, watching the departing flurry of skirts.

"They gossip and giggle till I can't bear it, but yes, they're very handy," said the Provincara, the disapproving purse of her lips belied by the warmth of her eyes.

"Your granddaughter is a delightful young lady."

"To a man of a certain age, Cazaril, all young ladies start to look delightful. It's the first symptom of senility."

"True, my lady." His lips twitched up.

"She's worn out two governesses and looks to be bent on destroying a third, by the way the woman complains of her. And yet . . ." the Provincara's tart voice grew slower, "she needs to be strong. Someday, inevitably, she will be sent far from me. And I will no longer be able to help her . . . protect her . . ."

An attractive, fresh young royesse was a pawn, not a player, in the politics of Chalion. Her bride-price would come high, but a politically and financially favorable marriage might not necessarily prove a good one in more intimate senses. The Dowager Provincara had been fortunate in her personal life, but in her long years had doubtless had opportunity to observe the whole range of marital fates awaiting highborn women. Would Iselle be sent to far Darthaca? Married off to some cousin in the too-close-related royacy of Brajar? Gods forbid she should be bartered away to the Roknari to seal some temporary peace, exiled to the Archipelago.

She studied him sidelong, in the light from the lavish branches of candles she had always favored. "How old are you now, Castillar? I thought you were about thirteen when your father sent you to serve my dear Provincar."

"About that, yes, Your Grace. I'm thirty-five."

"Ha. You should shave off that nasty mess growing out of your face, then. It makes you look fifteen years older than you are."

Cazaril considered some quip about a turn in the Roknari galleys being very aging to a man, but he wasn't quite up to it. Instead he said, "I hope I did not annoy the royse with my maunderings, my lady."

"I believe you actually made young Teidez stop and think. A rare event. I wish his tutor could manage it more often." She drummed her thin fingers briefly on the cloth and drained the last of her tiny glass of wine. She set it down, and added, "I don't know what flea-ridden inn you've put up at down in town, Castillar, but I'll dispatch a page for your things. You'll lodge here tonight."

"Thank you, Your Grace. I accept with gratitude." *And alacrity.* Thank the gods, oh, five times five, he was gathered in, at least temporarily. He hesitated, embarrassed. "But, ah . . . it won't be necessary to trouble your page."

She raised a brow at him. "That's what they exist for. As you may recall."

"Yes, but"—he smiled briefly, and gestured down himself— "these are my things."

At her pained look, he added weakly, "I had less, when I fell off the Ibran galley in Zagosur." He'd been dressed in a breechclout of surpassing filthiness, and scabs. The acolytes had burned the rag at their first opportunity.

"Then my page," said the Provincara in a precise voice, still regarding him levelly, "will escort you to your chamber. My lord Castillar."

She added, as she made to rise, and her cousin-companion hastened to assist her, "We'll speak again tomorrow."

❧THE CHAMBER WAS ONE IN THE OLD KEEP RESERVED for honored guests, more on account of having been slept in by several historical royas than for its absolute comfort; Cazaril had served its guests himself a hundred times. The bed had three mattresses, straw, feather, and down, and was dressed in the softest washed linen and a coverlet worked by ladies of the household. Before the page had left him, two maids arrived, bearing wash water, drinking water, towels, soap, a tooth-stick, and an embroidered nightgown, cap, and slippers. Cazaril had been planning to sleep in the dead man's shirt.

It was abruptly all too much. Cazaril sat down on the edge of the bed with the nightgown in his hands and burst into wracking sobs. Gulping, he gestured the unnerved-looking servitors to leave him.

"What's the matter with *him?*" he heard the maid's voice, as their footsteps trailed off down the corridor, and the tears trailed down the inside of his nose.

The page answered disgustedly, "A madman, I suppose."

After a short pause, the maid's voice floated back faintly, "Well, he'll fit right in here, then, won't he . . ."

3

The sounds of the household stirring—calls from the courtyard, the distant clank of pots—woke Cazaril in the predawn gray. He opened his eyes to a moment of panicked disorientation, but the reassuring embrace of the feather bed drew him down again into drowsy repose. Not a hard bench. Not moving up and down. Not moving at all, oh five gods, that was very heaven. So warm, on his knotted back.

The Daughter's Day celebrations would run from dawn till dark. Perhaps he would lie slugabed till the household had departed for the procession, then get up late. Creep around unobtrusively, lie in the sun with the castle cats. When he grew hungry, dredge up old memories from his days as a page—he'd used to know how to charm the cook for an extra tidbit . . .

A crisp knock on the door interrupted these pleasant meditations. Cazaril jerked, then relaxed again as Lady Betriz's voice followed: "My lord dy Cazaril? Are you awake? Castillar?"

"A moment, my lady," Cazaril called back. He wallowed to the bed's edge and tore himself from the loving clutch of the mattress. A woven rush mat on the floor kept the morning cold of the stone from nipping his bare feet. He shook the generous linen of the nightgown down over his legs, shuffled to the door, and opened it a crack. "Yes?"

She stood in the corridor with a candle shielded by a blown-glass lantern in one hand and a pile of cloth, leather straps, and something that clanked wedged awkwardly under her other arm. She was fully dressed for the day in a blue gown with a white vest-cloak that fell from shoulder to ankle. Her dark hair was braided up on her head with flowers and leaves. Her velvet brown eyes were merry, glinting in the candle's glow. Cazaril could not help but smile back.

"Her Grace the Provincara bids you a blessed Daughter's Day," she announced, and startled Cazaril into jumping backward by firmly kicking the door open. She rocked her loaded hips through, handed off the candle holder to him with a *Here, take this*, and dumped her burden on the edge of the bed: piles of blue and white cloth, and a sword with a belt. Cazaril set the candle down on the chest at the foot of the bed. "She sends you these to wear, and if it please you bids you join the household in the ancestors' hall for the dawn prayers. After which we will break our fast, which, she says, you know well where to find."

"Indeed, my lady."

"Actually, I asked Papa for the sword. It's his second-best one. He said it would be an honor to loan it to you." She turned a highly interested gaze upon him. "Is it true you were in the late war?"

"Uh . . . which one?"

"You've been in more than one?" Her eyes widened, then narrowed.

All of them for the last seventeen years, I think. Well, no. He'd sat out the most recent abortive campaign against Ibra in the dungeons of Brajar, and missed that foolish expedition the roya had sent in support of Darthaca because he'd been busy being inventively tormented by the Roknari general with whom the provincar of Guarida was bargaining so ineptly. Besides those two, he didn't think there had been a defeat in the last decade he'd missed. "Here and there, over the years," he answered vaguely. He was suddenly horridly conscious that there was nothing between his nakedness and her maiden eyes but a thin layer of linen. He twitched inward, clutching his arms across his belly, and smiled weakly.

"Oh," she said, following his gesture. "Have I embarrassed you? But Papa says soldiers have no modesty, on account of having to live all together in the field."

She returned her eyes to his face, which was heating. Cazaril got out, "I was thinking of your modesty, my lady."

"That's all right," she said cheerfully.

She didn't go away.

He nodded toward the pile of clothes. "I didn't wish to intrude upon the family during celebration. Are you sure . . . ?"

She clasped her hands together earnestly and intensified her gaze. "But you must come to the procession, and you must, you must, you *must* come to the Daughter's Day quarter-gifting at the temple. The Royesse Iselle is going to play the part of the Lady of Spring this year." She bounced on her toes in her importunity.

Cazaril smiled sheepishly. "Very well, if it please you." How could he resist all this urgent delight? Royesse Iselle must be rising sixteen; he wondered how old Lady Betriz was. *Too young for you, old fellow.* But surely he might watch her with a purely aesthetic appreciation, and thank the goddesses for her gifts of youth, beauty, and verve howsoever they were scattered. Brightening the world like flowers.

"And besides," Lady Betriz cinched it, "the Provincara bids you."

Cazaril seized the opportunity to light his candle from hers and, by way of a hint that it was time for her to go away and let him dress, handed the glass-globed flame back to her. The doubled light that made her more lovely doubtless made him less so. She'd just turned to go when he bethought him of his prudent question, unanswered last night.

"Wait, lady—"

She turned back with a look of bright inquiry.

"I didn't want to trouble the Provincara, or ask in front of the royse or royesse, but what grieves the Royina Ista? I don't want to say or do something wrong, out of ignorance . . ."

The light in her eyes died a little. She shrugged. "She's . . . weary. And nervous. Nothing more. We hope she will feel better, with the coming of the sun. She always seems to do better, in the summertime."

"How long has she been living here with her mother?"

"These six years, sir." She gave him a little half curtsey. "Now I have to go to Royesse Iselle. Don't be late, Castillar!" Her smile dimpled at him again, and she darted out.

He could not imagine that young lady being late anywhere. Her energy was appalling. Shaking his head, though the smile she'd left him still lingered on his lips, he turned to examine the new largesse.

He was certainly moving up to a better grade of castoffs. The tunic was blue silk brocade, the trousers heavy dark blue linen, and the knee-length vest-cloak white wool, all clean, the little mends and stains quite unobtrusive; dy Ferrej's festival gear outgrown, perhaps, or possibly even something packed away from the late provincar. The loose fit was forgiving of this change in ownership. With the sword hung at his left hip, familiar/unfamiliar weight, Cazaril hurried down out of the keep and across the gray courtyard to the household's ancestors' hall.

The air of the courtyard was chill and damp, the cobbles slippery under his thin boot soles. Overhead, a few stars still lingered. Cazaril eased open the big plank door to the hall and peered inside. Candles, figures; was he late? He slipped within, his eyes adjusting.

Not late but early. The tiers of little family memori boards at the front of the room had half a dozen old candle stubs burning before them. Two women, huddled into shawls, sat on the front bench watching over a third.

The Dowager Royina Ista lay before the altar in the attitude of deepest supplication, prone upon the floor, her arms outflung. Her fingers curled and uncurled; the nails were bitten down to the red. A muddle of nightgowns and shawls puddled around her. Her masses of crinkly hair, once gold, now darkened by age to a dull dun, spread out around her head like a fan. For a moment, Cazaril wondered if she had fallen asleep, so still did she lie. But in her pale face, turned sideways with her soft cheek resting directly on the floor, her eyes were open, gray and unblinking, filled with unshed tears.

It was a face of the most profound grief; Cazaril was put in mind of men's looks that he had seen, broken in not just body but soul by the dungeon or the horrors of the galleys. Or of his own, seen dimly in a polished steel mirror in the Mother's house in Ibra, when the acolytes had shaved his nerveless face and encouraged him to look, see, wasn't that better? Yet he was quite certain the royina had never been within smelling distance of a dungeon in her life, never felt the bite of the lash, never, perhaps, even felt a man's hand raised against her in anger. *What, then?* He stood still, lips parted, afraid to speak.

At a creak and a bustle behind him, he glanced round to see

the Dowager Provincara, attended by her cousin, slip inside. She flicked an eyebrow at him in passing; he jerked a little bow. The waiting women attending upon the royina started, and rose, offering ghostly curtseys.

The Provincara strode up the aisle between the benches and studied her daughter expressionlessly. "Oh, dear. How long has she been here?"

One of the waiting women half curtseyed again. "She rose in the night, Your Grace. We thought it better to let her come down than to fight her. As you instructed . . ."

"Yes, yes." The Provincara waved away this nervous excuse. "Did she get any sleep at all?"

"One or two hours, I think, my lady."

The Provincara sighed, and knelt by her daughter. Her voice went gentle, all the tartness drained out; for the first time, Cazaril heard the age in it.

"Ista, heart. Rise and go back to bed. Others will take over the praying today."

The prone woman's lips moved, twice, before words whispered out. "If the gods hear. If they hear, they do not speak. Their faces are turned from me, Mother."

Almost awkwardly, the old woman stroked her hair. "Others will pray today. We'll light all the candles new, and try again. Let your ladies put you back to bed. Up, now."

The royina sniffed, blinked, and, reluctantly, rose. At a jerk of the Provincara's head, the waiting ladies hurried forward to guide the royina out of the hall, gathering up her dropping shawls behind her. Cazaril searched her face anxiously as she passed, but found no signs of wasting illness, no yellow tinge to her skin or eyes, no emaciation. She scarcely seemed to see Cazaril; no recognition flickered in her eyes for the bearded stranger. Well, there was no reason she should remember him, merely one of dozens of pages in and out of dy Baocia's household over the years.

The Provincara's head turned back as the door closed behind her daughter. Cazaril was close enough to see her quiet sigh.

He made her a deeper bow. "I thank you for these festival garments, Your Grace. If . . ." he hesitated. "If there's anything I can do to ease your burdens, lady, or those of the royina, just ask."

She smiled, and took his hand and patted it rather absently, but didn't answer. She went to open the window shutters on the room's east side, to let in the peach-colored dawn glow.

Around the altar, Lady dy Hueltar blew out the candles and gathered up all the stubby ends in a basket brought for that purpose. The Provincara and Cazaril went to help her replace the sad lumps in each holder with a fresh, new beeswax candle. When the dozens of candles were standing up like young soldiers each in front of their respective tablets, the Provincara stepped back and gave a satisfied nod.

The rest of the household began arriving then, and Cazaril took a seat out of the way on a back bench. Cooks, servants, stableboys, pages, the huntsman and the falconer, the upper housekeeper, the castle warder, all in their best clothes, with as much blue and white as could be managed, filed in and sat. Then Lady Betriz led in Royesse Iselle, fully dressed and a trifle stiff in the elaborate, multilayered and brilliantly embroidered robes of the Lady of Spring, whose part she was selected to play today. They took an attentive seat on a front bench and managed not to giggle together. They were followed by a divine of the Holy Family from the temple in town, his vestments too changed from yesterday's black-and-gray robes of the Father to the blue-and-white of the Daughter. The divine led the assembly in a short service for the succession of the season and the peace of the dead here represented, and, as the first rays of sun fingered through the east window, ceremonially extinguished the last candle left burning, the last flame anywhere in the household.

All then adjourned for a cold breakfast set up on trestles in the courtyard. Cold, but not sparing; Cazaril reminded himself that he needn't try to make up for three years of privation in a day, and that he had some up- and downhill walking coming up soon. Still, he was happily replete when the royesse's white mule was led in.

It, too, was decorated with ribbons of blue and fresh early flowers braided into its mane and tail. Its hangings were gloriously elaborated with all the symbols of the Lady of Spring. Iselle in her Temple garments, her hair arranged to ripple down like an amber waterfall over her shoulders from under her crown of leaves and flowers, was loaded carefully into her saddle, and her drapes and panels arranged. This time, she used a mounting block and the assistance of a couple of hefty young pages. The divine took the mule's blue silk rope to lead her out the gate. The Provincara was hoisted aboard a sedate chestnut mare with showy white socks, also braided with ribbons and flowers, led by her castle warder. Cazaril muffled a belch, and at dy Ferrej's beckoning hastened to position himself after the mounted ladies, courteously offering his arm to the Lady dy Hueltar. The rest of the household, those who were going, also fell in behind on foot.

The whole merry mob wound down through the streets of town to the old east gate, where the procession was to formally begin. Some couple of hundred people waited there, including fifty or so mounted horsemen from the Daughter's guardsmen's associations drawn from all around the hinterlands of Valenda. Cazaril walked right under the nose of the burly soldier who'd dropped him that mistaken coin in the mud yesterday, but the man gazed back at him without recognition, merely a courteous nod for his silks and his sword. And his trim and his bath, Cazaril supposed. *How strangely we are blinded by the surfaces of things.* The gods, presumably, saw straight through. He wondered if the gods found this as uncomfortable as he sometimes did, these days.

He put his odd thoughts aside as the procession formed up. The divine turned Iselle's lead line over to the elderly gentleman who'd been selected to play the part of the Father of Winter. In the winter procession a young new father would have taken the god's place, his dark garb neat as a judge's, and he'd have ridden a fine black horse that the outgoing and ragged Son of Autumn led. Today's grandfather wore a collection of gray rags that made Cazaril's late wear look positively like a burgher's, his beard and hair and bare calves streaked with ashes. He smiled and made some joke up at Iselle; she laughed. The guardsmen formed up behind the pair, and the whole parade began its circuit of the old town walls, or as nearly as it could come to them with the new building all around. Some Temple acolytes followed between the guardsmen and the rest, to lead the singing, and encourage everyone to use the proper words and not the rude versions.

Any townspeople not in the procession played the audience, and threw, mostly, flowers and herbs. In the van, Cazaril could see the usual few young unmarried women dart in to touch the Daughter's garments for luck in finding a husband this season, and flurry off again, giggling. After a goodly morning walk—thank heavens for the mild lovely weather, one memorable spring they'd done this in a sleet storm—the whole straggling train snaked round to the east gate once more, and filed through to the temple in the town's heart.

The temple stood on the one side of the town square, surrounded by a bit of garden and a low stone wall. It was built in the usual four-lobed pattern, like a four-leafed clover around its central court. Its walls were the golden native stone that so eased Cazaril's heart, capped with the local red tile. One domed lobe held the altar for the god of each season; the Bastard's separate round tower directly back of his Mother's gate held his.

The Lady dy Hueltar ruthlessly dragged Cazaril to the front as the royesse was unloaded from her mule and led beneath the portico. He found Lady Betriz had taken up station on his other side. She craned her neck to follow Iselle. Beneath Cazaril's nose the fresh odor from the flowers and foliage twined around her head mingled with the warm scent of her hair, surely spring's own exhalation. The crowd pressed them onward through the wide-flung doors.

Inside, with the slanted shadows of morning still dimming the paved main courtyard, the Father of Winter cleaned the last of the ash from the raised hearth of the central holy fire and sprinkled it about his person. The acolytes hurried forward to lay the new tinder and wood, which the divine blessed. The ashy graybeard was then driven from the chamber with hoots, catcalls, little sticks with bells, and missiles of soft wool representing snowballs. It was considered an unlucky year, at least by the god's avatar, when the crowd could use real snowballs.

The Lady of Spring in the person of Iselle was then led forward to light the new fire from flint and steel. She knelt on the cushions provided, and bit her lip charmingly in her concentration as she mounded up the dry shavings and sacred herbs. All held their breaths; a dozen superstitions surrounded the matter of how many tries it took the ascending god's avatar to light the new fire each season.

Three quick strikes, a shower of sparks, a puff of young breath; the tiny flame caught. Quickly, the divine bent to light the new taper before any unfortunate failure could occur. None did. A murmur of relieved approval rose all round. The little flame was trans-

ferred to the holy hearth, and Iselle, looking smug and a trifle relieved, was helped to her feet. Her gray eyes seemed to burn as
brightly and cheerfully as the new flame.

She was then led to the throne of the reigning god, and the real
business of the morning began: collecting the quarterly gifts to the
temple that would keep it running for the next three months. Each
head of a household stepped forward to lay their little purse of
coins or other offering in the Lady's hands, be blessed, and have the
amount recorded by the temple's secretary at the table to Iselle's
right. They were then led off to receive in return their taper with
the new fire, to return to their house. The Provincara's household
was the first, by order of rank; the purse that the castle warder laid
in Iselle's hands was heavy with gold. Other men of worth stepped
forward. Iselle smiled and received and blessed; the chief divine
smiled and transferred and thanked; the secretary smiled and
recorded and piled.

Beside Cazaril, Betriz stiffened with . . . excitement? She
gripped Cazaril's left arm briefly. "The next one is that vile judge,
Vrese," she hissed in his ear. "Watch!"

A dour-looking fellow of middle years, richly dressed in dark
blue velvets and gold chains, stepped up to the Lady's throne with
his purse in his hand. With a tight smile, he held it out. "The House
of Vrese presents its offering to the goddess," he intoned nasally.
"Bless us in the coming season, my lady."

Iselle folded her hands in her lap. She raised her chin, looked
across at Vrese with an absolutely level, unsmiling stare, and said
in a clear, carrying voice, "The Daughter of Spring receives honest
hearts' offerings. She does not accept bribes. *Honorable* Vrese. Your
gold means more to you than anything. You may keep it."

Vrese stepped back a half pace; his mouth opened in shock,
and hung there. The stunned silence spread out in waves to the
back of the crowd, to return in a rising mutter of *What? What did
she say? I didn't hear . . . What?* The chief divine's face drained.
The recording secretary looked up with an expression of jolted
horror.

A well-attired man waiting toward the front of the line vented
a sharp crack of gleeful laughter; his lips drew back in an expression that had little to do with humor, but much with appreciation
of cosmic justice. Beside Cazaril, Lady Betriz bounced on her toes

and hissed through her teeth. A trail of choked snickers followed the whispers of explanation trickling back through the mob of townspeople like a small spring freshet.

The judge switched his glare to the chief divine, and made an odd little abortive jerk of his hand, the bagged offering in it, toward him instead. The divine's hands opened and clenched again, at his sides. He stared across beseechingly at the enthroned avatar of the goddess. "Lady Iselle," he whispered out of the corner of his mouth, not quite lowly enough, "you can't . . . we can't . . . does the *goddess* speak to you, in this?"

Iselle returned, not nearly so lowly, "She speaks in my heart. Doesn't she in yours? And besides, I asked her to sign me approval by giving me the first flame, and she did." Perfectly composed, she leaned around the frozen judge, smiled brightly at the next townsman in line, and invited, "You, sir?"

Perforce, the judge stepped aside, especially as the next man in line, grinning, had no hesitation at all in stepping up and shouldering past.

An acolyte, jerked into motion by a glare from his superior, hurried forward to invite the judge to step out somewhere and discuss this contretemps. His slight reach toward the offering purse was knifed right through by an icy frown tossed at him by the royesse; he clapped his hands behind his back and bowed the fuming judge away. Across the courtyard, the Provincara, seated, pinched the bridge of her nose between thumb and forefinger, wiped her hand over her mouth, and stared in exasperation at her granddaughter. Iselle merely raised her chin and continued blandly exchanging the goddess's blessings for the gifts of the quarter-day with a line of suddenly no longer bored nor perfunctory townsmen.

As she worked her way down through the town's households, such gifts in kind as chickens, eggs, and a bull-calf were collected outside, their bearers alone entering the sacred precincts to collect their blessing and their new fire. Lady dy Hueltar and Betriz went to join the Provincara on her courtesy bench, and Cazaril took up station behind it with the castle warder, who favored his demure daughter with a suspicious parental frown. Most of the crowd drifted away; the royesse continued cheerfully in her sacred duty down to the last and least, thanking a wood-gatherer, a charcoal burner, and a beggar—who for his gift sang a hymn—in the same even tones as she'd blessed the first men of Valenda.

❧THE STORM IN THE PROVINCARA'S FACE DIDN'T BREAK till the whole family party had returned to the castle for the afternoon feast.

Cazaril found himself leading her horse, as her castle warder dy Ferrej had taken a firm and prudent grip on the lead line of Iselle's white mule. Cazaril's plan to quietly absent himself was thwarted when, helped down off her chestnut mare by her servants, the Provincara demanded shortly, "Castillar, give me your arm." Her grip around it was tight and trembling. Through thinned lips, she added, "Iselle, Betriz, dy Ferrej, in here." She jerked her head toward the plank doors of the ancestors' hall, just off the castle courtyard.

Iselle had left her festal garments at the temple when the ceremonies had concluded, and was merely a young woman in pretty blue and white once more. No, Cazaril decided, watching her decided chin come up again; merely a royesse once more. Beneath that apprehensive surface glowed an alarming determination. Cazaril held the door as they all filed past, including Lady dy Hueltar. When he'd been a young page, Cazaril thought ruefully, his instinct for danger spilling down from on high would have sped him off at this point. But dy Ferrej stopped and waited for him, and he followed.

The hall was quiet, empty now, though warmly lit by the ranks of candles on the altar that would be allowed to burn all day today until entirely consumed. The wooden benches were polished to a subdued gleam in the candlelight by many pious—or restive—prior occupants. The Provincara stepped to the front of the room, and turned on the two girls, who drew together under her stern eye.

"All right. Which of you had *that* idea?"

Iselle took a half step forward, and gave a tiny curtsey. "It was mine, Grandmama," she said in almost, but not quite, as clear a voice as in the temple courtyard. She offered after another moment under that dour gaze, "Though Betriz thought of asking the first flame for confirmation."

Dy Ferrej wheeled on his daughter. "You knew this was coming up? And you didn't tell me?"

Betriz gave him a curtsey that was an echo of Iselle's, right down to the unbent backbone. "I had understood I was assigned to be the royesse's handmaiden, Papa. Not anybody's spy. If my first loyalty was to be to anyone but Iselle, no one ever told me. Guard her honor with your life, *you* said." After a moment she added more cautiously, undercutting this fine speech a trifle, "Besides, I couldn't *know* it was going to happen till after she had struck the first flame."

Dy Ferrej abandoned the young sophist and made a helpless gesture to the Provincara.

"You are older, Betriz," said the Provincara to her. "We thought you'd be a calming influence. Teach Iselle the duties of a pious maiden." Her lips twisted. "As when Beetim the huntsman couples the young hounds to the older ones. Alas that I did not give your upbringing over to him, instead of to these useless governesses."

Betriz blinked, and offered another curtsey. "Yes, my lady."

The Provincara eyed her, suspicious of concealed humor. Cazaril bit his lip.

Iselle took a deep breath. "If tolerating injustice and turning a blind eye to men's tragic and unnecessary damnations are among the first duties of a pious maiden, then the divines never taught it to me!"

"No, of course not," the Provincara snapped. For the first time, her harsh voice softened with a shade of persuasion. "But justice is not your *task*, heart."

"The men whose task it was appear to have neglected it. I am not a milkmaid. If I have a greater privilege in Chalion, surely I have a greater duty to Chalion as well. The divine and the good dedicat have both told me so!" She shot a defying look at the hovering Lady dy Hueltar.

"I was talking about you attending to your studies, Iselle," Lady dy Hueltar protested.

"When the divines talked of your pious duties, Iselle," dy Ferrej added, "they didn't mean . . . they didn't mean . . ."

"They didn't mean me to take them seriously?" she inquired sweetly.

Dy Ferrej sputtered. Cazaril sympathized. An innocent with

the moral advantage, and as feckless and ignorant of her dangers as the new pup the Provincara had compared her to—Cazaril was profoundly thankful that he had no part in this.

The Provincara's nostrils flared. "For now, you may both go to your chambers and stay there. I'd set you both to read scriptures for a penance, but . . . ! I will decide later if you will be permitted to come to the feast. Good Dedicat, follow after and make sure they arrive. Go!" She gestured imperiously. As Cazaril made to follow, her sweeping arm stopped in midair, and she pointed firmly downward. "Castillar, dy Ferrej, attend a moment." Lady Betriz shot a curious glance over her shoulder as she was ushered out. Iselle marched head high, and didn't look back.

"Well," said dy Ferrej wearily after a moment, "we did hope they would become friends."

Her young audience removed, the Provincara permitted herself a rueful smile. "Alas, yes."

"How old *is* the Lady Betriz?" Cazaril asked curiously, staring after the closing door.

"Nineteen," answered her father with a sigh.

Well, her age was not quite so disparate from his as Cazaril had thought, though her experience surely was.

"I really did think Betriz would be a good influence," dy Ferrej added. "It seems to have worked the other way around."

"Are you accusing my granddaughter of corrupting your daughter?" the Provincara inquired wryly.

"Say, *inspiring*, rather," dy Ferrej said, with a glum shrug. "Terrifying, that. I wonder . . . I wonder if we should part them?"

"There would follow much howling." Wearily, the Provincara seated herself on a bench, gesturing the men to do likewise: "Don't want a crick in my neck." Cazaril clasped his hands between his knees and waited her pleasure, whatever it was to be. She must have dragged him along in here for *something*. She stared thoughtfully at him for a long moment.

"You have a fresh eye, Cazaril," she said at last. "Do you have any suggestions?"

Cazaril's brows climbed. "I've had the training of young soldiers, lady. Never of young maidens. I'm quite out of my depth, here." He hesitated, then spoke almost despite himself. "It looks to me to be a trifle too late to teach Iselle to be a coward. But you might draw her attention to how little firsthand evidence she jumped from. How could she be so sure the judge was as guilty as rumor would have him? Hearsay, gossip? Even some apparent evidence can lie." Cazaril thought ruefully of the bath man's assumptions about the witness of his back. "It won't help for today's incident, but it might slow her down in future." He added in a drier voice, "And you might look to be more careful what gossip you discuss in front of her."

Dy Ferrej winced.

"In front of either one of them," said the Provincara. "Four ears, one mind—or one conspiracy." She pursed her lips and narrowed her eyes at him. "Cazaril . . . you speak and write Darthacan, do you not?"

Cazaril blinked at this sidewise jink in the conversation. "Yes, my lady . . . ?"

"And Roknari?"

"My, ah, court Roknari is a little rusty at present. Granted, my *vile* Roknari is quite fluent."

"And geography? You know the geography of Chalion, of Ibra, of the Roknari princedoms?"

"Five gods, that I do, my lady. What I haven't ridden over, I've walked, what I haven't walked, I've been dragged across. Or through. I've had geography ground into my skin. And I've rowed round half the Archipelago at least."

"And you write, you cipher, you keep books—you've done letters, reports, treaties, logistical orders . . ."

"My hand may be a trifle shaky at present, but yes, I've done all that," he admitted with belatedly rising wariness. Where was she going with this interrogation?

"Yes, yes!" She clapped her hands together; Cazaril flinched at the sharp noise. "The gods have surely landed you upon my wrist. Bastard's demons take me if I haven't the wit to jess you."

Cazaril smiled bewildered inquiry.

"Cazaril, you said you sought a post. I have one for you." She sat back triumphantly. "Secretary-tutor to the Royesse Iselle!"

Cazaril felt his jaw unhinge. He blinked stupidly at her. "What?"

"Teidez already has his own secretary, who keeps the books of his chambers, writes his letters, such as they are . . . it's time Iselle possessed her own warder, at the gate between her women's world and the greater one she'll have to deal with. And besides, none of those stupid governesses have ever been able to handle her. She needs a man's authority, that's what. You have the rank, you have the experience . . ." The Provincara . . . grinned, was all one could call that horrifying gleeful expression. "What do you think, my lord Castillar?"

Cazaril swallowed. "I think . . . I think if you lent me a razor now, for me to cut my throat with, it would save ever so many steps. Please Your Grace."

The Provincara snorted. "Good, Cazaril, good. I *do* so like a man who doesn't underestimate his situation."

Dy Ferrej, who'd at first looked startled and alarmed, eyed Cazaril with new interest.

"I'll wager *you* could direct her mind to her Darthacan declensions. You've been there, after all, which none of these fool women have," the Provincara went on, gaining enthusiasm. "Roknari, too, though we all pray she'll never need that. Read Brajaran poetry to her, you used to like that, I remember. Deportment—you've served at the roya's court, the gods know. Come, come, Cazaril, don't look at me like a lost calf. It would be easy work for you, in your convalescence. Eh, don't imagine I can't see how sick you've been," she added at his little negating gesture. "You wouldn't have to answer but two letters a week at most. Less. And you've ridden courier—when *you* rode out with the girls, I wouldn't have to listen to a lot of wheezing and whining afterward about saddle galls from those women with thighs like dough. As for keeping the books of her chamber—why, after running a fortress, it should be child's play for you. What say you, dear Cazaril?"

The vision was at once enticing and appalling. "Couldn't you give me a fortress under siege, instead?"

The humor faded in her face. She leaned forward, and tapped him on the knee; her voice dropped, and she breathed, "She will be, soon enough." She paused, and studied him. "You asked if there was anything you could do to ease my burdens. For the most part, the answer is no. You can't make me young, you can't make . . . many things better." Cazaril wondered anew how the strange fragile health of her daughter weighed upon her. "But can't you give me this one little yes?"

She begged him. *She* begged *him*. That was all wrong. "I am yours to command, of course, lady, of course. It's just . . . it's just that . . . are you sure?"

"You are not a stranger here, Cazaril. And I am in the most desperate need of a man I can trust."

His heart melted. Or maybe it was his wits. He bowed his head. "Then I am yours."

"Iselle's."

Cazaril, his elbows on his knees, glanced up and across at her, at the thoughtfully frowning dy Ferrej, and back at the old woman's intent face. "I . . . see."

"I believe you do. And that, Cazaril, is why I shall have you for her."

4

So it was Cazaril found himself,
the next morning, introduced into the
young ladies' schoolroom by the
Provincara herself. This sunny little chamber was on the east side
of the keep, on the top floor occupied by Royesse Iselle, Lady Betriz, their waiting woman, and a maid. Royse Teidez had chambers
for his similar subhousehold in the new building across the courtyard, rather more generously proportioned, Cazaril suspected, and
with better fireplaces. Iselle's schoolroom was simply furnished
with a pair of small tables, chairs, a single bookcase half-empty, and
a couple of chests. With the addition of Cazaril, feeling overtall and
awkward under the low-beamed ceiling, and the two young
women, it was as full as it would hold. The perpetual waiting
woman had to take her sewing into the next chamber, though the
doors were left propped open between them.

It seemed Cazaril was to have a class, not just a pupil. A maiden
of Iselle's rank would almost never be left alone, and certainly not
with a man, even a prematurely aged and convalescent one of her
own household. Cazaril didn't know how the two ladies felt about
this tacit arrangement, but he was secretly relieved. Never had he
felt more repulsively male—uncouth, clumsy, and degraded. In all,
this cheerful, peaceful feminine atmosphere was about as far from
a Roknari galley rower's bench as it was possible for Cazaril to
imagine, and he had to swallow a lump of delirious joy at the con-
trast as he ducked his head under the lintel and stepped inside.

The Provincara announced him briskly as Iselle's new secretary-tutor, "Just as your brother has," a clearly unexpected gift that Iselle, after a blink of surprise, accepted without the least demur. By her calculating look, the novelty and increased status of being instructed by a man was quite pleasing to her. Lady Betriz, too, Cazaril was heartened to note, looked alert and interested rather than wary or hostile.

Cazaril trusted he appeared scholarly enough to fool the young ladies, the wool merchant's neat brown gown secured today by the castle warder's silver-studded belt without the sword. He'd had the forethought to supply himself with all the books in Darthacan that a fast rummage through the remains of the late provincar's library could supply, some half dozen random volumes. He dropped them with an impressive thump upon one of the little tables and favored both new pupils with a deliberately sinister smile. If this was to be anything like training young soldiers, young horses, or young hawks, the key was to take the initiative from the first moment, and keep it thereafter. He could be as hollow as a drum, so long as he was as loud.

The Provincara departed as briskly as she'd arrived. In the interest of pretending he had a plan while devising one, Cazaril started right in by testing the royesse's command of Darthacan. He had her read a random page from one of the volumes, as it chanced on a topic that Cazaril knew well: mining and sapping fortified lines during sieges. With much help and prompting, Iselle stumbled through three laborious paragraphs. Two or three questions Cazaril put to her in Darthacan challenging her to explicate the contents of what she'd just read left her sputtering and floundering.

"Your accent is terrible," he told her frankly. "A Darthacan would find you nearly unintelligible."

Her head came up, and she glared at him. "My *governess* said I was quite good. She said that I had a very melodic intonation."

"Yes; you speak like a South Ibran fishwoman hawking her wares. They are very melodic, too. But any Darthacan lordling, and they are all arrogant as wasps about their dreadful tongue, would laugh in your face." At least, they had in Cazaril's, once. "Your governess flattered you, Royesse."

She frowned across at him. "I take it you do not fancy yourself a flatterer, Castillar?"

Her tone and terms were a bit more double-leveled than he'd expected. His ironic return bow, from his seat on a chest drawn up to her table's other side, was pulled shorter and a little less apologetic than he'd intended by the yank of his adhesions. "I trust I am not a complete lout. But if you desire a man to tell you comfortable lies about your prowess, and so fetter any hope of true excellence, I'm sure you may find one anywhere. Not all prisons are made of iron bars. Some are made of feather beds. Royesse."

Her nostrils flared; her lips thinned. Belatedly, it occurred to Cazaril that perhaps this was the wrong approach. She was a tender young thing, barely more than a girl—perhaps he ought to soften—and if she complained of him to the Provincara, he might lose—

She turned the page. "Let us," she said in an icy voice, "go on."

Five gods, he'd seen *exactly* that same look of frustrated fury in the eyes of the young men who'd picked themselves up, spat the dirt from their mouths, and gone on to become his best lieutenants. Maybe this wasn't going to be so difficult after all. With great effort, he cranked a broad grin downward into a grave frown and nodded august tutorly permission. "Continue."

An hour flew by in this pleasant, easy employment. Well, easy for him. When he noticed the royesse rubbing her temples, and lines deepening between her brows that had nothing to do with mere offense, he desisted and took the book back from her.

Lady Betriz had followed along at Iselle's side, her lips moving silently. Cazaril had her repeat the exercise. With Iselle's example before her, she was quicker, but alas she suffered from the same broad South Ibran accent, probably from the same South Ibran prior instructress, as Iselle. Iselle listened intently as they waded through corrections.

They had all earned their noon dinner by that time, Cazaril felt; but he had one more displeasing task to accomplish, strictly charged to him by the Provincara. He leaned back, as the girls stirred and made to rise, and cleared his throat.

"That was quite a spectacular gesture you brought off yesterday at the temple, Royesse."

Her wide mouth curved up; her curiously thick eyelids narrowed in pleasure. "Thank you, Castillar."

He let his own smile grow astringent. "A most showy insult, to put upon a man constrained to stand and not answer back. At least the idlers were vastly amused, judging by their laughter."

Her lips constricted into an uneasy purse. "There is much ill done in Chalion that I can do nothing about. It was little enough."

"If it was well, it was well-done," he conceded with a deceptively cordial nod. "Tell me, Royesse, what steps did you take beforehand, to assure yourself of the man's guilt?"

Her chin stopped in mid-rise. "Ser dy Ferrej . . . said it of him. And I know him to be honest."

"Ser dy Ferrej said, and I recall his words precisely, for he uses his words so, that he'd heard it *said* the judge had taken the duelist's bribe. He did not claim firsthand knowledge of the deed. Did you check with him, after dinner, to find out how he came by his belief?"

"No . . . If I'd told anyone what I was planning, they would have forbidden me."

"You, ah, told Lady Betriz, though." Cazaril favored the dark-eyed woman with a nod.

Stiffening, Betriz replied warily, "It's why I suggested asking the first flame."

Cazaril shrugged. "The first flame, ah. But your hand is young and strong and steady, Lady Iselle. Are you sure that first flame wasn't all your doing?"

Her frown deepened. "The townsmen applauded . . ."

"Indeed. On average, one-half of all supplicants to come before a judge's bench must depart angry and disappointed. But not, by that, necessarily wronged."

That one hit the target, by the change in her face. The shift from defiant to stricken was not especially pleasurable to watch. "But . . . but . . ."

Cazaril sighed. "I'm not saying you were wrong, Royesse. This time. I'm saying you were running blindfolded. And if it wasn't headlong into a tree, it was only by the mercy of the gods, and not by any care of yours."

"Oh."

"You may have slandered an honest man. Or you may have struck a blow for justice. I don't know. The point is . . . *neither do you.*"

Her *oh* this time was so repressed as to be unvoiced.

The horribly practical part of Cazaril's mind that had eased him through so many scrapes couldn't help adding, "And right *or* wrong, what I also saw was that you made an enemy, and left him alive behind you. Great charity. Bad tactics." Damn, but that was no remark to make to a gentle maiden . . . with an effort, he kept from clapping his hands over his mouth, a gesture that would do nothing to prop up his pose as a high-minded and earnest corrector.

Iselle's brows went up and stayed up, for a moment, this time. So did Lady Betriz's.

After an unnervingly long and thoughtful silence, Iselle said quietly, "I thank you for your good counsel, Castillar."

He returned her an approving nod. Good. If he'd got through that sticky one all right, he was halfway home with her. And now, thank the gods, on to the Provincara's generous table . . .

Iselle sat back and folded her hands in her lap. "You are to be my secretary, as well as my tutor, Cazaril, yes?"

Cazaril sank back. "Yes, my lady? You wish some assistance with a letter?" He almost added suggestively, *After dinner?*

"Assistance. Yes. But not with a letter. Ser dy Ferrej said you were once a courier, is that right?"

"I once rode for the provincar of Guarida, my lady. When I was younger."

"A courier is a spy." Her regard had grown disquietingly calculating.

"Not necessarily, though it was sometimes hard to . . . convince people otherwise. We were trusted messengers, first and foremost. Not that we weren't supposed to keep our eyes open and report our observations."

"Good enough." The chin came up. "Then my first task for you, as my secretary, is one of observation. I want you to find out if I made a mistake or not. I can't very well go down into town, or ask around—I have to stay up on top of this hill in my"—she grimaced—"feather bed. But you—you can do it." She gazed across at him with an expression of the most disturbing faith.

His stomach felt suddenly as hollow as a drum, and it had nothing to do with the lack of food. Apparently, he had just put on slightly too good a show. "I . . . I . . . immediately?"

She shifted uncomfortably. "Discreetly. As opportunity presents."
Cazaril swallowed. "I'll try what I can do, my lady."

❧ON HIS WAY DOWN THE STAIRS TO HIS OWN CHAM-
ber, one floor below, a vision surfaced in Cazaril's thoughts from
his days as a page in this very castle. He'd fancied himself a bit of
a swordsman, on account of being a shade better than the half
dozen other young highborn louts who'd shared his duties and his
training in the provincar's household. One day a new young page
had arrived, a short, surly fellow; the provincar's swordmaster had
invited Cazaril to step up against him at the next training session.
Cazaril had developed himself a pretty thrust or two, including a
flourish that, with a real blade, would have neatly nipped the ears
off most of his comrades. He'd tried his special pass on the new fellow, coming to a happy halt with the dulled edge flat against the
newcomer's head—only to look down and see his opponent's light
practice blade bent nearly double against his gut padding.

That page had gone on, Cazaril had heard, to become the
swordmaster for the roya of Brajar. In time, Cazaril had to own
himself an indifferent swordsman—his interests had always been
too broad-scattered for him to maintain the necessary obsession.
But he'd never forgotten that moment, looking down in surprise at
his mock-death.

It bemused him that his first lesson with the delicate Iselle had
churned up that old memory. Odd little flickers of intensity, to
burn in such disparate eyes . . . what had that short page's name
been . . . ?

Cazaril found that a couple more tunics and trousers had arrived on his bed while he was out, relics of the castle warder's
younger and thinner days, unless he missed his guess. He went to
put them away in the chest at the foot of his bed and was reminded
of the dead wool merchant's book, folded inside the black vest-
cloak there. He picked it up, thinking to walk it down to the temple this afternoon, but then set it back. Possibly, within its ciphered
pages, might lurk some of that moral certainty the royesse sought
of him—that he had pricked her to seek of him—some clearer evidence for or against the shamed judge. He would examine it him-

self, first. Perhaps it would provide some guidance to the secrets of Valenda's local scene.

🦑AFTER DINNER, CAZARIL LAY DOWN FOR A MARVELOUS little nap. He was just coming to luxuriant wakefulness again when Ser dy Ferrej knocked on his door, and delivered to him the books and records of the royesse's chambers. Betriz followed shortly with a box of letters for him to put in order. Cazaril spent the remainder of the afternoon starting to organize the randomly piled lot, and familiarize himself with the matters therein.

The financial records were fairly simple—the purchase of this or that trivial toy or bit of trumpery jewelry; lists of presents given and received; a somewhat more meticulous listing of jewels of genuine value, inheritances, or gifts. Clothing. Iselle's riding horse, the mule Snowflake, and their assorted trappings. Items such as linens or furniture were subsumed, presumably, in the Provincara's accounts, but would in future be Cazaril's charge. A lady of rank was normally sent off to marriage with cartloads—Cazaril hoped not boatloads—of fine goods, and Iselle was surely due to begin the years of accumulation against that future journey. Should he list himself as Item One in that bridal inventory?

He pictured the entry: *Sec't'y-tutor, One ea. Gift from Grandmama. Aged thirty-five. Badly damaged in shipping. Value . . . ?*

The bridal procession was a one-way journey, normally, although Iselle's mother the dowager royina had returned . . . *broken,* Cazaril tried not to think. The Lady Ista puzzled and disturbed him. It was said that madness ran in some noble families. Not Cazaril's—his family had run to financial fecklessness and unlucky political alliances instead, just as devastating in the long run. Was Iselle at risk . . . ? *Surely not.*

Iselle's correspondence was scant but interesting. Some early, kindly little letters from her grandmother, from before the widowed royina had moved her family back home from court, full of advice on the general order of *be good, obey your mother, say your prayers, help take care of your little brother.* One or two notes from uncles or aunts, the Provincara's other children—Iselle had no other relatives on her father the late Roya Ias's side, Ias having been the only surviving child of his own ill-fated father. A regular series of birthday and holy day letters from her much older half brother, the present roya, Orico.

Those were in the roya's own hand, Cazaril noted with approval, or at least, he trusted the roya did not employ any secretary with such a crabbed and difficult fist. They were for the most part stiff little missives, the effort of a man full-grown attempting to be kindly to a child, except when they broke into descriptions of Orico's beloved menagerie. Then they became spontaneous and flowing for the space of a paragraph or two, in enthusiasm and, perhaps, trust that here at least was an interest the two half siblings might share on the same level.

This pleasant task was interrupted in turn late in the afternoon with the word, brought by a page, that Cazaril's presence was now required to ride out with the royesse and Lady Betriz. He hastily donned the borrowed sword and found the horses saddled and waiting in the courtyard. Cazaril hadn't had a leg across a horse for nearly three years; the page eyed him with surprise and disfavor when Cazaril asked for a mounting block, to ease himself gingerly aboard. They gave him a nice mild-mannered beast, the same bay gelding he'd seen the royesse's waiting woman riding that first afternoon. As they formed up, the waiting woman leaned from a window in the keep and waved them out with a piece of linen and evident goodwill. But the ride proved much milder and more placid than he'd anticipated, a mere jaunt down to the river and back. Since he declared at the outset of the excursion that all conversation by the party must be conducted in Darthacan, it was also largely silent, adding to the general restfulness.

And then supper, and then to his chamber, where he pottered about trying on his new old clothing, and folding it away, and attempting the first few pages of deciphering the poor dead fool of a wool merchant's book. But Cazaril's eyes grew heavy over this task, and he slept like a block till morning.

❧As it had begun, so it went on. In the morning, lessons with the two lovely young ladies in Darthacan or Roknari or geography or arithmetic or geometry. For geography, he filched away the good maps from Teidez's tutor and entertained the royesse with suitably edited accounts of some of his more exotic past journeys around Chalion, Ibra, Brajar, great Darthaca, or the five perpetually quarreling Roknari princedoms along the north coast.

His more recent slave's-eye views of the Roknar Archipelago, he edited much more severely. Iselle's and Betriz's open boredom with court Roknari, he discovered, was susceptible to exactly the same cure as he'd used on the couple of young pages from the provincar of Guarida's household he'd once been detailed to teach the language. He traded the ladies one word of rude Roknari (albeit not the *most* rude) for every twenty of court Roknari they demonstrated themselves to have memorized. Not that they would ever get to use that vocabulary, but it might be well for them to be able to recognize things said in their hearing. And they giggled charmingly.

Cazaril approached his first assigned duty, quietly investigating the probity of the provincial justiciar, with trepidation. Oblique inquiries of the Provincara and dy Ferrej filled in background without supplying certainty, as neither had crossed the man in his professional capacity, merely in unexceptionable social contacts. A few excursions down into town to try to find anyone who'd known Cazaril seventeen years ago and would speak to him frankly proved a little disheartening. The only man who recognized him with certainty at sight was an elderly baker who'd maintained a long and lucrative career selling sweets to all the castle's parade of pages, but he was an amiable fellow not inclined to lawsuits.

Cazaril started working through the wool merchant's notebook leaf by leaf, as quickly as his other duties permitted him. Some truly disgusting early experiments in calling down the Bastard's demons had been entirely ineffective, Cazaril was relieved to observe. The dead duelist's name never appeared but with some excoriating adjectives attached, or sometimes just the adjectives alone; the live judge's name did not turn up explicitly. But before Cazaril had the tangle even half-unraveled, the question was taken out of his inexpert hands.

An Officer of Inquiry from the Provincar of Baocia's court arrived, from the busy town of Taryoon, to which the Dowager's son had moved his capital upon inheriting his father's gift. It had taken,

Cazaril counted off in his head later, just about as many days as one could expect for a letter from the Provincara to her son to be written, dispatched, and read, for orders to be passed down to Baocia's Chancellery of Justice, and for the Inquirer to ready himself and his staff for travel. Privilege indeed. Cazaril was unsure of the Provincara's allegiance to the processes of law, but he wagered the business of leaving loose enemies untidily about had plucked some, ah, housewifely nerve of hers.

The next day the judge Vrese was discovered to have ridden off in the night with two servants and some hastily packed bags and chests, leaving a disrupted household and a fireplace full of ashes from burned papers.

Cazaril tried to discourage Iselle from taking this as proof either, but that was a bit of a stretch even for his slow judgment. The alternative—that Iselle *had* been touched by the goddess that day—disturbed him to contemplate. The gods, the learned theologians of the Holy Family assured men, worked in ways subtle, secret, and above all, parsimonious: through the world, not in it. Even for the bright, exceptional miracles of healing—or dark miracles of disaster or death—men's free will must open a channel for good or evil to enter waking life. Cazaril had met, in his time, some two or three persons who he suspected might be truly godtouched, and a few more who'd plainly thought they were. They had not any of them been *comfortable* to be around. Cazaril trusted devoutly that the Daughter of Spring had gone away satisfied with her avatar's action. *Or just gone away . . .*

Iselle had little contact with her brother's household across the courtyard, except to meet at meals, or when they made up a party for a ride out into the countryside. Cazaril gathered the two children had been closer, before the onset of puberty had begun to drive them into the separate worlds of men and women.

The royse's stern secretary-tutor, Ser dy Sanda, seemed unnecessarily unnerved by Cazaril's empty rank of castillar. He laid claim to a higher place at table or in procession above the mere ladies' tutor with an insincerely apologetic smile that served—every meal—to draw more attention than it purported to soothe. Cazaril considered trying to explain to the man just how much he didn't care, but doubted he'd get through, so contented himself with merely smiling back, a response which confused dy Sanda terribly as he kept trying to place it as some sort of subtle tactic. When dy Sanda showed up in Iselle's schoolroom one day to demand his maps be returned, he seemed to expect Cazaril to defend them as though they were secret state papers. Cazaril produced them promptly, with gentle thanks. Dy Sanda was forced to depart with his huff barely half-vented.

Lady Betriz's teeth were set. "That fellow! He acts like, like . . ."

"Like one of the castle cats," Iselle supplied, "when a strange cat comes around. What have you done to make him hiss at you so, Cazaril?"

"I promise you, I haven't pissed outside his window," Cazaril offered earnestly, a remark that made Betriz choke on a giggle—ah, that was better—and look around guiltily to be sure the waiting woman was too far off to hear. Had that been too crude? He was sure he didn't quite have the hang of young ladies yet, but they had not complained of him, despite the Darthacan. "I suppose he imagines I would prefer his job. He can't have thought it through."

Or perhaps he had, Cazaril realized abruptly. When Teidez had been born, his heirship to his new-wed half brother Orico had been much less apparent. But as year had followed year, and Orico's royina still failed to conceive a child, interest—possibly unhealthy interest—in Teidez must surely have begun to grow in the court of Chalion. Perhaps that was why Ista had left the capital, taking her children out of that fervid atmosphere to this quiet, clean country town. A wise move, withal.

"Oh, no, Cazaril," said Iselle. "Stay up here with us. It's much nicer."

"Indeed, yes," he assured her.

"It's not just. You've twice Ser dy Sanda's wits, and ten times his travels! Why do you endure him so, so . . ." Betriz seemed at a loss for words. "Quietly," she finally finished. She stared away for a moment, as if afraid he would construe she'd swallowed a term less flattering.

Cazaril smiled crookedly at his unexpected partisan. "Do you think it would make him happier if I presented myself as a target for his foolishness?"

"Clearly, yes!"

"Well, then. Your question answers itself."

She opened her mouth, and closed it. Iselle nearly choked on a short laugh.

Cazaril's sympathy for dy Sanda increased, however, one morning when he turned up, his face so drained of blood as to be almost green, with the alarming news that his royal charge had vanished away, not to be found in house or kitchen, kennel or stable. Cazaril buckled on his sword and readied himself to ride out with the searchers, his mind already quartering the countryside and the town, weighing the options of injuries, bandits, the river . . . taverns? Was Teidez old enough yet to attempt a whore? Reason enough to scrape off his clinging attendants.

Before Cazaril was moved to point out the range of possibilities to dy Sanda, whose mind was utterly fixated on bandits, Teidez himself rode in to the courtyard, muddy and damp, a crossbow slung over his shoulder, a boy groom following behind, and a dead fox hung over his saddlebow. Teidez stared at the half-assembled cavalcade with surly horror.

Cazaril abandoned his attempt to climb on his horse without pulling something that hurt, lowered himself to a seat on his mounting block with the bay gelding's reins in his hand, and watched in fascination as four grown men began to belabor the boy and the obvious.

Where have you been? scarcely needed asked, *Why did you do that?* likewise, *Why didn't you tell anyone?* grew more apparent by the minute. Teidez endured it with his teeth closed, for the most part.

When dy Sanda paused for breath, Teidez thrust his limp and ruddy prey at Beetim the huntsman. "Here. Skin this for me. I want the pelt."

"Pelt's no good at this season, young lord," said Beetim severely. "The hair's all thin, and falls out." He shook his finger at the vixen's dark dugs, heavy with milk. "And it's bad luck to take a mother animal in the Daughter's season. I'll have to burn its whiskers, or its ghost'll be back, stirring up my dogs all night long. And where are the cubs, eh? You should've slain them as well, while you were at it, it's right cruel to leave them to starve. Or have you two gone and hidden them somewhere, eh?" His glower took in the shrinking boy groom.

Teidez threw his crossbow to the cobbles, and snarled in exasperation, "We *looked* for the den. We couldn't find it."

"Yes, and you—!" dy Sanda turned on the unlucky groom. "You

know you should have come to me—!" He abused the groom in much blunter terms than he'd dared to vent upon the royse, ending with the command, "Beetim, go beat the boy for his stupidity and insolence!"

"With a will, m'lord," said Beetim grimly, and stalked away toward the stables, the fox's scruff in one hand and the cowering groom's in the other.

The two senior grooms led the horses back to their stalls. Cazaril gave up his mount gladly and considered his breakfast—now, it appeared, not to be indefinitely delayed. Dy Sanda, anger succeeding his terror, confiscated the crossbow and drove the sullen Teidez indoors. Teidez's voice floated back in a last counterargument before the door banged closed upon the pair, "But I'm so *bored* . . .!"

Cazaril puffed a laugh. Five gods, but what a horrible age that was to be for any boy. All full of impulses and energy, plagued with incomprehensible arbitrary adults with stupid ideas that did not involve skipping morning prayers to go fox hunting on a fair spring morning—he glanced up at the sky overhead, brightening to a washed cerulean as the dawn mists burned away. The quietude of the Provincara's household, balm to Cazaril's soul, was doubtless acid to poor constricted Teidez.

Any word of advice from the newly employed Cazaril was not likely to be well received by dy Sanda, as matters stood between them at present. But it seemed to Cazaril that if dy Sanda was looking to guard his future influence over the royse when he came to a man's estate with its full power and privilege of a high lord—at the very least—of Chalion, he was going about it exactly backward. Teidez was more likely to shed him at the first opportunity.

Still, dy Sanda was a conscientious man, Cazaril had to grant. A viler man of like ambition might well be pandering to Teidez's appetites instead of attempting to control them, winning not loyalty but addiction. Cazaril had met a noble scion or two so corrupted by his attendants . . . but not in dy Baocia's household. While the Provincara was in charge, Teidez was unlikely to encounter such parasites. On that comforting reflection, Cazaril pushed off the block and climbed to his feet.

5

The Royesse Iselle's sixteenth birthday fell at the midpoint of spring, some six weeks after Cazaril had come to Valenda. The birthday present sent down this year from the capital at Cardegoss by her brother Orico was a fine dappled gray mare, an inspiration either well calculated or very lucky, for Iselle flew into transports over the shimmering beast. Cazaril had to concede it was a royal gift. And he was able to avoid the problem of his damaged handwriting a little longer, as it was no trouble at all to persuade Iselle to make her thank-you in her own hand, to send with the royal courier's return.

But Cazaril found himself subjected in the days following to the most minute and careful, not to say embarrassing, inquiries from Iselle and Betriz after his health. Little gifts of the best fruit or viands were sent down the table to tempt his appetite; he was encouraged to go early to bed, and drink a little wine, but not too much; both ladies persuaded him out to frequent short walks in the garden. It wasn't till dy Ferrej let fall a casual joke to the Provincara in his hearing that Cazaril caught on that Iselle and her handmaiden had been constrained to temper their gallops out of consideration for the new secretary's supposedly frail health. Cazaril's wits overtook his indignation just barely in time to confirm this canard with a straight face and a convincingly stiff gait. Their feminine attentions, however blatantly self-interested, were too lovely to scorn. And . . . it wasn't that much of an act.

Both the improving weather and, truth to tell, his improving condition baited him into relenting. After all, soon enough the summer heat would be upon them, and slow life down again. After watching both girls stick to their horses over logs and down the twisting trails by the river, flashing along in ripples of gold and green from the half shade of the new leaves overhead, his concern for their safety eased. It was *his* horse, shying sideways after startling a doe out of a thicket, that dumped him violently into a mess of rocks and tree roots, knocking his wind out and popping an adhesion in his back. He lay wheezing, the woods blurred with tears of pain, till two frightened female faces wavered into his view against the lace of leaves and sky.

It took the pair of them and the help of a fallen tree to get him loaded back up on his recaptured horse. The return trip up the hill to the castle was as demure and ladylike, not to mention guilty, a walk as ever the governesses could have wished. The world had stopped twisting around his head in odd little jerks by the time they rode through the arched gate, but the torn adhesion was a burning agony marked by a lump the size of an egg beneath his tunic. It would likely darken to black and take weeks to subside. Arriving safe at last in the courtyard, he had no attention for anything but the mounting block, the groom, and again getting off the damned horse alive. Secure on the ground he stood for a moment, head bent against the saddlebow, grimacing with pain.

"Caz!"

The familiar voice smote his ears out of nowhere. His head came up; he blinked around. Striding toward him, his arms held out, was a tall, athletic man with dark hair, dressed in an elegant red brocade tunic and high riding boots. "Five gods," whispered Cazaril, and then, "*Palli?*"

"Caz, Caz! I kiss your hands! I kiss your feet!" The tall man seized him, nearly knocking him over, made the first half of his greeting literal, but traded the second for an embrace instead. "Caz, man! I'd thought you were dead!"

"No, no . . . Palli . . ." His pain three-fourths forgotten, he grabbed the dark-haired man's hands in turn, and turned to Iselle and Betriz, who'd abandoned their horses to the grooms and drifted up in open curiosity. "Royesse Iselle, Lady Betriz, permit me to introduce the Ser dy Palliar—he was my good right arm at Gotorget—five gods, Palli, what are you doing *here*?"

"I could ask you the same, with more reason!" Palli replied, and made his bow to the ladies, who eyed him with increasing approval. The two years and more since Gotorget had done much to improve his already-pleasant looks, not that they hadn't all looked like depraved scarecrows at the end of the siege. "Royesse, my lady, an honor—but it's the March dy Palliar now, Caz."

"Oh," said Cazaril, and gave him an immediate, apologetic nod. "My condolences. Is it a recent loss?"

Palli returned an understanding duck of his chin. "Almost two years gone, now. The old man had suffered an apoplectic stroke while we were still closed up in Gotorget, but he hung on till just after I made it home, thanks be to the Father of Winter. He knew me, I was able to see him at the last, tell him of the campaign—he offered up a blessing for you, you know, on his last day, though we both thought we were praying for the lost dead. Caz, man, where did you *go*?"

"I . . . wasn't ransomed."

"Not ransomed? How, not ransomed? How could *you* not be ransomed?"

"It was an error. My name was left off the list."

"Dy Jironal said the Roknari reported you died of a sudden fever."

Cazaril's smile grew tight. "No. I was sold to the galleys."

Palli's head jerked back. "Some error! No, wait, that makes no sense—"

Cazaril's grimace, and his hand pressed palm down before his chest, stopped Palli's protest on his lips, though it didn't quench the startled look in his eyes. Palli always could take a hint, if you clouted him with it hard enough. The twist of his mouth said, *Very well, but I will have this out of you later*—! By the time he turned to Ser dy Ferrej, coming up to observe this reunion with an interested expression, his cheerful smile was back in place.

"My lord dy Palliar is taking wine with the Provincara in the garden," the castle warder explained. "Do join us, Cazaril."

"Thank you."

Palli took his arm, and they turned to follow dy Ferrej out of the courtyard and half-around the keep, to the little plot where the

Provincara's gardener grew flowers. In good weather she made it her favorite bower for sitting outdoors. Three strides, and Cazaril was trailing; Palli shortened his step abruptly at Cazaril's stumble, and eyed him sidelong. The Provincara waited their return with a patient smile, enthroned under an arching trellis of climbing roses not yet in bloom. She waved them to the chairs the servants had brought out. Cazaril lowered himself onto a cushion with a wince and an awkward grunt.

"Bastard's demons," said Palli under his breath, "did the Roknari cripple you?"

"Only half. Lady Iselle—oof!—seems bent on completing the task." Gingerly, he eased himself back. "And that fool horse."

The Provincara frowned at the two young ladies, who had tagged along uninvited. "Iselle, were you galloping?" she inquired dangerously.

Cazaril waved a diverting hand. "It was all the fault of my noble steed, my lady—attacked, it thought, by a horse-eating deer. It went sidewise, I didn't. Thank you." He accepted a glass of wine from the servant with deep appreciation and sipped quickly, trying not to let it slosh. The unpleasant shaky feeling in his gut was passing off, now.

Iselle cast him a grateful glance, which her grandmother did not miss. The Provincara sniffed faint disbelief. By way of punishment, she said, "Iselle, Betriz, go and change out of those riding clothes and into something suitable for supper. We may be country folk here; we need not be savages." They dragged off, with a couple of backward glances at the fascinating visitor.

"But how came you here, Palli?" Cazaril asked, when the double distraction had passed around the corner of the keep. Palli, too, stared after them, and seemed to have to shake himself back awake. *Close your mouth, man,* Cazaril thought in amusement. *I have to.*

"Oh! I'm riding up to Cardegoss, to dance attendance at court. M'father always used to break his journeys here, being thick with the old Provincar—when we passed near Valenda, I made to presume, and sent a messenger. And m'lady"—he nodded to the Provincara—"was kind enough to bid me bide."

"I'd have cuffed you if you'd failed to make your duty to me," said the Provincara amiably, with admirable illogic. "I'd not seen your father nor you for far too many years. I was sorry to hear of his passing."

Palli nodded. He continued to Cazaril, "We plan to rest the horses overnight and go on tomorrow at a leisurely pace—the weather's too fine to be in a rush. There are pilgrims on the roads to every shrine and temple—and those who prey on 'em, alas—there were bandits reported in the hill passes, but we didn't find 'em."

"You looked?" said Cazaril, bemused. *Not* finding bandits had been all his desire, on the road.

"Hey! I am the lord dedicat of the Daughter's Order at Palliar now, I'll have you know—in my father's shoes. I have duties."

"You ride with the soldier-brothers?"

"More like with the baggage train. It's all keeping the books, and collecting rents, and chasing the damned equipment, and *logistics*. The joys of command—well, you know. You taught them to me. One part glory to ten parts shoveling manure."

Cazaril grinned. "That good a ratio? You're blessed."

Palli grinned back and accepted cheese and cakes from the servant. "I lodged my troop down in town. But you, Caz! As soon as I said, *Gotorget*, they asked me if we'd met—you could have knocked me over with a straw when m'lady said you'd turned up here, having walked—walked!—from Ibra, and looking like something the cat hawked up."

The Provincara gave a small, unrepentant shrug at Cazaril's faintly reproachful glance her way.

"I've been telling them war stories for the past half hour," Palli went on. "How's your hand?"

Cazaril curled it in his lap. "Much recovered." He hastened to change the subject. "What's forward at court, for you?"

"Well, I'd not had the chance to make formal oath to Orico since m'father died, and also, I'm to represent the Daughter's Order of Palliar at the investiture."

"Investiture?" said Cazaril blankly.

"Ah, has Orico finally given out the generalship of the Daughter's Order?" asked dy Ferrej. "Since the old general died, I hear every high family in Chalion has been badgering him for the gift."

"I should imagine," said the Provincara. "Lucrative and powerful enough, even if it is smaller than the Son's."

"Oh, aye," said Palli. "It's not been announced yet, but it's known—it's to be Dondo dy Jironal, the younger brother of the Chancellor."

Cazaril stiffened, and sipped wine to hide his dismay.

After a rather long pause, the Provincara said, "What an odd choice. One usually expects the general of a holy military order to be more . . . personally austere."

"But, but," said dy Ferrej, "Chancellor *Martou* dy Jironal holds the generalship of the Order of the Son! Two, in one family? It's a dangerous concentration of power."

The Provincara murmured, "Martou is also to become the Provincar dy Jironal, if rumor is true. As soon as old dy Ildar stops lingering."

"I hadn't heard *that*," said Palli, sounding startled.

"Yes," said the Provincara dryly. "The Ildar family is not too happy. I believe they'd been counting on the provincarship for one of the nephews."

Palli shrugged. "The brothers Jironal certainly ride high in Chalion, by Orico's favor. I suppose if I were clever, I would find some way of grabbing on to their cloak-hems, and riding along."

Cazaril frowned into his wine and groped for a way to divert the topic. "What other news do you hear?"

"Well, these two weeks gone, the Heir of Ibra has raised his banner in South Ibra—again—against the old fox, his father. Everyone had thought last summer's treaty would hold, but it seems they had some secret falling-out, last autumn, and the roya repudiated it. Again."

"The Heir," said the Provincara, "presumes. Ibra does have another son, after all."

"Orico supported the Heir the last time," observed Palli.

"To Chalion's cost," murmured Cazaril.

"It seemed to me Orico was taking the long view. In the end," said Palli, "surely the Heir must win. One way or another."

"It will be a joyless victory for the old man if his son loses," said dy Ferrej in a tone of slow consideration. "No, I wager they'll spend more men's lives, and then make it up again between them over the bodies."

"A sad business," said the Provincara, tightening her lips. "No good can come of it. Eh, dy Palliar. Tell me some good news. Tell me Orico's royina is with child."

Palli shook his head ruefully. "Not as I've heard, lady."

"Well, then, let us go to our supper and talk no more politics. It makes my old head ache."

His muscles had seized up while he was sitting, despite the wine; Cazaril almost fell over, trying to rise from his chair. Palli caught him by the elbow and steadied him, and frowned deeply. Cazaril gave him a tiny shake of his head and went off to wash and change. And examine his bruises in private.

🐦SUPPER WAS A CHEERFUL MEAL, ATTENDED BY MOST of the household. Dy Palliar, no slouch at table when it came to either food or talk, held the attention of everyone, from the Lord Teidez and Lady Iselle down to the youngest page, with his tales. Despite the wine he kept his head in the high company, and told only the merry stories, with himself more as butt than hero. The account of how he'd followed Cazaril on a night sortie against the Roknari sappers, and so discouraged them for a month thereafter, drew wide-eyed stares upon Cazaril as well as himself. They clearly had a hard time picturing the royesse's timid, soft-spoken secretary grinning in the dirt and the soot, scrambling through the burning rubble with a dirk in his hand. Cazaril realized he disliked the stares. He wanted to be . . . invisible, here. Twice Palli tried to toss the conversational ball to him, to take a turn at the entertaining, and twice he fielded it back to Palli or to dy Ferrej. After the second attempt fell flat, Palli desisted from trying to draw him out.

The meal ran very late, but at last came the hour Cazaril had been both longing for and dreading, when all parted for the night, and Palli knocked on his chamber door. Cazaril bade him enter, pushed the trunk to the wall, tossed a cushion upon it for his guest, and settled himself upon his bed; both he and it creaked audibly. Palli sat and stared across at him in the dim double candlelight, and began with a directness that revealed the trend of his mind all too clearly.

"Error, Caz? Have you thought about that?"

Cazaril sighed. "I had nineteen months to think of it, Palli. I rubbed every possibility as thin as an old coin in my brain. I thought of it till I was sick to death of the thinking, and called it done. It's done."

This time, Palli brushed the hint firmly aside. "Do you think it was the Roknari taking revenge upon you, by hiding you from us and saying you died?"

"That's one." *Except that I saw the list.*

"Or did someone leave you off the list on purpose?" Palli persisted.

The list was in Martou dy Jironal's own hand. "That was my final conclusion."

Palli's breath blew out. "Vile! A *vile* betrayal, after what we suffered—dammit, Caz! When I get up to court, I am going to tell March dy Jironal of this. He's the most powerful lord in Chalion, the gods know. Together, I wager we can get to the bottom of—"

"No!" Cazaril lurched upright from his cushions, terrified. "Don't, Palli! Don't even tell dy Jironal I exist! Don't discuss it, don't mention me—if the world thinks I'm dead, so much the better. If I'd realized that was so, I would have stayed in Ibra. Just . . . drop it."

Palli stared. "But . . . Valenda is hardly the end of the world. Of course people will learn you're alive."

"It's a quiet, peaceful place. I'm not bothering anyone here."

Other men were as brave, some were stronger; it was Palli's wits that had made him Cazaril's favorite lieutenant at Gotorget. It only needed the one thread to start him unraveling . . . his eyes narrowed, glinting in the soft candlelight. "*Dy Jironal?* Himself? Five gods, what did you ever do to *him?*"

Cazaril shifted uncomfortably. "I think it was not personal. I think it was just a little . . . favor, for someone. A little, easy favor."

"Then two men must know the truth. Gods, Caz, which two?"

Palli would go nosing in—Cazaril must either tell him nothing—too late already—or else enough to stop him. Nothing halfway, Palli's brain would keep plucking at the puzzle—it was doing so even now.

"Who would hate you so? You were always the most agreeable man—you were downright famous for refusing duels, and leaving the bullroarers to look like the fools they were—for making peace, for wheedling out the most amazing treaty terms, for avoiding faction—Bastard's hell, you didn't even make bets on games! *Little, easy favor!* What could possibly drive such an implacable cruel hatred of *you?*"

Cazaril rubbed his brow, which was beginning to ache, and not from tonight's wine. "Fear. I think."

Palli's lips screwed up in astonishment.

"And if it becomes known you know, they'll fear you too. It's not something I wish to see fall on you, Palli. I want you to steer clear."

"If it's that degree of fear, the fact that we've even talked together will make me suspect. Their fear, plus my ignorance—gods, Caz! Don't send me blindfolded into battle!"

"I want never to send any man into battle again!" The fierceness in his own voice took even Cazaril by surprise. Palli's eyes widened. But the solution, the way to use Palli's own ravenous curiosity against him, came to Cazaril in that moment. "If I tell you what I know, and how I know it, will you give me your word—your word!—to drop it? Don't pursue it, don't mention it, don't mention me—no dark hints, no dancing about the issue—"

"What, as you are doing now?" said Palli dryly.

Cazaril grunted, half in amusement, half in pain. "Just so."

Palli sat back against the wall, and rubbed his lips. "Merchant," he said amiably. "To make me buy a pig in a bag, without ever seeing the animal."

"Oink," murmured Cazaril.

"I only want to buy the squeal, y'know—damn, all right. I never knew you to lead us over wet ground unknowing, nor into ambush. I'll trust your judgment—to the exact extent you trust my discretion. My word on *that.*"

A neat counterthrust. Cazaril could not but admire it. He sighed. "Very well." He sat silent for a moment after this—welcome—dual surrender, marshaling his thoughts. Where to begin? Well, it wasn't as though he hadn't gone over it, and over it, and over it in his mind. A most polished tale, for all it had never crossed his lips before.

"It's quickly enough told. I first met Dondo dy Jironal to speak to four, no, it's five now, five years ago. I was in Guarida's train in that little border war against the mad Roknari prince Olus—you know, the fellow who made a habit of burying his enemies up to the waist in excrement and burning them alive?—the one who was murdered about a year later by his own bodyguards?"

"Oh, yes. I'd heard of him. Ended head down in the excrement, they say."

"There are several versions. But he was still in control at *that* time. Lord dy Guarida had cornered Olus's army—well, rabble— up in the hills at the edge of his princedom. Lord Dondo and I were sent as the envoys, under the flag of parley, to deliver an ultimatum to Olus and arrange the terms and ransoms. Things went . . . badly, in the conference, and Olus decided he only required one messenger to return his defiance to the assembled lords of Chalion. So he stood us up, Dondo and me, in his tent surrounded by four of his monster guards with swords and gave us a choice. Whichever of us would cut off the other's head would be permitted to ride with it back to our lines. If we both refused, we both would die, and he'd return both our heads by catapult."

Palli opened his mouth, but the only comment he managed was, "Ah."

Cazaril took a breath. "I was given the first chance. I refused the sword. Olus whispered to me, in this weird oily voice, 'You cannot win this game, Lord Cazaril.' I said, 'I know, m'hendi. But I can make you lose it.' He was quiet for a little, but then he just laughed. Then he turned round and gave the chance to Dondo, who was green as a corpse by then . . ."

Palli stirred, but didn't interrupt; he signaled Cazaril mutely to go on.

"One of the guards knocked me to my knees and stretched my head, by the hair, over a footstool. Dondo—took his cut."

"On the guard's arm?" said Palli eagerly.

Cazaril hesitated. "No," he said at last. "But Olus, at the last moment, thrust his sword between us, and Dondo's sword came down on its flat, and slid—" Cazaril could still hear the sharp scraping *skree* of metal on metal, in his memory's ear. "I ended up with a bruise across the back of my neck that was black for a month. Two of the other guards wrestled the sword back from Dondo. And then we were both mounted up on our horses and sent back to dy Guarida's camp. As my hands were being tied to my saddle, Olus came up to me again, and whispered, 'Now we shall see who loses.'

"It was a very silent ride back. Until we were in sight of camp.

And Dondo turned and looked at me for the first time, and said, 'If you ever tell this tale, I will kill you.' And I said, "Don't worry, Lord Dondo. I only tell *amusing* tales at table.' I should have just sworn silence. I know better now, and yet . . . maybe even that would not have been enough."

"He owes you his life!"

Cazaril shook his head, and looked away. "I've seen his soul stripped naked. I doubt he can ever forgive me for that. Well, I didn't speak of it, of course, and he let it lie. I thought that was the end of it. But then came Gotorget, and then came . . . well. What came after Gotorget. And now I am doubly damned. If Dondo ever learns, if he ever realizes that I know exactly how I came to be sold to the galleys, what do you think my life will be worth then? But if I say nothing, do nothing, nothing to remind him . . . perhaps he has forgotten, by now. I just want to be left alone, in this quiet place. He surely has more pressing enemies these days." He turned his face back to Palli, and said tensely, "Don't you ever mention me to either of the Jironals. Ever. You never heard this story. You scarcely know me. If you ever loved me, Palli, *leave it be.*"

Palli's lips were pressed together; his oath would hold him, Cazaril thought. But he made a little unhappy gesture nonetheless. "As you will, but, but . . . damn. Damn." He stared for long across the dim chamber at Cazaril, as if searching for who-knew-what in his face. "It's not just that dreadful excuse for a beard. You are much changed."

"Am I? Well, so."

"How . . ." Palli looked away, looked back. "How bad was it? Really? In the galleys."

Cazaril shrugged. "I was fortunate in my misfortunes. I survived. Some did not."

"One hears all sorts of horrific stories, how the slaves are terrorized, or . . . misused . . ."

Cazaril scratched his slandered beard. It was *too* filling in, a bit, he fancied. "The stories are not so much untrue as twisted, exaggerated—exceptional events mistaken as daily bread. The best captains treated us as a good farmer treats his animals, with a sort of impersonal kindness. Food, water—heh—exercise—enough cleanliness to keep us free of disease and in good condition. Beating a man senseless makes him unfit to pull his oar, you know. Anyway, that sort of physical . . . discipline was only required in port. Once at sea, the sea supplied all."

"I don't understand."

Cazaril's brows flicked up. "Why break a man's skin, or his head, when you can break his heart simply by putting him overboard, in the water with his legs dangling down like worms for the great fishes? The Roknari only had to wait a very little to have us swim after and beg and plead and weep for our slavery again."

"You were always a strong swimmer. Surely that helped you bear it better than most?" Palli's voice was hopeful.

"The opposite, I'm afraid. The men who sank like stones went mercifully quickly. Think about it, Palli. I did." He still did, sitting up bolt upright in the dark in this bed from some nightmare of the water, closing over his head. Or worse . . . not. Once, the wind had come up unexpectedly while the oar-master had been playing this little game with a certain recalcitrant Ibran, and the captain, anxious for port before the storm, had refused to circle back. The Ibran's fading screams had echoed over the water as the ship drew away, growing fainter and fainter. . . . The captain had docked the oar-master the cost of the slave's replacement, as punishment for his misjudgment, which had made him surly for weeks.

After a moment Palli said, "Oh."

Oh indeed. "Grant you, my pride—and my mouth—did win me one beating when I first went aboard, but I still fancied myself a lord of Chalion then. I was broken of that . . . later."

"But . . . you weren't . . . they didn't make you an object of . . . I mean, use you after a degrading . . . um."

The light was too dim to tell if Palli reddened, but it finally dawned on Cazaril that he was trying to inquire in this worried and tongue-tumbled fashion if Cazaril had been raped. Cazaril's lips twisted in sympathy. "You are confusing the Roknari fleets with those of Darthaca, I think. I'm afraid those legends represent wishful thinking on someone's part. The Roknari heresy of the four gods makes a crime of the sort of odd loves the Bastard rules, here. The Roknari theologians say the Bastard is a demon, like his father, and not a god, after his holy mother, and so call us all devil worshippers—which is a deep offense to the Lady of Summer, I think, as well as to the poor Bastard himself, for did he ask to be born? They torture and hang men caught in sodomy, and the better

Roknari shipmasters do not tolerate it aboard in either men or slaves."

"Ah." Palli settled in relief. But then, being Palli, thought to ask, "And the worse Roknari shipmasters?"

"Their discretion could become deadly. It didn't happen to me—I fancy I was too bony—but a few of the young men, the softer boys . . . We slaves knew they were our sacrifice, and we tried to be kind to them when they were returned to the benches. Some cried. Some learned to use the mischance for favors . . . few of us begrudged them the extra rations or trivial treats so dearly bought. It was a dangerous game, for the Roknari inclined to them in secret were like to turn on them at any moment, and slay them as if they could so slay their own sin."

"You make my hair stand on end. I thought I knew my way around the world, but . . . eh. But at least you were spared the worst."

"I don't know what is the worst," said Cazaril thoughtfully. "I was once used after a vile humor for the space of one hellish afternoon that made what happened to some of the boys look like a friendly gesture, but no Roknari risked hanging for it." Cazaril realized he'd never told anyone of the incident, not the kind acolytes of the temple hospital, not, certainly, anyone in the Provincara's household. He'd had no one he *could* talk to, till now. He continued almost eagerly. "My corsair made the mistake of tackling a lumbering Brajaran merchanter, and spotted its escorting galleys too late. As we were being chased off, I failed at my oar, fainted in the heat. To make some use of me despite all, the oar-master hauled me out of my chains, stripped me, and hung me over the stern rail with my hands tied to my ankles, to mock our pursuers. I couldn't tell if the crossbow bolts that thumped into the rail or the stern around me were good or bad aim on the Brajaran archers' parts, nor by what god's mercy I didn't end my life with a few in my ass. Maybe they thought I was Roknari. Maybe they were trying to end my misery." For the sake of Palli's widening eyes, Cazaril skipped certain of the more grotesque details. "You know, we lived with fear for months on end at Gotorget, till we were used to it, a sort of nagging ache in the gut that we learned to ignore, but that never quite went away."

Palli nodded.

"But I found out that . . . this is odd. I don't quite know how to say it." He'd never had a chance to try to put it into words, out where he could see it, till now. "I found there is a place beyond fear. When the body and the mind just can't sustain it anymore. The world, time . . . *reorder* themselves. My heartbeat slowed down, I stopped sweating and salivating . . . it was almost like some holy trance. When the Roknari hung me up, I'd been weeping in fear and shame, in agony for the disgust of it all. When the Brajarans finally veered off, and the oar-master took me down, all blistered from the sun . . . I was laughing. The Roknari thought I had gone mad, and so withal did my poor benchmates, but I didn't think so. The whole world was all . . . new.

"Of course, the whole world was only a few dozen paces long, and made of wood, and rocked on the water . . . all time was the turning of a glass. I planned my life by the hour as closely as one plans a year, and no further than an hour. All men were kind and beautiful, each in his way, Roknari and slave alike, lordly or vile blood, and I was a friend to all, and smiled. I wasn't afraid anymore. I did take care never to faint at my oar again, though."

His voice slowed, thoughtfully. "So whenever fear comes back into my heart, I am more pleased than anything, for I take it as a sign that I am not mad after all. Or maybe, at least, getting better. Fear is my friend." He looked up, with a quick, apologetic smile.

Palli was sitting plastered back against the wall, his legs tense, his dark eyes round as saucers, smiling fixedly. Cazaril laughed out loud.

"Five gods, Palli, forgive me. I did not mean to make you a donkey for my confidences, to carry them safely away." Or perhaps he had, for Palli would be going away tomorrow, after all. "They make a motley menagerie to burden you with. I'm sorry."

Palli waved away his apology as if batting a stinging fly. His lips moved; he swallowed, and managed, "Are you sure it wasn't just sunstroke?"

Cazaril chuckled. "Oh, I had the sunstroke, too, of course. But if it doesn't kill you, sunstroke passes off in a day or two. This lasted . . . months." Until the last incident with that terrified defiant Ibran boy, and Cazaril's resultant final flogging. "We slaves—"

"Stop that!" cried Palli, running his hands through his hair.

"Stop what?" asked Cazaril in puzzlement.

"Stop *saying* that. *We slaves.* You are a lord of Chalion!"

Cazaril's smile twisted. He said gently, "We lords, at our oars, then? We sweating, pissing, swearing, grunting gentlemen? I think not, Palli. On the galleys we were not lords or men. We were men or animals, and which proved which had no relation I ever saw to birth or blood. The greatest soul I ever met there had been a tanner, and I would kiss his feet right now with joy to learn he yet lived. We slaves, we lords, we fools, we men and women, we mortals, we toys of the gods—all the same thing, Palli. They are all the same to me now."

After a long, indrawn breath, Palli changed the subject abruptly to the little matters of managing his escort from the Daughter's military order. Cazaril found himself comparing useful tricks for treating leather rot and thrush infections in horses' hooves. Soon thereafter Palli retired—or fled—for the night. An orderly retreat, but Cazaril recognized its nature all the same.

Cazaril lay down with his pains and his memories. Despite the feast and the wine, sleep was a long time coming. Fear might be his friend, if that wasn't just bluff and bluster for Palli's sake, but it was clear the dy Jironal brothers were not. *The Roknari reported you'd died of a fever* was a lie outright, and, cleverly, quite uncheckable by now. Well, he was surely sheltered here in quiet Valenda.

He hoped he'd cautioned Palli sufficiently to walk warily at the court in Cardegoss and not put a foot in a pile of old manure unawares. Cazaril rolled over in the darkness and sent up a whispered prayer to the Lady of Spring for Palli's safety. And to all the gods and the Bastard, too, for the deliverance of all upon the sea tonight.

At *the Temple pageant cele-*
brating the advent of summer, Iselle
was not invited to reprise her role of
the Lady of Spring because that part was traditionally taken by a
woman new-wed. A very shy and demure young bride handed off
the throne of the reigning god's avatar to an equally well-behaved
matron heavy with child. Cazaril saw out of the corner of his eye
the divine of the Holy Family heave a sigh of relief as the ceremony
concluded, this time, without any spiritual surprises.

Life slowed. Cazaril's pupils sighed and yawned in the stuffy
schoolroom as the afternoon sun baked the stones of the keep, and
so did their teacher; one sweaty hour he abruptly surrendered and
canceled for the season all classes after the noon nuncheon. As Betriz had said, the Royina Ista did seem to do better as the days
lengthened and softened. She came more often to the family's
meals and sat almost every afternoon with her lady attendants in
the shade of the gnarled fruit trees at the end of the Provincara's
flower garden. She was not, however, permitted by her guardians
to climb to the dizzy, breezy perches upon the battlements favored
by Iselle and Betriz to escape both the heat and the disapproval of
various aging persons disinclined to mount stairs.

Driven from his own bedchamber by its dog-breath closeness
on a hazy hot day following an unusually heavy night's rain,
Cazaril ventured into the garden seeking a more comfortable perch
himself. The book under his arm was one of the few in the castle's

meager library he had not previously read, not that Ordol's *The Fivefold Pathway of the Soul: On the True Methods of Quintarian Theology* was exactly one of his passions. Perhaps its leaves, fluttering loosely in his lap, would make his probable nap look more scholarly to passersby. He rounded the rose arbor and halted as he discovered the royina, accompanied by one of her ladies with an embroidery frame, occupying his intended bench. As the women looked up he dodged a couple of delirious bees and made an apologetic bow to them for his unintended intrusion.

"Stay, Castillar dy . . . Cazaril, is it?" murmured Ista, as he turned to withdraw. "How does my daughter go on in her new studies?"

"Very well, my lady," said Cazaril, turning back and ducking his head. "She is very quick at her arithmetic and geometry, and very, um, persistent in her Darthacan."

"Good," said Ista. "That's good." She stared away briefly across the sun-bleached garden.

The companion bent over her frame to tie off a thread. Lady Ista did not embroider. Cazaril had heard it whispered by a maidservant that she and her ladies had worked for half a year upon an elaborate altar cloth for the Temple. Just as the last stitches were set, the royina had suddenly seized it and burned it in the fireplace of her chamber when her women had left her alone for a moment. True tale or not, her hands held no needle today, but only a rose.

Cazaril searched her face for deeper recognition. "I wondered . . . I have meant to ask you, my lady, if you remembered me from the days I served your noble father as a page here. A score of years ago, now, so it would be no wonder if you had forgotten me." He ventured a smile. "I had no beard then." Helpfully, he pressed his hand over the lower half of his face.

Ista smiled back, but her brows drew down in an effort of recognition that was clearly futile. "I'm sorry. My late father had many pages, over the years."

"Indeed, he was a great lord. Well, no matter." Cazaril shifted his book from hand to hand to hide his disappointment, and smiled more apologetically. He feared her nonrecall had nothing to do with her nervous state. He had more likely simply never registered upon her in the first place, an eager young woman looking forward and upward, not down or back.

The royina's companion, hunting in her color box, murmured, "Drat," and glanced up in appraisal at Cazaril. "My lord dy Cazaril," she said, smiling invitingly. "If it would be no trouble to you, might you stay and keep my lady good company while I run up to my room and find my dark green silk?"

"No trouble at all, lady," said Cazaril automatically. "That is, um . . ." He glanced at Ista, who gazed back at him levelly, with an unsettling tinge of irony. Well, it wasn't as though Ista were given to shrieking and raving. Even the tears he had sometimes seen in her eyes welled silently. He gave the companion a little half bow as she rose; she seized him by the arm and took him a little way around the arbor.

She stood on tiptoe to whisper in his ear. "All will be well. Just don't mention Lord dy Lutez. And stay by her, till I return. If *she* starts going on again about old dy Lutez, just . . . don't leave her." She darted off.

Cazaril considered this hazard.

The brilliant Lord dy Lutez had been for thirty years the late Roya Ias's closest advisor: boyhood friend, brother in arms, boon companion. Over time Ias had loaded him with every honor that was his to command, making him provincar of two districts, chancellor of Chalion, marshal of his household troops, and master of the rich military order of the Son—all the better to control and compel the rest, men murmured. It had been whispered by enemies and admirers alike that dy Lutez was roya in Chalion in all but name. And Ias his royina . . .

Cazaril sometimes wondered if it had been weakness or cleverness on Ias's part, to let dy Lutez do the dirty work and take the heat of the high lords' grumbling, leaving his master with the name only of *Ias the Good*. Though not, Cazaril conceded, *Ias the Strong*, nor *Ias the Wise*, nor, the gods knew, ever *Ias the Lucky*. It was dy Lutez who had arranged Ias's second marriage to the Lady Ista, surely giving lie to the persistent rumor among the highborn of Cardegoss of an unnatural love between the roya and his lifelong friend. And yet . . .

Five years after the marriage, dy Lutez had fallen from the roya's grace, and all his honors, abruptly and lethally. Accused of treason, he'd died under torture in the dungeons of the Zangre, the great royal keep at Cardegoss. Outside of the court of Chalion, it was whispered that his real treason had been to love the young Royina Ista. In more intimate circles, a considerably more hushed whisper had it that Ista had at last persuaded her husband to destroy her hated rival for his love.

However the triangle was arranged, in the shrinking geometry of death it had collapsed from three points to two, and then, as Ias turned his face to the wall and died not a year after dy Lutez, one alone. And Ista had taken her children and fled the Zangre, or was exiled therefrom.

Dy Lutez. *Don't mention dy Lutez.* Don't mention, therefore, most of the history of Chalion for the past generation and a half. Right.

Cazaril returned to Ista and, somewhat warily, sat in the departed companion's chair. Ista had taken to shredding her rose, not wildly, but very gently and systematically, plucking the petals and laying them upon the bench beside her in a pattern mimicking their original form, circle within circle in an inward spiral.

"The lost dead visited me in my dreams last night," Ista continued conversationally. "Though they were only false dreams. Do yours ever visit you so, Cazaril?"

Cazaril blinked, and decided she was too aware for this to be dementia, even if she was a trifle elliptical. And besides, he had no trouble catching her meaning, which would surely not be the case if she were mad. "Sometimes I dream of my father and mother. For a little time, they walk and talk as in life . . . so I regret to wake again, and lose them anew."

Ista nodded. "False dreams are sad that way. But true dreams are cruel. The gods spare you from ever dreaming their true dreams, Cazaril."

Cazaril frowned, and cocked his head. "All my dreams are but confused throngs, and disperse like smoke and vapors upon my waking."

Ista bent her head to her denuded rose; she now was spreading the golden powdery stamens, fine as snips of silk thread, in a tiny fan within the circle of petals. "True dreams sit like lead upon the heart and stomach. Weight enough to . . . *drown* our souls in sorrow. True dreams walk in the waking day. And yet betray us still, as certainly as any man of flesh might swallow back his vomited promises, like a dog its cast-up dinner. Don't put your trust in dreams, Castillar. Or in the promises of men." She raised her face from her array of petals, her eyes suddenly intent.

Cazaril cleared his throat uncomfortably. "Nay, lady, that would be foolish. But it's pleasant to see my father, from time to time. For I shall not meet him any other way again."

She gave him an odd, tilted smile. "You don't fear your dead?"

"No, my lady. Not in dreams."

"Perhaps your dead are not very fearsome folk."

"For the most part, no, ma'am," he agreed.

High in the wall of the keep, a casement window swung wide, and Ista's companion leaned out and stared down into the garden. Apparently reassured by the sight of her lady in gentle conversation with her shabby courtier, she waved and disappeared again.

Cazaril wondered how Ista passed the time. She did not sew, apparently, nor did she seem much of a reader, nor did she keep musicians of her own. Cazaril had seen her sporadically at prayers, some weeks spending hours in the ancestors' hall, or at the little portable altar kept in her chambers, or, far more rarely, escorted by her ladies and dy Ferrej down to the temple in town, though never at its crowded moments. Other times weeks would pass when she seemed to keep no observances to the gods at all. "Have you much consolation in prayers, lady?" he asked curiously.

She glanced up, and her smile flattened a trifle. "I? I have not much consolation anywhere. The gods have surely made a mock of me. I would return the favor, but they hold my heart and my breath hostage to their whims. My children are prisoners of fortune. And fortune is gone mad, in Chalion."

He offered hesitantly, "I think there are worse prisons than this sunny keep, lady."

Her brows rose, and she sat back. "Oh, aye. Were you ever to the Zangre, in Cardegoss?"

"Yes, when I was a younger man. Not lately. It was a vast warren. I spent half my time lost in it."

"Strange. I was lost in it, too . . . it is haunted, you know."

Cazaril considered this matter-of-fact comment. "I shouldn't be surprised. It is the nature of a great fortress that as many die in it as build it, win it, lose it . . . men of Chalion, the renowned Roknari masons before us, the first kings, and men before them I'm sure who crept into its caves, on back into the mists of time. It is that

sort of prominence." High home of royas and nobles for generations—rank on rank of men and women had ended their lives in
the Zangre, some quite spectacularly . . . some quite secretly. "The
Zangre is older than Chalion itself. It surely . . . accumulates."

Ista began gently pressing the thorns from her rose stem, and
lining them up in a row like the teeth of a saw. "Yes. It *accumulates*.
That's the word, precisely. It collects calamity like a cistern, as its
slates and gutters collect rainwater. You will do well to avoid the
Zangre, Cazaril."

"I've no desire to attend court, my lady."

"I desired to, once. With all my heart. The gods' most savage
curses come upon us as answers to our own prayers, you know.
Prayer is a dangerous business. I think it should be outlawed." She
began to peel her rose stem, thin green strips pulling away to reveal fine white lines of pith.

Cazaril had no idea what to say to this, so merely smiled hesitantly.

Ista began to pull the whip of pith apart lengthwise. "A
prophecy was told of the Lord dy Lutez, that he should not drown
except upon a mountaintop. And that he never feared to swim
thereafter, no matter how violent the waves, for everyone knows
there is no water upon a mountaintop; it all runs away to the valleys."

Cazaril swallowed panic, and looked around surreptitiously for
the returning attendant. She was not yet in sight. Lord dy Lutez, it
was said, had died under the water torture in the dungeons of the
Zangre. Beneath the castle stones, but still high enough above the
town of Cardegoss. He licked slightly numb lips, and tried, "You
know, I never heard that while the man was alive. It is my opinion
that some tale-spinner made it up later, to sound shivery. Justifica-
tions . . . tend to accrue posthumously to so spectacular a fall as his
was."

Her lips parted in the strangest smile yet. She drew the last
threads of the stem pith apart, aligned them upon her knee, and
stroked them flat. "Poor Cazaril! How did you grow so wise?"

Cazaril was saved from trying to think of an answer for this by
Ista's attendant, who emerged again from the door of the keep
with a hank of colored silk in her hands. Cazaril leapt to his feet
and nodded to the royina. "Your good lady returns . . ."

He gave a little bow in passing to the attendant, who whispered urgently to him, "Was she sensible, my lord?"

"Yes, perfectly." *In her way . . .*

"Nothing of dy Lutez?"

"Nothing . . . remarkable." Nothing *he* cared to remark upon, certainly.

The attendant breathed relief and passed on, fixing a smile on her face. Ista regarded her with bored tolerance as she began chattering about all the items that she'd had to overturn and hunt through to find her strayed thread. It crossed Cazaril's mind that no daughter of the Provincara's, nor mother of Iselle's, could possibly be short of wit.

If Ista spoke to very many of her duller company with the cryptic leaps of thought she'd sprung on him, it was little wonder rumors circulated of madness, and yet . . . her occasional opacity of discourse felt more like cipher than babble to him. Of an elusive internal consistency, if only one held the key to it. Which, granted, he did not. Not that that wasn't also true of some sorts of madness he had seen . . .

Cazaril clutched his book and went off to seek some less disturbing shade.

❧SUMMER ADVANCED AT A LAZY PACE THAT EASED Cazaril's mind and body both. Only poor Teidez chafed at the inactivity, hunting being curtailed by the heat, the season, and his tutor. He did pot rabbits with a crossbow in the dawn mists around the castle, to the earnest applause and approval of all the castle's gardeners. The boy was so out-of-season—hot and restless and plump—if ever there was a born dedicat to the Son of Autumn, god of the hunt, war, and cooler weather, Cazaril judged it was surely Teidez.

Cazaril was a little surprised to be accosted on the way to nuncheon one warm noon by Teidez and his tutor. Judging by both their reddened faces, they were in the middle of another of their tearing arguments.

"Lord Caz!" Teidez hailed him breathlessly. "Didn't the old provincar's swordmaster *too* take the pages to the abattoir, to slay the young bulls—to teach them courage, in a real fight, not this, this, dancing about in the dueling ring!"

"Well, yes . . ."

"See, what did I tell you!" Teidez cried to dy Sanda.

"We practiced in the ring, too," Cazaril added immediately, for the sake of solidarity, should dy Sanda need it.

The tutor grimaced. "Bull-baiting is an old country practice, Royse. Not befitting training for the highborn. You are destined to be a gentleman—at the least!—not a butcher's apprentice."

The Provincara kept no swordmaster in her household these days, so she'd made sure the royse's tutor was a trained man. Cazaril, who had occasionally watched his practice sessions with Teidez, respected dy Sanda's precision. Dy Sanda's swordsmanship was pretty enough, if not quite brilliant. Sporting. Honorable. But if dy Sanda also knew the desperate brutal tricks that kept men alive on the field, he had not shown them to Teidez.

Cazaril grinned wryly. "The swordmaster wasn't training us to be gentlemen. He was training us to be soldiers. I'll give his old method this credit—any battlefield I was ever on was a lot more like a butcher's yard than it was like a dueling ring. It was ugly, but it taught us our business. And there was no waste to it. I can't think it mattered at the end of the day to the bulls whether they died after being chased around for an hour by a fool with a sword, or were simply stalled and thwacked on the head with a mallet." Though Cazaril had not cared to stretch the business out, as some of the young men had, making macabre and dangerous play with the maddened animals. With a little practice he had learned to dispatch his beast with a sword thrust nearly as quickly as the butcher might. "Grant you, on the battlefield we didn't eat what we killed, except sometimes the horses."

Dy Sanda sniffed disapproval at his wit. He offered placatingly to Teidez, "We might take the hawks out tomorrow morning, my lord, if the weather holds fine. And if you finish your cartography problems."

"A ladies' sport—with hawks and pigeons—pigeons! What do I care for pigeons!" In a voice of longing Teidez added, "At the roya's court at Cardegoss, they hunt wild boar in the oak forests in the fall. That's a real sport, a man's sport. They say those pigs are dangerous!"

"Very true," said Cazaril. "The big tuskers can disembowel a dog—or a horse. Or a man. They're much faster than you expect."

"Did you ever hunt at Cardegoss?" Teidez asked him eagerly.

"I followed my lord dy Guarida a few times there."

"Valenda has no boars." Teidez sighed. "But we do have bulls! At least it's *something*. Better than pigeons—or rabbits!"

"Oh, potting rabbits is a useful soldier's training, too," Cazaril offered consolingly. "In case you ever have to hunt rats for table. It's much the same skill."

Dy Sanda glared at him. Cazaril smiled and bowed out of the argument, leaving Teidez to his badgering.

Over nuncheon, Iselle took up a descant version of a similar song, though the authority she assailed was her grandmother and not her tutor.

"Grandmama, it's so *hot*. Can't we go swimming in the river as Teidez does?"

As the summer simmered on, the royse's afternoon rides with his gentleman-tutor and his grooms and the pages had been exchanged for afternoon swims at a sheltered pool in the river upstream of Valenda—the same spot overheated denizens of the castle had frequented when Cazaril had been a page. The ladies were, of course, excluded from these excursions. Cazaril had politely declined invitations to join the party, pleading his duties to Iselle. The true reason was that stripping naked to swim would display all the old disasters written in his flesh, a history he did not care to expound upon. The misunderstanding with the bath man still mortified him, in memory.

"Certainly not!" said the Provincara. "That would be entirely immodest."

"Not *with* him," said Iselle. "Make up our own party, a ladies' party." She turned to Cazaril. "You said the ladies of the castle swam when you were a page!"

"Servants, Iselle," said her grandmother wearily. "Lesser folk. It's not a pastime for you."

Iselle slumped, hot and red and pouting. Betriz, spared the unbecoming flush, drooped at her place, looking pale and wilted instead. Soup was served. Everyone sat eyeing their steaming bowls with revulsion. Maintaining the standards—as always—the Provincara picked up her spoon and took a determined sip.

Cazaril said suddenly, "But the Lady Iselle *can* swim, can she not, your grace? I mean, she presumably was taught, when she was younger?"

"Certainly not," said the Provincara.

"Oh," said Cazaril. "Oh, dear." He glanced around the table. Royina Ista was not with them, this meal; relieved of concern for a certain obsessive subject, he decided that he dared. "That puts me in mind of a most horrible tragedy."

The Provincara's eyes narrowed; she did not take the bait. Betriz, however, did. "Oh, what?"

"It was when I was riding for the provincar of Guarida, during a skirmish with the Roknari prince Olus. Olus's troops came raiding over the border under the cover of night, and a storm. I was told off to evacuate the ladies of dy Guarida's household before the town was encircled. Near dawn, after riding half the night, we crossed a high freshet. One of his provincara's ladies-in-waiting was swept off when her horse fell, and was carried away by the force of the waters, together with the page who went after her. By the time I'd got my horse turned around, they were out of sight . . . We found the bodies downstream next morning. The river was not that deep, but she panicked, not having any idea how to swim. A little training might have turned a fatal accident into merely a frightening one, and three lives saved."

"Three lives?" said Iselle. "The lady, the page . . ."

"She had been with child."

"Oh."

A very daunted silence fell.

The Provincara rubbed her chin, and eyed Cazaril. "A true story, Castillar?"

"Yes," Cazaril sighed. Her flesh had been bruised and battered, cold, blue-tinged, inert as clay beneath his clutching fingers, her sodden clothes heavy, but not as heavy as his heart. "I had to tell her husband."

"Huh," grunted dy Ferrej. The table's most reliable raconteur, he did not try to top this tale.

"It's not an experience I ever wish to repeat," added Cazaril.

The Provincara snorted and looked away. After a moment, she said, "My granddaughter cannot go sporting about naked in the river like an eel."

Iselle sat up. "But suppose we wore, oh, linen shifts."

"It's true, if one needed to swim in an emergency, one would most likely have clothes still on," Cazaril said helpfully.

Betriz added wistfully under her breath, "And we could cool off twice. Once when we swam, and once when we sat about drying out."

"Cannot some lady of the household instruct her?" Cazaril coaxed.

"They do not swim either," said the Provincara firmly.

Betriz nodded confirmation. "They just wade." She glanced up. "Could *you* teach us how to swim, Lord Caz?"

Iselle clapped her hands. "Oh, yes!"

"I . . . uh . . ." Cazaril stammered. On the other hand . . . in *that* company, he might keep his shirt on without comment. "I suppose so . . . if your ladies went along." He glanced across at the Provincara. "And if your grandmother would permit me."

After a long silence, the Provincara growled grudgingly, "Mind you don't all catch chills."

Iselle and Betriz, prudently, suppressed hoots of triumph, but they cast Cazaril sparkling glances of gratitude. He wondered if they thought he had made up the story of the night-ride drowning.

🐟THE LESSONS BEGAN THAT AFTERNOON, WITH CAZA-ril standing in the middle of the river trying to persuade two rather stiff young women that they would not drown instantly if they got their hair wet. His fear that he had overdone the dire safety warnings gradually passed as the women at length relaxed and learned to let the waters buoy them up. They were naturally more buoyant than Cazaril, though his months at the Provincara's table had driven a deal of the wolf-gauntness from his bearded face.

His patience proved justified. By the end of the summer, they were splashing and diving like otters in the drought-shrunken stream. Cazaril had merely to sit in the shallows in water up to his waist and call occasional suggestions.

His choice of vantage had only partly to do with staying cool. The Provincara was right, he had to allow—swimming *was* lewd. And loose linen shifts, thoroughly wetted down and clinging to lithe young bodies, made fair mockery of the modesty they attempted to preserve, a stunning effect he carefully did not point out to his two blithe charges. Worse, the effect cut two ways. Wet linen trews clinging to *his* loins revealed a state of mind—um, body—um, *recovering health*—that he earnestly prayed they would not notice. Iselle didn't seem to, anyway. He was not entirely sure about Betriz. Their middle-aged lady-in-waiting Nan dy Vrit, who declined the lessons but waded about in the shallows fully dressed with her skirts hoisted to her calves, missed nothing in the play, and was clearly hard-pressed to control her snickers. Charitably, she seemed to grant him his good faith, and did not laugh at him out loud, nor tattle on him to the Provincara. At least . . . he didn't think she did.

Cazaril was uncomfortably conscious that his awareness of Betriz was increasing day by day. Not yet to the point of slipping anonymous bad poetry under her door, thank the gods for the shreds of his sanity. Playing the lute under her window was, perhaps fortunately, no longer within his gift. And yet . . . in the long summer quiet of Valenda, he had begun to dare to think of a life beyond the turning of an hourglass.

Betriz did smile at him—that was true, he did not delude himself. And she was kind. But she smiled at and was kind to her horse, too. Her honest friendly courtesy was hardly ground enough to build a dream mansion upon, let alone bring bed and linens and try to move in. Still . . . she *did* smile at him.

He stifled the idea repeatedly, but it kept popping up—along with other things, alas, especially during swimming lessons. But he'd sworn off ambition—he didn't have to make a fool of himself anymore, dammit. His embarrassing arousal might be a sign of returning strength, but what good did it do him? He was as landless and penniless as in his days here as a page, and with far fewer hopes. He was mad to entertain fantasies of either lust or love, and yet . . . Betriz's father was a landless man of good blood, living a life of service. Surely he could not despise a like sojourner.

Not despise Cazaril, no—dy Ferrej was too wise for that. But he was also wise enough to know his daughter's beauty and connection with the royesse was a dowry that could bring her something rather better in the way of a husband than fortuneless Cazaril, or even the local petty gentry's sons who served the

Provincara's household as pages now. Betriz clearly considered the boys to be annoying puppies anyway. But some of them had elder brothers, heirs of their modest estates . . .

Today he sank down in the water to his chin and pretended not to watch through his eyelashes as Betriz scrambled up onto a rock, translucent linen dripping, black hair streaming down over her trembling curves. She stretched her arms to the sun before belly-flopping forward to splash Iselle, who ducked and shrieked and splashed her back. The days were shortening now, the nights were cooling, and likewise the afternoons. The festival of the ascent of the Son of Autumn was at hand. It had been too cool to swim all last week—only a few days were likely left warm enough to make these private wet river excursions tolerable. Fast gallops, and the hunt, would soon entice his ladies to drier delights. And his good sense would return to him like a strayed dog. Wouldn't it?

🐟THE SLANTING LIGHT AND CHILLING AIR DROVE THE lingering swimming party from the water to dry a while on the stony banks. Cazaril was so drenched in mellow ease that he didn't even make them conduct their idle chitchat in Darthacan or Roknari. At last he pulled on his heavy riding trousers and boots— good new boots, a gift from the Provincara—and his sword belt. He tightened the browsing horses' girths and removed their hobbles, and helped the ladies mount. Reluctantly, with many backward glances at the sylvan river glade falling behind, the little cavalcade wound up the hill to the castle.

In a spurt of recklessness, Cazaril pressed his horse forward to match pace with Betriz's. She glanced across at him, quick fugitive dimple winking. Was it want of courage, or want of wits that turned his tongue to wood in his mouth? Both, he decided. He and the Lady Betriz attended Iselle together daily. If some ponderous attempt of his at dalliance should prove unwelcome, might it damage the precious ease that had grown between them in the royesse's service? No—he must, he would say something—but her horse broke into a trot at the sight of the castle gate, and the moment was lost.

As they entered the courtyard, the scrape of their horses'

hooves echoing hollowly on the cobbles, Teidez burst from a side door, crying "Iselle! Iselle!"

Cazaril's hand leapt to his sword hilt in shock—the boy's tunic and trousers were bespattered with blood—then fell away again at the sight of the dusty and grimy dy Sanda trudging along behind his charge. Teidez's gory appearance was merely the result of an afternoon training session at Valenda's butcher's yard. It wasn't horror that drove his excited cries, but rapture. The round face he turned up to his sister was shining with joy.

"Iselle, the most wonderful thing has happened! Guess, guess!"

"How am I to guess—" she began, laughing.

Impatiently he waved this away; his news tumbled from his lips. "A courier from Roya Orico just arrived. You and I are ordered to attend upon him this fall at court in Cardegoss! And Mother and Grandmama are *not* invited! Iselle, we're going to escape from Valenda!"

"We're going to the *Zangre?*" Iselle whooped, and slid from her saddle to grab her brother's reeking hands and whirl with him around the courtyard. Betriz leaned on her saddlebow and watched, her lips parted in thrilled delight.

Their lady-in-waiting pursed her lips in much less delight. Cazaril caught Ser dy Sanda's eye. The royse's tutor's mouth was set in a grim frown.

Cazaril's stomach lurched, as the coins of conclusion dropped. The Royesse Iselle was ordered to court; therefore her little household would accompany her to Cardegoss. Including her handmaiden Lady Betriz.

And her secretary.

7

The royse and royesse's caravan
approached Cardegoss from the south
road. They struggled up a rise to find
the whole of the plain between the cradling mountains rolling out
below their feet.

Cazaril's nostrils flared as he drew in the sharp wind. Cold rain
last night had scoured the air clean. Tumbling banks of slate-blue
clouds shredded away to the east, echoing the lines of the wrinkled
blue-gray ranges hugging the horizon. Light from the west thrust
across the plains like a sword stroke. Rising up on its great rock jut-
ting out above the angle where two streams met, dominating the
rivers, the plains, the mountain passes, and the eyes of all behold-
ers, the Zangre caught the light and blazed like molten gold against
the dark retreating cloud banks. Its ochre stone towers were
crowned and capped with slate roofs the color of the scudding
clouds, like an array of iron helmets upon a valiant band of soldiers.
Favored seat of the royas of Chalion for generations, the Zangre appeared from this vantage all fortress, no palace, as dedicated to the
business of war as any soldier-brother sworn to the holy orders of
the gods.

Royse Teidez urged his black horse forward next to Cazaril's
bay and stared eagerly at their goal, his face lit with a kind of awed
avarice. Hunger for the promise of a larger life, free of the careful
constraints of mothers and grandmothers, Cazaril supposed, certainly. But Teidez would have to be much duller than he appeared

not to be wondering right now if this luminous miracle of stone could be his, someday. Why, indeed, had the boy been called to court, if Orico, despairing at last of ever getting heirs of his own body, was not meaning to groom him as his successor?

Iselle halted her dappled gray and stared nearly as eagerly as Teidez. "Strange. I remembered it as larger, somehow."

"Wait till we get closer," Cazaril advised dryly.

Ser dy Sanda, in the van, motioned them forward, and the whole train of riders and pack mules started down the muddy road once more: the two royal youths, their secretary-guardians, Lady Betriz, servants, grooms, armed outriders in the green-and-black livery of Baocia, extra horses, Snowflake—who might at this point more aptly be named Mudpot—and all their very considerable baggage. Cazaril, veteran of a number of hair-tearingly aggravating noble ladies' processions, regarded the progress of the convoy as a wonder of dispatch. It had taken only five days to ride from Valenda, four and a half, really. Royesse Iselle, ably backed by Betriz, had driven her subhousehold with verve and efficiency. Not one of the journey's inevitable delays could be laid to her feminine caprice.

In fact both Teidez and Iselle had pushed their entourage to its best speed from the moment they'd ridden out of Valenda and galloped ahead to outdistance Ista's heart-wrenching wails, audible even over the battlements. Iselle had clapped her hands over her ears and steered her horse with her knees till she'd escaped the echo of her mother's extravagant grief.

The news that her children were ordered from her had thrown the dowager royina, if not into madness outright, into deep distraction and despair. She had wept, and prayed, and argued, and, at length, gone silent, a relief of sorts. Dy Sanda had confided to Cazaril how she'd cornered him and tried to bribe him into flying with Teidez, where and how being unclear. He described her as gibbering, clutching, barely short of foam-flecked.

She had cornered Cazaril, too, in his chamber packing his saddlebags the night before the departure. Their conversation went rather differently; or at least, whatever it had been, it wasn't gibbering.

She had regarded him for a long, silent, and unnerving moment before saying abruptly, "Are you afraid, Cazaril?"

Cazaril considered his reply, and finally answered simply and truthfully, "Yes, my lady."

"Dy Sanda is a fool. You, at least, are not."

Not knowing what to say to this, Cazaril inclined his head politely.

She inhaled, her eyes gone huge, and said, "Protect Iselle. If ever you loved me, or your honor, protect Iselle. Swear it, Cazaril!"

"I swear."

Her eyes searched him, but rather to his surprise she did not demand more elaborate protestations, or reassuring repetitions.

"From what shall I protect her?" Cazaril asked cautiously. "What do you fear, Lady Ista?"

She stood silent in the candlelight.

Cazaril recalled Palli's effective entreaty. "Lady, please do not send me blindfolded into battle!"

Her lips puffed, as from a blow to the stomach; but then she shook her head in despair, whirled away, and rushed from the room. Her attendant, obviously worried to the point of exasperation, had blown out her breath and followed her.

Despite the memory of Ista's infectious agitation, Cazaril found his spirits lifted from their mire of dread by the young people's excitement as their goal neared. The road met the river that flowed out of Cardegoss, and ran alongside it as they descended into a wooded area. At length, Cardegoss's second stream joined the main. A chill draft coursed through the shaded valley. On the side of the river opposite the road, three hundred feet of cliff face erupted from the ground and soared aloft. Here and there, little trees clung desperately to crevices, and ferns spilled down over the rocks.

Iselle paused to stare up, and up. Cazaril reined his horse in beside hers. From here, one could not even see the beginnings of the human masons' puny defensive additions decorating the top of this natural fortress wall.

"Oh," said Iselle.

"My," added Betriz, joining them craning in their necks.

"The Zangre," said Cazaril, "has never in its history been taken by assault."

"I see," breathed Betriz.

A few floating yellow leaves, promise of autumn to come,

whirled away down the dark stream. The party pressed their horses forward, climbing up out of the valley to where a great stone arch, leading to one of the seven gates of the city, spanned the stream. Cardegoss shared the stream-carved plateau with the fortress. The town ramparts flared back along the tops of the ravines like the shape of a boat with the Zangre at its prow, then turned inward in a long wall forming the stern.

In the clear light of this crisp afternoon, the city failed signally to look sinister. Markets, glimpsed down side streets, were bright with food and flowers, thronged with men and women. Bakers and bankers, weavers and tailors and jewelers and saddlers, together with such trades and crafts that were not required by their need for running water to be down by the riversides, offered their wares. The royal company rode through the misnamed Temple Square, which had five sides, one for each of the big regional mother-houses of the gods' holy orders. Divines, acolytes, and dedicats strode along, looking more harried and bureaucratic than ascetic. In the square's vast paved center, the familiar cloverleaf-and-tower shape of Cardegoss's Temple of the Holy Family bulked, impressively more extensive than the homey little version in Valenda.

To Teidez's ill-concealed impatience, Iselle demanded a stop here, and sent Cazaril scurrying into the temple's echoing inner courtyard to lay an offering of coins upon the altar of the Lady of Spring in gratitude for their safe journey. An acolyte took charge of it with thanks and stared curiously at Cazaril; Cazaril mumbled a brief distracted prayer and hurried back out to mount again.

Climbing the long shallow slope toward the Zangre, they passed through streets where houses of the nobility, built of dressed stone and with elaborate iron grilles protecting windows and gates, loomed shoulder to shoulder, high and square. The dowager royina had lived in one such, for a time in her early widowhood. Iselle excitedly identified three possible candidates for her childhood home, until, overcome with confusion, she made Cazaril promise to determine later which had been hers.

At last they rode up to the great gate of the Zangre itself. A natural cleft across the plateau opened just before it into a sharp shadowed crevice, more daunting than any moat. On the far side, huge boulders formed the lowest course of stones in the walls; irregular, but fitting so tightly a knife blade could not have slid between

them. Atop them, fine Roknari work, its delicate traceries of geo-
metric decoration seeming sugar rather than stone. Atop that, yet
more crisp-cut stone, towering higher and higher as if men com-
peted with the gods who had thrown up the great rock the whole
edifice stood upon. The Zangre was the only castle Cazaril had
ever been in where he suffered whirling vertigo standing at the
bottom looking *up*.

A horn sounded from above, and soldiers in the livery of Roya
Orico saluted as they rode across the drawbridge and through the
narrow archway into the courtyard. Lady Betriz clutched her reins
and stared around with her lips parted. The courtyard was domi-
nated by a huge high rectangular tower, newest and crispest, the
addition of the reign of Roya Ias and Lord dy Lutez. Cazaril had always wondered if its great size was a measure of the men's
strength . . . or their fears. A little beyond it, almost as high, a round
tower loomed at one corner of the main block. Its slate roof was
tumbled in, and its tall top ragged and broken.

"Dear gods," said Betriz, staring at the half ruin, "what happened there? Why don't they repair it?"

"Ah," said Cazaril, thrown into tutorial mode, considerably
more for his own reassurance than Betriz's. "That's the tower of
Roya Fonsa the Wise." Known more commonly, after his death, as
Fonsa the Fairly-Wise. "They say he used to walk upon it all night,
trying to read the will of the gods and the fate of Chalion in the
stars. On the night he worked his miracle of death magic upon the
Golden General, a great storm and gouts of lightning threw down
the roof, and set a fire that didn't burn out until morning despite
the torrents of rain."

When the Roknari had first invaded from the sea, they had
overrun most of Chalion, Ibra, and Brajar in their first violent
burst, even past Cardegoss, to the very feet of the southern mountain ranges. Darthaca itself had been threatened by their advance
parties. But from the ashes of the weak Old Kingdoms and the
harsh cradle of the hills new men had emerged, fighting for generations to regain what had been lost in those first few years. War-
rior-thieves, they made an economy of raiding; noble fortunes were
not made, but stolen. Turnabout, for the Roknari idea of tax collection was a column of soldiers taking all in their winding path at
sword's point, like locusts in arms. Bribe and counterbribe turned

the columns back, until Chalion was become an odd interlocking dance of counting armies and armed accountants. But over time, the Roknari were pushed back north toward the sea again, leaving behind as legacy a residue of castles and brutality. At length the invaders were reduced to the five squabbling princedoms hugging the north coast.

The Golden General, the Lion of Roknar, had looked to reverse the ebb of his history. By war, guile, and marriage he had in ten blazing years united all five princedoms for almost the first time since the Roknari had landed. Barely thirty, he'd gathered a great tide of men into his hands, preparing to sweep south once more, declaring he would wipe the Quintarian heretics and the worship of the Bastard from the face of the land with fire and sword. Desperate and disunited, Chalion, Ibra, and Brajar were losing against him on every front.

More ordinary forms of assassination failing, death magic was tried upon the golden genius a dozen times and more, without result. Fonsa the Wise, from deep study, reasoned that the Golden General must be the chosen of one of the gods; no sacrifice less than that of a king could balance his thundering destiny. Fonsa had lost five sons and heirs one after another in the wars to the north. Ias, his last and youngest, was locked in bitter struggle with the Roknari for the final mountain passes blocking their invasion routes. One stormy night, taking only a divine of the Bastard who was in his confidence and a loyal young page, Fonsa had mounted his tower, locking its door behind him . . .

The courtiers of Chalion had pulled three charred bodies from the rubble the following morning; only the differing heights allowed them to tell divine from page from roya. Shocked and terrified, the trembling court had awaited its fate. The courier from Cardegoss, galloping north with the news of loss and woe, met the courier galloping south from Ias with news of victory. Funeral and coronation were celebrated simultaneously within the Zangre's walls.

Cazaril stared around at those walls now. "When Royse— now Roya—Ias returned from the war," he went on to Betriz, "he ordered the lower windows and doors of his dead father's tower bricked up, and proclaimed that no one should enter it again."

A dark, flapping shape launched itself from the tower's top, and Betriz squeaked and ducked.

"Crows have nested in it ever since," Cazaril noted, tilting his head back to watch the black silhouette wheel against the intense blue sky. "I believe it's the same flock of sacred crows the divines of the Bastard feed in the temple yard. Intelligent birds. The acolytes make pets of them and teach them to speak."

Iselle, who had drawn closer as Cazaril had discoursed upon her royal grandfather's fate, asked, "What do they say?"

"Not much," Cazaril admitted, with a quick grin at her. "I never saw one that had a vocabulary of more than three squawks. Although some of the acolytes insisted they were saying more."

Warned by the outrider dy Sanda had sent on ahead, a swarm of grooms and servants rushed out to assist the arriving guests. The Zangre's castle warder, with his own hands, positioned a mounting bench for Royesse Iselle. Perhaps thrown into consciousness of her dignity by this gentleman's bending gray head, she used the step for a change, parting from her horse with ladylike grace. Teidez tossed his reins to a bowing groom and stared about with shining eyes. The warder made rapid conference with dy Sanda and Cazaril of a dozen practical details, from stabling the horses and grooms to—Cazaril grinned briefly—stabling the royse and royesse.

The warder escorted the royal children to their rooms in the left wing of the main block, followed by a parade of servants lugging the baggage. Teidez and his entourage were given half a floor; Iselle and her ladies, the floor above them. Cazaril was assigned a small room on the gentlemen's floor, but at the very end. He wondered if he was expected to guard the staircase.

"Rest and refresh yourselves," the warder said. "The roya and royina will receive you at a celebratory banquet this evening, attended by all the court." A rush of servants bringing wash water, clean linens, bread, fruit, pastries, cheese, and wine assured the visitors from Valenda that they were not abandoned to starve between now and then.

"Where are my royal brother and sister-in-law?" Iselle asked the warder.

The warder made her a little bow. "The royina is resting. The roya is visiting his menagerie, which is a great consolation to him."

"I'd like to see it," she said, a little wistfully. "He has often written me of it."

"Tell him so. He'll like to show it to you," the warder assured her with a smile.

The ladies' party was soon deeply involved in a frantic turning out of luggage to select garments for the banquet, an exercise that quite clearly did not require Cazaril's inexpert assistance. He directed the servant to place his trunk in his narrow room and depart, dropped his saddlebags on his bed, and rooted through them to find the letter to Orico the Provincara had strictly charged him to deliver, into the roya's hand and no other, at his earliest possible moment upon arrival. He paused only to wash the road dirt from his hands and spare a quick glance out his window. The deep ravine on this side of the castle seemed to plunge straight down below his sill. A dizzying glint of water from the stream was just visible through the treetops far below.

Cazaril only lost his way once on the way to the menagerie, which was outside the walls and across the gardens, an adjunct of the stables. If nothing else he could identify it by the sharp, acrid smell of strange manures neither human nor equine. Cazaril stared into an arched aisle of the stone building, his eyes adjusting to its cool shade, and diffidently entered.

A couple of former stalls were converted to cages for a pair of wonderfully glossy black bears. One was asleep on a pile of clean golden straw; the other stared up at him, lifting its muzzle and sniffing hopefully as Cazaril passed. On the other side of the aisle stalls housed some very strange beasts that Cazaril could not even put a name to, like tall leggy goats, but with long curving necks, mild and liquid eyes, and thick soft fur. In a room to one side, a dozen large, brilliantly colored birds on perches preened and muttered, and other tiny, equally bright ones twittered and flitted in cages lining the wall. Across from the aviary, in an open bay, he found human occupants at last: a neat groom in the roya's livery, and a fat man sitting cross-legged on a table, holding a leopard by its jeweled collar. Cazaril gasped and froze as the man ducked his head right next to the great cat's open jaws.

The man was currying the beast vigorously. A cloud of yellow and black hairs rose from the pair as the leopard writhed on the table in what Cazaril recognized, after a blink, as feline ecstasy.

Cazaril's eye was so locked by the leopard, it took him another moment to recognize the man as Roya Orico.

The dozen years since Cazaril had last glimpsed him had not been kind. Orico had never been a handsome man, even in the vigor of his youth. He was a little below average in height, with a short nose unfortunately broken in a riding accident in his teens and now looking rather like a squashed mushroom in the middle of his face. His hair had been auburn and curly. It was now roan, still curly but much thinner. His hair was the only thing about him that was thinner; his body was grossly broadened. His face was pale and puffy, with baggy eyelids. He chirped at his spotted cat, who rubbed its head against the roya's tunic, shedding more hairs, then licked the brocade vigorously with a tongue the size of a washcloth, evidently pursuing a large gravy stain that had trailed down over the roya's impressive paunch. The roya's sleeves were rolled up, and half a dozen scabbed scratches scored his arms. The great cat caught a bare arm, and held it in its yellow teeth briefly, but did not close its jaws. Cazaril unwound his clutching fingers from his sword hilt, and cleared his throat.

As the roya turned his head, Cazaril fell to one knee. "Sire, I bear you respectful greetings from the Dowager Provincara of Baocia, and this her letter." He held out the paper, and added, just in case no one had mentioned it to him yet, "Royse Teidez and Royesse Iselle are arrived safely, sire."

"Oh, yes." The roya jerked his head at the elderly groom, who went to relieve Cazaril of the letter with a graceful bow.

"Her Grace the Dowager instructed me to deliver it into your hand," Cazaril added uncertainly.

"Yes, yes—just a moment—" With some effort, Orico bent over his belly to give the cat one quick hug, then clipped a silver chain to its collar. Chirping some more, he urged it to leap lightly from the table. He dismounted more heavily, and said, "Here, Umegat."

This was evidently the groom's name, not the cat's, for the man stepped forward and took the silver leash in exchange for the letter. He led the beast to its cage a little way down the aisle, unceremoniously shoving it in with a knee to its rump when it paused to rub on the bars. Cazaril breathed a little easier when the groom locked the cage.

Orico broke the seal, scattering wax on the swept tiled floor.

Absently, he motioned Cazaril to his feet and read slowly down the Provincara's spidery handwriting, pausing to move the paper closer or farther and squinting now and then. Cazaril, falling easily back into his old courier mode, folded his hands behind his back and waited patiently to be questioned or dismissed at Orico's will.

Cazaril eyed the groom—head groom?—as he waited. Even without the clue of the name, the man was obviously of Roknari descent. Umegat had been tallish, but was now a little stooped. His skin, which must have been burnished gold in his youth, was leathery, its color faded to ivory. Fine wrinkles wreathed his eyes and mouth. His curly bronze hair, going gray, was tightly bound to his head in two braids that ran from his temples over his crown to meet in the back in a neat queue, an old Roknari style. It made him look pure Roknari, though half-breeds abounded in Chalion; Roya Orico himself had a couple of Roknari princesses up his family tree on both the Chalionese and Brajaran sides, the source of the family hair. The groom wore the service livery of the Zangre, tunic and leggings and a knee-length tabard with the symbol of Chalion, a royal leopard rampant upon a stylized castle, stitched upon it. He looked considerably tidier and more fastidious than his master.

Orico finished the letter, and sighed. "Royina Ista upset, was she?" he said to Cazaril.

"She was naturally disturbed to be parted from her children," said Cazaril cautiously.

"I was afraid of that. Can't be helped. As long as she is disturbed in Valenda, and not in Cardegoss. I'll not have her here, she's too . . . difficult." He rubbed his nose on the back of his hand, and sniffed. "Tell Her Grace the Provincara she has all my esteem, and assure her that I have concerned myself with her grandchildren's good fates. They have their brother's protection."

"I plan to write to her tonight, sire, to assure her of our safe arrival. I will convey your words."

Orico nodded shortly, rubbed his nose again, and squinted at Cazaril. "Do I know you?"

"I . . . shouldn't think so, sire. I am lately appointed by the Dowager Provincara to be secretary to the Royesse Iselle. I had served the late provincar of Baocia as a page, in my youth," he added, by way of recommendation. He did not mention his service in dy Guarida's train, which might well trigger the roya's more recent memory, not that he had ever been more than one of the crowd of dy Guarida's men. A little unplanned disguise was surely lent him by his recent beard, his gray-flecked hair, his general debilitation—if Orico didn't recognize him, was there a chance that others also might not? He wondered how long he could go here at Cardegoss without giving his own name. Too late to change it, alas.

He could remain anonymous a little while longer, it appeared, for Orico nodded in apparent satisfaction and waved his hand in dismissal. "You'll be at the banquet, then. Tell my fair sister I look forward to seeing her there."

Cazaril bowed obediently and withdrew.

He chewed worriedly upon his lower lip as he made his way back to the gate of the Zangre. If all the court was to attend tonight's welcoming banquet, Chancellor the March dy Jironal, Orico's chief staff and support, would not be absent; and where the march went, his brother Lord Dondo usually attended upon him.

Maybe they won't remember me either. It had been well over two years since the fall—*shameful sale*—of Gotorget, and longer than that since the unpleasant incident in mad Prince Olus's tent. Cazaril's existence could never have been more than a petty irritation to these powerful lords. They could not know that he had realized his sale to the galleys had been calculated betrayal and not mischance. If he did nothing to draw attention to himself, they would not be reminded of what they had forgotten, and he would be safe.

A fool's hope.

Cazaril's shoulders hunched, and his stride lengthened.

🦅BACK IN HIS HIGH CHAMBER, CAZARIL FINGERED HIS sober brown wool robe and black vest-cloak longingly. But, obedient to the orders sent down from the floor above via a breathless maidservant, he donned much gaudier garb, an eggshell-blue tunic with turquoise brocade vestments and dark blue trousers from the old provincar's store, still smelling faintly of the spices they'd been packed with as proof against moths. Boots and sword completed a courtier's attire, even if it lacked the wealth of rings and chains.

At Teidez's urgent behest Cazaril stumped upstairs to check if his ladies were ready yet, there to discover that he was part of an ensemble. Iselle was arrayed in her finest favored blue-and-white gown and robes, and Betriz and the lady-in-waiting wore layers featuring turquoise and night-blue respectively. Someone in the party had come down on the side of restraint, and Iselle was decked in jewels befitting a maiden, mere diamond sparks in her ears, a brooch at her cleavage, one enameled belt, and only two rings. Betriz displayed some of the rest of the inventory, on loan. Cazaril stood straighter and regretted his resplendency less, determined to hold up his part for Iselle.

After only some seven or eight delays for last-minute exchanges and adjustments of clothing or decoration, Cazaril herded them all downstairs to join Teidez and his little entourage of rank, consisting of dy Sanda, the Baocian captain who had guarded their journey, and his chief sergeant at arms, the latter pair in their best livery, all with jewel-hilted swords. Swishing and clinking, they followed the royal page who was sent to guide them to Orico's throne room.

They paused briefly in the antechamber, where they formed up in proper order under the whispered instructions from the castle warder. Doors swung wide, sweet horns sounded, and the warder announced in stentorian breaths, "The Royse Teidez dy Chalion! The Royesse Iselle dy Chalion! Ser dy Sanda—" and on down the pack in strict order of rank, ending with "Lady Betriz dy Ferrej, Castillar Lupe dy Cazaril, Sera Nan dy Vrit!"

Betriz glanced up sideways at Cazaril, her brown eyes suddenly merry, and murmured under her breath, "Lupe? Your first name is *Lupe?*"

Cazaril considered himself excused from attempting to reply by their situation—just as well, as it would doubtless have come out thoroughly garbled. The room was thronged with courtiers and ladies, glittering and rustling, the air thick with perfume, incense, and excitement. In this crowd, he realized, his garments *were* modest and unobtrusive—in his austere brown and black, he'd have looked a crow among peacocks. Even the walls were dressed in red brocade.

On a raised dais at the end of the room, sheltered by a red brocade canopy fringed with gold braid, Roya Orico and his royina were seated on gilded chairs, side by side. Orico was looking much better this evening, washed up and in clean clothes, even with a dash of color in his puffy cheeks; very nearly kingly beneath his gold circlet crown, after a stodgy middle-aged fashion. Royina Sara was elegantly dressed in matching scarlet robes and sat very upright, almost prim, in her seat. Now in her mid-thirties, her earlier prettiness was fading and worn. Her expression was a little wooden, and Cazaril wondered how mixed her feelings must be at this royal reception. In her long infertility, she had failed her chief duty to the royacy of Chalion—if the failure was hers. Even when Cazaril had been on the fringes of court years ago, it was whispered that Orico had never got a bastard, though at the time this lack was attributed to an excessive loyalty to his marriage bed. Teidez's elevation was also the royal couple's public acknowledgment of a most private despair.

Teidez and Iselle advanced to the dais in turn. They exchanged fraternal kisses of welcome upon the hands with the roya and royina, though the full formal kisses of submission upon forehead, hands, and feet were not required of them tonight. Each member of their entourage was also granted the boon of kneeling and kissing the royal hands. Sara's was chill as wax, beneath Cazaril's respectful lips.

Cazaril stood behind Iselle and braced his back to endure, as the royal siblings prepared to receive a long line of courtiers, none of whom could be insulted by being left out or denied a personal introduction or touch. Cazaril's breath stopped in his throat as he recognized the first and foremost pair of men to advance.

The March dy Jironal was dressed in the full court robes of the general of the holy military order of the Son, in layers of brown, orange, and yellow. Dy Jironal was not much changed from when Cazaril had last seen him three years ago, when Cazaril had accepted the keys of Gotorget and the trust of its command from his hand in his field tent. He was still spare, graying, cool of eye, tense with energy, likely to forget to smile. The broad sword belt that crossed his chest was thick with enamel and jewels in the symbols of the Son, weapons and animals and wine casks. The heavy gold chain of the office of the chancellor of Chalion circled his neck.

Three large seal-rings decorated his hands, that of his own rich house, of Chalion, and of the Son's Order. No others cluttered his fingers—a wealth of jewels could not possibly have added more impact to that casual display of power.

Lord Dondo dy Jironal also wore the robes of a holy general, in the blue and white of the Daughter's Order. Stockier than his brother, with an unfortunate tendency to profuse sweat, at forty he still radiated the family dynamism. Except for his new honors he appeared unchanged, unaged, from when Cazaril had last seen him in his brother's camp. Cazaril realized he'd been hoping Dondo would at least have run to fat like Orico, given his infamous indulgences at table, in bed, and in every other possible pleasure, but he was only a little paunchy. The glitter on his hands, not to mention his ears, neck, arms, and gold-spurred boot heels, made up for whatever display of family wealth his brother disdained.

Dy Jironal's gaze passed over Cazaril without pause or recognition, but Dondo's black eyebrows drew down as he waited his turn, and he frowned at Cazaril's blankly affable features. His frown deepened abruptly. But Dondo's searching look was torn from Cazaril as his brother motioned a servant to bring forward the gifts he was presenting to Royse Teidez: a silver-mounted saddle and bridle, a fine hunting crossbow, and an ash boar spear with a wickedly gleaming, chased steel point. Teidez's excited thanks were entirely genuine.

Lord Dondo, after his formal introductions, snapped his fingers, and a servant holding a small casket stepped forward and opened it. With a gesture worthy of theater, he drew from it an enormously long string of pearls which he held high for all to see. "Royesse, I welcome you to Cardegoss in the name of my holy order, my glorious family, and my noble person! May I present you with double your length in pearls"— he brandished the string, which was indeed as long as the surprised Iselle was high— "and give thanks to the gods that you are not a taller lady, or I should be bankrupted!" A chuckle ran through the courtiers at his joke. He smiled engagingly at her, and murmured, "May I?" Without waiting for reply, he bent forward and laid the rope over her head; she flinched a little as his hand briefly touched her cheek, but fingered the gleaming spheres and smiled back in astonishment. She stammered out pretty thanks, and Dondo bowed—*too* low, Cazaril thought sourly; the gesture seemed tinged with subtle mockery, to his eye.

Only then did Dondo take a moment to murmur in his

brother's ear. Cazaril could not make out the low words, but he thought he saw Dondo's bearded lips shape the word *Gotorget*. Dy Jironal's glance at Cazaril grew startled and sharp, for an instant, but then both men had to make way for the next noble lord in line.

A daunting number of rich or clever welcoming gifts were pressed upon the royse and royesse. Cazaril found himself taking charge of Iselle's lot, and with Betriz's help making detailed notes as to their givers, to add to the household inventory later. Courtiers swarmed around the youths, Cazaril thought dryly, like flies around spilled honey. Teidez was elated to the point of giggling; dy Sanda was a little stiff, both gratified and strained. Iselle, though also clearly elated, conducted herself with fair dignity. She took alarm only once, when a Roknari envoy from one of the northern princedoms, tall and golden-skinned with his tawny hair dressed in elaborate braids, was introduced to her. His fine embroidered linen robes fluttered like banners with his sweeping bow. She curtseyed back with unsmiling but controlled courtesy, and thanked him for a beautiful belt of carved corals, jade, and gold links.

Teidez's gifts were more varied, though running heavily to weapons. Iselle's were mostly jewelry, although they included no less than three fine music boxes. At length all the gifts not imme-diately worn were placed on a table for display under the guard of a couple of pages—display of the givers' wealth, wit, or generosity, after all, being better than half their purpose—and the crowd of Cardegoss's elite filed into the banqueting hall.

The royse and royesse were conducted to the high table and seated on either side of Orico and his royina. They were flanked in turn by the Jironal brothers, Chancellor dy Jironal smiling a bit tightly at the fourteen-year-old Teidez, Dondo evidently trying to make himself pleasant to Iselle, though it could be seen that he laughed louder at his wit than she did. Cazaril was seated at one of the long tables perpendicular to the room's front, above the salt and not too far from his charge. He discovered the middle-aged man on his right to be an Ibran envoy.

"The Ibrans treated me well during my last sojourn in your country," Cazaril ventured politely after their mutual introduc-tions, deciding to avoid mentioning the details. "How came you to Cardegoss, my lord?"

The Ibran smiled in a friendly manner. "You are the Royesse

Iselle's man, eh? Well, besides the undoubted attractions of the hunting in Cardegoss in the fall, the roya of Ibra dispatched me to persuade Roya Orico not to support the Heir's new rebellion in South Ibra. The Heir accepts aid from Darthaca; I believe he will find it a gift that turns to bite him, in time."

"His Heir's rebellion is a painful contretemps for the roya of Ibra," Cazaril said, truthfully, but with studied neutrality. The old Fox of Ibra had double-dealt with Chalion enough times in the last thirty years to be considered a dubious friend and a dangerous enemy—though if this ghastly stop-and-start war with his son was the retribution of the gods for his slyness, the gods were surely to be feared. "I do not know Roya Orico's mind, but it seems to me that to back youth against age is to bet on a surety. They must make up again, or time will decide. For the old man to defeat his son is like to defeating himself."

"Not this time. Ibra has another son." The envoy glanced around and leaned closer to Cazaril, lowering his voice. "A fact that did not escape the attention of the Heir. To secure himself, he struck last fall at his younger brother, a foul and secret attack—although he claims now it was not ordered by him but was the wild work of minions who misunderstood some careless words. Understood them all too well, I'd say. The attempt to make away with young Royse Bergon was thwarted, thank the gods, and Bergon rescued. But the Heir has finally pushed his father's mercy over the line. There will be no peace between them this time short of South Ibra's abject surrender."

"A sad business," Cazaril said. "I hope they may all come to their senses."

"Aye," agreed the envoy. He smiled in dry appreciation, perhaps, of Cazaril's neat avoidance of declaring a preference, and let his patent persuasion rest.

The Zangre's food was wondrous, and left Cazaril close to cross-eyed with repletion. The court removed to the chamber where the dancing was to be held, where Roya Orico promptly fell asleep in his chair, to Cazaril's envy. The court musicians were excellent as ever. Royina Sara didn't dance either, but her cold face softened in apparent enjoyment of the music, and her hand kept time on her chair arm. Cazaril took his burdened digestion to a side wall, propped his shoulders comfortably, and watched younger and more vigorous, or less-stuffed-full, folk promenade, turn, and sway gracefully to the delicate strains. Neither Iselle nor Betriz nor even Nan dy Vrit lacked for partners.

Cazaril frowned as Betriz took her place in the figure with her third, no, fifth young lord. Royina Ista hadn't been the only concerned parent to corner him before he'd left Valenda; so had Ser dy Ferrej. *Watch out for my Betriz,* he had pleaded. *She ought to have her mother, or some older lady who knows the way of the world, but alas . . .* Dy Ferrej had been torn between fear of disaster and hope for opportunity. *Help her beware of unworthy men, roisterers, landless hangers-on, you know the type.* Like himself? Cazaril couldn't help wondering. *On the other hand, should she meet someone solid, honorable, I'd not be averse to her choosing with her heart . . . you know, a nice fellow, like, oh, say, your friend the March dy Palliar . . .* That airy example did not sound quite random enough, to Cazaril's ear. Had Betriz already formed a secret fondness? Palli, alas, was not present here tonight, having returned to his district after the installment of Lord Dondo in his holy generalship. Cazaril could have welcomed a friendly and familiar face in all this crowd.

He glanced aside at a movement, to find a face familiar and coolly smiling, but not one he welcomed. Chancellor dy Jironal gave him a slight bow of greeting; he pushed off the wall and returned it. His wits fought their way through a fog of food and wine to full alertness.

"Dy Cazaril. It *is* you. We had thought you were dead."

I'd wager so. "No, my lord. I escaped."

"Some of your friends feared you had deserted—"

None of my friends *would fear any such thing.*

"But the Roknari reported you had died."

"A foul lie, sir." Cazaril didn't say *whose* lie, his only daring. "They sold me to the galleys with the unransomed men."

"Vile!"

"I thought so."

"It's a miracle you survived the ordeal."

"Yes. It was." Cazaril blinked, and smiled sweetly. "Did you at least recover your ransom money, as the price of that lie? Or did some thief pocket it? I'd like to think that someone paid for the deception."

"I don't recall. It would have been the quartermaster's business."

"Well, it was all a dreadful mischance, but it has come right in the end."

"Indeed. I shall have to hear more of your adventures, sometime."

"When you will, my lord."

Dy Jironal nodded austerely, smiling, and moved on, evidently reassured.

Cazaril smiled back, pleased with his self-control—if it wasn't just his sick fear. He could, it seemed, smile, and smile, and not launch himself at the lying villain's throat—*I'll make a courtier yet, eh?*

His worst fears assuaged, Cazaril abandoned his futile attempt at invisibility, and nerved himself to ask Lady Betriz for one roundel. He knew himself tall and gangling and not graceful, but at least he was not falling-down drunk, which put him ahead of half the young men here by now. Not to mention Lord Dondo dy Jironal, who after monopolizing Iselle in the dance for a time had moved off with his roistering hangers-on to find either rougher pleasures or a quiet corridor to vomit in. Cazaril hoped the latter. Betriz's eyes sparkled with exhilaration as she swung with him into the figures.

At length, Orico woke up, the musicians flagged, and the evening drew to a close. Cazaril mobilized pages, Lady Betriz, and Sera dy Vrit to help carry off Iselle's booty and store it safe away. Teidez, scorning the dancing, had indulged in the spectacular array of sweets more than in drink, though dy Sanda might still have to deal with a bout of violent illness before dawn as a result. But it was clear the boy was more drunk on attention than on wine.

"Lord Dondo told me that anyone would have taken me for eighteen!" he told Iselle triumphantly. His growth spurt this past summer that had shot him up above his older sister had been occasion for much crowing on his part, and snorting on Iselle's. He trod off toward his bedchamber with feet barely touching the floor.

Betriz, her hands full of jewelry, asked Cazaril as they placed the gauds into Iselle's lockable boxes in her antechamber, "So why don't you use your name, Lord Caz? What's so wrong with Lupe? It's really quite a, a *strong* man's name, withal."

"Early aversion," he sighed. "My older brother and his friends used to torment me by yipping and howling until they'd driven me to tears of rage, which made me madder still—alas, by the time I'd grown tall enough to beat him, he'd outgrown the game. I thought that was most unfair of him."

Betriz laughed. "I see!"

Cazaril reeled off to the quiet of his own bedchamber, to realize he had failed to pen his faithfully promised note of reassurance to the Provincara. Torn between bed and duty, he sighed and pulled out his pens and paper and wax, but his account was much shorter than the entertaining report he had planned, a few terse lines ending, *All is well in Cardegoss.*

He sealed it, found a sleepy page to deliver it to whatever morning courier rode out of the Zangre, and fell into bed.

8

The first night's welcoming banquet was followed all too soon by the next day's breakfast, dinner, and an evening fête that included a masque. More sumptuous meals cascaded down the ensuing days, till Cazaril, instead of thinking Roya Orico sadly run to fat, began to marvel that the man could still walk. At least the initial bombardment of gifts upon the royal siblings slowed. Cazaril caught up on his inventory and began to think about where and upon what occasions some of this largesse should eventually be rebestowed. A royesse was expected to be openhanded.

He woke on the fourth morning from a confused dream of running about the Zangre with his hands full of jewelry that he could not get delivered to the right persons at the right times, and which had somehow included a large talking rat that gave him impossible directions. He rubbed away the sand of sleep from his eyes, and considered swearing off either Orico's fortified wines, or sweets that included too much almond paste, he wasn't sure which. He wondered what meals he'd have to face today. And then laughed out loud at himself, remembering siege rations. Still grinning, he rolled out of bed.

He shook out the tunic he'd worn yesterday afternoon, and unlaced the cuff to rescue the drying half loaf of bread that Betriz had bade him tuck in its wide sleeve when the royal picnic down by the river had been cut short by seasonable but unwelcome af-

ternoon rain showers. He wondered bemusedly if harboring provisions was what these courtiers' sleeves had been designed for,
back when this garment was new. He peeled off his nightshirt,
pulled on his trousers and tied their strings, and went to wash at
his basin.

A confused flapping sounded at his open window. Cazaril
glanced aside, startled by the noise, to see one of the castle crows
land upon the wide stone sill and cock its head at him. It cawed
twice, then made some odd little muttering noises. Amused, he
wiped his face on his towel, and, picking up the bread, advanced
slowly upon the bird to see if it was one of the tame ones that
might take food from his hand.

It seemed to spy the bread, for it didn't launch itself again as
he approached. He held out a fragment. The glossy bird regarded
him intently for a moment, then pecked the crumb rapidly from
between his fingers. Cazaril controlled his flinch as the sharp black
beak poked, but did not pierce, his hand. The bird shifted and
shook its wings, spreading a tail that was missing two feathers. It
muttered some more, then cawed again, a shrill harsh noise echoing in the little chamber.

"You shouldn't say *caw, caw,*" Cazaril told it. "You should say,
Caz, Caz!" He entertained himself and, apparently, the bird, for
several minutes attempting to instruct it in its new language, even
meeting it halfway by trilling *Cazaril! Cazaril!* in what he fancied
a birdish accent, but despite lavish bribes of bread it seemed even
more resistant than Iselle to Darthacan.

A knock at his chamber door interrupted the lesson, and he
called absently, "Yes?"

The door popped open; the crow flapped backward and fell
away through the window. Cazaril leaned out a moment to watch
its flight. It plummeted, then spread its wings with a snap and
soared again, wheeling away upon some morning updraft rising
along the ravine's steep face.

"My lord dy Cazaril, th—" The voice froze abruptly. Cazaril
pushed up from the windowsill and turned to find a shocked-looking
page standing in his doorway. Cazaril realized with a cold flush of
embarrassment that he had not yet donned his shirt.

"Yes, boy?" Without appearing to hurry, he reached casually for
the tunic, shook it out again, and pulled it on. "What is it?" His

drawl did not invite comment or query upon the year-old mess on his back.

The page swallowed and found his voice again. "My lord dy Cazaril, the Royesse Iselle bids you attend upon her in the green chamber immediately following breakfast."

"Thank you," said Cazaril coolly. He nodded in sober dismissal. The page scampered off.

The morning excursion for which Iselle demanded Cazaril's escort turned out to be nothing farther afield than the promised tour of Orico's menagerie. The roya himself was to conduct his sister; entering the green chamber, Cazaril found him dozing in a chair in his postbreakfast nap. Orico snorted awake and rubbed his forehead as if it ached. He brushed sticky crumbs from his broad tunic, gathered up a square of linen wrapping some packet, and led his sister, Betriz, and Cazaril out the castle gate and off across the gardens.

In the stable yard, they encountered Teidez's morning hunting party forming up. Teidez had been begging for this treat practically since he'd arrived at the Zangre. Lord Dondo, it appeared, had organized the boy's wish, and now led the group, which included half a dozen other courtiers, grooms and beaters, three braces of dogs, and Ser dy Sanda. Teidez, atop his black horse, saluted his sister and royal brother cheerfully.

"Lord Dondo says it's likely too early to spot boar," he told them, "as the leaves are not yet fallen down. But we might get lucky." Teidez's groom, following on his own horse, was loaded down with a veritable arsenal of weaponry just in case, including the new crossbow and boar spear. Iselle, who evidently hadn't been invited, looked on with some envy.

Dy Sanda smiled in contentment, as much as he ever smiled, with this noble sport, as Lord Dondo whooped and guided the cavalcade out of the yard at a smart trot. Cazaril watched them ride off and tried to figure out what about the fine autumn picture they presented made him uneasy. It came to him that not one of the men surrounding Teidez was under thirty. None followed the boy for friendship, or even anticipated friendship; all were there for self-interest. If any of these courtiers had their wits about them, Cazaril decided, they ought to bring their sons to court now and turn them loose and let nature take its course. A vision not without its own perils, but . . .

Orico lumbered on around the stable block, the ladies and Cazaril following. They found the head groom Umegat, evidently forewarned, waiting decorously by the menagerie doors, open wide to the morning sun and breeze. He bowed his neatly braided head to his master and his guests.

" 'S Umegat," said Orico to his sister, by way of introduction. "Runs this place for me. Roknari, but a good man anyway."

Iselle controlled a visible twinge of alarm and inclined her head graciously. In passable court Roknari, albeit improperly in the grammatical mode of master to warrior rather than master to servant, she said, ~Blessings of the Holy Ones be upon you this day, Umegat.~

Umegat's eyes widened, and his bow deepened. He returned a ~Blessings of the High Ones upon you too, m'hendi,~ in the purest accent of the Archipelago, in the polite grammatical form of slave to master.

Cazaril's brows rose. Umegat was no Chalionese half-breed after all, it seemed. Cazaril wondered by what convoluted life's chances he'd ended up *here*. Interest roused, he ventured, ~You are a long way from home, Umegat,~ in the mode of servant to lesser servant.

A little smile turned the groom's lips. ~You have an ear, m'hendi. That is rare, in Chalion.~

~Lord dy Cazaril instructs me,~ Iselle supplied.

~Then you are well served, lady. But,~ turning to Cazaril, he shifted modes, now to that of slave to scholar, even more exquisitely polite than that of slave to master, ~Chalion is my home now, Wisdom.~

"Let us show my sister my creatures," put in Orico, evidently growing bored with the bilingual amenities. He held up his linen napkin and grinned conspiratorially. "I stole a honeycomb for my bears from the breakfast table, and it will soak through soon if I don't rid myself of it."

Umegat smiled back and conducted them into the cool stone building.

The place was even more immaculate this morning than the other day, tidier by far than Orico's banqueting halls. Orico excused himself and dodged aside at once into one of his bears' cages. The bear woke up and sat up on his haunches; Orico lowered himself to his haunches on the gleaming straw, and the two regarded one another. Orico was very nearly the same shape as the bear, withal. He unwrapped his napkin and broke off a chunk of honey-comb, and the bear snuffled over and began licking his fingers with a long pink tongue. Iselle and Betriz exclaimed at the bear's thick and beautiful fur, but made no move to join the roya in the cage.

Umegat directed them to the more obviously herbivorous goat-creatures, and this time the ladies did go into the stalls, to stroke the beasts and compliment them enviously on their big brown eyes and sweeping eyelashes. Umegat explained that they were called vellas, imported from somewhere beyond the Archipelago, and supplied carrots, which the ladies fed to the vellas with much giggling and mutual satisfaction. Iselle wiped the last carrot bits mixed with vella slime on her skirt, and they all followed Umegat toward the aviary. Orico, lingering with his bear, languidly waved them on without him.

A dark shape swooped from the sunlight into the stone-arched aisle and fetched up with a flap and a grumble on Cazaril's shoulder; he nearly jumped out of his boots. He craned his neck to find it was his crow from his window this morning, judging by the ragged slot in its tail feathers. It flexed its clawed feet in his shoulder and cried, "Caz, Caz!"

Cazaril burst into laughter. "About time, you foolish bird! But it will do you no good now—I'm all out of bread." He shrugged his shoulder, but the bird clung stubbornly, and cried, "Caz, Caz!" again, right in his ear, painfully loudly.

Betriz laughed, lips parted in amazement. "Who's your friend, Lord Caz?"

"It came to my window this morning, and I attempted to teach it, um, a few words. I didn't think I'd succeeded—"

"Caz, Caz!" the crow insisted.

"You should be so attentive to your Darthacan, my lady!" Cazaril finished. "Come, Ser dy Bird, away with you. I have no more bread. Go find yourself a stunned fish below the falls, or a nice smelly dead sheep, or something . . . shoo!" He dipped his shoulder, but the bird clung stubbornly. "They are most greedy birds, these castle crows. Country crows have to fly about and find their own dinners. These lazy creatures expect you to put it in their mouths."

"Indeed," said Umegat, with a sly smile, "the birds of the Zangre are veritable courtiers among crows."

Cazaril swallowed a bark of laughter slightly too late and sneaked another look at the impeccable Roknari—ex-Roknari—groom. Well, if Umegat had worked here long, he'd had plenty of time to study courtiers. "This worship would be more flattering if you were a more savory bird. Shoo!" He pushed the crow from his shoulder, but it only flapped to the top of his head and dug its claws into his scalp. "Ow!"

"Cazaril!" the crow cried shrilly from this new perch.

"You must be a master teacher of tongues indeed, my lord dy Cazaril." Umegat smiled more broadly. "I hear you," he assured the crow. "If you will duck your head, my lord, I will endeavor to remove your passenger."

Cazaril did so. Murmuring something in Roknari, Umegat persuaded the bird onto his arm, carried it to the doors, and flung it into the air. It flapped away, cawing, to Cazaril's relief, more ordinary caws.

They proceeded to the aviary, where Iselle found herself as popular among the brilliant little birds from the cages as Cazaril was with the ragged crow; they hopped upon her sleeve, and Umegat showed her how to coax them to take grains from between her teeth.

They turned next to the perch birds. Betriz admired a large bright green one with yellow breast feathers and a ruby throat. It clicked its thick yellow beak, wobbled from side to side, and stuck out a narrow black tongue.

"This is a fairly recent arrival," Umegat told them. "I believe it has had a difficult and wandering life. Tame enough, but it's taken time and patience to calm it down."

"Does it speak?" asked Betriz.

"Yes," said Umegat, "but only rude words. In Roknari, perhaps fortunately. I think it must have once been a sailor's bird. March dy Jironal brought it back from the north this spring, as war booty."

Reports and rumors of that inconclusive campaign had come to Valenda. Cazaril wondered if Umegat had ever been war booty—as he had been—and if that was how he'd first been brought to Chalion. He said dryly, "Pretty bird, but it seems a poor trade for three towns and control of a pass."

"I believe Lord dy Jironal gained rather more movables than that," Umegat said. "His baggage train, returning to Cardegoss, took an hour to file through the gates."

"I've had to deal with slow mules like that, too," murmured Cazaril, unimpressed. "Chalion lost more than dy Jironal gained on that ill-conceived venture."

Iselle's eyebrows bent. "Was it not a victory?"

"By what definition? We and the Roknari princedoms have been pushing and shoving over that border area for decades. It used to be good land—it's now a waste. Orchards and olive groves and vineyards burned, farms abandoned, animals turned loose to go wild or starve—it's peace, not war, that makes wealth for a country. War just transfers possession of the residue from the weaker to the stronger. Worse, what is bought with blood is sold for coin, and then stolen back again." He brooded, and added bitterly, "Your grandfather Roya Fonsa bought Gotorget with the lives of his sons. It was sold by March dy Jironal for three hundred thousand royals. It's a wondrous transmutation, where the blood of one man is turned into the money of another. Lead into gold is nothing to it."

"Can there never be peace in the north?" asked Betriz, startled by his unusual vehemence.

Cazaril shrugged. "Not while there is so much profit in war. The Roknari princes play the same game. It is a universal corruption."

"*Winning* the war would end it," said Iselle thoughtfully.

"Now there's a dream," sighed Cazaril. "If the roya could sneak it past his nobles without their noticing they were losing their future livelihoods. But no. It's just not possible. Chalion alone could not defeat all five princedoms, and even if by some miracle it did, it has no naval expertise to hold the coasts thereafter. If all the Quintarian royacies were to combine, and fight hard for a generation, some immensely strong and determined roya might push it through and unite the whole land. But the cost in men and nerve and money would be vast."

Iselle said slowly, "Greater than the cost of this endless sucking drain of blood and virtue to the north? Done once—done *right* once—would be done for all time."

"But there is none to do it. No man with the nerve and vision and will. The roya of Brajar is an aging drunkard who sports with his court ladies, the Fox of Ibra is tied down with civil strife, Chalion . . ." Cazaril hesitated, realizing his stirred emotions were luring him into impolitic frankness.

"Teidez," Iselle began, and took a breath. "Maybe it will be Teidez's gift, when he comes to full manhood."

Not a gift Cazaril would wish on any man, and yet the boy did seem to have some nascent talents in that direction, if only his education in the next few years could bring them into sharp and directed focus.

"Conquest isn't the only way to unite peoples," Betriz pointed out. "There's marriage."

"Yes, but no one can marry three royacies and five princedoms," Iselle said, wrinkling her nose. "Not all at once, anyway."

The green bird, perhaps irritated at losing the attention of its audience, chose this moment to vent a remarkably lewd phrase in rude Roknari. Sailor's bird, indeed—a galley-man's bird, Cazaril judged. Umegat smiled dryly at Cazaril's involuntary snort but raised his brows slightly as Betriz and Iselle clamped their lips shut and turned a suffused pink, caught each other's gazes, and nearly lost their gravity. Smoothly, he reached for a hood and popped it over the bird's head. "Good night, my green friend," he told it. "I think you are not quite ready for polite society, here. Perhaps Lord dy Cazaril should stop in and teach you court Roknari too, eh?"

Cazaril's thought that Umegat seemed perfectly capable of teaching court Roknari all by himself was interrupted when a surprisingly brisk step at the door of the aviary proved to be Orico, wiping bear spittle on his trousers and smiling. Cazaril decided the castle warder's comment that first day was right: his menagerie did seem to be a consolation to the roya. His eye was clear, and color brightened his face again, visibly improved from the soggy exhaustion he'd evidenced immediately after breakfast.

"You must come see my cats," he told the ladies. They all followed him into the stone aisle, where he proudly showed off cages containing a pair of fine golden cats with tufted ears from the mountains of south Chalion, and a rare blue-eyed albino mountain cat of the same breed with striking black ear tufts. This end of the aisle also held a cage containing a pair of what Umegat named Archipelago sand foxes, looking like skinny, half-sized wolves, but with enormous triangular ears and cynical expressions.

With a flourish, Orico turned finally to his obvious favorite, the leopard. Let out on its silver chain, it rubbed itself around the roya's legs and made odd little growly noises. Cazaril held his breath as, encouraged by her brother, Iselle knelt to pet it, her face right next to those powerful jaws. Those round, pellucid amber eyes looked anything but friendly to him, but their lids did half close in evident enjoyment, and the broad brick-colored nose quivered as Iselle scratched the beast vigorously under the chin, and ran her spread fingers through its fabulous spotted coat. When Cazaril knelt, however, its growl took what seemed to his ear a decidedly hostile edge, and its distant amber stare encouraged no such liberties. Cazaril prudently kept his hands to himself.

The roya choosing to linger to consult with his head groom, Cazaril walked his ladies back to the Zangre, as they argued amiably over which had been the most interesting beast in the menagerie.

"What did *you* think the most curious creature there?" Betriz charged him.

Cazaril took a moment before replying, but in the end decided on the truth. "Umegat."

Her mouth opened to object to this supposed levity, but then closed again as Iselle cast him a sharp look. A thoughtful silence descended, which reigned all the way to the castle doors.

❧THE SHORTENING OF THE DAYLIGHT RUNNING ON INTO autumn was felt to be no loss by the inhabitants of the Zangre, for the lengthening nights continued to be made brilliant by candle-light, feasting, and fêtes. The courtiers took turns outdoing one another providing the entertainments, freely spending money and wit. Teidez and Iselle were dazzled, Iselle, fortunately, not totally; with the aid of Cazaril's undervoiced running commentary, she began to look for hidden meanings and messages, watch for intents, calculate expenditures and expectations.

Teidez, as nearly as Cazaril could tell, swallowed it all down whole. Signs of indigestion showed themselves. Teidez and dy Sanda began to clash more and more openly, as dy Sanda fought a losing battle to maintain the disciplines he'd imposed on the boy in the Provincara's careful household. Even Iselle began to worry about the heightening tensions between her brother and his tutor, as Cazaril quickly deduced when Betriz cornered him one morning, apparently casually, in a window nook overlooking the confluence of the rivers and half the hinterland of Cardegoss.

After a few remarks upon the weather, which was seasonable, and the hunting, which was too, she swerved abruptly to the matter that brought her to him, lowering her voice and asking, "What was that dreadful row between Teidez and poor dy Sanda in your corridor last night? We could hear the uproar through the windows *and* through the floor."

"Um . . ." Five gods, how was he to handle this one? *Maidens*. He half wished Iselle had sent Nan dy Vrit. Well, surely that sensible widow was in on whatever distaff discussions went on overhead. Yes, and better to be blunt than misunderstood. And far better to be blunt with Betriz than with Iselle herself. Betriz, no child, and most of all not Teidez's only sister, could decide what was fit to pass on to Iselle's ears better than he could. "Dondo dy Jironal brought Teidez a drab for his bed last night. Dy Sanda threw her back out. Teidez was infuriated." Infuriated, embarrassed, possibly secretly relieved, and, later in the evening, sick on wine. Ah, the glorious courtly life.

"Oh," said Betriz. He'd shocked her a little, but not excessively, he was relieved to see. "Oh." She fell into a thoughtful silence for a few moments, staring out over the rolling golden plains beyond the river and its widening valley. The harvest was almost all in. She bit her lower lip and looked back at him in narrow-eyed concern. "It's not . . . it's surely not . . . there is something very odd in the spectacle of a forty-year-old man like Lord Dondo hanging on a fourteen-year-old boy's sleeve."

"To hang on a boy? Odd indeed. To hang on a royse, his future roya, future dispenser of position, wealth, preferment, military opportunity—well, there you have it. Grant you, if Dondo were to let go his space on that sleeve it would instantly be seized by three other men. It's the . . . the *manner* that's the matter."

Her lips twisted in disgust. "Indeed. A drab, ugh. And Lord Dondo . . . that's what is called a *procurer*, is it not?"

"Mm, and ruder names. Not that . . . not that Teidez is not on the brink of full manhood, and every man must learn sometime—"

"Their wedding night isn't good enough? *We* must learn it all then."

"Men . . . usually marry later," he attempted, deciding this was an argument he'd best stay away from and, besides, embarrassed by the memory of how late his own apprenticeship had been. "Yet normally, a man will have a friend, a brother, or at least a father or an uncle, to introduce him to, um. How to go on. With ladies. But Dondo dy Jironal is none of these things to Teidez."

Betriz frowned. "Teidez has none of those. Well, except . . . except Roya Orico, who is both father and brother, in a way."

Their eyes met, and Cazaril realized he didn't have to add aloud, *But not in a very useful way.*

She added, after an even more thoughtful moment, "And I can't *imagine* Ser dy Sanda . . ."

Cazaril muffled a snort. "Oh, poor Teidez. Nor can I." He hesitated, then added, "It's an awkward age. If Teidez had been at court all along, he would be used to this atmosphere, not be so . . . impressed. Or if he'd been brought here when he was older, he might have a more settled character, a firmer mind. Not that court isn't dazzling at any age, especially if you're suddenly plopped down in the center of the whole wheel. And yet, if Teidez is to be Orico's heir, it's time he began training up to it. How to handle pleasures as well as duties with proper balance."

"Is he being so trained? I do not see it. Dy Sanda tries, desperately, but . . ."

"He's outnumbered," Cazaril finished for her glumly. "That is the root of the trouble." His brow wrinkled, as he thought it through. "In the Provincara's household, dy Sanda had her backing, her authority to complete his own. Here in Cardegoss Roya Orico should take that part, but takes no interest. Dy Sanda has been left to struggle on his own against impossible odds."

"Does this court . . ." Betriz frowned, clearly trying to frame unfamiliar thoughts. "Does this court have a center?"

Cazaril vented a wary sigh. "A well-conducted court always has someone in moral authority. If not the roya, perhaps his royina, someone like the Provincara to set the tone, keep the standards. Orico is . . ." he could not say *weak*, dared not say *ill*, "not doing so, and Royina Sara . . ." Royina Sara seemed a ghost to Cazaril, pale and drifting, nearly invisible. "Doesn't either. That brings us to

Chancellor dy Jironal. Who is much absorbed by the affairs of state, and does not take it upon himself to curb his brother."

Betriz's eyes narrowed. "Are you saying he sets Dondo on?"

Cazaril touched his finger warningly to his lips. "Do you remember Umegat's little joke about the Zangre's courtly crows? Try it in reverse. Have you ever watched a mob of crows combine to rob another bird's nest? One will draw off the parent birds, while another darts in to take the eggs or chicks . . ." His voice went dry. "Fortunately, most of the courtiers of Cardegoss don't work together as cleverly as a flock of crows."

Betriz sighed. "I'm not even sure Teidez realizes it's not all for his own sake."

"I'm afraid dy Sanda, for all his very real concern, has not laid it all out in blunt enough terms. Grant you he'd need to be pretty blunt to get through the fog of flattery Teidez floats in right now."

"But you do it for Iselle, all the time," Betriz objected. "You say, watch this man, see what he does next, see why he moves so—the seventh or eighth time you turn out to be dead on the target, we cannot help but listen—and the tenth or twelfth time, to begin to see it, too. Can't dy Sanda do that for Royse Teidez?"

"It's easier to see the smudge on another's face than on one's own. This flock of courtiers is not pressing Iselle nearly so hard as they are Teidez. Thank the gods. They all know she must be sold out of court, probably out of Chalion altogether, and is not meat for them. Teidez will be their future livelihood."

On that inconclusive and unsatisfactory note, they were forced to leave it for a time, but Cazaril was glad to know Betriz and Iselle were growing alive to the subtler hazards of court life. The gaiety was dazzling, seductive, a feast to the eye that could leave the reason as drunk and reeling as the body. For some courtiers and ladies, Cazaril supposed, it actually was the cheerful, innocent—albeit expensive—game it seemed. For others, it was a dance of display, ciphered message, thrust and counterthrust as serious, if not so instantly deadly, as a duel. To stay afoot, one had to distinguish the players from the played. Dondo dy Jironal was a major player in his own right, and yet . . . if not every move he made was directed by his older brother, it was surely safe to say his every move was permitted by him.

No. Not *safe to say*. Merely *true to think*.

*   *   *

❧HOWEVER DIM HIS VIEW OF THE MORALS OF COURT, he had to grant that Orico's musicians were very good, Cazaril reflected, opening his ear greedily to them at the next evening dance. If Royina Sara had a consolation to match Orico's menagerie, it was surely the Zangre's minstrels and singers. She never danced, she rarely smiled, but she never missed a fête where music was played, either sitting next to her sodden and sleepy spouse, or, if Orico staggered off to bed early, lingering behind a carved screen with her ladies on the gallery opposite the musicians. Cazaril thought he understood her hunger for this solace, as he leaned against the chamber wall in what was becoming his usual spot, tapping his foot and benignly watching his ladies twirl about on the polished wooden floor.

Musicians and dancers stopped for breath after a brisk roundel, and Cazaril joined the smattering of applause led by the royina from behind her screen. A completely unexpected voice spoke next to his ear.

"Well, Castillar. You're looking more your old self!"

"Palli!" Cazaril controlled his surge forward, turning it into a sweeping bow instead. Palli, formally dressed in the blue trousers and tunic and white tabard of the Daughter's military order, boots polished and sword glittering at his waist, laughed and returned an equally ceremonious bow, though he followed it up with a firm, if brief, grip of Cazaril's hands. "What brings you to Cardegoss?" Cazaril asked eagerly.

"Justice, by the goddess! And a good job of it, too, a year in the making. I rode up in support of the lord dedicat the provincar dy Yarrin, on a little holy quest of his. I'll tell you more, but, ah"—Palli glanced around the crowded chamber, where the dancers were forming up again—"maybe not here. You seem to have survived your trip to court—you're over that little burst of nerves now, I trust?"

Cazaril's lips twisted. "So far. I'll tell you more, but—not here." A glance around assured him neither Lord Dondo nor his elder brother were present at the moment, though some half dozen men he knew to be their creatures were just as certain to report this meeting and greeting. So be it. "Let us find a cooler spot, then."

They strolled out casually together into the next chamber, and Cazaril led Palli to a window embrasure that overlooked a moonlit courtyard. On the courtyard's far side, a couple sat closely together, but Cazaril judged them out of both earshot and caring.

"So what is old dy Yarrin about that brings him hot to court?" asked Cazaril curiously. The provincar of Yarrin was the highest-ranking lord of Chalion to have chosen allegiance to the holy military order of the Daughter. Most young men with military leanings dedicated themselves to the far more glamorous Order of the Son, with its glorious tradition of battle against the Roknari invaders. Even Cazaril had sworn himself a lay dedicat to the Son, in his youth—and unsworn himself, when . . . *let it go*. The far smaller holy military order of the Daughter concerned itself with more domestic challenges, guarding the temples, patrolling the roads to the pilgrimage shrines; by extension, controlling banditry, pursuing horse and cattle thieves, assisting in the capture of murderers. Granted, what the goddess's soldiers lacked in numbers they frequently made up in romantic dedication to her. Palli was a natural, Cazaril thought with a grin, and had surely found his calling at last.

"*Spring* cleaning." Palli smiled like one of Umegat's sand foxes for a moment. "A smelly little mess inside the temple walls is going to get washed out at last. Dy Yarrin had suspected for some time that, with the old general sick and dying for so long, the order's comptroller here in Cardegoss was filtering the order's funds as they flowed through his fingers." Palli wiggled his, in illustration. "Into his personal purse."

Cazaril grunted. "Unfortunate."

Palli cocked an eyebrow at him. "This doesn't take you by surprise?"

Cazaril shrugged. "Not in the main. Such things happen now and then, when men are tempted beyond their strength. I'd not heard anything specific said against the Daughter's comptroller though, no, beyond the usual slanders against every official in Cardegoss, be he honest or not, that every fool repeats."

Palli nodded. "Dy Yarrin's been over a year, quietly collecting the evidence and the witnesses. We took the comptroller—and his books—by surprise about two hours ago. He's locked down now in the Daughter's house's own cellar, under guard. Dy Yarrin will present the whole case to the order's council tomorrow morning. The comptroller will be stripped of his post and rank by tomorrow afternoon and delivered to the Chancellery of Cardegoss for punishment by tomorrow night. Ha!" His fist closed in anticipated triumph.

"Well done! Will you stay on, after that?"

"I hope to stay a week or two, for the hunting."

"Oh, excellent!" Time to talk, and a man of wit and certain honor to talk with—double luxury.

"I'm lodging in town at Yarrin Palace—I can't linger long here tonight, though. I just came up to the Zangre with dy Yarrin while he made his bow—and his report—to Roya Orico and General Lord Dondo dy Jironal." Palli paused. "I take it by your very healthy appearance that your worries about the Jironals turned out to be groundless?"

Cazaril fell silent. The breeze through the embrasure was growing chill. Even the lovers across the courtyard had gone in. He finally said, "I take care not to cross either of the Jironals. In any way."

Palli frowned, and seemed to hold some speech jostling just behind his lips.

A pair of servants wheeled a cart holding a crock of hot mulled wine, redolent of spices and sugar, through the antechamber toward the dancing chamber. A giggling young lady exited, closely pursued by a laughing young courtier; they both vanished out the other side, though their blended laughter lingered in the air. Strains of music sounded again, floating down from the gallery like flowers.

Palli's frown quirked away. "Did Lady Betriz dy Ferrej also accompany Royesse Iselle from Valenda?"

"Didn't you see her, among the dancers?"

"No—I saw you first, long stick that you are, propping up the walls. When I'd heard the royesse was here, I came looking in the chance you would be, too, though from the way you talked when last we met I couldn't be sure I'd find you. Do you think I might seize a dance before dy Yarrin is done closeting himself with Orico?"

"If you think you have the strength to fight your way through the mob that surrounds her, perhaps," said Cazaril dryly, waving him on. "They usually defeat me."

Palli managed this without apparent effort, and soon was handing a surprised and laughing Betriz in and out of the figures with cheery panache. He took a turn with Royesse Iselle as well. Both ladies seemed delighted to meet him again. Drawing breath afterward, he was greeted by some four or five other lords he apparently knew, until a page approached and touched him on the elbow, and murmured some message in his ear. Palli made his bows and left, presumably to join his fellow lord dedicat dy Yarrin and escort him back to his mansion.

Cazaril hoped the Daughter's new holy general, Lord Dondo dy Jironal, would be glad and grateful to have his house cleaned for him tomorrow. He hoped it fervently.

9

Cazaril spent the following day in smiling anticipation of the delight Palli's visit to court would bring to his routine. Betriz and Iselle also spoke in praise of the young march, which gave Cazaril brief pause. Palli would show to his best in this splendid setting.

And what of it? Palli was a landed man, with money, looks, charm, honorable responsibilities. Suppose he and the Lady Betriz were to hit it off. Was either of them less than what the other deserved? Nevertheless, Cazaril found his mind, unwilled, revolving plans for pleasures with Palli that somehow did not include his ladies.

But to his disappointment, Palli did not appear at court that evening—nor did the provincar of Yarrin. Cazaril supposed their wearing day of presenting evidence at the Daughter's house to whatever committee of justice had assembled there had run into complexities, and stretched past dinner. If the case took longer than Palli's first optimistic estimate, well, it would at least extend his visit to Cardegoss.

He did not see Palli again until the next morning, when the march appeared abruptly at the open door of Cazaril's office, which was an antechamber to the succession of rooms occupied by Royesse Iselle and her ladies. Cazaril stared up from his writing desk in surprise. Palli had discarded his court attire, and was dressed for the road in well-worn tall boots, thick tunic, and a short cloak for riding.

"Palli! Sit down—" Cazaril gestured to a stool.

Palli pulled it up across from him and lowered himself with a tired grunt. "Only for a moment, old friend. I could not leave without bidding you farewell. I, dy Yarrin, and our troops are commanded to be quit of Cardegoss before noon today, under pain of expulsion from the Daughter's holy order." His smile was tight as a stretched hawser.

"*What?* What has happened?" Cazaril laid down his quill, and pushed aside the book of Iselle's increasingly complex household accounts.

Palli ran a hand through his dark hair and shook his head as if in disbelief. "I'm not sure I can speak of it without bursting. It was all I could do last night not to pull out my sword and run the smirking son of a bitch through his soft guts on the spot. Caz, they threw out dy Yarrin's case! Confiscated all his evidence, dismissed all his witnesses—uncalled! unheard!—let that lying, thieving worm of a comptroller out of the cellar—"

"Who has?"

"Our *holy* general, Dondo dy Jironal, and his, his, his *creatures* on the Daughter's council, his cowed dogs—goddess blind me if I've ever before seen such a set of cringing curs—a disgrace to her pure colors!" Palli clenched his fist upon his knees, sputtering. "We all knew the order's house in Cardegoss has been in disarray for some time. I suppose we should have petitioned the roya to dismiss the old general when he first grew too ill to keep it all in hand, but no one had the heart to kick him so—we all thought a new, younger, vigorous man would turn it all out again and start fresh. But this, this, this is *worse* than neglect. It's active malfeasance! Caz, they cleared the comptroller and dismissed dy Yarrin—they scarcely glanced at his letters and ledgers, dear goddess the papers filled two trunks—I swear the decision was made before the meeting was called!"

Cazaril had not heard Palli stammer with rage like this since the day the news of the sale of Gotorget had been delivered to the starving, battered garrison by the roya's stout courier, passed through the Roknari lines. He sat back and pulled his beard.

"I suspect—no, I'm certain in my heart—Lord Dondo was paid off for his judgment. If he is not simply the comptroller's new master—and two trunks of evidence now being used to feed the fires on the Lady's altar—Caz, our new holy general is running the Daughter's Order as his personal milch cow. I was told by an acolyte yesterday—on the stairs, and the man shook as he whispered it to me—he's placed out six troops of the Daughter's men to the Heir of Ibra in South Ibra—as plain paid mercenaries. That's not their mandate, that's not the goddess's work—it's worse than stealing money, it's stealing blood!"

A rustle, and an indrawn breath, drew both men's glances to the inner doorway. Lady Betriz stood there with her hand upon the frame, and the Royesse Iselle peeked over her shoulder. Both ladies' eyes were round.

Palli opened and shut his mouth, swallowed, then jumped to his feet and bowed to them. "Royesse. Lady Betriz. Alas that I must take my leave of you. I return to Palliar this morning."

"We shall regret the loss of your company, March," said the royesse faintly.

Palli wheeled to Cazaril. "Caz—" He gave an apologetic little nod. "I'm sorry I disbelieved you about the Jironals. You weren't crazed after all. You were right on every point."

Cazaril blinked, nonplussed. "I thought you *had* believed me . . ."

"Old dy Yarrin was as canny as you. He suspected this trouble from the first. I'd asked him why he thought we needed to bring so large a troop to enter Cardegoss—he murmured, 'No boy—it is to *leave* Cardegoss.' I didn't understand his joke. Till now." Palli vented a bitter laugh.

"Will you be—will you not be returning here?" asked Betriz in a rather breathy voice. Her hand went to her lips.

"I swear before the goddess—" Palli touched his hand to forehead, lip, navel, and groin, and then spread it flat over his heart in the fivefold sacred gesture, "I will not return to Cardegoss except it be to Dondo dy Jironal's funeral. Ladies—" He stood at attention and gave them a bow. "Caz—" He grasped Cazaril's hands across the table and bent to kiss them; hastily, Cazaril returned the honor. "Farewell." Palli turned and strode from the room.

The space he had vacated seemed to collapse around his absence, as if four men had just left. Betriz and Iselle were drawn into it; Betriz tiptoed to the outer door and peered around it, to spy the last of his clomping retreat down the corridor.

Cazaril picked up his quill and drew the feather end nervously through his fingers. "How much of that did you hear?" he asked the ladies.

Betriz glanced back at Iselle, and replied, "All of it, I think. His voice was not pitched low." She returned slowly across the antechamber, her face troubled.

Cazaril groped for some way to caution these unintended auditors. "It was the business of a closed council of a holy military order. Palli should not have spoken of it outside the Daughter's house."

Iselle said, "But isn't he a lord dedicat, a member of that council—doesn't he have as much right—duty!—to speak as any of them?"

"Yes, but . . . in the heat of his temper, he has made serious accusations against his own holy general that he has not the . . . power to prove."

Iselle gave him a sharp look. "Do you believe him?"

"My belief is not the issue."

"But—if it's true—it's a crime, and worse than a crime. An insulting impiety, and a violation of the trust not only of the roya and the goddess above, but of all who are sworn to obey in their names below."

She sees the consequences in both directions! Good! No, wait, no. "We haven't seen the evidence. Maybe the council was justified in discarding it. We cannot know."

"If we can't see the evidence as March dy Palliar has, can we judge the men and reason backward to it?"

"No," said Cazaril firmly. "Even a habitual liar may tell the truth from time to time, or an honest man be tempted to lie by some extraordinary need."

Betriz, startled, said, "Do you think your friend was lying?"

"As he is my friend, no, of course not, but . . . but he might be mistaken."

"This is all too murky," said Iselle decisively. "I shall pray to the goddess for guidance."

Cazaril, remembering the last time she'd done that, said hastily, "You need not reach that high for guidance, Royesse. You inadvertently overheard a confidence. You have a plain duty not to repeat it. In word *or* deed."

"But if it's true, it *matters*. It matters greatly, Lord Caz!"

"Nevertheless, liking and disliking do not constitute proof any more than hearsay does."

Iselle frowned thoughtfully. "It's true I do not like Lord Dondo. He smells odd, and his hands are always hot and sweaty."

Betriz added, with a grimace of distaste, "Yes, and he's always touching one with them. Ugh!"

The quill snapped in Cazaril's hand, spraying a small spatter of ink drops on his sleeve. He set the pieces aside. "Oh?" he said, in what he trusted was a neutral tone. "When was this?"

"Oh, everywhere, at the dances, at dinner, in the halls. I mean, many gentlemen here flirt, some quite agreeably, but Lord Dondo . . . *presses*. There are enough fine ladies here at court nearer his own age. I don't know why he doesn't go try to charm them."

Cazaril almost asked her if thirty-five seemed as ancient to her as forty, but bit it short, and said instead, "He desires influence over Royse Teidez, of course. And therefore desires whatever good grace he can obtain from Teidez's sister, directly or through her attendants."

Betriz's breath puffed out in relief. "Oh, do you think that's so? It made me quite ill to think he might *really* be in love with me. But if he's only flattering me for his advantage, *that's* all right."

Cazaril was still laboring to work this through when Iselle said, "He has a very odd idea of my character if he thinks seducing my attendants will gain my good graces! And I do not think he needs any more influence over Teidez, if what I've seen so far is a sample. I mean—if it were good influence, shouldn't we see good results? We ought to see Teidez growing firmer in his studies, clearer in health, opening his mind to a wider world of *some* kind."

Cazaril also bit back the observation that Teidez was certainly getting that last from Lord Dondo, in a way.

Iselle went on with growing passion, "Shouldn't Teidez be apprenticing statecraft? At least seeing the Chancellery work, sitting in on councils, listening to envoys? Or if not statecraft, real warcraft? Hunting is fine, but shouldn't he be learning military drill with men? His spiritual diet seems all candy and no meat. What kind of roya do they mean to train him to be?"

Possibly, one just like Orico—sodden and sickly—who will not compete with Chancellor dy Jironal for power in Chalion. But what Cazaril said aloud was, "I do not know, Royesse."

"How can I know? How can I know anything?" She stepped back and forth across the chamber, her spine tense with frustration, her skirts swishing. "Mama and Grandmama would wish me to watch out for him. Cazaril, can you at least find out if it's true about selling the Daughter's men to the Heir of Ibra? That at least can't be any kind of subtle secret!"

She was right about that. Cazaril swallowed. "I'll try, my lady. But—then what?" He made his voice stern, for emphasis. "Dondo dy Jironal is a power you dare not treat with anything but strictest courtesy."

Iselle swirled round, and stared intently at him. "No matter how corrupt that power is?"

"The more corrupt, the less safe."

Iselle raised her chin. "So, Castillar, tell me—how safe, in your judgment, is Dondo dy Jironal?"

He was caught out, his mouth at half cock. *So say it—Dondo dy Jironal is the second-most-dangerous man in Chalion, after his brother.* Instead, he picked up a new quill from the clay jar and began shaping its tip with the penknife. After a moment or two he got out, "I do not like his sweaty hands either."

Iselle snorted. But Cazaril was saved from further cross-examination by a call from Nan dy Vrit, some vital little matter of scarves and straying seed pearls, and the two ladies went back into their chambers.

🦋On cool afternoons when no more-exciting hunting party went out, Royesse Iselle vented her restless energy by gathering up her little household and going for rides in the oak woods near Cardegoss. Cazaril, along with Lady Betriz and a couple of wheezing grooms, was cantering in the wake of her dappled mare down a green ride, the crisp air spangled with golden falling leaves, when his ear picked up a thunder of new hooves gaining ground behind them. He glanced over his shoulder, and his stomach lurched; a cavalcade of masked men was pelting down the track. The yelling crew overtook them. He had his sword half-out before he recognized the horses and equipage as belonging to some of the Zangre's younger courtiers. The men were dressed in an amazing array of rags, bare arms and legs smeared with a dirt suspiciously reminiscent of boot blacking.

Cazaril drew a long breath, and bent briefly over his saddlebow, willing his heart to slow, as the grinning mob "captured" the royesse and Lady Betriz, and tied their prisoners, including Cazaril, with silk ribands. He wished fervently someone would warn *him*, at least, about these pranks in advance. The laughing Lord dy Rinal had come, though he apparently did not realize it, to within a fraction of a reflex of receiving a length of razor steel across his throat. His sturdy page, galloping up on Cazaril's other side, might have died on the backstroke, and Cazaril's sword sheathed itself in a third man's belly before, had they been real bandits, they could have combined to take him down. And all before Cazaril's brain had formulated his first clear thought, or his mouth opened to scream warning. They all laughed heartily at the look of terror they'd surprised on his face, and teased him about drawing steel; he smiled sheepishly, and decided not to explain just what aspect of it all had drained the blood from his face.

They rode to their "bandit camp," a large clearing in the forest where a number of servants from the Zangre, also dressed in artistic rags, roasted deer and lesser game on spits over open fires. Bandit ladies, shepherdesses, and some rather stately beggar girls hailed the kidnappers' return. Iselle squeaked in laughing outrage when the bandit king dy Rinal clipped a lock of her curling hair and held it up for ransom. The masque was not yet finished, for upon this cue a troop of "rescuers" in blue and white, led by Lord Dondo dy Jironal, galloped into the camp. Vigorous mock swordplay ensued, including some alarming and messy moments involving pig's bladders filled with blood, before all the bandits were slain—some still complaining about the unfairness of it—and the lock of hair rescued by Dondo. A mock divine of the Brother then went about miraculously raising the bandits back to life with a skin of wine, and the entire company settled down upon cloths spread on the ground for some serious feasting and drinking.

Cazaril found himself sharing a cloth with Iselle, Betriz, and Lord Dondo. He sat cross-legged toward the edge, nibbled venison and bread, and watched and listened as Dondo entertained the royesse with what was, to his ear, heavy-handed wit. Dondo begged Iselle to award him her shorn lock as his prize for her daring rescue, and offered up in return, with a snap of his fingers to his hovering page, a tooled leather case containing two beautiful jeweled tortoiseshell combs.

"A treasure for a treasure, and all is quits," Dondo told her, and ostentatiously tucked the curl of hair away in an inner pocket of his vest-cloak, over his heart.

"It's a cruel gift, though," Iselle parried, "to give me combs but leave me no hair to hold with them." She held a comb up and turned it, glittering and translucent, in the sunlight.

"But you may grow new hair, Royesse."

"But can you grow new treasure?"

"As easily as you can grow new hair, I assure you." He leaned on his elbow by her side, and grinned up at her, his head nearly in her lap.

Iselle's amused smile faded. "Do you find your new post so profitable, then, Holy General?"

"Indeed."

"You are miscast, then. Perhaps you should have played the bandit king today."

Dondo's smile thinned. "If the world were not so, how could I ever buy enough pearls to please the pretty ladies?"

Spots of color flared in Iselle's cheeks, and she lowered her eyes. Dondo's smile grew satisfied. Cazaril, his tongue clamped between his teeth, reached for a silver flagon of wine, with an eye to accidentally in this emergency spilling it down the back of Iselle's neck. Alas, the flagon was empty. But to his intense relief, Iselle took a bite of bread and meat next, and chewed instead on it. It was notable, though, that she drew her skirts aside from Lord Dondo when next she shifted position.

The chill of the autumn evening was rising with the shadows from the low places when the replete company rode slowly back to the Zangre after the bandits' picnic. Iselle reined in her dappled mare and fell back beside Cazaril for a moment.

"Castillar. Did you ever discover for me the truth of the rumor of the Daughter's troops being sold for mercenaries?"

"One or two other men have said so, but it is not what I would call confirmed news." It was, in fact, quite thoroughly confirmed, but Cazaril judged it imprudent to say so to Iselle just at this moment.

She frowned silently, then spurred her horse forward to catch up with Lady Betriz again.

❧THAT NIGHT THE SPARER-THAN-USUAL EVENING BAN-quet broke up without dancing, and tired courtiers and ladies went off to an early bed or private pleasures. Cazaril found Dondo dy Jironal falling into step beside him in an antechamber.

"Walk with me a little, Castillar. I think we need to talk."

Cazaril shrugged obligingly, and followed Dondo, feigning not to notice the two choice young bravos, a couple of Dondo's riper friends, who padded along a few paces behind them. They exited the tower block at the narrow end of the fortress, onto an irregular little quadrangle of a courtyard overlooking the confluence of the rivers. At a hand signal from Dondo, his two friends waited by the door, leaning against the stone wall like bored and tired sentries.

Cazaril calculated the odds. He had reach on Dondo, and de-spite his subsequent illness, his months pulling the oar on the galleys had left his wiry arms much stronger than they looked. Dondo was doubtless better trained. The bravos were young. A little drunk, but young. At three-to-one, swordplay might not even be required. An unagile secretary, too full of wine after supper, taking a walk on the battlements, could slip and fall in the dark, bouncing off the rock face three hundred feet down to the water below; his broken body might be found next day without a single telltale stab wound in it.

A few lanterns in wall brackets cast flickering orange light across the paving stones. Dondo gestured invitingly to a carved granite bench against the outer wall. The stone was gritty and chill against Cazaril's legs as he sat, the night breeze dank on his neck. With a little grunt, Dondo seated himself, too, automatically flip-ping his vest-cloak aside to free his sword hilt.

"So, Cazaril," Dondo began. "I see you are quite close in the confidence of the Royesse Iselle, these days."

"The post of her secretary is one of great responsibility. Of her tutor, even more so. I take it quite seriously."

"No surprise there—you always took everything too seriously. Too much of a good thing can be a fault in a man, you know."

Cazaril shrugged.

Dondo sat back and crossed his legs at the ankles, as if making himself comfortable for a chat with some intimate. "For example"—he waved a hand toward the tower block now rising before them—"a girl of her age and style should be just starting to warm to men, and yet I find her strangely chill. A mare like that is made for breeding—she has good wide hips, to cradle a man." He gave his own a little double jerk, for illustration. "One hopes she has escaped that unfortunate taint in the blood, and it's not an early sign of the sort of, ah, difficulties of mind that overset her poor mother."

Cazaril decided not to touch this one. "Mm," he said.

"One hopes. And yet, if that is not the case, one is almost led to wonder if some . . . overserious person has taken to poisoning her mind against me."

"This court is full of gossip. And gossipers."

"Indeed. And, ah . . . just how *do* you speak of me to her, Cazaril?"

"Carefully."

Dondo sat back, and folded his arms. "Good. That's good." He paused for a time. "And yet, withal, I think that I should prefer warmly. Warmly would be better."

Cazaril moistened his lips. "Iselle is a very clever and sensitive girl. I'm sure she could sense if I were lying. Better to leave it as it is."

Dondo snorted. "Ah, here we come to it. I suspected you might still be holding a grudge against me for that evil little game of mad Olus's."

Cazaril made a little negating gesture. "No. It is forgotten, my lord." The proximity of Dondo, as close as in Olus's tent, his slightly peculiar scent, brought it back in intense detail, blaring through Cazaril's memory, the panting despair, the *skree*, the heavy blow . . . "It was a long time ago."

"Huh. I do like a man with a malleable memory, and yet . . . I still feel you need more heat. I suppose you're still a poor man, as ever. Some fellows never catch the tricks of getting on in the world." Dondo unfolded his arms, and, with some little difficulty, twisted a ring off one of his thick, damp fingers. Its gold was thin, but a large bevel-cut flat green stone gleamed in its setting. He held it out to Cazaril. "Let this warm your heart to me. And your tongue."

Cazaril didn't move. "I have all I need from the royesse, my lord."

"Indeed." Dondo's black brows knotted; his dark eyes glittered in the lanternlight between his narrowed lids. "Your position does give you considerable opportunity to fill your pockets, I suppose."

Cazaril closed his teeth, hiding his tremble of outrage. "If you decline to believe in my probity, my lord, you might at least reflect upon Royesse Iselle's future, and believe I still possess the wits the gods gave me. Today she has a household. Another day, it may be some royacy, or a princedom."

"Indeed, think you so?" Dondo sat back with a strange grin, then laughed aloud. "Ah, poor Cazaril. If a man neglects his bird in the hand for the flock he sees in the tree, he's very like to end with no bird at all. How clever is that?" He set the ring coyly down on the stone between them.

Cazaril opened both his hands and held them out palm up in front of his chest in a gesture of release. He returned them firmly to his knees, and said with undeceptive mildness, "Save your treasure, my lord, to buy yourself a man with a lower price. I'm sure you can find one."

Dondo scooped his ring back up and frowned fiercely at Cazaril. "You haven't changed. Still the same sanctimonious prig. You and that fool dy Sanda are much alike. No wonder, I suppose, considering that old woman in Valenda who chose you both." He rose and stalked indoors, shoving the ring back on his finger. The two men waiting glanced across curiously at Cazaril and turned to follow.

Cazaril sighed, and wondered if his moment of furious satisfaction had been bought at too high a price. It might have been wiser to take the bribe and leave Lord Dondo calm, happy in the belief that he'd bought another man, one just like himself, easy to understand, certain of control. Feeling very tired, he pushed himself to his feet and went back inside to mount the stairs to his bedchamber.

He was just putting his key in his lock when dy Sanda passed him in the corridor, yawning. They exchanged cordial-enough murmurs of greeting.

"Stay a moment, dy Sanda."

Dy Sanda glanced back over his shoulder. "Castillar?"

"Are you careful to keep your door locked these days, and your key about your person?"

Dy Sanda's brows rose, and he turned. "I have a trunk with a good, stout lock, that serves for all I have to guard."

"That's not enough. You need to block your whole room."

"So that nothing can be stolen? I have little enough that—"

"No. So that nothing stolen can be placed therein."

Dy Sanda's lips parted; he stood a moment, as this sank in, and raised his eyes to meet Cazaril's. "Oh," he said at last. He gave Cazaril a slow nod, almost a bow. "Thank you, Castillar. I hadn't thought of that."

Cazaril returned the nod, and went inside.

10

Cazaril sat in his bedchamber with a profligacy of candles and the classic Brajaran verse romance *The Legend of the Green Tree*, and sighed in contentment. The Zangre's library had been famous in the days of Fonsa the Wise but neglected ever since—this volume, judging by the dust, hadn't been pulled off the shelves since the end of Fonsa's reign. But it was the luxury of enough candles to make reading late at night a pleasure and not a strain, as much as Behar's versifying, that gave his heart joy. And a little guilt the charges for good wax candles upon Iselle's household accounts were going to add up after a time, and look a trifle odd. Behar's thundering cadences echoing in his head, he moistened his finger and turned a page.

Behar's stanzas weren't the only things around here thundering and echoing. He glanced upward, as rapid thumps and scrapes and the muffled sounds of laughter and calling voices penetrated from the ceiling. Well, enforcing reasonable bedtimes in Iselle's household was Nan dy Vrit's job, not his, thank the gods. He returned his eye to the poet's theologically symbolic visions, and ignored the clatter, till the pig squealed shrilly.

Even the great Behar could not compete with *that* mystery. His lips drawing back in a grin, Cazaril set the volume down on his coverlet and swung his still-trousered legs out of bed, fastened his tunic, wriggled his feet into his shoes, and picked up the candle with the glass chimney to light his way up the back stairs.

He met Dondo dy Jironal coming down. Dondo was dressed in his usual courtier's attire, blue brocade tunic and linen-woolen trousers, though his white vest-cloak swung from his hand, along with his sword in its scabbard and sword belt. His face was set and flushed. Cazaril's mouth opened to give some polite greeting, but his words died on his lips at Dondo's murderous glare. Dondo stormed on past him without a word.

Cazaril swung into the upstairs corridor to find all its wall sconces lit and an inexplicable array of people gathered. Not only Betriz, Iselle, and Nan dy Vrit, but Lord dy Rinal, one of his friends and another lady, and Ser dy Sanda were all crowded around laughing. They scattered to the walls as Teidez and a page blasted through their midst, in hot pursuit of a scrubbed and beribboned young pig trailing a length of scarf. The page tackled the animal at Cazaril's feet, and Teidez hooted triumph.

"In the bag, in the bag!" dy Sanda called.

He and Lady Betriz came up as Teidez and the page collaborated on inserting the squealing creature into a large canvas sack, where it clearly didn't want to go. Betriz bent to give the struggling animal a quick scratch behind its flapping ears. "My thanks, Lady Pig! You played your part superbly. But it's time to go back to your home now."

The page hoisted the heavy sack up over his shoulder, saluted the assembled company, and staggered off, grinning.

"*What* is going on up here?" demanded Cazaril, torn between laughter and alarm.

"Oh, it was the greatest jest!" cried Teidez. "You should have seen the look on Lord Dondo's face!"

Cazaril just had, and it hadn't inspired him with mirth. His stomach sank. "What have you done?"

Iselle tossed her head. "Neither my hints not Lady Betriz's plain words having served to discourage Lord Dondo's attentions, or to convince him they were unwelcome, we conspired to make him the assignation of love he desired. Teidez undertook to secure our player from the stable. So, instead of the virgin Lord Dondo was confidently expecting to find waiting when he went tiptoeing up to Betriz's bed in the dark, he found—Lady Pig!"

"Oh, you traduce the poor pig, Royesse!" cried Lord dy Rinal. "She may have been a virgin, too, after all!"

"I'm sure she was, or she would not have squealed so," the laughing lady on his arm put in.

"It's only too bad," said dy Sanda acidly, "she was not to Lord Dondo's taste. I confess I'm surprised. From all reports of the man, I'd have thought he'd lie down with anything." His eyes flicked sideways, to check the effect of these words on the grinning Teidez.

"And after we'd doused her with my *best* Darthacan perfume, too," sighed Betriz hugely. The merriment in her eyes was underscored by a glittering rage and sharp satisfaction.

"You should have told me," Cazaril began. Told him what? Of this prank? It was clear enough they knew he would have suppressed it. Of Dondo's continued *pressings?* Just how vile had they been? His fingernails bit into his palm. And what could he have done about them, eh? Gone to Orico, or Royina Sara? *Futile . . .*

Lord dy Rinal said, "It will be the best tale of the week in all of Cardegoss—and the best tail, too, if a curly one. Lord Dondo hasn't played the butt for years, and I do think it was past his turn. I can hear the oinking already. The man won't sit to a pork dinner for months without hearing it. Royesse, Lady Betriz"—he swept them a bow—"I thank you from the bottom of my heart."

The two courtiers and the lady took themselves off, presumably to spread the jest to whatever of their friends were still awake.

Cazaril, suppressing the first several remarks trying to rip from his lips, finally ground out, "Royesse, that was not wise."

Iselle frowned back, undaunted. "The man wears the robes of a holy general of the Lady of Spring yet undertakes to rob women of their virginity, sacred to Her, just as he robs . . . well, so you say we have no proof of what else he robs. We had proof enough of this, by the goddess! At least this may teach him the unwisdom of attempting to steal from *my* household. The Zangre is supposed to be a royal court, not a barnyard!"

"Cheer up, Cazaril," dy Sanda advised him. "The man cannot revenge his outraged vanity upon the royse and royesse, after all." He glanced around; Teidez had gone off up the corridor to collect the trampled ribbons the pig had shed in its attempted flight. He lowered his voice, and added, "And it was well worth the trouble for Teidez to see his, ah, *hero* in a less flattering light. When the amorous Lord Dondo stumbled out of Betriz's bedchamber with the strings of his trousers in his hands, he found all our witnesses lined up waiting. Lady Pig nearly knocked him down, escaping between his legs. He looked an utter fool. It's the best lesson I've been able to bring off all this month we've been here. Maybe we can start to regain some lost ground in that direction, eh?"

"I pray you may be right," said Cazaril carefully. He did not say aloud his reflection that the royse and the royesse were the *only* people Dondo could not revenge himself upon.

Nevertheless, there was no sign of retaliation in the next several days. Lord Dondo took the raillery of dy Rinal and his friends with a thin smile, but a smile nonetheless. Cazaril sat to every meal in the expectation of, at the very least, a certain pig served up roasted with ribbons round its neck to the royesse's table, but the dish did not appear. Betriz, at first infected by Cazaril's nerves, was reassured. Cazaril was not. For all his hot temper, Dondo had amply demonstrated just how long he could wait for his opportunities without forgetting his wounds.

To Cazaril's relief, the oinking about the castle corridors died down in less than a fortnight as new fêtes and pranks and gossip took its place. Cazaril began to hope Lord Dondo was going to swallow his so publicly administered medicine without spitting. Perhaps his elder brother, with larger horizons in view than the little society inside the Zangre's walls, had undertaken to suppress any inappropriate response. There was news enough from the outside world to absorb grown men's attention: sharpening of the civil war in South Ibra, banditry in the provinces, bad weather closing down the high passes unseasonably early.

In light of these last reports, Cazaril gave an eye to the logistics of transporting the royesse's household, should the court decide to leave the Zangre early and remove to its traditional winter quarters before the Father's Day. He was sitting in his office totting up horses and mules when one of Orico's pages appeared at the antechamber door.

"My lord dy Cazaril, the roya bids you attend upon him in Ias's Tower."

Cazaril raised his eyebrows, set down his quill, and followed the boy, wondering what service the roya desired of him. Orico's sudden fancies could be a trifle eccentric. Twice he had ordered Cazaril to accompany him on expeditions to his menagerie, there to perform no offices more complex than what a page or groom might well have done, holding his animals' chains or fetching brushes or feed. Well, no—the roya had also asked leading questions about his sister Iselle's doings, in an apparently desultory fashion. Cazaril had seized the opportunity to convey Iselle's horror of being bartered to the Archipelago, or to any other Roknari prince, and had hoped the roya's ear was more open than his sleepy demeanor would indicate.

The page guided him to the long room on the second floor of Ias's Tower that dy Jironal used for his Chancellery when the court was resident in the Zangre. It was lined with shelves crammed with books, parchments, files, and a row of the seal-locked saddlebags used by the royal couriers. The two liveried guards standing at attention followed them within and took up their posts inside the door. Cazaril felt their eyes follow him.

Roya Orico was seated with the chancellor behind a large table scattered about with papers. Orico looked weary. Dy Jironal was spare and intense, dressed today in ordinary court garb, but with his chain of office around his neck. A courtier, whom Cazaril recognized as Ser dy Maroc, master of the roya's armor and wardrobe, stood at one end of the table. One of Orico's pages, looking very worried, stood at the other.

Cazaril's escort announced, "The Castillar dy Cazaril, sire," and then, after a glance at his fellow page, backed away to make himself invisible by the far wall.

Cazaril bowed. "Sire, my lord Chancellor?"

Dy Jironal stroked his steel-streaked beard, glanced at Orico, who shrugged, and said quietly, "Castillar, you will oblige His Majesty, please, by removing your tunic, and turning around."

Cold unease knotted the words in his throat. Cazaril closed his lips, gave a single nod, and undid the frogs of his tunic. Tunic and vest-cloak he slipped off together and folded neatly over his arm. Face set, he made a military about-face, and stood still. Behind him, he heard two men stifle gasps, and a young voice mutter, "It *was* so. I *did* see." Oh. *That* page. Yes.

Someone cleared his throat; Cazaril waited for the hot flush to die from his cheeks, then wheeled around again. He said steadily, "Was that all, sire?"

Orico fidgeted, and said, "Castillar, it is whispered . . . you are accused . . . an accusation has been made . . . that you were convicted of the crime of rape in Ibra, and flogged in the stocks."

"That is a lie, sire. Who has said it?" He glanced at Ser dy Maroc, who had grown a trifle pale while Cazaril's back was turned. Dy Maroc was not in either of the Jironal brothers' direct employ, and he was not, so far as Cazaril knew, one of Dondo's riper creatures . . . might he have been bribed? Or was he an honest gull?

A clear voice rang from the corridor. "I will *too* see my brother, and at once! I have the right!"

Orico's guards surged forward, then hastily back again, as Royesse Iselle, trailed by a very pale Lady Betriz and Ser dy Sanda, burst into the chamber.

Iselle's quick glance took in the tableau of men. She raised her chin, and cried, "What is this, Orico? Dy Sanda tells me you have arrested my secretary! Without even warning me!"

By the peeved ripple of Chancellor dy Jironal's mouth, this intrusion had not been in his plans. Orico waved his thick hands. "No, no, not *arrested*. No one has arrested anyone. We are gathered to investigate an accusation."

"What accusation?"

"A very serious one, Royesse, and not for your ears," said dy Jironal. "You should withdraw."

Pointedly ignoring him, she pulled up a chair and plunked down into it, folding her arms. "If it's a serious accusation against the most trusted servant of my household, it is very much for my ears. Cazaril, what is this about?"

Cazaril gave her a slight bow. "A slander has apparently been circulated, by persons not yet named, that the scars on my back were punishment for a crime."

"Last fall," dy Maroc put in nervously. "In Ibra."

By Betriz's widening stare and caught breath, she had obtained a good close view of the ropy mess as she'd followed Iselle around Cazaril. Ser dy Sanda's lips too pursed in a wince.

"May I put my tunic back on, sire?" Cazaril added stiffly.

"Yes, yes." Orico waved a hasty assent.

"The nature of the crime, Royesse," dy Jironal put in smoothly, "is such as to cast very serious doubts on whether the man should be a trusted servant of your, or indeed, any lady's household."

"What, rape?" said Iselle scornfully. "*Cazaril?* That is the most absurd lie I have ever heard."

"And yet," said dy Jironal, "there are the flogging scars."

"The gift," said Cazaril through his teeth, "of a Roknari oar-master, in return for a certain ill-considered defiance. Last fall, and off the coast of Ibra, that much is true."

"Plausible, and yet . . . odd," said dy Jironal in a judicious tone. "The cruelties of the galleys are legendary, but one would not think a competent oar-master would damage a slave past use."

Cazaril half smiled. "I provoked him."

"How so, Cazaril?" asked Orico, leaning back and squeezing the fat of his chin with one hand.

"Wrapped my oar-chain around his throat and did my best to strangle him. I almost succeeded, too. But they pulled me off him a trifle too soon."

"Dear gods," said the roya. "Were you trying to commit suicide?"

"I . . . am not quite sure. I'd thought I was past fury, but . . . I had been given a new benchmate, an Ibran boy, maybe fifteen years old. Kidnapped, he said, and I believed him. You could tell he was of good family, soft, well-spoken, not used to rough places—he blistered dreadfully in the sun, and his hands bled on the oars. Scared, defiant, ashamed . . . he said his name was Danni, but he never told me his surname. The oar-master made to use him after a manner forbidden to Roknari, and Danni struck out at him. Before I could stop him. It was insanely foolish, but the boy didn't realize. . . . I thought—well, I wasn't thinking very clearly, but I thought if I struck harder I could distract the oar-master from retaliating upon him."

"By retaliating against you instead?" said Betriz wonderingly.

Cazaril shrugged. He'd kneed the oar-master hard enough in the groin, before wrapping the chain around his neck, to assure he wouldn't be amorous again for a week, but a week would have passed soon enough, and then what? "It was a futile gesture. *Would* have been futile, but for the chance of the Ibran naval flotilla crossing our bows the next morning, and rescuing us all."

Dy Sanda said encouragingly, "You have witnesses, then. Quite a large number of them, it sounds like. The boy, the galley slaves, the Ibran sailors . . . what became of the boy, after?"

"I don't know. I lay ill in the Temple Hospital of the Mother's Mercy in Zagosur for, for a while, and everyone was scattered and gone by the time I, um, left."

"A very heroic tale," said dy Jironal, in a dry tone well calculated to remind his listeners that this was Cazaril's version. He frowned judiciously and glanced around the assembled company, his gaze lingering for a moment upon dy Sanda, and the outraged Iselle. "Still . . . I suppose you might ask the royesse to give you a month's leave to ride to Ibra, and locate some of these, ah, conveniently scattered witnesses. If you can."

Leave his ladies unguarded for a month, *here*? And would he survive the trip? Or be slain and buried in a shallow grave in the woods two hours' ride out of Cardegoss, leaving the court to construe his guilt from his supposed flight? Betriz pressed her hand to whitened lips, but her glare was wholly for dy Jironal. Here, at least, was one who believed Cazaril's word and not his back. He stood a little straighter.

"No," he said at last. "I am slandered. My sworn word stands against hearsay. Unless you have some better support than castle gossip, I defy the lie. Or—where did you have the tale? Have you traced it to its source? Who accuses me—is it you, dy Maroc?" He frowned at the courtier.

"Explain it, dy Maroc," dy Jironal invited, with a careless wave.

De Maroc took a breath. "I had it from an Ibran silk merchant that I dealt with for the roya's wardrobe—he recognized the castillar, he said, from the flogging block in Zagosur, and was very shocked to see him here. He said it was an ugly case—that the castillar had ravished the daughter of a man who took him in and gave him shelter, and he remembered it very well, therefore, because it was so vile."

Cazaril scratched his beard. "Are you sure he didn't simply mistake me for another man?"

Dy Maroc replied stiffly, "No, for he had your name."

Cazaril's eyes narrowed. No mistake here—it was a lie outright, bought and paid for. But whose tongue had been bought? The courtier's, or the merchant's?

"Where is this merchant now?" dy Sanda broke in.

"Led his pack train back to Ibra, before the snows."

Cazaril said, in a mild voice, "Just exactly when did you have this tale?"

Dy Maroc hesitated, apparently casting back, for his fingers twitched down by his side as if counting. "Three weeks gone, he rode out. It was just before he left that we talked."

I know who's lying now, yes. Cazaril's lip turned up, without humor. That there was a real silk merchant, who had really ridden out of Cardegoss on that date, he had no doubt. But the Ibran had departed well before Dondo's emerald bribe, and Dondo would not have troubled to invent this indirect route for getting rid of Cazaril until after he'd failed to purchase him direct. Unfortunately, this was not a line of reasoning Cazaril could adduce in his defense.

"The silk merchant," dy Maroc added, "could have had no reason to lie."

But you do. I wonder what it is? "You've known of this serious charge for over three weeks, yet only now have brought it to your lord's attention? How very odd of you, dy Maroc."

Dy Maroc glowered at him.

"If the Ibran's gone," said Orico querulously, "it's impossible to find out who is telling the truth."

"Then my lord dy Cazaril should surely be given the benefit of the doubt," said dy Sanda, standing sternly upright. "You may not know him, but the Provincara dy Baocia, who gave him this trust, did; he'd served her late husband some six or seven years, in all."

"In his youth," said dy Jironal. "Men do change, you know. Especially in the brutality of war. If there is any doubt of the man, he should not be trusted in such a critical and, dare I say it"—he glanced pointedly at Betriz—"tempting post."

Betriz's long, incensed inhalation was, perhaps fortunately, cut across by Iselle, who cried, "Oh, rubbish! In the midst of the brutality of war, you yourself gave this man the keys to the fortress of Gotorget, which was the anchor of Chalion's whole battle line in the north. You clearly trusted him enough *then*, March! Nor did *he* betray that trust."

Dy Jironal's jaw tightened, and he smiled thinly. "Why, how militant Chalion is grown, that our very maidens seek to give us better advice upon our strategies."

"They could hardly give us worse," growled Orico under his breath. Only a slight sideways flick of the eyes betrayed that dy Jironal had heard him.

Dy Sanda said, in a puzzled voice, "Yes, and why wasn't the castillar ransomed with the rest of his officers when you surrendered Gotorget, dy Jironal?"

Cazaril clenched his teeth. *Shut up, dy Sanda.*

"The Roknari reported he'd died," replied the chancellor shortly. "They'd hid him for revenge, I'd assumed, when I learned he yet lived. Though if the silk merchant spoke truth, maybe it was for embarrassment. He must have escaped them, and knocked about Ibra for a time, until his, um, unhappy arrest." He glanced at Cazaril, and away.

You know you lie. I know you lie. But dy Jironal did not, even now, know for certain if Cazaril knew he lied. It didn't seem much of an advantage. This was a weak moment for a countercharge. This slander already half cut the ground from under his feet, regardless of the outcome of Orico's inquiry.

"Well, I do not understand how his loss was allowed to pass without investigation," said dy Sanda, staring narrowly at dy Jironal. "He was the fortress's *commander.*"

Iselle put in thoughtfully, "If you assumed revenge, you must have judged he'd cost the Roknari dearly in the field, for them to use him so thereafter."

Dy Jironal grimaced, clearly misliking where this line of logic was leading. He sat back and waved away the digression. "We are come to an impasse, then. A man's word against a man's word, and nothing to decide it. Sire, I earnestly advise prudence. Let my lord dy Cazaril be given some lesser post or sent back to the Dowager of Baocia."

Iselle nearly sputtered. "And let the slander go unchallenged? No! I will not stand for it."

Orico rubbed his head, as if it ached, and shot side glances at his chilly chief advisor and his furious half sister. He vented a small groan. "Oh, gods, I hate this sort of thing . . ." His expression changed, and he sat upright again. "Ah! But of course. There is just the solution . . . just the *just* solution, heh, heh . . ." He beckoned to the page who had summoned Cazaril, and murmured in his ear. Dy Jironal watched, frowning, but apparently could not make out what had been said either. The page scampered out.

"What is your solution, sire?" asked dy Jironal apprehensively.

"Not my solution. The gods. We will let the gods decide who is innocent, and who lies."

"You're not thinking of putting this to trial by combat, are you?" asked dy Jironal in a voice of real horror.

Cazaril could only share that horror—and so did Ser dy Maroc, judging by the way the blood drained from his face.

Orico blinked. "Well, now, there's another thought." He glanced at dy Maroc and at Cazaril. "They appear evenly matched, withal. Dy Maroc is younger, of course, and does very well on the sand of my practice ring, but experience counts for something."

Lady Betriz glanced at dy Maroc and frowned in sudden worry. So did Cazaril, for the opposite reason, he suspected. Dy Maroc was indeed a very pretty duello dancer. Against the brutality of the battlefield, he would last, Cazaril calculated, maybe five minutes. Dy Jironal met Cazaril's eyes directly for almost the first time in this inquiry, and Cazaril knew he was making the identical calculation. Cazaril's stomach heaved at the thought of being forced to butcher the boy, even if he was a tool and a liar.

"I do not know if the Ibran lied or not," put in dy Maroc warily. "I only know what I heard."

"Yes, yes." Orico waved this away. "I think my plan will be better." He sniffed, rubbed his nose on his sleeve, and waited. A lengthy and unnerving silence fell.

It was broken when the page returned, announcing, "Umegat, sire."

The dapper Roknari groom entered and glanced in faint surprise at the people assembled, but trod directly to his master and made his bow. "How may I serve you, my lord?"

"Umegat," said Orico. "I want you to go outside and catch the first sacred crow you see, and bring it back in here. You"—he gestured at the page—"go with him for witness. Hurry, now, quick quick." Orico clapped his hands in his urgency.

Without evincing the least surprise or question, Umegat bowed again and padded back out. Cazaril caught dy Maroc giving the chancellor a piteous *Now what?* look; dy Jironal set his teeth and ignored it.

"Now," said Orico, "how shall we arrange this? I know—Cazaril, you go stand in one end of the room. Dy Maroc, you go stand in the other."

Dy Jironal's eyes shifted in uncertain calculation. He gave dy Maroc a slight nod, toward the end of the room with the open window. Cazaril found himself relegated to the dimmer, closed end.

"You all"—Orico gestured to Iselle and her cohort—"stand to the side, for witness. You and you and you too," this to the guards and the remaining page. Orico heaved to his feet and went about the table to arrange his human tableau to his close satisfaction. Dy Jironal stayed seated where he was, playing with a quill and scowling.

In much less time than Cazaril would have expected, Umegat returned, with a cranky-looking crow tucked under his arm and the excited page bouncing around him.

"Was that the first crow you saw?" Orico asked the boy.

"Yes, my lord," the page replied breathlessly. "Well, the whole flock was circling above Fonsa's Tower, so I suppose we saw six or eight at once. So Umegat just stood in the courtyard with his arm out and his eyes closed, quite still. And this one came down to him and landed right on his sleeve!"

Cazaril's eyes strained, trying to see if the muttering bird might, just possibly, be missing two tail feathers.

"Very good," said Orico happily. "Now, Umegat, I want you to stand in the exact center of the room, and when I give the signal, release the sacred crow. We'll see which man he flies to, and then we'll know! Wait—everyone should say a prayer in their hearts first to the gods for guidance."

Iselle composed herself, but Betriz looked up. "But sire. What shall we know? Is the crow to fly to the liar, or the honest man?" She stared hard at Umegat.

"Oh," said Orico. "Hm."

"And what if it just flies around in circles?" said dy Jironal, an exasperated edge leaking into his voice.

Then we'll know the gods are as confused as all of the rest of us, Cazaril did not say out loud.

Umegat, stroking the bird to calm it, gave a slight bow. "As the truth is sacred to the gods, let the crow fly to the honest man, sire." He did not glance at Cazaril.

"Oh, very good. Carry on, then."

Umegat, with what Cazaril was beginning to suspect was a fine sense of theater, positioned himself precisely between the two accused men, and held the bird out on his arm, slowly removing his controlling hand. He stood a moment with a look of pious quietude on his face. Cazaril wondered what the gods made of the cacophony of conflicting prayers no doubt arising from this room at this instant. Then Umegat tossed the crow into the air, and let his arms hang down. It squawked and spread its wings, and fanned a tail missing two feathers.

Dy Maroc held his arms widespread, hopefully, looking as if he wondered if he was allowed to tackle the creature out of the air as it swooped by him. Cazaril, about to cry *Caz, Caz* to be safe, was suddenly overcome with theological curiosity. He already knew the truth—what else might this test reveal? He stood still and straight, lips parted, and watched in disturbed fascination as the crow ignored the open window and flapped straight to his shoulder.

"Well," he said quietly to it, as it dug in its claws and shifted from side to side. "Well." It tilted its black beak, regarding him with expressionless, beady eyes.

Iselle and Betriz jumped up and down and whooped, hugging each other and nearly frightening the bird off again. Dy Sanda smiled grimly. Dy Jironal gritted his teeth; dy Maroc looked faintly appalled.

Orico dusted his plump hands. "Good. That settles *that*. Now, by the gods, I want my dinner."

🕊ISELLE, BETRIZ, AND DY SANDA SURROUNDED CAZARIL like an honor guard and marched him out of Ias's Tower to the courtyard.

"How did you know to come to my rescue?" Cazaril asked them. Surreptitiously, he glanced up; no crows were circling, just now.

"I had it from a page that you were to be arrested this morning," said dy Sanda, "and I went at once to the royesse."

Cazaril wondered if dy Sanda, like himself, kept a private budget to pay for early news from various observers around the Zangre. And why his own arrangements hadn't worked a trifle better in this case. "I thank you, for covering my"—he swallowed the word, *back*—"blind side. I should have been dismissed by now, if you all hadn't come to stand up for me."

"No thanks needed," said dy Sanda. "I believe you'd have done as much for me."

"My brother needed someone to prop him," said Iselle a trifle bitterly. "Else he bows to whatever force blows most proximately."

Cazaril was torn between commending her shrewdness and suppressing her frankness. He glanced at dy Sanda. "How long—do you know—has this story about me been circulating in the court?"

He shrugged. "Some four or five days, I think."

"This was the first *we* heard of it!" said Betriz indignantly.

Dy Sanda opened his hands in apology. "Likely it seemed too raw a thing to pour in your maiden ears, my lady."

Iselle scowled. Dy Sanda accepted reiterated thanks from Cazaril and took his leave to check on Teidez.

Betriz, who had grown suddenly quiet, said in a stifled voice, "This was all my fault, wasn't it? Dondo struck at you to avenge himself for the pig. Oh, Lord Caz, I'm *sorry!*"

"No, my lady," said Cazaril firmly. "There is some old business between Dondo and me that goes back to before . . . before Gotorget." Her face lightened, to his relief; nevertheless, he seized the chance to add prudently, "Grant you, the prank with the pig didn't help, and you should not do anything like that again."

Betriz sighed, but then smiled just a little bit. "Well, he did stop pressing himself upon me. So it helped that much."

"I can't deny that's a benefit, but . . . Dondo remains a powerful man. I beg you—both—to take care to walk wide around him."

Iselle's eyes flicked toward him. She said quietly, "We're under siege here, aren't we. Me, Teidez, all our households."

"I trust," sighed Cazaril, "it is not quite so dire. Just go more carefully from now on, eh?"

He escorted them back to their chambers in the main block, but did not take up his calculations again. Instead, he strode back down the stairs and out past the stables to the menagerie. He found Umegat in the aviary, persuading the small birds to take dust baths in a basin of ashes as proof against lice. The neat Roknari, his tabard protected by an apron, looked up at him and smiled.

Cazaril did not smile back. "Umegat," he began without preamble, "I have to know. Did you pick the crow, or did the crow pick you?"

"Does it matter to you, my lord?"

"Yes!"

"Why?"

Cazaril's mouth opened, and shut. He finally began again, almost pleadingly. "It was a trick, yes? You tricked them, by bringing the crow I feed at my window. The gods didn't really reach into that room, right?"

Umegat's brows rose. "The Bastard is the most subtle of the gods, my lord. Merely because something is a trick, is no guarantee you are not god-touched." He added apologetically, "I'm afraid that's just the way it works." He chirped at the bright bird, apparently now done with its flutter in the ashes, coaxed it onto his hand with a seed drawn from his apron pocket, and popped it back into its nearby cage.

Cazaril followed, arguing, "It was the crow that I fed. Of course it flew to me. You feed it too, eh?"

"I feed all the sacred crows of Fonsa's Tower. So do the pages and ladies, the visitors to the Zangre, and the acolytes and divines of all the Temple houses in town. The miracle of those crows is that they're not all grown too fat to fly." With a neat twist of his wrist, Umegat secured another bird and tipped it into the ash bath.

Cazaril stood back from him as ashes puffed, and frowned. "You're Roknari. Aren't you of the Quadrene faith?"

"No, my lord," said Umegat serenely. "I've been a devout Quintarian since my late youth."

"Did you convert when you came to Chalion?"

"No, when I was still in the Archipelago."

"How . . . came it about that you were not hanged for heresy?"

"I made it to the ship to Brajar before they caught me." Umegat's smile crimped.

Indeed, he still had his thumbs. Cazaril's brows drew down, as he studied the man's fine-drawn features. "What was your father, in the Archipelago?"

"Narrow-minded. Very pious, though, in his foursquare way."

"That is not what I meant."

"I know, my lord. But he's been dead these twenty years. It doesn't matter anymore. I am content with what I am now."

Cazaril scratched his beard, as Umegat traded for another bright bird. "How long have you been head groom of this menagerie, then?"

"From its beginning. About six years. I came with the leopard, and the first birds. We were a gift."

"Who from?"

"Oh, from the archdivine of Cardegoss, and the Order of the Bastard. Upon the occasion of the roya's birthday, you see. Many fine animals have been added, since then."

Cazaril digested that, for a little. "This is a very unusual collection."

"Yes, my lord."

"How unusual?"

"Very unusual."

"Can you tell me more?"

"I beg you will not ask me more, my lord."

"Why not?"

"Because I do not wish to lie to you."

"Why not?" *Everyone else does.*

Umegat drew in his breath and smiled crookedly, watching Cazaril. "Because, my lord, the crow picked me."

Cazaril's return smile grew a trifle strained. He gave Umegat a small bow and withdrew.

II

Cazaril was just exiting his bedchamber on the way to breakfast, some three mornings later, when a breathless page accosted him, grabbing him by the sleeve.

"M' lord dy Cazaril ! The castle warder begs you 'tend on him at once, in the courtyard!"

"Why? What's the matter?" Obedient to this urgency, Cazaril swung into motion beside the boy.

"It's Ser dy Sanda. He was set upon last night by footpads, and robbed and stabbed!"

Cazaril's stride lengthened. "How badly was he injured? Where does he lie?"

"Not injured, m'lord. Slain!"

Oh, gods, no. Cazaril left the page behind as he clattered down the staircase. He hurried into the Zangre's front courtyard in time to see a man in the tabard of the constable of Cardegoss, and another man dressed as a farmer, lower a stiff form from the back of a mule and lay it out on the cobbles. The Zangre's castle warder, frowning, squatted down by the body. A couple of the roya's guards watched from a few paces back, warily, as if knife wounds might prove contagious.

"What has happened?" demanded Cazaril.

The farmer, in his courtier's garb taking, pulled off his wool hat in a sort of salute. "I found him by the riverside this morning, sir, when I took my cattle down to drink. The river curves—I often find things hung up upon the shoal. 'Twas a wagon wheel, last week. I always check. Not bodies too often, thank the Mother of Mercy. Not since that poor lady who drowned herself, two years back—" He and the constable's man exchanged nods of reminiscence. "This one has not a drowned look."

Dy Sanda's trousers were still sodden, but his hair was done dripping. His tunic had been removed by his finders—Cazaril saw the brocade folded up over the mule's withers. The mouths of his wounds had been cleaned of blood by the river water, and showed now as dark puckered slits in his pale skin, in his back, belly, neck. Cazaril counted over a dozen strikes, deep and hard.

The castle warder, sitting on his heels, pointed to a bit of frayed cord knotted around dy Sanda's belt. "His purse was cut off. In a hurry, they were."

"But it wasn't just a robbery," said Cazaril. "One or two of these blows would have put him on the ground, stopped resistance. They didn't need to . . . they were making sure of his death." *They* or *he*? No real way to know, but dy Sanda could not have been either easy or safe to bring down. He rather thought *they*. "I suppose his sword was taken." Had he ever had time to draw it? Or had the first blow fallen on him by surprise, from a man he walked beside in trust?

"Taken or lost in the river," said the farmer. "He would not have floated down to me so soon if it had still been dragging him down."

"Did he have rings or jewelry?" asked the constable's man.

The castle warder nodded. "Several, and a gold ear loop." They were all gone now.

"I'll want a description of them all, my lord," the constable's man said, and the warder nodded understanding.

"You know where he was found," said Cazaril to the constable's man. "Do you know where he was attacked?"

The man shook his head. "Hard to say. Somewhere in the bottoms, maybe." The lower end of Cardegoss, both socially and topographically, huddled on both sides of the wall that ran between the two rivers. "There are only half a dozen places someone might pitch a body over the town walls and be sure the stream would take it off. Some are more lonely than others. When did anyone here see him last?"

"I saw him at supper," said Cazaril. "He said nothing to me about going into town." There were a couple of places right here in the Zangre where a body might also be pitched into the rivers below. . . . "Has he broken bones?"

"Not as I felt, sir," said the constable's man. Indeed, the pale corpse did not show great bruises.

Inquiry of the castle guards disclosed that dy Sanda had left the Zangre, alone and on foot, about the mid-watch last night. Cazaril gave up a budding plan to check every foot of the castle's great lengths of corridors and niches for new bloodstains. Later in the afternoon the constable's men found three people who'd said they'd seen the royse's secretary drinking in a tavern in the bottoms, and depart alone; one swore he'd left staggering drunk. That witness, Cazaril would have liked to have had alone for a time in one of the Zangre's stony, scream-absorbing cells off the old, old tunnels going down to the rivers. Some better kind of truth might have been pounded out of him there. Cazaril had never seen dy Sanda drink to drunkenness, ever.

It fell to Cazaril to inventory and pack dy Sanda's meager pile of worldly goods, to be sent off by carter to the man's surviving older brother somewhere in the provinces of Chalion. While the city constable's men searched the bottoms, futilely, Cazaril was sure, for the supposed footpads, Cazaril turned out every scrap of paper in dy Sanda's room. But whatever lying assignation had lured him to the bottoms, he'd either received verbally or taken with him.

Dy Sanda having no relatives near enough to wait upon, the funeral was held the next day. The services were somberly graced by both the royse and royesse and their households, so a few courtiers anxious for their favor likewise attended. The ceremony of departure, held in the Son's chamber off the main courtyard of the temple, was brief. It was borne in upon Cazaril what a lonely man dy Sanda had been. No friends thronged to the head of his bier to speak long eulogies for each other's comfort. Only Cazaril spoke a few formal words of regret on behalf of the royesse, managing to get through them without the embarrassment of referring to the paper, upon which he had so hastily composed them that morning, tucked in his sleeve.

Cazaril stood down from the bier to make way for the blessing of the animals, going to stand with the little crowd of mourners before the altar. Acolytes, dressed each in the colors of their chosen gods, brought in their creatures and stood round the bier at five evenly spaced points. In country temples, the most motley assortment of animals was used for this rite; Cazaril had once seen it carried through—successfully—for the dead daughter of a poor man by a single overworked acolyte with a basket of five kittens with colored ribbons tied round their necks. The Roknari often used fish, though in the number of four, not five; the Quadrene divines marked them with dye and interpreted the will of the gods by the patterns they made swimming about in a tub. Whatever the means used, the omen was the one tiny miracle the gods granted every person, no matter how humble, at their last passing.

The temple of Cardegoss had the resources to command the most beautiful of sacred animals, selected for appropriate color and gender. The Daughter's acolyte in her blue robes had a fine female crested blue jay, new-hatched last spring. The Mother's woman in green held on her arm a great green bird, close relative, Cazaril thought, to Umegat's prize in the roya's menagerie. The acolyte of the Son in his red-orange robes led a glorious young dog-fox, whose burnished coat seemed to glow like fire in the somber shadows of the echoing, vaulted chamber. The Father's acolyte, in gray, was led in by a stout, elderly, and immensely dignified gray wolf. Cazaril expected the Bastard's acolyte in her white robes to bear one of Fonsa's sacred crows, but instead she cradled a pair of plump, inquisitive-looking white rats in her arms.

The divine prostrated himself for the gods to make their sign, then stood back at dy Sanda's head. The brightly robed acolytes each in turn urged their creatures forward. At a jerk of the acolyte's wrist the blue jay fluttered up, but then back down to her shoulder, as did the Mother's green bird. The dog-fox, released from its copper chain, sniffed, trotted to the bier, whined, hopped up, and curled itself at dy Sanda's side. It rested its muzzle over the dead man's heart, and sighed deeply.

The wolf, obviously very experienced in these matters, evinced no interest. The Bastard's acolyte released her rats upon the paving stones, but they merely ran back up her sleeve, nuzzled her ears, and caught their claws in her hair and had to be gently disengaged.

No surprises today. Unless persons had dedicated themselves especially to another god, the childless soul normally went to the Daughter or the Son, deceased parents to the Mother or the Father.

Dy Sanda was a childless man and had ridden as lay dedicat of the Son's military order himself in his youth. It was the natural order of things that his soul would be taken up by the Son. Although it was not unknown for this moment of a funeral to be the first notice surviving family had that the member they buried had an unexpected child somewhere. The Bastard took up all of His own order—and all those souls disdained by the greater gods. The Bastard was the god of last resort, ultimate, if ambiguous, refuge for those who had made disasters of their lives.

Obedient to the clear choice of Autumn's elegant fox, the acolyte of the Son stepped forward to close the ceremonies, calling down his god's special blessing upon dy Sanda's sundered soul. The mourners filed past the bier and placed small offerings on the Son's altar for the dead man's sake.

Cazaril nearly drove his fingernails through his palms, watching Dondo dy Jironal go through the motions of pious grief. Teidez was shocked and quiet, regretting, Cazaril hoped, all the hot complaints he'd heaped on his rigid but loyal secretary-tutor's head while he lived; his offering was a notable heap of gold.

Iselle and Betriz, too, were quiet, both then and later. They passed little comment upon the buzzing court gossip that surrounded the murder, except for refusing invitations to go into town and finding excuses to check on Cazaril's continued existence four or five times of an evening.

The court murmured over the mystery. New and more draconian punishments were mooted for such dangerous, lowlife scum as cutpurses and footpads. Cazaril said nothing. There was no mystery in dy Sanda's death to him, except how to bring home its proof to the Jironals. He turned it over and over in his mind, but the way defeated him. He dared not start the process until he had every step laid clear to the end, or he might as well slit his own throat and be done with it.

Unless, he decided, some luckless footpad or cutpurse was falsely accused. Then he would . . . what? What was *his* word worth now, after the misfired slander about his flogging scars? Most of the court had been impressed by the testimony of the crow—some had not. Easy enough to tell which was which, by the way some gentlemen drew aside their cloaks from Cazaril, or ladies recoiled from his touch. But no sacrificial peasants were brought forth by the constable's office, and the revived gaiety of the court closed over the unpleasant incident like a scab over a wound.

Teidez was assigned a new secretary, hand-selected from the roya's own Chancellery by the senior dy Jironal himself. He was a narrow-faced fellow, altogether the chancellor's creature, and he made no move to make friends with Cazaril. Dondo dy Jironal publicly undertook to distract the young royse from his sorrow by providing him with the most delectable entertainments. Just how delectable, Cazaril had all too good a view of, watching the drabs and ripe comrades pass in and out of Teidez's chamber late at night. Once, Teidez stumbled into Cazaril's room, apparently not able to tell one door from another, and vomited about a quart of red wine at his feet. Cazaril guided him, sick and blind, back to his servants for cleanup.

Cazaril's most troubled moment, however, was the evening his eye caught a green glint on the hand of Teidez's guard captain, the man who had ridden with them from Baocia. Who before riding out had sworn to mother and grandmother, formally and on one knee, to guard both young people with his life . . . Cazaril's hand snaked out to grab the captain's hand in passing, bringing him up short. He gazed down at the familiar flat-cut stone.

"Nice ring," he said after a moment.

The captain pulled his hand back, frowning. "I thought so."

"I hope you didn't pay too much for it. I believe the stone is false."

"It is a true emerald, my lord!"

"If I were you, I'd have it to a gem-cutter, and check. It's a continuing source of amazement to me, the lies that men will tell these days for their profit."

The captain covered one hand with the other. "It is a good ring."

"Compared to what you traded for it, I'd say it is trash."

The captain's lips pressed closed. He shrugged away and stalked off.

If this is a siege, thought Cazaril, *we're losing.*

❧THE WEATHER TURNED CHILL AND RAINY, THE RIVERS swelling, as the Son's season ran toward its close. At the musicale after supper one sodden evening, Orico leaned over to his sister, and murmured, "Bring your people to the throne room tomorrow at noon, and attend dy Jironal's investiture. I'll have some happy announcements afterward to make to the whole court. And wear your most festive raiment. Oh, and your pearls—Lord Dondo was saying only last night, he never sees you wear his pearls."

"I do not think they become me," Iselle replied. She glanced sideways at Cazaril, seated nearby, and then down at her hands tightening in her lap.

"Nonsense, how can pearls not become any maiden?" The roya sat back to applaud the sprightly piece just ending.

Iselle kept her lips closed upon this suggestion until Cazaril had escorted his ladies as far as his office antechamber. He was about to bid them to sleep well, and depart, yawning, to his own bed, when she burst out, "I am *not* wearing that thief Lord Dondo's pearls. I would give them back to the Daughter's Order, but I swear they would be an insult to the goddess. They're tainted. Cazaril, what can I do with them?"

"The Bastard is not a fussy god. Give them to the divine of his foundling hospital, to sell for the orphans," he suggested.

Her lips curved. "Wouldn't *that* annoy Lord Dondo. And he couldn't even protest! Good idea. You shall take them to the orphans, with my goodwill. And for tomorrow—I'll wear my red velvet vest-cloak over my white silk gown, that will certainly be festive, and my garnet set Mama gave me. None can chide me for wearing my mother's jewels."

Nan dy Vrit said, "But what do you suppose your brother meant by *happy announcements*? You don't think he's determined upon your betrothal already, do you?"

Iselle went still, blinking, but then said decisively, "No. It can't be. There must be months of negotiations first—ambassadors, letters, exchanges of presents, treaties for the dowry—*and* my assent won. My portrait taken. And I *will* have a portrait of the man, whoever he may turn out to be. A true and honest portrait, by an artist I send myself. If my prince is fat, or squinty, or bald, or has a lip that hangs loose, so be it, but I will not be lied to in paint."

Betriz made a face at the image this conjured. "I do hope you'll win a handsome lord, when the time does come."

Iselle sighed. "It would be nice, but given most of the great lords I've seen, not likely. I should settle for healthy, I think, and not plague the gods with impossible prayers. Healthy, and a Quintarian."

"Very sensible," Cazaril put in, encouraging this practical frame of mind with an eye to easing his life in the near future.

Betriz said uneasily, "There have been a great many envoys from the Roknari princedoms in and out of court this fall."

Iselle's mouth tightened. "Mm."

"There are not a great many Quintarian choices, amongst the highest lords," Cazaril conceded.

"The roya of Brajar is a widower again," Nan dy Vrit put in, pursing her lips in doubt.

Iselle waved this away. "Surely not. He's fifty-seven years old, has gout, and he already has an heir full-grown and married. Where's the point of my having a son friendly to his Uncle Orico—or his Uncle Teidez, if it should chance so—if he's not ruling his land?"

"There's Brajar's grandson," said Cazaril.

"Seven years old! I'd have to wait seven more years—"

Not, Cazaril thought, *altogether a bad thing.*

"Now is too soon, but that is too long. Anything could happen in seven years. People die, countries go to war . . ."

"It's true," said Nan dy Vrit, "your father Roya Ias betrothed you at the age of two to a Roknari prince, but the poor lad took a fever and died soon after, so that never came to anything. Or you would have been taken off to his princedom these two years ago."

Betriz said, a little teasingly, "The Fox of Ibra's a widower, too."

Iselle choked. "*He's* over seventy!"

"Not fat, though. And I suppose you wouldn't have to endure him for very long."

"Ha. He could live another twenty years just for spite, I think—he's full enough of it. And his Heir is married, too. I think his second son is the only royse in the lands who's near to my age, and he's not the heir."

"You won't be offered an Ibran this year, Royesse," said Cazaril. "The Fox is exceedingly wroth with Orico for his clumsy meddling in the war in South Ibra."

"Yes, but . . . they say all the Ibran high lords are trained as naval officers," said Iselle, taking on an introspective look.

"Well, and how useful is that likely to be to Orico?" Nan dy Vrit snorted. "Chalion has not one yard of coastline."

"To our cost," Iselle murmured.

Cazaril said regretfully, "When we had Gotorget, and held those passes, we were almost in position to swoop down and take the port of Visping. We've lost that leverage now . . . well, anyway. My best guess, Royesse, is that you are destined for a lord of Darthaca. So let's spend a little more time on those declensions this coming week, eh?"

Iselle made a face, but sighed assent. Cazaril smiled and bowed himself out. If she was not to espouse a ruling roya, he wouldn't altogether mind a Darthacan border lord for Iselle, he thought as he made his way down the stairs. At least a lord of one of its warmer northern provinces. Either power or distance would do to protect Iselle from the . . . difficulties, of the court of Chalion. And the sooner, the better.

For her, or for you?

For both of us.

✌FOR ALL THAT NAN DY VRIT PUT HER HAND OVER her eyes and winced, Cazaril thought Iselle looked very bright and warm in her carmine robes, with her amber curls cascading down her back nearly to her waist. Given the hint, he wore a red brocade tunic that had been the old provincar's and his white wool vest-cloak. Betriz, too, wore her favorite red; Nan, claiming eyestrain, had chosen a sober black and white. The reds clashed a trifle, but they certainly defied the rain.

They all scurried across the wet cobbles to Ias's great tower block. The crows from Fonsa's Tower were all gone to roost—no, not quite. Cazaril ducked as a certain foolish bird missing two feathers from its tail swooped down out of the drizzling mist past him, cawing, *Caz, Caz!* With an eye to defending his white cloak from birdish deposits, he fended it off. It circled back up to the ruined slates, screeching sadly.

Orico's red brocade throne room was brilliantly lit with wall sconces against the autumn gray; two or three dozen courtiers and ladies warmed it thoroughly. Orico wore his formal robes, and his crown, but Royina Sara was not at his side today. Teidez was given a seat in a lower chair at Orico's right hand.

The royesse's party kissed his hands and took their places, Iselle in a smaller chair to the left of Sara's empty one, the rest standing. Orico, smiling, began the day's largesse by awarding Teidez the revenues of four more royal towns for the support of his household, for which his younger half brother thanked him with proper hand-kisses and a brief set-speech. Dondo had not kept the royse up last night, so he was looking much less green and seedy than usual.

Orico then motioned his chancellor to his royal knee. As had been announced, the roya awarded the letters and sword, and received the oath, that made the senior dy Jironal into the provincar of Ildar. Several of Ildar's minor lords knelt and took oath in turn to dy Jironal. It was less expected when the two turned round at once and transferred the marchship of Jironal, together with its towns and tax revenues, immediately to Lord—now March—Dondo.

Iselle was surprised, but obviously pleased, when her brother next awarded her the revenues of six towns for the support of her household. Not before time, to be sure—her allowance till now had been notably scant for a royesse. She thanked him prettily, while Cazaril's brain lurched into calculation. Might Iselle afford her own guard company, instead of the loan of men from Baocia she'd shared till now with Teidez? And might Cazaril choose them himself? Could she take a house of her own in town, protected by her own people? Iselle returned to her chair on the dais and arranged her skirts, a certain tension easing from her face that had not been apparent till its absence.

Orico cleared his throat. "I'm pleased to come to the happiest of this day's rewards, well merited, and, er, much-desired. Iselle, up—" Orico stood, and held out his hand to his half sister; puzzled but smiling, she rose and stood with him before the dais.

"March dy Jironal, come forth," Orico continued. Lord Dondo, in the full robes of the Daughter's holy generalship and with a page in dy Jironal livery at his heels, came and stood at Orico's other hand. The skin on the back of Cazaril's neck began to creep, as he watched from the side of the room. *What is Orico about . . . ?*

"My much-beloved and loyal Chancellor and Provincar dy Jironal has begged a boon of blood from my house, and upon meditation, I have concluded it gives my heart joy to comply." He didn't look joyful. He looked nervous. "He has asked for the hand of my sister Iselle for his brother, the new march. Freely do I betroth and bestow it." He turned Dondo's thick hand palm up, Iselle's slim one palm down, pressed them together at the height of his chest, and stepped back.

Iselle's face drained of color and all expression. She stood utterly still, staring across at Dondo as though she could not believe her senses. The blood thudded in Cazaril's ears, almost roaring, and he could hardly draw his breath. *No, no, no . . . !*

"As a betrothal gift, my dear Royesse, I have guessed what your heart most desired to complete your trousseau," Dondo told her, and motioned his page forward.

Iselle, regarding him with that same frozen stare, said, "You guessed I wanted a coastal city with an excellent harbor?"

Dondo, momentarily taken aback, choked out a hearty laugh, and turned from her. The page flipped open the tooled leather box, revealing a delicate pearl-and-silver tiara, and Dondo reached in to hold it up before the eyes of the court. A smattering of applause ran through the crowd from his friends. Cazaril's hand clenched on his sword hilt. If he drew and lunged . . . he'd be struck down before he made it across the throne room.

As Dondo raised the tiara high to bring down upon Iselle's head, she recoiled like a shying horse. "*Orico . . .*"

"This betrothal is my will and desire, dear sister," said Orico, in edged tones.

Dondo, apparently unwilling to chase her about the room with the tiara, paused, and shot a meaningful glance at the roya.

Iselle swallowed. It was clear her mind was frantically churning over responses. She'd stifled her first scream of outrage, and had not the trick of falling down in a convincing dead faint. She stood trapped and conscious. "Sire. As the provincar of Labran said when the forces of the Golden General poured over his walls . . . this is entirely a surprise."

A very hesitant titter ran through the courtiers at this witticism.

Her voice lowered, and she murmured through her teeth, "You didn't tell me. You didn't *ask* me."

Orico returned, equally sotto voce, "We'll talk of it after this."

After another frozen moment, she accepted this with a small nod. Dondo managed to complete his divestiture of the pearl tiara. He bent and kissed her hand. Wisely, he did not demand the usual return kiss; from the look of astonished loathing on Iselle's face, there seemed a good chance she might have bitten him.

Orico's court divine, in the seasonal robes of the Brother, stepped forward and called down a blessing upon the pair from all the gods.

Orico announced, "In three days' time, we will all meet again here and witness this union sworn and celebrated. Thank you all."

"Three days! *Three days!*" said Iselle, her voice breaking for the first time. "Don't you mean three *years*, sire?"

"Three days," said Orico. "Prepare yourself." He prepared himself to duck out of the throne room, motioning his servants about him. Most of the courtiers departed with the dy Jironals, offering congratulations. A few of the more boldly curious lingered, ears pricking for the conversation between brother and sister.

"What, in three *days*! There is not even time to send a courier to Baocia, let alone to have any reply from my mother or grandmother—"

"Your mother, as all know, is too ill to stand the strain of a trip to court, and your grandmother must stay in Valenda to attend upon her."

"But I don't—" She found herself addressing the broad royal back, as Orico scurried from the throne room.

She plunged after him into the next chamber, Betriz, Nan, and Cazaril following anxiously. "But Orico, I don't *wish* to marry Dondo dy Jironal!"

"A lady of your rank does not marry to please herself, but to bring advantage to her house," he told her sternly, when she brought him to bay only by dint of rushing around in front of him and planting herself in his path.

"Is that indeed so? Then perhaps you can explain to me what advantage it brings to the House of Chalion to throw me—to *waste* me—upon the younger son of a minor lord? My husband should have brought us a royacy for his dowry!"

"This binds the dy Jironals to me—and to Teidez."

"Say rather, it binds us to them! The advantage is a trifle one-sided, I think!"

"You said you did not wish to marry a Roknari prince, and I have not given you to one. And it wasn't for lack of offers—I've refused two this season. Think on that, and be grateful, dear sister!"

Cazaril wasn't sure if Orico was threatening or pleading.

He went on, "You didn't wish to leave Chalion. Very well, you shall not leave Chalion. You wanted to marry a Quintarian lord—I have given you one, a holy general at that! Besides," he went on with a petulant shrug, "if I gave you to a power too close to my borders, they might use you as an excuse to claim some of my lands. I do well, with this, for the future peace of Chalion."

"Lord Dondo is forty years old! He's a corrupt, impious thief! An embezzler! A libertine! Worse! Orico, you *cannot* do this to me!" Her voice was rising.

"I'll not hear you," said Orico, and actually put his hands over his ears. "Three days. Compose your mind and see to your wardrobe." He fled her as if she were a burning tower. "I'll not hear this!"

He meant it. Four times that afternoon she attempted to seek him in his quarters to further her plea, and four times he had his guards repulse her. After that, he rode out of the Zangre altogether, to take up residence in a hunting lodge deep in the oak woods, a move of remarkable cowardice. Cazaril could only hope its roof leaked icy rain on the royal head.

Cazaril slept badly that night. Venturing upstairs in the morning, he found three frayed women who appeared to have not slept at all.

Iselle, heavy-eyed, drew him by the sleeve into her sitting chamber, sat him down on the window seat, and lowered her voice to a fierce whisper.

"Cazaril. Can you get four horses? Or three? Or two, or even one? I've thought it through. I spent all night thinking it through. The only answer is to fly."

He sighed. "I thought it through, too. First, I am watched. When I went to leave the Zangre last night, two of the roya's guards followed me. To protect me, they said. I might be able to kill or bribe one—I doubt two."

"We could ride out as if we were hunting," argued Iselle.

"In the rain?" Cazaril gestured to the steady mizzle still coming down outside the high window, fogging the valley so that one could not even see the river below, turning the bare tree branches to black ink marks in the gray. "And even if they let us ride out, they'd be sure to send an armed escort."

"If we could get any kind of a head start—"

"And if we could, what then? If—when!—they overtook us on the road, the first thing they would do is pull me from my horse and cut off my head, and leave my body for the foxes and crows. And then they would take you back. And if by some miracle they didn't catch us, where would we go?"

"A border. Any border."

"Brajar and South Ibra would send you right back, to please Orico. The five princedoms or the Fox of Ibra would take you hostage. Darthaca . . . presupposes we could make it across half of Chalion and all of South Ibra. I fear not, Royesse."

"What else can I do?" Her young voice was edged with desperation.

"No one can force a marriage. Both parties must freely assent before the gods. If you have the courage to simply stand there and say *No*, it cannot go forth. Can you not find it in yourself to do so?"

Her lips tightened. "Of course I could. Then what? Now I think you are the one who has not thought it through. Do you think Lord Dondo would just give up, at that point?"

He shook his head. "It's not valid if they force it, and everyone knows it. Just hold on to that thought."

She shook her head in something between grief and exasperation. "You don't understand."

He'd have taken that for the wail of youth everywhere, till Dondo himself came that afternoon to the royesse's chamber to persuade his betrothed to a more seemly compliance. The doors were left open to the royesse's sitting room, but an armed guard stood at each, keeping back both Cazaril on one side and Nan dy Vrit and Betriz on the other. He did not catch one word in three of the furious undervoiced argument that raged between the thickset courtier and the red-haired maiden. But at the end of it Dondo stalked out with a look of savage satisfaction on his face, and Iselle collapsed on the window seat nearly unable to breathe, so torn was she between terror and fury.

She clutched Betriz and choked out, "He said . . . if I did not make the responses, he would take me anyway. I said, Orico would never let you rape his sister. He said, why not? He let us rape his wife. When Royina Sara would not conceive, and could not conceive, and Orico was too impotent to get a bastard no matter how many ladies and maidens and whores they brought to him, and, and even more disgusting things, the Jironals finally persuaded him to let them in upon her, and try . . . Dondo said, he and his brother tried every night for a year, one at a time or both together, till she threatened to kill herself. He said he would roger me till he'd planted his fruit in my womb, and when I was ripe to bursting, I'd hang on him as husband hard enough." She blinked blurry eyes at Cazaril, her lips drawn back on clenched teeth. "He said, my belly would grow very big indeed, because I am short. How much courage do I need for that simple *No*, Cazaril, do you think? And what happens when courage makes no difference at all, at all?"

I thought the only place that courage didn't matter was on a Roknari slave galley. I was wrong. He whispered abjectly, "I do not know, Royesse."

Trapped and desperate, she fell to fasting and prayer; Nan and Betriz helped to set up a portable altar to the gods in her chambers and collected all the symbols of the Lady of Spring they could find to decorate it. Cazaril, trailed by his two guards, walked down into Cardegoss and found a flower-seller with forced violets, out of season, and brought them back to put in a glass jar of water on the altar. He felt stupid and helpless, though the royesse dropped a tear on his hand when she thanked him. Taking neither food nor drink, she lay back down on the floor in the attitude of deepest supplication, so like Royina Ista when Cazaril had first caught sight of her in the Provincara's ancestors' hall that he was unnerved, and fled the room. He spent hours, walking about the Zangre, trying to think, thinking only of horrors.

Late that evening, the Lady Betriz called him up to the office antechamber that was rapidly becoming a place of hectic nightmare.

"I have the answer!" she told him. "Cazaril, teach me how to kill a man with a knife."

"What?"

"Dondo's guards know enough not to let you close to him. But I will be standing beside Iselle on her wedding morning, to be her witness, and make the responses. No one will expect it of *me*. I'll hide the knife in my bodice. When Dondo comes close, and bends to kiss her hand, I can strike at him, two, three times before anyone can stop me. But I don't know just how and where to cut, to be sure. The neck, yes, but what part?" Earnestly, she drew a heavy dirk out from behind her skirts and held it out to him. "Show me. We can practice, till I have it very smooth and fast."

"Gods, no, Lady Betriz! Give up this mad plan! They would strike you down—they'd *hang* you, afterward!"

"Provided only I was able to kill Dondo first, I'd go gladly to the gallows. I swore to guard Iselle with my life. Well, so." Her brown eyes burned in her white face.

"No," he said firmly, taking the knife and not giving it back. Where had she obtained it, anyway? "This is no work for a woman."

"I'd say it's work for whoever has a chance at it. My chance is best. Show me!"

"Look, no. Just . . . wait. I'll, I'll try something, find what I can do."

"*Can* you kill Dondo? Iselle is in there praying to the Lady to slay either her or Dondo before the wedding, she doesn't care anymore which. Well, *I* care which. I think it should be Dondo."

"I entirely agree. Look, Lady Betriz. Wait, just wait. I'll see what I can do."

If the gods will not answer your prayers, Lady Iselle, by the gods I will try to.

He spent hours the following day, the last before the marriage, trying to stalk Lord Dondo through the Zangre like a boar in a forest of stone. He never got within striking distance. In midafternoon, Dondo returned to the Jironals' great palace in town, and Cazaril could not get past its walls or gates. The second time Dondo's bravos threw him out, one held him while another struck him enough times in the chest, belly, and groin to make his return to the Zangre a slow weave, supporting himself like a drunk with a hand out to nearby walls. The roya's guards, whom he had scraped off in a dodge through Cardegoss's alleys, arrived in time to watch both the beating and the crawl home. They did not interfere with either.

In a burst of inspiration, he bethought himself of the secret passage that had run between the Zangre and the Jironals' great palace when it had been the property of Lord dy Lutez. Ias and dy Lutez had been reputed to use it daily, for conference, or nightly, for assignations of love, depending on the teller. The tunnel, he discovered, was now about as secret as Cardegoss's main street, and had guards on both ends, and locked doors. His attempt at bribery won him shoves and curses, and the threat of another beating.

Some assassin I am, he thought bitterly, as he reeled into his bedchamber as dusk descended, and fell groaning into his bed. Head pounding, body aching, he lay still for a time, then at last roused himself enough to light a candle. He ought to go upstairs, and check on his ladies, but he didn't think he could bear the weeping. Or the reporting of his failure to Betriz, or what she would demand of him after that. If he could not kill Dondo, what right had he to try to thwart her effort?

I would gladly die, if only I could stop this abomination to-morrow . . .

Do you mean that?

He sat stiffly, wondering if that last voice was quite his own. His tongue had moved a little behind his lips, as usual for when he was babbling to himself. *Yes.*

He lurched around to the end of his bed, fell to his knees, and flipped open the lid of his trunk. He dived down amongst the folded garments, scented with cloves as proof against moths, until he came to a black velvet vest-cloak folded around a brown wool robe. Folded around a ciphered notebook that he had never finished deciphering when the crooked judge had fled Valenda, that it had seemed too late to return to the Temple without embarrassing explanations. Feverishly, he drew it out, and lit more candles. *There's not much time left.* About a third of it was left untranslated. *Forget all the failed experiments. Go to the last page, eh?*

Even in the bad cipher, the wool merchant's despair came through, in a kind of strange shining simplicity. Eschewing all his previous bizarre elaborations, he had turned at the last not to magic, but to plain prayer. Rat and crow only to carry the plea, candles only to light his way, herbs only to lift his heart with their scents, and compose his mind to purity of will; a will then put aside, laid wholehearted on the god's altar. *Help me. Help me. Help me.*

Those were the last words entered in the notebook.

I can do that, thought Cazaril in wonder.

And if he failed . . . there would still be Betriz and her knife.

I will not fail. I've failed practically everything else in my life. I will not fail death.

He slipped the book under his pillow, locked his door behind him, and went to find a page.

The sleepy boy he selected was waiting in the corridor upon the pleasure of the lords and ladies at their dinner in Orico's banqueting hall, where Iselle's nonappearance was doubtless the subject of much gossip, not even kept to a whisper since none of the principals were present. Dondo roistered privately in his palace with his hangers-on; Orico still cowered out in the woods.

He fished a gold royal from his purse and held it up, smiling through the O of his thumb and finger. "Hey, boy. Would you like to earn a royal?"

The Zangre pages had learned to be wary; a royal was enough to buy some truly intimate services from those who sold such. And enough to be a caution, to those who didn't care to play those games. "Doing what, my lord?"

"Catch me a rat."

"A rat, my lord? Why?"

Ah. Why. *Why, so that I can work the crime of death magic upon the second most powerful lord in Chalion, of course!* No.

Cazaril leaned his shoulders against the wall, and smiled down confidingly. "When I was in the fortress of Gotorget, during the siege three years ago—did you know I was its commander? until my brave general sold it out from under us, that is—we learned to eat rats. Tasty little things, if you could catch enough of them. I really miss the flavor of a good, candle-roasted rat haunch. Catch me a really big, fat one, and there will be another to match this." Cazaril dropped the coin in the page's hand, and licked his lips, wondering how crazed he looked right now. The page was edging farther from him. "You know where my chamber is?"

"Yes, m'lord?"

"Bring it there. In a bag. Quick as you can. I'm hungry." Cazaril lurched off, laughing. Really laughing, not feigning it. A weird, wild exhilaration filled his heart.

It lasted until he reached his bedchamber again and sat to plan the rest of his ploy, his dark prayer, his suicide. It was night; the crow would not fly to his window at night, even for the piece of bread he'd snatched from the banqueting hall before returning to the main block. He turned the bread roll over in his hands. The crows roosted in Fonsa's Tower. If they wouldn't fly to him, he could crawl to them, over the roof slates. Sliding in the dark? And then back to his chamber, with a squawking bundle under his arm?

No. Let the bundle be the bagged rat. If he did the deed there, in the shadow of the broken roof upon whatever scorched and shaking platform still stood inside, he'd only have to make the trip one way. And . . . death magic had worked there once before, eh? Spectacularly, for Iselle's grandfather. Would Fonsa's spirit lend his aid to his granddaughter's unholy soldier? His tower was a fraught place, sacred to the Bastard and his pets, especially at night, midnight in the cold rain. Cazaril's body need never be found, nor buried. The crows could feast upon his remains, fair trade for the depredation he planned upon their poor comrade. Animals were innocent, even the grisly crows; that innocence surely made them all a little sacred.

The dubious page arrived much quicker than Cazaril had thought he might, with a wriggling bag. Cazaril checked its contents—the snapping, hissing rat must have weighed a pound and a half—and paid up. The page pocketed his coin and walked off, staring over his shoulder. Cazaril fastened the mouth of the bag tight and locked it in his chest to prevent the condemned prisoner's escape.

He put off his courtier's garb and put on the robe and vestcloak the wool merchant had died in, just for luck. Boots, shoes, barefoot? Which would be more secure, upon the slippery stones and slates? Barefoot, he decided. But he slipped on his shoes for one last, practical expedition.

"Betriz?" he whispered loudly through the door of his office antechamber. "Lady Betriz? I know it's late—can you come out to me?"

She was still fully dressed for the day, still pale and exhausted. She let him grip her hands, and leaned her forehead briefly against his chest. The warm scent of her hair took him back for a dizzy instant to his second day in Valenda, standing by her in the Temple crowd. The only thing unchanged from that happy hour was her loyalty.

"How does the Royesse?" Cazaril asked her.

She looked up, in the dim candlelight. "She prays unceasingly to the Daughter. She has not eaten or drunk since yesterday. I don't know where the gods are, nor why they have abandoned us."

"I couldn't kill Dondo today. I couldn't get near him."

"I'd guessed as much. Or we would have heard something."

"I have one more thing to try. If it doesn't work . . . I'll return in the morning, and we'll see what we can do with your knife. But I just wanted you to know . . . if I don't come back in the morning, I'm all right. And not to worry about me, or look for me."

"You're not abandoning us?" Her hands spasmed around his.

"No, never."

She blinked. "I don't understand."

"That's all right. Take care of Iselle. Don't trust the Chancellor dy Jironal, ever."

"I don't need you to tell me *that*."

"There's more. My friend Palli, the March dy Palliar, knows the true story of how I was betrayed after Gotorget. How I came to be enemies with Dondo . . . won't matter, but Iselle should know, his elder brother deliberately struck me from the list of men to be ransomed, to betray me to the galleys and my death. There's no doubt. I saw the list, in his own hand, which I knew well from his military orders."

She hissed through clenched teeth. "Can nothing be done?"

"I doubt it. If it could be proved, some half the lords of Chalion would likely refuse to ride under his banner thereafter. Maybe it would be enough to topple him. Or not. It's a quarrel Iselle can store up in her quiver; someday she may be able to fire it." He stared down at her face, turned up to his, ivory and coral and deep, deep ebony eyes, huge in the dim light. Awkwardly, he bent and kissed her.

Her breath stopped, then she laughed in startlement and put her hand to her mouth. "I'm sorry. Your beard scratches."

"I . . . forgive me. Palli would make you a most honorable husband, if you're inclined to him. He's very true. As true as you. Tell him I said so."

"Cazaril, what are you—"

Nan dy Vrit called from the Royesse's chambers, "Betriz? Come here, please?"

He must part with everything now, even regret. He kissed her hands, and fled.

❧THE NIGHT SCRAMBLE OVER THE ROOF OF THE ZANgre, from main block to Fonsa's Tower, was every bit as stomach-churning as Cazaril had anticipated. It was still raining. The moon shone fitfully behind the clouds, but its gloomy radiance didn't help much. The footing was either gritty or breath-catchingly slippery under his naked soles, and numbingly cold. The worst part was the final little jump across about six feet to the top of the round tower. Fortunately, the leap was angled down and not up, and he didn't end a simple suicide, wasted, spattered on the cobbles far below.

Bag jerking in his hand, breath whistling past his cold lips, he half squatted, trembling, after the jump, leaning into a bank of roof slates slick with rain beneath his hands. He pictured one working loose, shattering on the stones below, drawing the guards' attention upward. . . . Slowly, he worked his way around until the dark gap of the open roof yawned beside him. He sat on the edge, and felt with his feet. He could touch no solid surface. He waited for a little moonlight; was that a floor, down there? Or a bit of rail? A crow muttered, in the dark.

He spent the next ten minutes, teetering, hands shaking, trying to light the candle stub from his pocket, by feel, with flint and tinder in his lap. He burned himself, but won a little flame at last.

It was a rail, and a bit of crude flooring. Someone had built up heavy timbering inside the tower after the fire, to work on some reinforcement of the stones so they didn't fall down on people's heads, presumably. Cazaril held his breath and dropped to a solid, if small and splintery, platform. He wedged his candle stub in a gap between two boards and lit another from it, got out his bread and Betriz's razor-edged dirk, and stared around. Catch a crow. Right. It had sounded so simple, back in his bedchamber. He couldn't even *see* the crows in these flickering shadows.

A flap by his head, as a crow landed on the railing, nearly stopped his heart. Shivering, he held out a bit of bread. It snatched the fragment from his hand and flew off again. Cazaril cursed, then drew some deep breaths and organized himself. Bread. Knife. Candles. Wriggling cloth bag. Man on his knees. Serenity in his heart? Hardly.

Help me. Help me. Help me.

The crow, or its twin brother, returned. "Caz, Caz!" it cried, not very loudly. But the sound echoed down the tower and back up, weirdly resonant.

"Right," huffed Cazaril. "Right."

He wrestled the rat from its bag, laid the knife against its throat, and whispered, "Run to your lord with my prayer." Sharp and quick, he let its lifeblood out; the warm dark liquid ran over his hand. He laid the little corpse down at his knee.

He held out his arm to his crow; it hopped aboard, and bent to lap the rat blood from his hand. Its black tongue, darting out, startled him so much that he flinched, and nearly lost the bird again. He folded its body under his arm, and kissed it on the head. "Forgive me. My need is great. Maybe the Bastard will feed you the bread of the gods, and you can ride on His shoulder, when you reach Him. Fly to your lord with my prayer." A quick twist broke the crow's neck. It fluttered briefly, quivering, then went still in his hands. He laid it down in front of his other knee.

"Lord Bastard, god of justice when justice fails, of balance, of all things out of season, of my need. For dy Sanda. For Iselle. For all who love her—Lady Betriz, Royina Ista, the old Provincara. For the mess on my back. For truth against lies. Receive my prayer." He had no idea if those were the right words, or if there were any right words. His breath was coming short; maybe he was crying. Surely he was crying. He found himself bending over the dead animals. A terrible pain was starting in his belly, cramping, burning in his gut. Oh. He hadn't known this was going to *hurt* . . .

Anyway, it's a better death than from a flight of Brajaran crossbow bolts in my ass on the galley, for no reason.

Politely, he remembered to say, "For your blessings, too, we thank you, god of the unseason," just like in his bedside prayers as a boy.

Help me, help me, help me.

Oh.

The candle flames guttered and died. The dark world darkened further, and went out.

12

Cazaril's eyes pulled open against the glue that rimmed their lids. He stared up without comprehension at a ragged gray rift in the sky, framed in black. He licked crusted lips, and swallowed. He lay on his back on hard boards—the bracing frame inside Fonsa's Tower. Recollection of the night came rushing back to him.

I live.

Therefore, I have failed.

His right hand, reaching blindly about him, encountered an inert little mound of cold feathers, and recoiled. He lay panting in remembered terror. A cramp gnawed his gut, a dull ache. He was shivering, damp, chilled through, as cold as any corpse. But not a corpse. He breathed. And so, likewise, must Dondo dy Jironal, on . . . was this his wedding morning?

As his eyes slowly adjusted, he saw he was not alone. Lined up along the crude rail that bounded the workmen's platform, a dozen or more crows perched in the shadows, utterly silent, nearly still. They all seemed to be staring down at him.

Cazaril touched his face, but no wounds bled there—no bird had tried an experimental peck yet. "No," he whispered shakily. "I am not your breakfast. I'm sorry." One rustled its wings uneasily, but none of them flapped away at the sound of his voice. Even when he sat up, they shifted about but did not take to the air.

All was not drowned blackness since the night before—fragments of a dream coursed through his memory. He had dreamed that he was Dondo dy Jironal, roistering with his friends and their whores in some torchlit and candle-gilded hall, the board gleaming with silver goblets, his thick hands glittering with rings. He had toasted the blood-sacrifice of Iselle's maidenhood with obscene jests, and drunk deeply . . . then he'd been taken with a cough, a scratching in his throat that needled rapidly to pain. His throat had swelled, closing shut, choking him, cutting off his air, as if he were being strangled from the inside out. The flushed faces of his companions had whirled about him, their laughter and derision turning to panic as it was forced upon them by his purpling livid features that he was not clowning. Cries, wine cups knocked over, shocked fearful hisses of *Poison!* No last words squeezed through that inward-strangled throat, past that thickening tongue. Just silent convulsions, laboring heart racing, viselike pain in the chest and head, black clouds shot with red boiling up in his darkening vision . . .

It was only a dream. If I live, so does he.

Cazaril lay back down upon the hard boards, curled around his bellyache, for half the turning of a glass, exhausted, despairing. The row of crows kept watch over him in unnerving silence. It gradually came to him that he would have to go back. And he hadn't planned a return route.

He might climb down the bracing frames . . . but that would leave him standing in the bottom of a bricked-up tower atop a years-long accumulation of guano and detritus, crying to be let out. Could anyone even hear him through the thick stone? Would they take his muffled voice for an echo of the crows' caws, or the howling of a ghost?

Up, then? Back the way he'd come in?

He stood at last, pulling himself up by the rail—even now, the crows did not fly away—and stretched his cramped and aching muscles. He had to physically shove a couple of crows from the railing to clear a place to stand; they flapped off indignantly, but still with that uncanny silence. He rucked up the brown gown, tucked hem in belt. When he balanced on the rail, it was a short reach to the tower's rim. He grasped, heaved. His arms were strong, and his body was lean. One hideous moment of consciousness of the air below his bare kicking legs, and he was up over the stones and out onto the slates. The fog was so thick, he could barely see down into the courtyard below. Dawn, or just after dawn, he guessed; the lesser denizens of the castle would already be awake, this tag-end-of-autumn morning. The crows followed him solemnly, flapping up one by one through the gap in the roof to find perches on stone or slate. Their heads turned to track his progress.

He had a vision of them, mobbing him to spoil his next leap from the tower up to the main block, revenging their comrade. And then another vision, as his feet scrambled and his arms shook, of letting go, letting it all go, and falling to his welcome death on the stones below. A wrenching cramp coiled in his gut, driving out his breath in a gasp.

He would have let go then, except for the sudden terror that he might survive the fall, leg-smashed and crippled. Only that drove him up over the eaves to the slates of the main block's roof. His muscles cracked as he lifted himself. His hands were scraped raw by their frantic gripping.

He was not sure, in this paling fog, which of the dozen dormer windows erupting out of the slates he'd emerged from last night. Suppose someone had come along and closed and locked it, since? He inched slowly along, trying each one. The crows followed, stalking along the gutters, flapping up in brief hops, their clawed feet slipping on the slates, too, at times. The mist beaded, glistening, on their feathers, and in his beard and hair, silver sequins on his black vest-cloak. The fourth casement window swung open to his scrabbling fingers. It *was* the unused lumber room. He slid through, and slammed it upon his black-liveried escort just in time to stop a couple of the birds from flying in after him. One bounced off the glass with a thud.

He crept down the stairs to his floor without encountering any early servants, stumbled into his chamber, and closed the door behind him. Tight-bladdered and cramping, he used his chamber pot; his bowels voided frightening blood clots. His hands trembled as he washed them in his basin. When he went to fling the bloodied wash water out into the ravine, the opening window dislodged two silent, sentinel crows from the stone sill. He closed it tight again and locked the latch.

He weaved to his bed like a man drunk on his feet, fell into it, and wrapped his coverlet around himself. As his shivering continued, he could hear the sounds of the castle's servants carrying water or linens or pots, feet plodding up stairs and down corridors, an occasional low-voiced call or order.

Was Iselle being waked now, on the floor above, to be washed and attired, bound in ropes of pearls, chained in jewels, for her dreadful appointment with Dondo? Had she even slept? Or wept all night, prayed to gods gone deaf? He should go up, to offer what comfort he could. Had Betriz found another knife? *I cannot bear to face them*. He curled tighter and shut his eyes in agony.

He was still lying in bed, gasping in breaths perilously close to sobs, when booted steps sounded in the corridor, and his door banged open. Chancellor dy Jironal's voice snarled, "I know it's him. It has to be him!"

The steps stalked across his floorboards, and his coverlet was snatched from him. He rolled over and stared up in surprise at dy Jironal's steel-bearded, panting face glaring down at him in astonishment.

"You're alive!" cried dy Jironal. His voice was indignant.

Half a dozen courtiers, a couple of whom Cazaril recognized as Dondo's bravos, crowded dy Jironal's shoulder to gape at him. They had their hands upon their swords, as if prepared to correct this mistaken animation of Cazaril's at dy Jironal's word. Roya Orico, clad in a nightgown, a shabby old cloak clutched about his neck by his fat fingers, stood at the back of the mob. Orico looked . . . strange. Cazaril blinked, and rubbed his eyes. A kind of aura surrounded the roya, not of light, but of darkness. Cazaril could see him perfectly clearly, so he could not call it a cloud or a fog, for it obscured nothing. And yet it was there, moving as the man moved, like a trailing garment.

Dy Jironal bit his lip, his eyes boring into Cazaril's face. "If not you—who, then? It has to be someone . . . it has to be someone close to . . . that girl! The foul little murderess!" He spun around and stormed out, curtly motioning his men to follow him.

"What's afoot?" Cazaril demanded of Orico, who had turned to waddle after them.

Orico looked back over his shoulder, and spread his hands in a wide, bewildered shrug. "Wedding's off. Dondo dy Jironal was murdered around midnight last night—by death magic."

Cazaril's mouth opened; nothing came out but a weak, "Oh." He sank back, dazed, as Orico shuffled out after his chancellor.

I don't understand.

If Dondo is slain, and yet I live . . . I cannot have been granted a death miracle. And yet Dondo is slain. How?

How else but that someone had beaten Cazaril to the deed?

Belatedly, his wits caught up with dy Jironal's.

Betriz?

No, oh no . . . !

He surged out of bed, fell heavily to the floor, scrambled to his feet, and staggered after the crowd of enraged and baffled courtiers.

He arrived at his invaded office antechamber to hear dy Jironal bellowing, "Then bring her out, that I may see!" to a disheveled and frightened-looking Nan dy Vrit, who nevertheless blocked the doorway to the inner rooms with her body as though ready to defend a drawbridge. Cazaril nearly fainted with relief when Betriz, frowning fiercely, came up behind Nan's shoulder. Nan was in her nightdress, but Betriz, rumpled and weary-looking, was still wearing the same green wool gown she'd had on last night. Had *she* slept? *But she lives, she lives!*

"Why do you make this uncouth roaring here, my lord?" Betriz demanded coldly. "It is unseemly and untimely."

Dy Jironal's lips parted in his beard; he was clearly taken aback. After a moment, his teeth snapped closed. "Where is the royesse, then? I must see the royesse."

"She is sleeping a little, for the first time in days. I'll not have her disturbed. She'll have to exchange dreams for nightmare soon enough." Betriz's nostrils flared with open hostility.

Dy Jironal's back straightened; his breath hissed in. "Wake her? *Can* you wake her?"

Dear gods. Might Iselle have . . . ? But before this new panic closed down Cazaril's throat, Iselle herself appeared, pushed between her ladies, and walked coolly forward into the antechamber to face dy Jironal.

"I do not sleep. What do you want, my lord?" Her eyes passed over her brother Orico, hovering at the edge of the mob, and dismissed him with contempt, returning to dy Jironal. Her brows tensed in wariness. No question but that she understood whose power forced her to her unwelcome wedding.

Dy Jironal stared from woman to woman, all indisputably alive before him. He wheeled around and stared again at Cazaril, who was blinking at Iselle. Aura flared around her, too, just like Orico, but hers was more disturbed, a churning of deep darkness and luminous pale blue, like the aurora he'd once seen in the far southern night sky.

"Whoever," grated dy Jironal. "Wherever. I'll find the filthy coward's corpse if I have to search all of Chalion."

"And then what?" inquired Orico, rubbing his unshaven jowls. "Hang it?" He returned a raised-brow look of irony for dy Jironal's driven glare; dy Jironal whirled and stamped back out. Cazaril stepped aside to let the entourage pass, his gaze flicking covertly from Orico to Iselle, comparing the two . . . hallucinations? No one else here pulsed like that. *Maybe I'm sick. Maybe I'm mad.*

"Cazaril," said Iselle in urgent bewilderment as soon as the men had cleared the outer door—Nan hurried to shut it behind the invaders—"what has happened?"

"Someone killed Dondo dy Jironal last night. By death magic."

Her lips parted, and her hands clasped together like a child just promised its heart's desire. "Oh! Oh! Oh, this is *welcome* news! Oh, thank the Lady, oh, *thank* the Bastard—I will send such gifts to his altar—oh, Cazaril, who—?"

At Betriz's look of wild surmise in his direction, Cazaril grimaced. "Not me. Obviously." *Though not for want of trying.*

"Did you—" Betriz began, then pressed her lips closed. Cazaril's grimace tilted in appreciation of her delicacy in not inquiring, out loud before two witnesses, if he'd plotted a capital crime. He hardly needed to speak; her eyes blazed with speculation.

Iselle paced back and forth, almost bouncing with relief. "I think I felt it," she said in a voice of great wonder. "In any case, I felt something . . . midnight, around midnight, you said?" No one had said so here. "An easing of my heart, as if something in me knew my prayers were heard. But I never expected *this*. I'd asked the Lady for *my* death . . ." She paused, and touched her hand to her broad white forehead. "Or what She willed." Her voice slowed. "Cazaril . . . did I . . . could I have done this? Did the goddess answer me so?"

"I . . . I don't see how, Royesse. You prayed to the Lady of Spring, did you not?"

"Yes, and to Her Mother of Summer, both. But mostly to Spring herself."

"The Great Ladies grant miracles of life, and healing. Not death." Normally. And all miracles were rare and capricious. Gods. Who knew their limits, their purposes?

"It didn't feel like death," Iselle confessed. "And yet I was eased. I took a little food and didn't throw it up, and I slept for a time."

Nan dy Vrit nodded confirmation. "And glad I was of it, my lady."

Cazaril took a deep breath. "Well, dy Jironal will solve the mystery for us, I'm sure. He'll hunt down every person to die last night in Cardegoss—in all of Chalion, I have no doubt—until he finds out his brother's murderer."

"Bless the poor soul who put his vile plans in such disarray." Formally, Iselle touched forehead, lip, navel, groin, and heart, spreading her fingers wide. "And at such a cost. May the Bastard's demons grant him what mercy ever they can."

"Amen," said Cazaril. "Let's just hope dy Jironal finds no close comrades or family to wreak his vengeance upon." He wrapped his arms around his belly, which was cramping again.

Betriz came near him and stared him in the face, her hand going out but then falling back hesitantly. "Lord Caz, you look dreadful. Your skin is the color of cold porridge."

"I'm . . . ill. Something I ate." He took a breath. "So we prepare today not for grievous wedding but joyous funeral. I trust you ladies will contain your glee in public?"

Nan dy Vrit snorted. Iselle motioned her to silence, and said firmly, "Solemn piety, I promise you. And if it is thanksgiving and not sorrow in my heart, only the gods shall know."

Cazaril nodded, and rubbed his aching neck. "Usually, a victim of death magic is burned before nightfall, to deny the body, the divines say, to uncanny things that might want to move in. Apparently, such a death invites them. It will be a terribly hurried funeral for such a high lord. They'll have to assemble all before dark." Iselle's coruscating aura was making him almost nauseated. He swallowed, and looked away from her.

"Then, Cazaril," said Betriz, "for pity's sake go lie down till then. We're safe, all unexpectedly. You need do no more." She took him by his cold hands, clasped them briefly, and smiled in wry concern. He managed a wan return smile, and retreated.

*　　　*　　　*

❧HE CRAWLED BACK INTO HIS BED. HE HAD LAIN THERE perhaps an hour, bewildered and still shivering, when his door swung open and Betriz tiptoed in to stare down at him. She laid a hand across his clammy forehead.

"I was afraid you'd taken a fever," she said, "but you're chilled."

"I was, um . . . chilled, yes. Must have thrown off my blankets in the night."

She touched his shoulder. "Your clothes are damp through." Her eyes narrowed. "When was the last time you ate?"

He could not remember. "Yesterday morning. I think."

"I see." She frowned at him a moment longer, then whirled and went out.

Ten minutes later, a maid arrived with a warming pan full of hot coals and a feather quilt; a few minutes after that, a manservant with a can of hot water and firm instructions to see him washed and put back to bed in dry nightclothes. This, in a castle gone mad with the disruption of every courtier and lady at once trying to prepare themselves for an unscheduled public appearance of utmost formality. Cazaril questioned nothing. The servant had just finished tucking him into the hot dry envelope of his sheets when Betriz reappeared with a crockery bowl on a tray. She propped his door open and seated herself on the edge of his bed.

"Eat this."

It was bread soaked in steaming milk, laced with honey. He accepted the first spoonful in bemused surprise, then struggled up on his pillows. "I'm not *that* sick." Attempting to regain his dignity, he took the bowl from her; she made no objection, as long as he continued to eat. He discovered he was ravenous. By the time he'd finished, he'd stopped shivering.

She smiled in satisfaction. "Your color's much less ghastly now. Good."

"How fares the royesse?"

"Vastly better. She's . . . I want to say, collapsed, but I don't mean overcome. The blessed release that comes when an unbearable pressure is suddenly removed. It's a joy to look upon her."

"Yes. I understand."

Betriz nodded. "She's resting now, till time to dress." She took the empty bowl from him, set it aside, and lowered her voice. "Cazaril, what did you *do* last night?"

"Nothing. Evidently."

Her lips thinned in exasperation. But what use was it to lay the burden of his secret upon her now? Confession might relieve his soul, but it would put hers in danger in any subsequent investigation that demanded oath-sworn testimony from her.

"Lord dy Rinal had it that you paid a page to catch you a rat last night. It was that news that sent Chancellor dy Jironal pelting up to your bedchamber, dy Rinal told me. The page said you'd claimed you wanted it to eat."

"Well, so. It's no crime for a man to eat a rat. It was a little memorial feast, for the siege of Gotorget."

"Oh? You just said you'd eaten nothing since yesterday morning." She hesitated, her eyes anxious. "The chambermaid also said there was blood in your pot that she emptied this morning."

"Bastard's demons!" Cazaril, who had slid down into his covers, struggled up again. "Is *nothing* sacred to castle gossip? Can't a man even call his chamber pot his own here?"

She held out a hand. "Lord Caz, don't joke. How sick are you?"

"I had a bellyache. It's eased off now. A passing thing. So to speak." He grimaced, and decided not to mention the hallucinations. "Obviously, the blood in the pot was from butchering the rat. And the bellyache just what I deserved, for eating such a disgusting creature. Eh?"

She said slowly, "It's a good story. It all hangs together."

"So, there."

"But Caz—people will think you're *strange*."

"I can add them to the collection along with the ones who think I rape girls. I suppose I need a third perversion, to balance me properly." Well, there was being suspected of attempting death magic. That could balance him over a gallows.

She sat back, frowning deeply. "All right. I won't press you. But I was wondering . . ." She wrapped her arms around herself, and regarded him intently. "If two—theoretical—persons were to attempt death magic on the same victim at the same time, might they each end up . . . *half*-dead?"

Cazaril stared back—no, *she* didn't look sick—and shook his head. "I don't think so. Given all the various vain attempts that people have made to compel the gods with death magic, if it could happen that way, it surely would have before now. The Bastard's death demon is always portrayed in the Temple carvings with a yoke over his shoulders and two identical buckets, one for each soul. I don't think the demon can choose differently." Umegat's words came back to him, *I'm afraid that's just the way it works.* "I'm not even sure the god can choose differently."

Her eyes narrowed further. "*You* said, if you weren't back this morning, not to worry for you, or look for you. *You* said you'd be all right. You *also* said, if the bodies are not burned properly, terrible uncanny things happen to them."

He shifted uncomfortably. "I made provision." *Of sorts.*

"What provision? You sneaked away, leaving none who cared for you to know where to look or even whether to pray!"

He cleared his throat. "Fonsa's crows. I climbed over the roof to Fonsa's Tower to, ah, say my prayers last night. If, if things had, ah, come out differently, I figured they'd clear up the mess, just as their brethren clean up a battlefield, or a stray sheep lost over a cliff."

"*Cazaril!*" she cried in indignation, then hastily lowered her voice to a near whisper. "Caz, that's, that's . . . you mean to tell me you crawled off all alone, to die in despair, expecting to leave your body to be eaten by . . . that's *horrid!*"

He was startled to see tears welling in her eyes. "Hey, now! It's not so bad. Right soldierly, *I* thought." His hand began to reach for the drops on her cheeks, then hesitated and fell back to his coverlet.

Her fists clenched in her lap. "If you *ever* do anything like that again without telling me—telling anyone—I'll, I'll . . . slap you silly!" She knuckled her eyes, rubbed her face, and sat up, her spine stern. Her voice returned abruptly to a conversational tone. "The funeral has been set for an hour before sunset, at the temple. Do you mean to go, or will you stay in bed?"

"If I can walk at all, I'm going. I mean to see it through. Every enemy of Dondo's will be there, if only to prove *they* didn't do it. It's going to be a remarkable event to behold."

❧THE FUNERAL RITES AT THE TEMPLE OF CARDEGOSS were far more heavily attended for Dondo dy Jironal than they had been for poor lonely dy Sanda. Roya Orico himself, soberly garbed, led the mourners from the Zangre walking in loose procession down the hill. Royina Sara was carried in a sedan chair. Her face was as blank as though carved from an ice block, but her raiment was a shout of color, festival gear from three holidays jumbled together, draped and spangled with what looked like half the jewels from her jewel case. Everyone pretended not to notice.

Cazaril eyed her covertly, but not for the sake of her bizarrely chosen clothing. It was the other garment, the shadow-cloak, visible-invisible twin to Orico's, that tugged and twisted at his mind's eye. Teidez wore another such dark aura, blurring along with his steps down the cobbled streets. Whatever the black mirage was, it seemed to run in the family. Cazaril wondered what he would see if he could look upon Dowager Royina Ista right now.

The archdivine of Cardegoss himself, in his five-colored robes, conducted the ceremony, so crowded it was held in the temple's main courtyard. The procession from the Jironals' palace placed the bier with Dondo's body down a few paces in front of the gods' hearth, a round stone platform with a pierced copper tent raised over it on five slim pillars to protect the holy fire from the elements. A shadowless gray light filled the court as the cold wet day sank toward foggy evening. The air was hazy violet with a clashing mélange of the incenses burned in the prayers and rites of cleansing.

Dondo's stiff body, laid out on the bier and banked around with flowers and herbs of good fortune and symbolic protection— too late, Cazaril thought—had been dressed in the blue-and-white robes of his holy generalship of the Daughter's military order. The sword of his rank lay unsheathed upon his chest, his hands clasped over the hilt. His body did not seem particularly swollen or misshapen—dy Rinal whispered the gruesome rumor that it had been tightly wrapped with linen bands before being dressed. The corpse's face was hardly more puffy than from one of Dondo's morning hangovers. But he would have to be burned with his rings still on. They'd never pry them from those sausage fingers without the aid of a butcher's knife.

Cazaril had managed the walk down from the Zangre without stumbling, but his stomach was cramping again now, unpleasantly distended against his belt. He took what he hoped was an unobtrusive place standing behind Betriz and Nan in the crowd from the castle. Iselle was pulled away to stand between the chancellor and Roya Orico in the position of a chief mourner that her brief betrothal bequeathed her. She was still shimmering like an aurora in Cazaril's aching eyes. Her face was stern and pale. The sight of Dondo's body had apparently drained her of any impulse to an unseemly display of joy.

Two courtiers stepped forth to deliver seemingly heartfelt eulogies upon Dondo that Cazaril entirely failed to relate to the erratic real life of the man cut down here. Chancellor dy Jironal was too overcome to speak very long, though whether with grief or rage or both it was hard to tell beneath that steely surface. He did announce a purse of a thousand royals reward for information leading to the identification of his brother's murderer, the only overt reference made this day to the abrupt manner of Dondo's death.

It was clear that a large purse had been laid down on the temple altar. What seemed all the dedicats, acolytes, and divines of Cardegoss were massed in robed blocks to chant the prayers and responses in both unison and harmony, as though extra holiness were to be obtained by volume. One of the singers, in the green-robed squad of altos, caught Cazaril's inner eye. She was middle-aged and dumpy, and she glowed like a candle seen through green glass. She looked up once directly at Cazaril, then away, back to the harried divine who directed their orisons.

Cazaril nudged Nan and whispered, "Who is that woman acolyte on the end of the second row of the Mother's singers, do you know?"

She glanced over. "One of the Mother's midwives. I believe she's said to be very good."

"Oh."

When the sacred animals were led forth, the crowd grew attentive. It was by no means clear which god would take up the soul of Dondo dy Jironal. His predecessor in the Daughter's generalship, though a father and grandfather, had been claimed at once by the Lady of Spring in whose long service he had died. Dondo himself had served in the Son's military order as an officer in his youth. And he was known to have sired a scattering of bastards, as well as two scorned daughters by his late first wife, left to be raised by country kin. And—unspoken thought—as his soul had been carried off by the Bastard's death demon, it had surely passed through the Bastard's hands. Might those hands have closed upon it?

The acolyte-groom carrying the Daughter's jay stepped forth at Archdivine Mendenal's gesture, and raised her wrist. The bird bobbed, but clung stubbornly to her sleeve. She glanced up at the archdivine, who frowned and gave her a little nod toward the bier. Her nostrils flared in faint protest, but she obediently stepped forward, wrapped both hands around the jay, and set it firmly down upon the corpse's chest.

She lifted her hands. The jay lifted its tail, dropped a blob of guano, and shot skyward, trailing its embroidered silk jesses, screeching piercingly. At least three men in Cazaril's hearing choked and hissed but, at the sight of the chancellor's set teeth, did not laugh aloud. Iselle's eyes blazed like cerulean fires, and she cast her glance demurely downward; her aura roiled. The acolyte stepped back, head tipped up, following the bird's flight anxiously. The jay came to roost on the ornaments at the top of one of the ring of porphyry pillars circling the court, and screeched again. The acolyte glared at the archdivine; he waved her hastily away, and she bowed and retreated to go try to coax the bird back to her hand.

The Mother's green bird also refused to leave its handler's arm. Archdivine Mendenal did not repeat the previous disastrous experiment, but merely nodded her back to her place in the circle of creatures.

The Son's acolyte dragged the fox by its chain to the edge of the bier. The animal whined and snapped, its black claws scrabbling noisily on the tiles as it struggled to get away. The archdivine waved him back.

The stout gray wolf, sitting on its haunches with its great red tongue lolling out of its unmuzzled jaws, growled deeply as its gray-robed handler suggestively lifted its silver chain. The vibrato resonated around the stone courtyard. The wolf lowered itself to its belly on the tiles, and stretched out its paws. Gingerly, the acolyte lowered his hands and stood down; his glance at the archdivine shouted silently, *I'm not touching this*. Mendenal didn't argue.

All eyes turned expectantly to the Bastard's white-robed acolyte with her white rats. Chancellor dy Jironal's lips were pressed flat and pale with his impotent fury, but there was nothing he could do or say. The white lady took a breath, stepped forward to the bier, and lowered her sacred creatures to Dondo's chest to sign the god's acceptance of the unacceptable, disdained, discarded soul.

The moment her hands released the silky white bodies, both rats sprang away to either side of the bier as though shot from catapults. The acolyte dodged right and left as though unable to decide which sacred charge to chase after first, and flung up her hands. One rat scurried for the safety of the pillars. The other scampered into the crowd of mourners, which stirred around its track; a couple of ladies yipped nervously. A murmur of astonishment, disbelief, and dismay ran through the array of courtiers and ladies, and a stream of shocked whispers.

Betriz's was among them. "Cazaril," she said anxiously, crowding back under his arm to hiss in his ear, "what does it mean? The Bastard *always* takes the leftovers. Always. It is His, His . . . it's His *job*. He *can't* not take a severed soul—I thought He already *had*."

Cazaril was stunned, too. "If no god has taken up Lord Dondo's soul . . . then it's still in the world. I mean, if it's not *there*, then it has to be *here*. Somewhere . . ." An unquiet ghost, a revenant spirit. *Sundered and damned.*

The ceremonies stopped dead as the archdivine and Chancellor dy Jironal retreated around the hearth for a low-voiced conversation, or possibly argument, from the rise and chop of swallowed words that drifted back to the curious crowd waiting. The archdivine popped around the hearth to call an acolyte of the Bastard to him; after a whispered conference, the white-garbed young man departed at a run. The gray sky overhead was darkening. A subdivine, in a burst of initiative, struck up an unscheduled hymn from the robed singers to cover the gap. By the time they'd finished, dy Jironal and Mendenal had returned.

Still they waited. The singers embarked on another hymn. Cazaril found himself wishing he'd used Ordol's *Fivefold Pathway* for something other than a prop to cover his naps; alas, the book was still back in Valenda. If Dondo's spirit had not been taken by the servant-demon back to its master, where was it? And if the demon could not return except with both its soul-buckets filled, where was the sundered soul of Dondo's unknown murderer now?

For that matter, where was the *demon?* Cazaril had never read much theology. For some reason now obscure to him, he'd thought it an impractical study, suited only to unworldly dreamers. Till he'd waked to this nightmare.

A scritching noise from his boot made him look down. The sacred white rat was stretching itself up his leg, its pink nose quivering. It rubbed its little pointed face rapidly against Cazaril's shin. He bent and picked it up, meaning to return it to its handler. It writhed ecstatically in his cupped hands, and licked his thumb.

To Cazaril's surprise, the wheezing acolyte returned to the temple courtyard leading the groom Umegat, dressed as usual in the tabard of the Zangre. But it was Umegat who stunned him.

The Roknari shone with a white aura like a man standing in front of a clear glass window at a sea dawn. Cazaril shut his eyes, though he knew he didn't see this with his eyes. The white blaze still moved behind his lids. Over there, a darkness that wasn't darkness, and two more, and an unrestful aurora, and off to the side, a faint green spark. His eyes sprang open. Umegat stared straight at him for the fraction of a second, and Cazaril felt flensed. The roya's groom moved on, to present himself with a diffident bow to the archdivine, and step aside for some whispered conference.

The archdivine called the Bastard's acolyte to him, who had recaptured one of her charges; she gave up the rat to Umegat, who cradled it in one arm and glanced toward Cazaril. The Roknari groom trod over to him, humbly excusing himself through the crowd of courtiers, who barely glanced at him. Cazaril could not understand why they did not open before that bow wave of his white aura like the sea before a spinnaker-driven ship. Umegat held out his open hand. Cazaril blinked down stupidly at it.

"The sacred rat, my lord?" prompted Umegat gently.

"Oh." The creature was still sucking on his fingers, tickling them. Umegat pulled the reluctant animal off Cazaril's sleeve as though removing a burr and just prevented its mate from springing across to take its place. Juggling rats, he walked quietly back to the bier, where the archdivine waited. Was Cazaril losing his mind—*don't answer that*—or did Mendenal barely keep himself from bowing to the groom? The Zangre's courtiers seemed to see nothing unreasonable in the archdivine calling in the roya's most expert animal-handler in this awkward crisis. All eyes were locked on the rats, not on the Roknari. The unreason was all Cazaril's.

Umegat held the creatures in his arms and whispered to them, and approached Dondo's body. A long moment, while the rats, though quiescent, made no move to claim Dondo for their god. At last Umegat backed away, and shook his head apologetically to the archdivine, and gave up the rats to their anxious young woman.

Mendenal prostrated himself between the hearth and the bier for a moment of abject prayer, but rose again soon. Dedicats were bringing out tapers to light the wall lanterns around the darkening courtyard. The archdivine called forth the pallbearers to take up the bier to Dondo's waiting pyre, and the singers filed out in procession.

Iselle returned to Betriz and Cazaril. She rubbed the back of her hand across eyes rimmed with dark circles. "I don't think I can bear any more of this. Dy Jironal can see to his brother's roasting. Take me home, Lord Caz."

The royesse's little party split off from the main body of mourners, not the only wearied persons to do so, and exited through the front portico into the damp dusk of the autumn day.

The groom Umegat, waiting with his shoulders propped against a pillar, shoved himself upright, came toward them, and bowed. "My lord dy Cazaril. Might I have a brief word?"

It almost surprised Cazaril that the aura did not reflect off the wet pavement at his feet. He gave Iselle an apologetic salute and went aside with the Roknari. The three women waited at the edge of the portico, Iselle leaning on Betriz's arm.

"My lord, at your earliest convenience, I beg that I might have some private audience with you."

"I'll come to you at the menagerie as soon as I have Iselle settled." Cazaril hesitated. "Do you know that you are lit like a burning torch?"

The groom inclined his head. "So I have been told, my lord, by the few with eyes to see. One can never see oneself, alas. No mundane mirror reflects this. Only the eyes of a soul."

"There was a woman inside who glowed like a green candle."

"Mother Clara? Yes, she just spoke to me of you. She is a most excellent midwife."

"What is that, that anti-light, then?" Cazaril glanced toward where the women lingered.

Umegat touched his lips. "Not here, if you please, my lord."

Cazaril's mouth formed a silent *Oh*. He nodded.

The Roknari swept him a lower bow. As he turned to pad quietly into the gathering gloom, he added over his shoulder, "*You* are lit like a burning city."

13

The royesse was so drained by the ordeal of Lord Dondo's odd funeral that she was stumbling by the time they had climbed to the castle again. Cazaril left Nan and Betriz making sensible plans to put Iselle straight to bed and have the servants bring a plain dinner to their chambers. He made his way back out of the main block to the Zangre's gates. Pausing, he glanced out over the city to see if a column of smoke was still rising from the temple. He fancied he saw a faint orange reflection on the lowering clouds, but it was too dark by now to make out anything more.

His heart leapt in shock at the sudden flapping around him as he crossed the stable yard, but it was only Fonsa's crows, mobbing him again. He fended off two that attempted to land on his shoulder, and tried to wave them away, hissing and stamping. They hopped back out of reach, but would not leave, following him, conspicuously, all the way to the menagerie.

One of Umegat's undergrooms was waiting by the wall lanterns bracketing the aisle door. He was a little, elderly, thumbless man, who gave Cazaril a wide smile that showed a truncated tongue, accounting for a welcome that was a kind of mouthed hum, the meaning made clear by his friendly gestures. He slid the broad door back just enough to admit Cazaril before him, and shooed away the crows who tried to follow, scooping the most persistent one back out the gap with a flip of his foot before closing it.

The groom's candlestick, shielded by a blown-glass tulip, had a

thick handle made for him to wrap his fingers around. By this light
he guided Cazaril down the menagerie's aisle. The animals in their
stalls snuffled and thumped as Cazaril passed, pressing to the bars
to stare at him from the shadows. The leopard's eyes shone like
green sparks; its ratcheting growl echoed off the walls, not low and
hostile, but pulsing in a weirdly inquiring singsong.

The menagerie's grooms had their sleeping quarters on half the
building's upper floor, the other half being devoted to the storage
of fodder and straw. A door stood open, candlelight spilling from it
into the dark corridor. The undergroom knocked on the frame;
Umegat's voice responded, "Good. Thank you."

The undergroom gave way with a bow. Cazaril ducked through
the door to see a narrow but private chamber with a window looking out over the dark stable yard. Umegat pulled the curtain across
the window and bustled around a rude pine table that held a
brightly patterned cloth, a wine jug and clay cups, and a plate with
bread and cheese. "Thank you for coming, Lord Cazaril. Enter,
please, seat yourself. Thank you, Daris, that will be all." Umegat
closed the door. Cazaril paused on the way to the chair Umegat's
gesture had indicated to stare at a tall shelf crammed with books,
including titles in Ibran, Darthacan, and Roknari. A bit of gold let-
tering on a familiar-looking spine on the top shelf caught his eye,
The Fivefold Pathway of the Soul. Ordol. The leather binding was
worn with use, the volume, and most of its company, free of dust.
Theology, mostly. *Why am I not surprised?*

Cazaril lowered himself onto the plain wooden chair. Umegat
turned up a cup and poured a heavy red wine into it, smiled briefly,
and held it out to his guest. Cazaril closed his shaking hands
around it with vast gratitude. "Thank you. I need that."

"I should imagine so, my lord." Umegat poured a cup for himself and sat across the table from Cazaril. The table might be plain
and poor, but the generous braces of wax candles upon it gave a
rich, clear light. A reading man's light.

Cazaril raised the cup to his lips and gulped. When he set it
down, Umegat immediately topped it up again. Cazaril closed his
eyes and opened them. Open or shut, Umegat still glowed.

"You are an acolyte—no. You're a divine. Aren't you," said Cazaril.

Umegat cleared his throat apologetically. "Yes. Of the Bastard's
Order. Although that is not why I am here."

"Why are you here?"

"We'll come to that." Umegat bent forward, picked up the waiting knife, and began to saw off hunks of bread and cheese.

"I thought—I hoped—I wondered—if you might have been sent by the gods. To guide and guard me."

Umegat's lip quirked up. "Indeed? And here I was wondering if you had been sent by the gods to guide and guard *me*."

"Oh. That's . . . not so good, then." Cazaril shrank a little in his seat, and took another gulp of wine. "Since when?"

"Since the day in the menagerie that Fonsa's crow practically jumped up and down on your head crying *This one! This one!* My chosen god is, dare I say it, fiendishly ambiguous at times, but that was a little hard to miss."

"Was I glowing, then?"

"No."

"When did I start, um, doing that?"

"Sometime between the last time I saw you, which was late yesterday afternoon when you came back to the Zangre limping as though you'd been thrown from a horse, and today at the temple. I believe you may have a better guess than I do as to the *exact* time. Will you not take a little food, my lord? You don't look well."

Cazaril had eaten nothing since Betriz had brought him the milk sops at noon. Umegat waited until his guest's mouth was full of cheese and chewy crust before remarking, "One of my varied tasks as a young divine, before I came to Cardegoss, was as an assistant Inquirer for the Temple investigating alleged charges of death magic." Cazaril choked; Umegat went on serenely, "Or death miracle, to put it with more theological accuracy. We uncovered quite a number of ingenious fakes—usually poison, though the, ah, dimmer murderers sometimes tried cruder methods. I had to explain to them that the Bastard does not ever execute unrepentant sinners with a dirk, nor a large hammer. The true miracles were much more rare than their notoriety would suggest. But I never encountered an authentic case where the victim was an innocent. To put it more finely still, what the Bastard granted was miracles of justice." His voice had grown crisper, more decisive, the servility evaporating out of it along with most of his soft Roknari accent.

"Ah," Cazaril mumbled, and took another gulp of wine. *This is the most wit-full man I have met in Cardegoss, and I've spent the last three months looking past him because he wears a servant's garb.* Granted, Umegat apparently did not wish to draw attention to himself. "That tabard is as good as a cloak of invisibility, you know."

Umegat smiled, and took a sip of his wine. "Yes."

"So . . . are you an Inquirer now?" Was it all over? Would he be charged, convicted, executed for his murderous, if vain, attempt on Dondo?

"No. Not anymore."

"What *are* you, then?"

To Cazaril's bewilderment, Umegat's eyes crinkled with laughter. "I'm a saint."

Cazaril stared at him for a long, long moment, then drained his cup. Amiably, Umegat refilled it. Cazaril was certain of very little tonight, but somehow, he didn't think Umegat was mad. Or lying.

"A saint. Of the Bastard."

Umegat nodded.

"That's . . . an unusual line of work, for a Roknari. How did it come about?" This was inane, but with two cups of wine on an empty stomach, he was growing light-headed.

Umegat's smile grew sadly introspective. "For you—the truth. I suppose the names no longer matter. This was a lifetime ago. When I was a young lord in the Archipelago, I fell in love."

"Young lords and young louts do that everywhere."

"My lover was about thirty then. A man of keen mind and kind heart."

"Oh. Not in the Archipelago, you don't."

"Indeed. I had no interest in religion whatsoever. For obvious reasons, he was a secret Quintarian. We made plans to flee together. I reached the ship to Brajar. He did not. I spent the voyage seasick and desperate, learning—I thought—to pray. Hoping he'd made it to another vessel, and we'd meet in the port city we'd chosen for our destination. It was over a year before I found out how he'd met his end, from a Roknari merchant trading there whom we had once both known."

Cazaril took a drink. "The usual?"

"Oh, yes. Genitals, thumbs—that he might not sign the fifth god—" Umegat touched forehead, navel, groin, and heart, folding his thumb beneath his palm in the Quadrene fashion, denying the fifth finger that was the Bastard's—"they saved his tongue for last, that he might betray others. He never did. He died a martyr, hanged."

Cazaril touched forehead, lip, navel, groin, and heart, fingers spread wide. "I'm sorry."

Umegat nodded. "I thought about it for a time. At least, those times when I wasn't drunk or vomiting or being stupid, eh? Youth, eh. It didn't come easily. Finally, one day, I walked to the temple and turned myself in." He took a breath. "And the Bastard's Order took me in. Gave a home to the homeless, friends to the friendless, honor to the despised. And they gave me work. I was . . . charmed."

A Temple divine. Umegat was leaving out a few details, Cazaril felt. Forty years or so of them. But there was nothing inexplicable about an intelligent, energetic, dedicated man rising through the Temple hierarchy to such a rank. It was the part about shining like a full moon over a snowfall that was making his head reel. "Good. Wonderful. Great works. Foundling hospitals and, um, inquiries. Now explain why you glow in the dark." He had either drunk too much, or not nearly enough, he decided glumly.

Umegat rubbed his neck and pulled gently on his queue. "Do you understand what it means to be a saint?"

Cazaril cleared his throat uncomfortably. "You must be very virtuous, I suppose."

"No, in fact. One need not be good. Or even nice." Umegat looked wry of a sudden. "Grant you, once one experiences . . . what one experiences, one's tastes change. Material ambition seems immaterial. Greed, pride, vanity, wrath, just grow too dull to bother with."

"Lust?"

Umegat brightened. "Lust, I'm happy to say, seems largely unaffected. Or perhaps I might grant, love. For the cruelty and selfishness that make lust vile become tedious. But personally, I think it is not so much the growth of virtue, as simply the replacement of prior vices with an addiction to one's god." Umegat emptied his cup. "The gods love their great-souled men and women as an artist loves fine marble, but the issue isn't virtue. It is will. Which is chisel and hammer. Has anyone ever quoted you Ordol's classic sermon of the cups?"

"That thing where the divine pours water all over everything? I first heard it when I was ten. I thought it was pretty entertaining when he got his shoes wet, but then, I was ten. I'm afraid our Temple divine at Cazaril tended to drone on."

"Attend now, and you shall not be bored." Umegat inverted his clay cup upon the cloth. "Men's will is free. The gods may not invade it, any more than I may pour wine into this cup through its bottom."

"No, don't waste the wine!" Cazaril protested, as Umegat reached for the jug. "I've seen it demonstrated before."

Umegat grinned, and desisted. "But have you really understood how powerless the gods are, when the lowest slave may exclude them from his heart? And if from his heart, then from the world as well, for the gods may not reach in except through living souls. If the gods could seize passage from anyone they wished, then men would be mere puppets. Only if they borrow or are given will from a willing creature, do they have a little channel through which to act. They can seep in through the minds of animals, sometimes, with effort. Plants . . . require much foresight. Or"—Umegat turned his cup upright again, and lifted the jug—"sometimes, a man may open himself to them, and let them pour through him into the world." He filled his cup. "A saint is not a virtuous soul, but an empty one. He—or she—freely gives the gift of their will to their god. And in renouncing action, makes action possible." He lifted his cup to his lips, stared disquietingly at Cazaril over the rim, and drank. He added, "Your divine should not have used water. It just doesn't hold the attention properly. Wine. Or blood, in a pinch. Some liquid that matters."

"Um," managed Cazaril.

Umegat sat back and studied him for a time. Cazaril didn't think the Roknari was looking at his flesh. *So, tell me, what's a renegade Roknari Temple divine scholar-saint of the Bastard doing disguised as a groom in the Zangre's menagerie?* Out loud, he managed to pare this down to a plaintive, "What *are* you doing here?"

Umegat shrugged. "What the god wills." He took pity on Cazaril's exasperated look, and added, "What He wills, it seems, is to keep Roya Orico alive."

Cazaril sat up, fighting the slurry that the wine seemed to be making of his brains. "Orico, sick?"

"Yes. A state secret, mind you, although one that's grown obvious enough to anyone with wits and eyes. Nevertheless—" Umegat laid his finger to his lips in a command of discretion.

"Yes, but—I thought healing was the province of the Mother and the Daughter."

"Were the roya's illness of natural causes, yes."

"Unnatural causes?" Cazaril squinted. "The dark cloak—can you see it, too?"

"Yes."

"But Teidez has the shadow, too, and Iselle—and Royina Sara is tainted as well. What evil thing is it, that you would not let me speak of it in the street?"

Umegat put his cup down, tugged on his bronze-gray queue, and sighed. "It all goes back to Fonsa the Fairly-Wise and the Golden General. Which is, I suppose, history and tale to you. I lived through those desperate times." He added conversationally, "I saw the general once, you know. I was a spy in his princedom at the time. I hated everything he stood for, and yet . . . had he given me a word, a mere word, I think I might have crawled after him on my knees. He was more than just god-touched. He was avatar incarnate, striding toward the fulcrum of the world in the perfected instant of time. Almost. He was reaching for his moment when Fonsa and the Bastard cut him down." Umegat's cultured voice, lightly reminiscent, had dropped to remembered awe. He stared into the middle distance of his memory.

His gaze jumped out of the lost past and back to Cazaril. Remembering to smile, he held out his hand, thumb up, and waggled it gently from side to side. "The Bastard, though the weakest of His family, is the god of balance. The opposition that gives the hand its clever grip. It is said that if ever one god subsumes all the others, truth will become single, and simple, and perfect, and the world will end in a burst of light. Some tidy-minded men actually find this idea attractive. Personally, I find it a horror, but then I always did have low tastes. In the meantime, the Bastard, unfixed in any season, circles to preserve us all." Umegat's fingers tapped one by one, Daughter-Mother-Son-Father, against the ball of his thumb.

He went on, "The Golden General was a tidal wave of destiny, gathering to crash upon the world. Fonsa's soul could match his soul, but could not balance his vast fate. When the death demon carried their souls from the world, that fate overflowed to settle upon Fonsa's heirs, a miasma of ill luck and subtle bitterness. The black shadow you see is the Golden General's unfulfilled destiny, curdling around his enemies' lives. His death curse, if you will."

Cazaril wondered if this explained why all of Ias's and Orico's military campaigns that he'd ever been in had fared so ill. "How . . . how may the curse be lifted?"

Umegat sighed. "In six years, no answer has been given me. Perhaps it will run out in the deaths of all who flowed from Fonsa's loins."

But that's . . . the roya, Teidez—Iselle!

"Or perhaps," Umegat continued, "even then, it will continue to trickle down through time like a stream of poison. It should have killed Orico years ago. Contact with the sacred creatures cleanses the roya from the corrosion of the curse, but only for a little time. The menagerie delays his destruction, but the god has never told me why." Umegat's voice went glum. "The gods don't write letters of instruction, you know. Not even to their saints. I've suggested it, in my prayers. Sat by the hour with the ink drying on my quill, entirely at His service. And what does He send instead? An overexcited crow with a one-word vocabulary."

Cazaril winced in guilt, thinking of that poor crow. In truth, he felt far worse about the crow's death than Dondo's.

"So that's what I'm doing here," said Umegat. He glanced up keenly at Cazaril. "And so. What are *you* doing here?"

Cazaril spread his hands helplessly. "Umegat, I don't know." He added plaintively, "Can't you tell? You said . . . I was lit up. Do I look like you? Or like Iselle? Or Orico, even?"

"You look like nothing I've seen since I was lent the inner eye. If Iselle is a candle, you are a conflagration. You are . . . actually quite disturbing to contemplate."

"I don't feel like a conflagration."

"What do you feel like?"

"Right now? Like a pile of dung. Sick. Drunk." He swirled the red wine in the bottom of his cup. "I have this belly cramp that comes and goes." It was quiescent at the moment, but his stomach was still swollen. "And tired. I haven't felt this tired since I was sick in the Mother's house in Zagosur."

"I think," Umegat spoke carefully, "that it is very, very important that you tell me the truth."

His lips still smiled, but his gray eyes seemed to burn. It occurred to Cazaril then that a good Temple Inquirer *would* likely be charming, and adept at worming confidences from people in his investigations. Smooth at getting them drunk.

You laid down your life. It's not fair to whine for it back now.

"I attempted death magic upon Dondo dy Jironal last night."

Umegat looked neither shocked nor surprised, merely more intent. "Yes. Where?"

"In Fonsa's Tower. I crawled over the roof slates. I brought my own rat, but the crow . . . it came to me. It wasn't afraid. I'd fed it, you see."

"Go on . . ." breathed Umegat.

"I slew the rat, and broke the poor crow, and I prayed on my knees. And then I hurt. I wasn't expecting that. And I couldn't breathe. The candles went out. And I said, *Thank you*, because I felt . . ." He could not speak of what he'd felt, that strange peace, as if he'd lain down in a place of safety to rest forever. "And then I passed out. I thought I was dying."

"And then?"

"Then . . . nothing. I woke up in the dawn fog, sick and cold and feeling an utter fool. No, wait—I'd had a nightmare about Dondo choking to death. But I knew I'd failed. So I crawled back to bed. And then dy Jironal came bursting in . . ."

Umegat drummed his fingers on the table a moment, staring at him through slitted eyes. And then he stared with his eyes closed. Open again. "My lord, may I touch you?"

"All right . . ." Briefly, as the Roknari bent over him, Cazaril feared some unwelcome attempt at intimacy, but Umegat's touch was as professional as any physician's; forehead, face, neck, spine, heart, belly . . . Cazaril tensed, but Umegat's hand descended no farther. When he finished, Umegat's face was set. The Roknari went to fetch another jug of wine from a basket by the door before returning to his chair.

Cazaril attempted to fend the jug from his cup. "I've had enough. I'll be stumbling if I take any more."

"My grooms can walk you back to your chambers in a little while. No?" Umegat filled his own cup instead, and sat again. He ran his finger over the tabletop in a little pattern, repeated three times—Cazaril wasn't sure if it was a charm or just nerves—and finally said, "By the testimony of the sacred animals, no god accepted the soul of Dondo dy Jironal. Normally, that is a sign that an unquiet spirit is abroad in the world, and relatives and friends—and enemies—rush to buy rites and prayers from the Temple. Some for the sake of the dead—some for their own protection."

"I am sure," said Cazaril a little bitterly, "Dondo will have all the prayers that money can buy."

"I hope so."

"Why? What . . . ?" *What do you see? What do you know?*

Umegat glanced up, and inhaled. "Dondo's spirit was taken by the death demon, but not passed to the gods. This we know. It is my conjecture that the death demon could not return to its master because it was prevented from taking the second and balancing soul."

Cazaril licked his lips, and husked fearfully, "How, prevented?"

"At the instant of attempting to do so, I believe the demon was captured—constrained—bound, if you will—by a second and simultaneous miracle. Judging by the distinctive colors boiling off you, it was from the holy and gracious hand of the Lady of Spring. If I am right, the acolytes of the Temple can all go back to bed, for Dondo's spirit is not abroad. It is bound to the death demon, who is bound in turn to the locus of the second soul. Which is presently bound to its still-living body." Umegat's finger rose to point directly at Cazaril. "There."

Cazaril's jaw fell open. He stared down at his aching, swollen belly, and back up at the fascinated . . . saint. Briefly, he was put in mind of Fonsa's entranced crows. Violent denial boiled to his lips, and caught there, stopped by his inner sight of Umegat's clear aura. "I didn't pray to the Daughter last night!"

"Apparently, someone did."

Iselle. "The royesse said she prayed. Did you see her as I saw her today—" Cazaril made inarticulate motions with his hands, not knowing what words to use to describe that roiling perturbation. "Is that what you see in me? Does Iselle see me as I do her?"

"Did she say anything about it?" asked Umegat.

"No. But neither did I."

Umegat gave him that sidewise stare again. "Did you ever see, when you were in the Archipelago, the nights when the sea was Mother-touched? The way the wake glowed green in the breaking waves of a ship's passage?"

"Yes . . ."

"What you saw around Iselle was such a wake. The passage of the Daughter, like a lingering perfume in the air. What I see in you is not a passage but a Presence. A blessing. Far more intense. Your corona is slowly dying down—the sacred animals should be less enthralled by you in a day or two—but at the center there sits a tight blue core of sapphire, into which I cannot see. I think it is an encapsulation." He brought his cupped hands together like a man enclosing a live lizard.

Cazaril swallowed, and panted, "Are you saying the goddess has turned my belly into a perfect little annex of hell? One demon, one lost soul, sealed together like two snakes in a bottle?" His clawed hands went to his stomach, as if ready to rip his guts apart on the spot. "And you call it a *blessing*?"

Umegat's eyes remained serious, but his brows crimped in sympathy. "Well, what is a blessing but a curse from another point of view? If it's any consolation to you, I imagine Dondo dy Jironal is even less happy about this development than you are." He added after a thoughtful moment, "I can't imagine the demon is too pleased with it, either."

Cazaril nearly convulsed out of his chair. "Five gods! How do I rid myself of this—this—this—horror?"

Umegat held up a restraining hand. "I . . . suggest . . . that you not be in a great rush about that. The consequences could be tangled."

"How, tangled? How could anything be more tangled than *this* monstrosity?"

"Well"—Umegat leaned back and tented his hands together—"the most obvious way to break the, ah, blessing, would be by your death. With your soul freed from its material locus, the demon could fly away with you both."

A chill stole over Cazaril, as he remembered how his belly cramp had almost betrayed him to a fall when jumping the roof gap at dawn. He took refuge from his drunken terror in a dryness to match Umegat's. "Oh, wonderful. Have you any other cures to suggest, physician?"

Umegat's lips twitched, and he acknowledged the jibe with a brief wave of his fingers. "Likewise, should the miracle cease that you presently host—should the Lady's hand lift," Umegat mimed someone opening their hands as if to release a bird, "I think the demon would immediately attempt to complete its destiny. Not that it has a choice—the Bastard's demons have no free will. You can't argue with or persuade them. In fact, there's no use talking to one at all."

"So you're saying that I could die at any moment!"

"Yes. And this is different from your life yesterday in what way?" Umegat cocked his head in dry inquiry.

Cazaril snorted. It was cold comfort . . . but comfort still, in a backhanded sort of way. Umegat was a sensible saint, it seemed. Which was not what Cazaril would have expected . . . had he ever met a saint before? *How would I know? I walked right past this one.*

Umegat's voice took on a tinge of scholarly curiosity. "Actually, this could answer a question I've long had. Does the Bastard command a troop of death demons, or just one? If all death miracles in the world cease while the demon is bound in you, it would be compelling evidence for the singularity of that holy power."

A ghastly laugh pealed from Cazaril's lips. "My service to Quintarian theology! Gods—Umegat—what am I to do? There has never been any of this, this god-touched madness in *my* family. I'm not fit for this business. *I* am not a saint!"

Umegat opened his lips, but then closed them again. He finally said, "One grows more accustomed with use. The first time I hosted a miracle I wasn't too happy either, and I'm in the trade, so to speak. My personal recommendation to you, tonight, is to get pie-eyed drunk and go to sleep."

"So I can wake in the morning both demon-ridden *and* with a hangover?" Granted, he couldn't imagine getting to sleep under any other circumstances, apart from a blow to the head.

"Well, it worked for me, once. The hangover is a fair trade for being so immobilized one cannot do anything stupid for a little while." Umegat looked away for a moment. "The gods do not grant miracles for our purposes, but for theirs. If you are become their tool, it is for a greater reason, an urgent reason. But you are the tool. You are not the work. Expect to be valued accordingly."

While Cazaril was still trying, unsuccessfully, to unravel that, Umegat leaned forward and poured fresh wine into Cazaril's cup. Cazaril was beyond resistance.

It took two undergrooms, an hour or so later, to guide his slithering steps across the wet cobbles of the stable yard, past the gates, and up the stairs, where they poured his limp form into his bed. Cazaril wasn't sure just when he parted from his beleaguered consciousness, but never had he been more glad to do so.

14

Cazaril had to allow Umegat's wine this much merit—it did mean he spent the first few hours of the next morning wishing for death rather than dreading it. He knew his hangover was passing off when fear began to regain the upper hand.

He found oddly little regret in his heart for his own lost life. He'd seen more of the world than most men ever did, and he'd had his chances, though the gods knew he'd made little enough of them. Marshaling his thoughts, as he sheltered under his covers, he realized with some wonder that his greatest dismay was for the work he'd be forced to leave undone.

Fears he'd had no time for during the day he'd stalked Dondo now crowded into his mind. Who would guard his ladies, if he were to die now? How much time was going to be granted to him to try to find some better bastion for them? On whom could they be safely bestowed? Betriz might find protection as the wife, say, of a stout country lord like March dy Palliar. But Iselle? Her grandmother and mother were too weak and distant, Teidez too young, Orico, apparently, entirely the creature of his chancellor. There could be no security for Iselle until she was out of this cursed court altogether.

Another cramp riveted his attention again on the lethal little hell in his belly, and he peered worriedly down under the tent of his sheet at his knotted stomach. How much was this dying going to hurt? He had not passed so much blood this morning. He blinked around his chamber in the early-afternoon light. The odd hallucinations, pale blurred blobs at the corners of his vision that he had earlier blamed on last night's wine, were still present. Maybe they were another symptom?

A brisk knock sounded at his chamber door. Cazaril crawled from his warm refuge and, walking only a little bent over, went to unlock it. Umegat, bearing a stoppered ewer, bade him good afternoon, stepped within, and closed the door behind him. He was still faintly radiant: alas, yesterday hadn't been a bizarre bad dream after all.

"My word," the groom added, staring about in astonishment. He waved his hand. "Shoo! Shoo!"

The pale blurred blobs swirled about the chamber and fled into the walls.

"What *are* those things?" Cazaril asked, easing back into his bed. "Do you see them, too?"

"Ghosts. Here, drink this." Umegat poured from the ewer into the glazed cup from Cazaril's washbasin set, and handed it across. "It will settle your stomach and clear your head."

About to reject it with loathing, Cazaril discovered it to be not wine but some sort of cold herbed tea. He tasted it cautiously. Pleasantly bitter, its astringency made a most welcome sluicing in his sticky mouth. Umegat pulled a stool over to his bedside and settled cheerfully. Cazaril squeezed his eyes shut, and open again. "Ghosts?"

"I've never seen so many of the Zangre's ghosts collected in one place. They must be attracted to you just like the sacred animals."

"Can anyone else see them?"

"Anyone with the inner eye. That's three in Cardegoss, to my knowledge."

And two of them are here. "Have they been around all this time?"

"I glimpse them now and then. They're usually more elusive. You needn't be afraid of them. They are powerless and cannot hurt you. Old lost souls." In response to Cazaril's rather stunned stare, Umegat added, "When, as happens from time to time, no god takes up a sundered soul, it is left to wander the world, slowly losing its mindfulness of itself and fading into air. New ghosts first take the form they had in life, but in their despair and loneliness they cannot maintain it."

Cazaril wrapped his arms around his belly. "Oh." His mind tried to gallop in three directions at once. So what was the fate of those souls the gods did accept? And just what exactly was happening to the enraged spirit so miraculously and hideously lodged in him? And . . . the Dowager Royina Ista's words came back to him. *The Zangre is haunted, you know.* Not metaphor or madness after all, it appeared, but simple observation. How much else, then, of the eerie things she'd said might be not derangement, but plain truth—seen with altered eyes?

He glanced up to find Umegat regarding him thoughtfully. The Roknari inquired politely, "And how are you feeling today?"

"Better this afternoon than this morning." He added a little reluctantly, "Better than yesterday."

"Have you eaten?"

"Not yet. Later, perhaps." He rubbed a hand over his beard. "What's happening out there?"

Umegat sat back and shrugged. "Chancellor dy Jironal, finding no candidates in the city, has ridden out of Cardegoss in search of the corpse of his brother's murderer and any confederates left alive."

"I trust he will not seize some innocent in error."

"An experienced Inquirer from the Temple rides with him, which should suffice to prevent such mistakes."

Cazaril digested this. After a moment, Umegat added, "Also, a faction in the military order of the Daughter's house has sent couriers riding out to all its lord dedicats, calling them to a general council. They mean not to allow Roya Orico to foist another commander like Lord Dondo onto them."

"How should they defy him? Revolt?"

Umegat hastily waved away this treasonable suggestion. "Certainly not. Petition. Request."

"Mm. But I thought they protested last time, to no avail. Dy Jironal will not be wanting to let control of that order slip from his hands."

"The military order is backed by the whole of its house, this time."

"And, ah . . . what have you been doing today?"

"Praying for guidance."

"And did you get an answer?"

Umegat smiled ambiguously at him. "Perhaps."

Cazaril considered for a moment how best to phrase his next remark. "Interesting gossip you're privy to. I take it, then, that it would now be redundant for me to go down to the temple and confess to Archdivine Mendenal for Dondo's murder?"

Umegat's brows went up. "I suppose," he said after a moment, "that it should not surprise me that the Lady of Spring has chosen a sharp-edged tool."

"You are a divine, a trained Inquirer. I didn't imagine you could, or would, evade your oaths and disciplines. You immobilized me to give yourself time to report, and confer." Cazaril hesitated. "That I am not presently under arrest should tell me . . . something about that conference, but I'm not at all sure what."

Umegat studied his hands, spread on his knees. "As a divine, I defer to my superiors. As a saint, I answer to my god. Alone. If He trusts my judgment, so perforce must I. And so must my superiors." He looked up, and now his gaze was unsettlingly direct. "That the goddess has set your feet on some journey on her behalf— courier—is abundantly plain from Her hour-by-hour preservation of your life. The Temple is at . . . not your service, but Hers. I think I can promise you, none shall interfere with you."

Cazaril was stung into a wail. "But what am I supposed to be *doing?*"

Umegat's voice grew almost apologetic. "Speaking just from my own experience, I would surmise—your daily duties as they come to you."

"That's not very helpful."

"Yes. I know." Umegat's lips twitched in a dry humor. "So the gods humble the would-be wise, I think." He added after a moment, "Speaking of daily duties, I must return now to mine. Orico is unwell today. Feel free to visit the menagerie anytime you are so moved, my lord dy Cazaril."

"Wait—" Cazaril held out a hand as Umegat rose. "Can you tell me—does Orico know of the miracle of the menagerie? Does he understand—does he even know he is accursed? I'll swear Iselle knows naught of it, nor Teidez." *Royina Ista, on the other hand . . .* "Or does the roya just know he feels better for contact with his animals?"

Umegat gave a little nod. "Orico knows. His father Ias told him, on his deathbed. The Temple has made many secret trials to break this curse. The menagerie is the only one that has seemed to do any good."

"And what of the Dowager Royina Ista? Is she shadowed like Sara?"

Umegat tugged his queue and frowned thoughtfully. "I could better guess if I'd ever met her face-to-face. The dy Baocia family removed her from Cardegoss shortly before I was brought here."

"Does Chancellor dy Jironal know?"

The frown deepened. "If he does, it was not from my lips. I have often cautioned Orico not to discuss his miracle, but . . ."

"If Orico has kept something from dy Jironal, it would be a first."

Umegat shrugged acknowledgment, but added, "Given the early disasters in his reign, Orico believes that any action he dares take will redound to the detriment of Chalion. The chancellor is the tongs by which the roya attempts to handle all matters of state without spilling his bane thereupon."

"Some might wonder if dy Jironal is the answer to the curse, or part of it."

"The proxy seemed to work at first."

"And lately?"

"Lately—we've redoubled our petitions to the gods for aid."

"And how have the gods answered?"

"It would seem—by sending you."

Cazaril sat up in renewed terror, clutching his bedclothes. "No one sent me! I came by chance."

"I'd like an accounting of those chances, someday soon. When you will, my lord." Umegat, with a deeply hopeful gaze that frightened Cazaril quite as much as any of his saintly remarks, bowed himself out.

❧AFTER A FEW MORE HOURS SPENT COWERING UNDER his quilts, Cazaril decided that unless a man could dither himself to death, he wasn't going to die this afternoon. Or if he was, there was nothing he could do about it. And his stomach was growling in a decidedly unsupernatural fashion. As the chill autumn light faded he crept out of bed, stretched his aching muscles, dressed himself, and went down to dinner.

The Zangre was extremely subdued. With the court plunged into deep mourning, no fêtes or music were offered tonight. Cazaril found the banqueting hall thin of company; neither Iselle's household nor Teidez's were present, Royina Sara absented herself, and Roya Orico, his dark shadow clinging about him, ate hastily and departed immediately thereafter.

The reason for Teidez's absence, Cazaril soon learned, was that Chancellor dy Jironal had taken the royse with him when he rode out on his mission of investigation. Cazaril blinked and fell silent at this news. Surely dy Jironal could not be attempting to continue the seduction by corruption his brother had taken so well in hand? Downright austere by comparison to Dondo, he had not the taste or style for such puerile pleasures. It was impossible to imagine him roistering with a juvenile. Was it too much to hope he might be reversing his strategy for ascendancy over Teidez's mind, taking the boy up after a true fatherly manner, apprenticing him to state-craft? The young royse was half-sick with idleness as well as disso-lution; almost any exposure to men's work must be medicine for him. More probably, Cazaril thought wearily, the chancellor sim-ply dared not let his future handle upon Chalion out of his grip for an instant.

Lord dy Rinal, seated across from Cazaril, twisted his lips at the half-empty hall and remarked, "Everyone's deserting. Off to their country estates, if they have 'em, before the snow flies. It's going to be a gloomy Father's Day celebration, I warrant. Only the tailors and seamstresses are busy, furbishing up mourning garb."

Cazaril reached through the ghost-smudge that was hovering next to his plate and washed down the last bite of his repast with a gulp of well-watered wine. Four or five of the revenants had trailed after him to the hall and now clustered about him like cold children crowding a hearth. He had chosen somber clothing him-self tonight, automatically; he wondered if he should trouble him-self to obtain the full correct lavenders and blacks such as dy Rinal, always fashionable, now sported. Would the abomination locked in his belly take it as hypocrisy, or as a gesture of respect? Would it even know? New-riven from its body, how much of its repulsive nature did Dondo's soul now retain? These weathered old spirits seemed to watch him from the outside; was Dondo watching him from the inside? He grinned briefly, as an alternative to startling poor dy Rinal with a fit of screaming. He managed a politely inquiring, "Do you stay or go?"

"I go, I think. I'll ride down with Marchess dy Heron as far as Heron itself, and then cut over the lower passes to home. The old lady might be glad enough of another sword in her party that she'd even invite me to stay." He took a swallow of wine and lowered his voice. "If not even the Bastard would take Lord Dondo off our hands, you realize he must still be about somewhere. One trusts he'll just haunt Jironal's palace where he died, but really, he could be anywhere in Cardegoss. And he was vicious enough before he was murdered; he's bound to be vengeful now. Slain the night before his wedding, gods!"

Cazaril made a neutral noise.

"The chancellor seems set on calling it death magic, but I shouldn't wonder if it was poison after all. No way of telling, now the body's burned, I suppose. Convenient for somebody, that."

"But he was surrounded by his friends. Surely no one could have administered—were you there?"

Dy Rinal grimaced. "After Lady Pig? No. Thanks be to all her squeals, I was not present at that butchering." Dy Rinal glanced around, as if afraid a ghost with a grudge might be sneaking up on him even now. That there were half a dozen within his arm's reach was evidently not apparent to him. Cazaril brushed one away from his face, trying not to let his eyes focus on what, to his companion, must seem empty air.

Ser dy Maroc, the roya's wardrobe-master, strolled up to their table saying, "Dy Rinal! Have you heard the news from Ibra?" Belatedly, he observed Cazaril leaning with elbows on the board opposite and hesitated, flushing slightly.

Cazaril smiled sourly. "One trusts you're getting your gossip from Ibra from more reliable sources these days, Maroc?"

Dy Maroc stiffened. "If the Chancellery's own courier be one, yes. He came in pell-mell while my head tailor was refitting Orico's mourning garb, that he had to let out by four fingerbreadths—anyway, it's official. The Heir of Ibra died last week, all suddenly, of the coughing fever in South Ibra. His faction has collapsed, and rushes to make treaty with the old Fox, or save their lives by sacrificing each other. The war in South Ibra is ended."

"Well!" Dy Rinal sat up and stroked his beard. "Do we call that good news, or bad? Good for poor Ibra, the gods know. But our Orico has chosen the losing side *again*."

Dy Maroc nodded. "The Fox is rumored to be most wroth with Chalion, for stirring the pot and keeping it boiling, not that the Heir needed help putting wood on that fire."

"Perhaps the old roya's taste for strife shall be buried with his firstborn," said Cazaril, not too hopefully.

"So the Fox has a new Heir, that child of his age—what was the boy's name?" said dy Rinal.

"Royse Bergon," Cazaril supplied.

"Aye," said dy Maroc. "A young one indeed. And the Fox could drop at any moment, leaving an untried boy on the throne."

"Not so untried as all that," said Cazaril. "He's seen the prosecution of one siege and the breaking of another, riding in his late mother's train, and survived a civil war. And one would think a son of the Fox could not be stupid."

"The first one was," said dy Rinal, unassailably. "To leave his supporters in such naked disarray."

"One cannot blame death of the coughing fever on a lack of wit," said Cazaril.

"Assuming it really was the coughing fever," said dy Rinal, pursing his lips in new suspicion.

"What, d'you think the Fox would poison his own son?" said dy Maroc.

"His agents, man."

"Well, then, he might have done it sooner, and saved Ibra a world of woe—"

Cazaril smiled thinly, and pushed up from the table, leaving dy Rinal and dy Maroc to their tale-spinning. His wine-sickness was past, and he felt better for his dinner, but the shaky exhaustion that remained was not anything he was accustomed to calling *well*. In the absence of any summons from the royesse, he made his way back to his bed.

Wearied beyond fear, he fell asleep soon enough. But around midnight, he was brought awake with a gasp. A man's screams echoed distantly in his head. Screams, and broken weeping, and choked howls of rage—he bolted upright, heart pounding, turning his head to locate the sound. Faint and strange—might it be coming from across the ravine from the Zangre, or down by the river below his window? No one from the castle seemed to respond, no footsteps, or cries of inquiry from the guards . . . In another few moments, Cazaril realized he was not hearing the tormented howls with his ears, any more than he saw the pale smudges floating around his bed with his eyes. And he recognized the voice.

He lay back down, panting and curled around himself, and endured the uproar for another ten minutes. Was the damned soul of Dondo preparing to break free of the Lady's miracle and haul him off to hell? He was about to leave his bed and run to the menagerie, all in his nightdress, pound on the doors and wake up Umegat and beg the saint for help—could Umegat do anything about this?—when the cries faded again.

It was about the hour of Dondo's death, he realized. Perhaps the spirit took up some special powers at this time? He couldn't tell if it had or had not done so last night, he'd been so sodden drunk. One uneasy nightmare had blended in mad fragments with all the others.

It might have been worse, he told himself as his heart gradually slowed again. Dondo might have been given an articulate voice. The thought of Dondo's ghost made nightly free to speak to him, whether in rage or abuse or vile suggestion, broke his courage as the plain howls had not, and he wept for a little in the sheer terror of the imagining.

Trust the Lady. Trust the Lady. He whispered some incoherent prayers, and slowly regained control of himself. If She had brought him this far for some purpose, surely She would not abandon him now.

A new horrible thought occurred to him, as he told Umegat's sermon over in his mind. If the goddess only entered the world by Cazaril renouncing his will on Her behalf, could wanting desperately to live, an act of will if ever there was one, be enough to exclude Her, and Her miracle? Her protective encapsulation might pop like a soap bubble, releasing a paradox of death and damnation . . . Following this logic loop around and around was enough to keep him awake for hours, as the night slowly wore itself out.

The square of his chamber's window was growing faintly gray before he dropped again into blessed unconsciousness.

❧SO IT WAS THAT, FLANKED BY HIS GHOSTLY OUTRIDERS, he climbed the stairs late the following morning to his office antechamber. He felt stupid and eroded from lack of sleep, and he looked forward without enthusiasm to a week's worth of neglected correspondence and bookkeeping, dropped in disordered piles on his desk from the hour of Iselle's disastrous betrothal.

He found his ladies up betimes. In the sitting room just past the frontier of his office, all his good new schoolroom maps were spread out on a table. Iselle leaned on her hands, staring down at them. Betriz, her arms folded under her breasts, stood watching over her shoulder and frowning. Both young women, and Nan dy Vrit, who sat sewing, wore the blacks and lavenders of strict formal court mourning, a prudent dissimulation of which Cazaril approved.

As he entered, he saw next to Iselle's hand a scattering of paper scraps with scribbled lists, some items scratched through, some circled or ticked with checks. Iselle scowled and pointed to a spot on the map marked with a sturdy hat pin, and said over her shoulder to her handmaiden, "But that's no better than—" She broke off when she saw Cazaril. The dark, invisible cloak still clung about her; only an occasional faint thread of blue light still glinted in its sluggish folds. The ghost-blobs veered violently away from it and, only partly to Cazaril's relief, vanished from his second sight.

"Are you all right, Lord Caz?" Iselle inquired, looking at him with her brows drawing down. "You don't look well."

Cazaril bowed greeting. "My apologies for absenting myself yesterday, Royesse. I was taken with a . . . a colic. It has mostly passed off now."

Nan dy Vrit, from her seat in the corner, looked up from her sewing with an unfriendly stare to remark, "The chamber woman had it that you were taken with a bad head from drinking and carousing with the stable grooms. She said she saw you come in so drunk after Lord Dondo's funeral you could barely stagger."

Conscious of Betriz's unhappy scrutiny, he said apologetically,

"Drinking yes; carousing, no. It won't happen again, milady." He added a little dryly, "It didn't answer anyway."

"It's a scandal to the royesse, that her secretary be seen so inebriated that he—"

"Hush, Nan," Iselle interrupted this lecture impatiently. "Leave be."

"What's this, Royesse?" Cazaril gestured at the pin-studded map.

Iselle drew a long breath. "I've thought it through. I've been thinking for days. As long as I remain unwed, plots will swirl about me. I don't doubt dy Jironal will produce some other candidate to try to bind me and Teidez to his clan. And other factions—now it's revealed that Orico would willingly bestow me on a lesser lord, every lesser lord in Chalion will begin badgering him for my hand. My only defense, my only certain refuge, is if I am married already. And *not* to a lesser lord."

Cazaril's brows rose. "I confess, Royesse, my own thoughts have been running something along those lines."

"And swiftly, swiftly, Cazaril. Before they can come up with someone even *more* disgusting than Dondo." Her voice was edged with stress.

"Even our dear chancellor must find *that* a daunting challenge," he murmured diffidently, and had the satisfaction of drawing a brief bark of laughter from her. He pursed his lips. "The need is great, I grant you, but the danger is not so instantly pressing as all that. Dy Jironal himself will block the lesser lords for you, I am sure. Your first line of defense must be to block dy Jironal's next candidate. Although, thinking over his family, it's not clear to me who he can offer up. His sons are both married, or he might have put forth one of them in place of Dondo. Or offered himself, were he not wed."

"Wives die," said Betriz darkly. "Sometimes, they even die conveniently."

Cazaril shook his head. "Dy Jironal has planned his family alliances with care. His daughters-in-law—his wife, too—are his links to some of the greatest families in Chalion, the daughters and sisters of powerful provincars. I don't say he wouldn't seize a vacancy, but he dare not be seen or even suspected of creating one. And his grandsons are toddlers. No, dy Jironal must play a waiting game."

"What about his nephews?" said Betriz.

Cazaril, after a pause for thought, shook his head again. "Too loose a connection, not controlled enough. He desires a subordinate, not a rival."

"I decline," said Iselle through her teeth, "to wait a decade to be wed to a boy fifteen years younger than I am."

Cazaril glanced involuntarily at Lady Betriz. He himself was fifteen years older than—he thrust the discouraging thought from his mind. The evil barrier between them now was less surmountable than merely that of youth versus age. *Life does not wed death.*

"We've placed a pin in the map for every unwed ruler or heir we can think of between here and Darthaca," said Betriz.

Cazaril advanced and looked over the map. "What, even the Roknari princedoms?"

"I wanted to be complete," said Iselle. "Without them, well . . . there weren't very many choices. I admit, I don't much like the idea of a Roknari prince. Leaving aside their horrid squared-off religion, their custom of choosing as heir any son at all, whether of true wife or concubine, makes it nearly impossible to tell if one is wedding a future ruler or a future drone."

"Or a future corpse," said Cazaril. "Half the victories Chalion ever gained over the Roknari were the result of some embittered failed candidate stabbing his princely half brother in the back."

"But that leaves only four true Quintarians of rank," put in Betriz. "The roya of Brajar, Bergon of Ibra, and the twin sons of the high march of Yiss just across the Darthacan border. Who are twelve years old."

"Not impossible," said Iselle judiciously, "but March dy Yiss would have no natural reason to ally with Teidez, later, against the Roknari. He shares no borders with the princedoms and does not suffer from their depredations. And he pays fealty to Darthaca, who has no interest in seeing a strong, united alliance of Ibran states arise to put an end to the perpetual war in the north."

Cazaril was pleased to hear his own analysis coming back to him in the royesse's mouth; she'd paid more attention during her geography lessons than he'd thought. He smiled encouragingly.

"And besides," Iselle added crossly, "Yiss has no coastline either." Her hand drifted unhappily across the map to the east. "My cousin the roya of Brajar is quite old, and they say is grown too sodden with drink to ride to war. And his grandson is too young."

"Brajar does have good ports," said Betriz. She added more dubiously, although in the tone of one pointing out an advantage, "I suppose he wouldn't live very long."

"Yes, but what help could I be to Teidez as a mere dowager royina? It's not as though I might tell a, a stepgrandson how to deploy his troops!" Iselle's hand trailed back to the opposite coast. "And the Fox of Ibra's eldest son is married, and his younger not the heir, and the country is convulsed with civil strife."

"Not anymore," said Cazaril abruptly. "Did no one tell you the news that came yesterday from Ibra? The Heir is dead. Struck down in South Ibra—the coughing fever. No one doubts that young Royse Bergon will take his place. He's been loyal to his father throughout the whole mess."

Iselle turned her head and stared at him, her eyes widening. "Really . . . ! How old is Bergon, again? Fifteen, was he not?"

"He must be rising sixteen now, Royesse."

"Better than fifty-seven!" Her fingers walked lightly up the coast of Ibra along the string of maritime cities to the great port of Zagosur, where they stopped, resting upon a certain pin with a carved mother-of-pearl head. "What do you know of Royse Bergon, Cazaril? Is he well-favored? Did you ever see him when you were in Ibra?"

"Not with my own eyes. They say he's a handsome boy."

Iselle shrugged impatiently. "All royses are always described as handsome, unless they're absolutely grotesque. Then it's said they have *character*."

"I believe Bergon to be reasonably athletic, which argues for at least a pleasantly healthy appearance. They say he has been trained at seamanship." Cazaril saw the glow of youthful enthusiasm starting in her eyes, and felt constrained to add, "But your brother Orico has been at this half war with the roya of Ibra for the past seven years. The Fox has no love for Chalion."

Iselle pressed her hands together. "But what better way to end a war than with a marriage treaty?"

"Chancellor dy Jironal is bound to oppose it. Quite aside from wanting you for his own family connection, he wants Teidez to have no ally, now or in the future, stronger than himself."

"By that reasoning, he must oppose any good match I can suggest." Iselle leaned over the map again, her hand sweeping in a long arc encompassing Chalion and Ibra both—two-thirds of the lands between the seas. "But if I could bring Teidez and Bergon together . . ." Her palm pressed flat and slowly slid along the north coast across the five Roknari princedoms; pins popped from the paper and scattered. "Yes," she breathed. Her eyes narrowed, and her jaw tightened. When she again looked up at Cazaril, her eyes were blazing. "I shall put it to my brother Orico at once, before dy Jironal returns. If I can get his word on it, publicly declared, surely even dy Jironal cannot make him take it back?"

"Think it through first, Royesse. Think of all the issues. One drawback is surely the ghastly father-in-law." Cazaril's brow wrinkled. "Though I suppose time will remove him. And if anyone is capable of overcoming his emotions in favor of policy, it's the old Fox."

She turned from the table to pace hastily back and forth across the chamber, heavy skirts swishing. Her dark aura clung about her.

Royina Sara shared the vilest dregs of Orico's curse; she must presumably have entered into it upon her marriage to the roya. If Iselle married out of Chalion, would she shed her curse reciprocally, leaving it behind? Was this a way for her to escape the geas? His rising excitement was cut by caution. Or would the Golden General's old dark destiny follow her across the borders to her new country? He must consult with Umegat, and soon.

Iselle stopped and stared out the window embrasure where she had sat to endure Dondo's hideous wooing. Her eyes narrowed. At last she said decisively, "I must try. I cannot, will not, leave my fate to drift downstream to another disastrous falls and make no push to steer it. I will petition my royal brother, and at once."

She wheeled for the door and beckoned sharply, like a general urging on his troops. "Betriz, Cazaril, attend upon me!"

15

After some time casting about
the Zangre they ran Orico to earth, to
Cazaril's surprise, in Royina Sara's
chambers on the top floor of Ias's Tower. The roya and royina were
seated at a small table by a window, playing at blocks-and-dodges
together. The simple game, with its carved board and colored mar-
bles, seemed a pastime for children or convalescents, not for the
greatest lord and lady in the land . . . not that Orico could be mistaken for a well man by any experienced eye. The royal couple's
eerie shadows seemed merely a redundant underscore to their
weary sadness. They played not for idleness, Cazaril realized, but
for distraction, diversion from the fear and woe that hedged them
all around.

Cazaril was taken aback by Sara's garb. Instead of the black-
and-lavender court mourning that Orico wore, she was dressed all
in white, the festival garb of the Bastard's Day, that intercalary hol-
iday inserted every two years after Mother's Midsummer to prevent the calendar's precessing from its proper seasons. The
bleached linens were far too light for this weather, and she huddled
into a large puffy white wool shawl to combat the chill. She looked
dark and thin and sallow in the pale wrappings. Withal, it was an
even more edged insult than the colorful gowns and robes she'd
hastily donned for Dondo's funeral. Cazaril wondered if she meant
to wear the Bastard's whites for the whole period of mourning.
And if dy Jironal would dare protest.

Iselle curtseyed to her royal brother and sister-in-law, and stood before Orico with eyes bright, hands clasped before her in an attitude of demure femininity belied by the steel in her spine. Cazaril and Lady Betriz, flanking her, also made their courtesies. Orico, turning from the game table, acknowledged his sister's greeting. He adjusted his paunch in his lap and eyed her uneasily. On closer view, Cazaril could see where his tailor had added a matched panel of lavender brocade beneath the arms to enlarge his tunic's girth, and the slight discoloration where the sleeve seams had been picked out and resewn. Royina Sara gathered her shawl and withdrew a little into the window seat.

With the barest preamble, Iselle launched into her plea for the roya to open formal negotiations with Ibra for the hand of the Royse Bergon. She emphasized the opportunity to make a bid for peace, thus repairing the breach created by Orico's ill-fated support of the late Heir, for surely neither Chalion nor exhausted Ibra were prepared to continue the conflict now. She pointed out how appropriate a match in age and rank Bergon was for her own years and station, and the advantage to Orico—she diplomatically did not add *and then Teidez*—in future years to have a relative and ally in Ibra's court. She painted a vivid word-picture of the harassment from lesser lords of Chalion vying for her hand that Orico might neatly sidestep by this ploy, a bit of eloquence that caused the roya to vent a wistful sigh.

Nonetheless, Orico began his expected equivocation by seizing on this last point. "But Iselle, your mourning protects you for a time. Not even Martou—I mean, Martou won't insult the memory of his brother by marrying off Dondo's bereaved fiancée over his hot ashes."

Iselle snorted at the *bereaved*. "Dondo's ashes will chill soon enough, and what then? Orico, you will never again force me to a husband without my assent—my *prior* assent, obtained beforehand. I won't let you."

"No, no," Orico agreed hastily, waving his hands. "That . . . that was a mistake, I see it now. I'm sorry."

Now, there's an understatement . . .

"I did not mean to insult you, dear sister, or, or the gods." Orico glanced around a little vaguely, as though afraid an offended god might pounce upon him out of some astral ambuscade at any moment. "I meant well, for you and for Chalion."

Belatedly, it dawned upon Cazaril that while no one at court but himself and Umegat knew just whose prayers had hurried Dondo . . . well, not out of the world, but out of his life—all knew that the royesse had been praying for rescue. None, Cazaril thought, suspected or accused her of working death magic—of course, neither did they suspect or accuse him—nevertheless, Iselle was here, and Dondo was gone. Every thinking courtier must be unnerved by Dondo's mysterious death, and some more than a little.

"No marriage shall be offered to you in future without your prior accordance," said Orico, with uncharacteristic firmness. "That, I promise you upon my own head and crown."

It was a solemn oath; Cazaril's brows rose. Orico meant it, apparently. Iselle pursed her lips, then accepted this with a slight, wary nod.

A faint dry breath, puffed through feminine nostrils—Cazaril's eyes went to Royina Sara. Her face was shadowed by the window embrasure, but her mouth twisted briefly in some small irony at her husband's words. Cazaril considered what solemn promises Orico had broken to her, and looked away, discomfited.

"By the same token," Orico skipped to his next evasion like a man crossing stepping-stones on a steam, "our mourning makes it too soon to offer you to Ibra. The Fox may construe an insult in this haste."

Iselle made a gesture of impatience. "But if we wait, Bergon is likely to be snatched up! The royse is now the Heir, he's of marriageable age, and his father wants safety on his borders. The Fox is bound to barter him for an ally—a daughter of the high march of Yiss, perhaps, or a rich Darthacan noblewoman, and Chalion will have lost its chance!"

"It's too soon. Too soon. I don't disagree that your arguments are good, and may have their day. Indeed, the Fox made diplomatic inquiries for your hand some years ago, I forget for which son, but all was broken off when the troubles in South Ibra erupted. Nothing is fixed. Why, my poor Brajaran mother was betrothed five different times before she was finally wed to Roya Ias. Take patience, calm yourself, and await a more seemly time."

"I think now is an excellent time. I want to see you make a decision, announce it, and stand by it—before Chancellor dy Jironal returns."

"Ah, um, yes. And that's another thing. I cannot possibly take a step of this grave nature without consultation with my chief noble and the other lords in council." Orico nodded to himself.

"You didn't consult the other lords the last time. *I* think you're most strangely afraid to do anything dy Jironal doesn't approve. Who is roya in Cardegoss, anyway, Orico dy Chalion or Martou dy Jironal?"

"I—I—I will think on your words, dear sister." Orico made craven little waving-away motions with his fat hands.

Iselle, after a moment spent staring at him with a burning intensity that made him writhe, accepted this with a small, provisional nod. "Yes, do think on my petition, my lord. I'll ask you again tomorrow."

With this promise—or threat—she made courtesy again to Orico and Sara and withdrew, Betriz and Cazaril trailing.

"Tomorrow and every day thereafter?" Cazaril inquired in an undervoice as she sailed down the corridor in a savage rustling of skirts.

"Every day till Orico yields," she replied through set teeth. "Plan on it, Cazaril."

❧WINTRY YELLOW LIGHT SLANTED THROUGH GRAY clouds later that afternoon as Cazaril made his way out of the Zangre to the stable block. He pulled his fine embroidered wool coat around him and drew in his neck like a turtle against the damp, cold wind. When he opened his mouth and exhaled, he could make his breath mist in a little cloud before him. He blew a few puffs at the ghosts that, pale almost to invisibility in the sunlight, bobbed perpetually after him. A damp frost rimed the cobbles beneath his feet. He pushed the menagerie's heavy door aside just enough to nip within and pulled it shut again immediately thereafter. He stood a moment, letting his eyes adjust to the darker interior, and sneezed from the sweet dust of the hay.

The thumbless groom set down a pail, hurried up to him, bowed, and made welcoming noises.

"I have come to see Umegat," Cazaril told him. The little old man bowed again and beckoned him onward. He led Cazaril down the aisle. The beautiful animals all lurched to the front of their stalls to snort at him, and the sand foxes jumped up and yipped excitedly as he passed.

A stone-walled chamber at the far end proved to be a tack room converted to a work and leisure room for the menagerie's servants. A small fire burned cheerfully in a fieldstone fireplace, taking the chill off. The faint, pleasant scent of woodsmoke combined with that of leather, metal polish, and soaps. The wool-stuffed cushions on the chairs to which the groom gestured him were faded and worn, and the old worktable was stained and scarred. But the room was swept, and the glazed windows, one on either side of the fireplace, had the little round panes set in their leads polished clean. The groom made noises and shuffled out again.

In a few minutes, Umegat entered, wiping his hands dry on a cloth and straightening his tabard. "Welcome, my lord," he said softly. Cazaril felt suddenly uncertain of his etiquette, whether to stand as for a superior or sit as for a servant. There was no court Roknari grammatical mode for secretary to saint. He sat up and half bowed from the waist, awkwardly, by way of compromise. "Umegat."

Umegat closed the door, assuring privacy. Cazaril leaned forward, clasping his hands upon the tabletop, and spoke with the urgency of patient to physician. "You see the ghosts of the Zangre. Do you ever hear them?"

"Not normally. Have you?" Umegat pulled out a chair and seated himself at right angles to Cazaril.

"Not these—" He batted away the most persistent one, which had followed him inside. Umegat pursed his lips and flipped his cloth at it, and it flitted off. "Dondo's." Cazaril described last night's internal uproar. "I thought he was trying to break out. Can he succeed? If the goddess's grip fails?"

"I am certain no ghost can overpower a god," said Umegat.

"That's . . . not quite an answer." Cazaril brooded. Perhaps Dondo and the demon meant to kill him from sheer exhaustion. "Can you at least suggest a way to shut him up? Putting my head under the pillow was no help at all."

"There is a kind of symmetry to it," observed Umegat slowly. "Outer ghosts that you may see but not hear, inner ghosts that you may hear but not see . . . if the Bastard has a hand in it, it may have something to do with maintaining balance. In any case, I am sure your preservation was no accident and would not be accidentally withdrawn."

Cazaril absorbed this for a moment. Daily duties, eh. Today's had brought some curious turns. He spoke now as comrade to comrade. "Umegat, listen, I've had an idea. We know the curse has followed the House of Chalion's male line, Fonsa to Ias to Orico. Yet Royina Sara wears nearly as dark a shadow as Orico does, and she is no spawn of Fonsa's loins. She must have married into the curse, yes?"

The fine lines of Umegat's face deepened with his frown. "Sara already bore the shadow when I first came, years ago, but I suppose . . . yes, it must have been so."

"Ista likewise, presumably?"

"Presumably."

"So—could Iselle marry *out* of the curse? Shed it with her marriage vows, when she leaves her family of birth behind and enters into the family of her husband? Or would the curse follow her to taint them both?"

Umegat's brows went up. "I don't know."

"But you don't know that it's impossible? I was thinking that it might be a way to salvage . . . something."

Umegat sat back. "Possibly. I don't know. It was never a ploy to consider, for Orico."

"I need to know, Umegat. Royesse Iselle is pushing Orico to open negotiations for her marriage out of Chalion."

"Chancellor dy Jironal will surely not allow *that.*"

"I would not underestimate her powers of persuasion. She is not another Sara."

"Neither was Sara, once. But you are right. Oh, my poor Orico, to be pressed between two such grinding stones."

Cazaril bit his lip, and paused a long time before venturing his next query. "Umegat . . . you've been observing this court for many years. Was dy Jironal always so poisonous a peculator, or has the curse slowly been corrupting him, too? Did the curse draw such a man to his position of power, or would any man trying to serve the House of Chalion become so corroded, in time?"

"You ask very interesting questions, Lord Cazaril." Umegat's graying brows drew down in thought. "I wish I had better answers. Martou dy Jironal was always forcible, intelligent, able. We shall leave aside consideration of his younger brother, who made his reputation as a strong arm in the field, not a strong head in the court. When he first took up the post of chancellor I would have judged the elder dy Jironal no more susceptible to the temptations of pride and greed than any other high lord of Chalion with a clan to provide for."

Faint enough praise, that. And yet . . .

"Yet I think . . ." Umegat seemed to continue Cazaril's very thought, his eyes rising to meet his guest's, "the curse has done him no good either."

"So . . . getting rid of dy Jironal is not the solution to Orico's woes? Another such man, perhaps worse, would simply rise in his place?"

Umegat opened his hands. "The curse takes a hundred forms, twisting each good thing that should be Orico's according to the weaknesses of its nature. A wife grown barren instead of fertile. A chief advisor corrupt instead of loyal. Friends fickle instead of true, food that sickens instead of strengthening, and on and on."

A secretary-tutor grown cowardly and foolish instead of brave and wise? Or maybe just fey and mad . . . If any man who came within the curse's ambit was vulnerable, was he destined to become Iselle's plague, as dy Jironal was Orico's? "And Teidez, and Iselle— must all her choices fall out as ill as Orico's, or does he bear a special burden, being the roya?"

"I think the curse has grown worse for Orico over time." The Roknari's gray eyes narrowed. "You have asked me a dozen questions, Lord Cazaril. Allow me to ask you one. How came you into the service of Royesse Iselle?"

Cazaril opened his mouth and sat back, his mind jumping first to the day the Provincara had ambushed him with her offer of employment. But no, before that came . . . and before that came . . . He found himself instead telling Umegat of the day a soldier of the Daughter astride a nervy horse had dropped a gold coin in the mud, and how he had arrived in Valenda. Umegat brewed tea at the little fire and pushed a steaming mug in front of Cazaril, who paused only to lubricate his drying throat. Cazaril described how

Iselle had discomfited the crooked judge on the Daughter's Day, and, at length, how they had all come to Cardegoss.

Umegat pulled on his queue. "Do you think your steps were fated from that far back? Disturbing. But the gods are parsimonious, and take their chances where they can find them."

"If the gods are making this path for me, then where is my free will? No, it cannot be!"

"Ah." Umegat brightened at this thorny theological point. "I have had another thought on such fates, that denies neither gods nor men. Perhaps, instead of controlling every step, the gods have started a hundred or a thousand Cazarils and Umegats down this road. And only those arrive who choose to."

"But am I the first to arrive, or the last?"

"Well," said Umegat dryly, "I can promise you you're not the first."

Cazaril grunted understanding. After a little time spent digesting this, he said suddenly, "But if the gods have given you to Orico, and me to Iselle—though I think Someone has made a holy mistake—who is given for the protection of Teidez? Shouldn't there be three of us? A man of the Brother, surely, though whether tool or saint or fool I know not—or have all the boy's hundred destined protectors fallen by the roadside, one by one? Maybe the man is just not here yet." A new thought robbed Cazaril of breath. "Maybe it was supposed to have been dy Sanda." He leaned forward, burying his face in his hands. "If I stay here talking theology with you much longer, I swear I'll end up drinking myself blind again, just to make my brain stop spinning round and round inside my skull."

"Addiction to drink is actually a fairly common hazard, among divines," said Umegat.

"I begin to see why." Cazaril tilted back his head to catch the last trickle of tea, grown cold in his cup, and set it down. "Umegat . . . if I must ask of every action not only if it is wise or good, but also if it's the one I'm supposed to choose, I shall go mad. Madder. I'll end up curled in a corner not doing anything at all, except maybe mumbling and weeping."

Umegat chuckled—cruelly, Cazaril thought—but then shook his head. "You cannot outguess the gods. Hold to virtue—if you can identify it—and trust that the duty set before you is the duty desired of you. And that the talents given to you are the talents you should place in the gods' service. Believe that the gods ask for nothing back that they have not first lent to you. Not even your life."

Cazaril rubbed his face, and inhaled. "Then I shall bend all my efforts to promoting this marriage of Iselle's, to break the hold of the curse upon her. I must trust my reason, or why else did the goddess choose a reasonable man for Iselle's guardian?" Though he added under his breath, "At least, I used to be a reasonable man . . ." He nodded, far more firmly than he felt, and pushed back his chair. "Pray for me, Umegat."

"Every hour, my lord."

❧IT WAS GROWING DARK WHEN LADY BETRIZ BROUGHT a taper into Cazaril's office and drifted about for a moment lighting his reading candles in their glass vases. He smiled and nodded thanks. She smiled back and blew out her taper, but then paused, not yet returning to the women's chambers. She stood, Cazaril observed, in the same spot where they had parted the night of Dondo's death.

"Things seem to be settling down a little now, thank the gods," she remarked.

"Yes. A little." Cazaril laid down his quill.

"I begin to believe all will be well."

"Yes." His stomach cramped. *No.*

A long pause. He picked up his quill again, and dipped it, although he had nothing more to write.

"Cazaril, must you believe you are about to die in order to bring yourself to kiss a lady?" she demanded abruptly.

He ducked his head, flushing, and cleared his throat. "My deepest apologies, Lady Betriz. It won't happen again."

He dared not look up, lest she try anew to break through his fragile barriers. Lest she succeed. *Oh, Betriz, do not sacrifice your dignity to my futility!*

Her voice grew stiff. "I'm very sorry to hear that, Castillar."

He kept his eyes on his ledger as her footsteps retreated.

*   *   *

🐟SEVERAL DAYS PASSED, AS ISELLE CONTINUED HER campaign upon Orico. Several nights passed, made ghastly for Cazaril by the howls of Dondo's soul in its private torment. This intestinal visitation did indeed prove to be nightly, a quarter of an hour reprising the terror of that death. Cazaril could not fall to sleep before the midnight interlude, in sick apprehension, nor for long after it, in shaken resonance, and his face grew gray with fatigue. The blurry old phantasms began to seem pleasant pets by comparison. There was no way he could drink enough wine, nightly, to sleep through it, so he set himself to endure.

Orico endured his sister's visitations with less fortitude. He took to avoiding her in increasingly bizarre ways, but she broke in upon him anyway, in chamber, kitchen, and once, to Nan dy Vrit's scandal, his steam bath. The day he rode out to his hunting lodge in the oak woods at dawn, Iselle followed promptly after breakfast. Cazaril was relieved to note that his own spectral retinue fell behind as they rode out of the Zangre, as though bound to their place of death.

It was clear that the fast gallop was an inexpressible joy to Iselle, as she shook out the knots and strains of her trammeled existence in the castle. A day in the saddle in the crisp early-winter air, going and returning from an otherwise futile interview, brightened her eye and put color in her cheeks. Lady Betriz was no less invigorated. The four Baocian guards told off to ride with them kept up, but only just, laboring along with their horses; Cazaril concealed agony. He passed blood again that evening, which he'd not done for some days, and Dondo's nightly serenade proved especially shattering because, for the first time, Cazaril's inward ear could make out words in the cries. They weren't words that made any sense, but they were distinguishable. Would more follow?

Dreading another such ride, Cazaril wearily climbed the stairs to Iselle's chambers late the next morning. He had just eased himself stiffly into his chair at his desk and taken up his account book, when Royina Sara appeared, accompanied by two of her ladies. She wafted past Cazaril in a cloud of white wool. He scrambled to his feet in surprise and bowed deeply; she acknowledged his existence with a faint, faraway nod.

A flurry of feminine voices in the forbidden chambers beyond announced her visit to her sister-in-law. Both the royina's ladies-in-waiting and Nan dy Vrit were exiled to the sitting room, where they sat sewing and quietly gossiping. After about half an hour, Royina Sara came out again and crossed through Cazaril's office antechamber with the same unsmiling abstraction.

Betriz followed shortly. "The royesse bids you attend upon her in her sitting chamber," she told Cazaril. Her black eyebrows were crimped tight with worry. Cazaril rose at once and followed her inside.

Iselle sat in a carved chair, her hands clenched upon its arms, pale and breathing heavily. "Infamous! My brother is infamous, Cazaril!" she told him as he made his bow and pulled a stool up to her knee.

"My lady?" he inquired, and let himself down as carefully as he could. Last night's belly cramp still lingered, and stabbed him if he moved too quickly.

"No marriage without my consent, aye, he spoke that truly enough—but none without dy Jironal's consent, either! Sara has whispered it to me. After his brother's death, but before he rode out of Cardegoss to seek the murderer, the chancellor closeted himself with my brother and persuaded him to make a codicil to his will. In the event of Orico's death, the chancellor is made regent for my brother Teidez—"

"I believe that arrangement has been known for quite some time, Royesse. There is a regency council set up to advise him, as well. The provincars of Chalion would not let that much power pass to one of their number without a check."

"Yes, yes, I knew that, but—"

"The codicil does not attempt to abolish the council, does it?" asked Cazaril in alarm. "*That* would set the lords in an uproar."

"No, that part is left all as it was. But formerly, I was to be the ward of my grandmother and my uncle the provincar of Baocia. Now, I am to be transferred to dy Jironal's own wardship. There is no council to check that! And listen, Cazaril! The term of his guardianship is set to be until I marry, and permission for my marriage is left entirely in his hands! He can keep me unwed till I die of old age, if he chooses!"

Cazaril concealed his unease and held up a soothing hand. "Surely not. He must die of old age long before you. And well before that, when Teidez comes to his man's estate and the full powers of the royacy, he can free you with a royal decree."

"Teidez's majority is set at twenty-five years, Cazaril!"

A decade ago, Cazaril would have shared her outrage at this lengthy term. Now it sounded more like a good idea. But not, granted, with dy Jironal in the saddle instead.

"I would be almost twenty-eight years old!"

Twelve more years for the curse to work upon her, and within her . . . no, it was not good by any measure.

"He could dismiss *you* from my household instantly!"

You have another Patroness, who has not chosen to dismiss me yet. "I grant you have cause for concern, Royesse, but don't borrow trouble before its time. None of this matters while Orico lives."

"He is not well, Sara says."

"He is not very fit," Cazaril agreed cautiously. "But he's not by any means an old man. He's barely more than forty."

By the expression on Iselle's face, she found that quite aged enough. "He is more . . . not-well than he appears. Sara says."

Cazaril hesitated. "Is she that intimate with him, to know this? I had thought them estranged."

"I don't understand them." Iselle knuckled her eyes. "Oh, Cazaril, it was *true* what Dondo told me! I thought, later, that it might have been just a horrid lie to frighten me. Sara was so desperate for a child, she agreed to let dy Jironal try, when Orico . . . could not, anymore. Martou was not so bad, she said. He was at least courteous. It was only when he could not get her with child either that his brother cajoled him to let him into the venture. Dondo was dreadful, and took pleasure in her humiliation. But Cazaril, Orico *knew*. He helped *persuade* Sara to this outrage. I don't understand, because Orico surely does not hate Teidez so much he'd wish to set dy Jironal's bastard in his place."

"No." *And yes.* A son of dy Jironal and Sara would not be a descendant of Fonsa the Fairly-wise. Orico must have reasoned that such a child might grow up to free the royacy of Chalion from the Golden General's death curse. A desperate measure, but possibly an effective one.

"Royina Sara," Iselle added, her mouth crooking, "says if dy Jironal finds Dondo's murderer, she plans to pay for his funeral, pension his family, and have perpetual prayers sung for him in the temple of Cardegoss."

"That's good to know," said Cazaril faintly. Although he had no family to pension. He hunched over a little and smiled to hide a grimace of pain. So, not even Sara, who had filled Iselle's maiden ears with details of shocking intimacy, had told her of the curse. And he was certain now that Sara, too, knew of it. Orico, Sara, dy Jironal, Umegat, probably Ista, possibly even the Provincara, and not one had chosen to burden these children with knowledge of the dark cloud that hung over them. Who was he to betray that implicit conspiracy of silence?

No one told me, either. Do I thank them now for their considera-tion? When, then, did Teidez's and Iselle's protectors plan to let them know of the geas that wrapped them round? Did Orico expect to tell them on his deathbed, as he'd been told by his father Ias?

Had Cazaril the right to tell Iselle secrets that her natural guardians chose to conceal?

Was he prepared to explain to her just *how* he had found it all out?

He glanced at Lady Betriz, seated now on another stool and anxiously watching her distressed royal mistress. Even Betriz, who knew quite well that he had attempted death magic, did not know that he had succeeded.

"I don't know what to try next," moaned Iselle. "Orico is *use-less.*"

Could Iselle escape this curse without ever having to know of it? He took a deep breath, for what he was about to say skirted treason. "You could take steps to arrange your marriage yourself."

Betriz stirred and sat up, her eyes widening at him.

"What, in secret?" said Iselle. "From my royal brother?"

"Certainly in secret from his chancellor."

"Is that legal?"

Cazaril blew out his breath. "A marriage, contracted and con-summated, cannot readily be set aside even by a roya. If a suffi-ciently large camp of Chalionese were persuaded to support you in it—and a considerable faction of opposition to dy Jironal exists ready-made—setting it aside would be rendered still harder." And if she were got out of Chalion and placed under the protection of, say, as shrewd a father-in-law as the Fox of Ibra, she might leave curse and faction both behind altogether. Arranging the matter so that she didn't simply trade being a powerless hostage in one court for being a powerless hostage in another was the hard part. *But at least an uncursed hostage, eh?*

"Ah!" Iselle's eyes lit with approval. "Cazaril, can it be done?"

"There are practical difficulties," he admitted. "All of which have practical solutions. The most critical is to discover a man you can trust to be your ambassador. He must have the wit to gain you the strongest possible position in negotiation with Ibra, the suppleness to avoid offending Chalion, nerve to pass in disguise across uneasy borders, strength for travel, loyalty to you and you alone, and courage in your cause that must not break. A mistake in this selection would be fatal." Possibly literally.

She pressed her hands together, and frowned. "Can you find me such a man?"

"I will bend my thoughts to it, and look about me."

"Do so, Lord Cazaril," she breathed. "Do so."

Lady Betriz said, in an oddly dry voice, "Surely you need not look far."

"It cannot be me." With a swallow, he converted *I could fall dead at your feet at any moment* to, "I dare not leave you here without protection."

"We shall all think on it," said Iselle firmly.

❧THE FATHER'S DAY FESTIVITIES PASSED QUIETLY. CHILL rain dampened the celebrations in Cardegoss, and kept many from the Zangre from attending the municipal procession, though Orico went as a royal duty and as a result contracted a head cold. He turned this to account by taking to his bed and avoiding everyone thereby. The Zangre's denizens, still in black and lavender for Lord Dondo, kept a sober Father's Feast, with sacred music but no dancing.

The icy rain continued through the week. Cazaril, one sodden afternoon, was combining practical application with tutorial by teaching Betriz and Iselle how to keep accounts, when a crisp rap on the chamber door overrode a page's diffident voice announcing, "The March dy Palliar begs to see my lord dy Cazaril."

"Palli!" Cazaril turned in his chair, and levered himself to his feet with a hand on the table. Bright delight flooded both his ladies' faces with sudden energy, driving out the ennui. "I wasn't expecting you in Cardegoss so soon!"

"Nor was I." Palli bowed to the women and favored Cazaril with a twisted grin. He dropped a coin in the page's hand and jerked his head; the boy bent double, in a gradation that indicated deep approval of the amount of the largesse, and scampered off.

Palli continued, "I took only two officers and rode hard; my troop from Palliar follows at a pace that will not destroy horses." He glanced around the chamber and shrugged his broad shoulders. "Goddess forfend! I didn't think I was speaking prophecy, last time I was here. Gives me a worse chill than this miserable rain." He cast off a water-spotted woolen cloak, revealing the blue-and-white garb of an officer of the Daughter's Order, and ran a rueful hand through the bright drops beading in his dark hair. He clasped hands with Cazaril, and added, "Bastard's demons, Caz, you look terrible!"

Cazaril could not, alas, respond to this with a *Very well put*. He instead turned off the remark with a mumble of, "It's the weather, I suppose. It makes everyone dull and drab."

Palli stood back and stared him up and down. "Weather? When last I saw you, your skin was not the color of moldy dough, you didn't have black rings around your eyes like a striped rock-rat, and, and, you looked pretty fit, not—pale, pinched, and potbellied." Cazaril straightened up, indignantly sucking in his aching gut, as Palli jerked a thumb at him and added, "Royesse, you should get your secretary to a physician."

Iselle stared at Cazaril in sudden doubt, her hand going to her mouth, as if really looking him for the first time in weeks. Which, he supposed, she was; her attentions had been thoroughly absorbed by her own troubles through these late disasters. Betriz looked from one of them to the other, and set her teeth on her lower lip.

"I don't need to see a physician," said Cazaril firmly, loudly, and quickly. *Or any other such interrogator, dear gods.*

"So all men say, in terror of the lancet and the purgative." Palli waved away this stung protest. "The last one of my sergeants who developed saddle boils, I had to march in to the old leech-handler at sword's point. Don't listen to him, Royesse. Cazaril"—his face sobered, and he made an apologetic half bow to Iselle—"may I speak to you privately for a moment? I promise I shall not keep him from you long, Royesse. I cannot linger."

Gravely, Iselle granted her royal permission. Cazaril, quick to catch the undertone in Palli's voice, led him not to his office antechamber but all the way down the stairs to his own chamber. The corridor was empty, happily. He closed his heavy door firmly behind them, to thwart human eavesdroppers. The senile spirit smudges kept their confidences.

Cazaril took the chair, the better to conceal his lack of grace in movement. Palli sat on the edge of the bed, folded his cloak beside him, and clasped his hands loosely between his knees.

"The Daughter's courier to Palliar must have made excellent time despite the winter muds," said Cazaril, counting days in his head.

Palli's dark brows rose. "You know of that already? I'd thought it a, ah, quite private call to conclave. Though it will become obvious soon enough, as the other lord dedicats arrive in Cardegoss."

Cazaril shrugged. "I have my sources."

"I don't doubt it. And so have I mine." Palli shook his finger at him. "You are the only intelligencer in the Zangre that I would trust, at present. What, under the gods' eyes, has been happening here at court? The most lurid and garbled tales are circulating regarding our late holy general's sudden demise. And delightful as the picture is, somehow I don't really think he was carried off bodily by a flight of demons with blazing wings called down by the Royesse Iselle's prayers."

"Ah . . . not exactly. He just choked to death in the middle of a drinking fest, the night before his wedding."

"On his poisonous, lying tongue, one would wish."

"Very nearly."

Palli sniffed. "The lord dedicats whom Lord Dondo put in a fury—who are not only all the ones he failed to buy outright, but also those who've grown ashamed of their purchase since—have taken his taking-off as a sign the wheel has turned. As soon as our quorum arrives in Cardegoss, we mean to steal a march on the chancellor and present our own candidate for holy general to Orico. Or perhaps a slate of three acceptable men, from which the roya might choose."

"That would likely go down better. It's a delicate balance between . . ." Cazaril cut off, *loyalty and treason*. "Too, dy Jironal has his own powers in the Temple, as well as in the Zangre. You don't want this infighting to turn too ugly."

"Even dy Jironal would not dare disrupt the Temple by setting soldiers of the Son upon soldiers of the Daughter," said Palli confidently.

"Mm," said Cazaril.

"At the same time, some of the lord dedicats—naming no names right now—want to go farther. Maybe assemble and present evidence of enough of both the Jironals' bribes, threats, peculations, and malfeasances to Orico that it would force him to dismiss dy Jironal as chancellor. Make the roya take a stand."

Cazaril rubbed his nose, and said warningly, "Forcing Orico to stand would be like trying to build a tower out of custard. I don't recommend it. Nor will he readily be parted from dy Jironal. The roya relies on him . . . more deeply than I can explain. Your evidence would need to be utterly overwhelming."

"Yes, which is part of what brings me to you." Palli leaned forward intently. "Would you be willing to repeat, under oath before the Daughter's conclave, the tale you told me in Valenda about how the Jironals sold you to the galleys?"

Cazaril hesitated. "I have only my word to offer as proof, Palli. Too weak to topple dy Jironal, I assure you."

"Not alone, no. But it might be just the coin to tip the scale, the straw to light the fire."

Just the straw to stand out from all the others? Did he *want* to be known as the pivot of this plot? Cazaril's lips screwed up in dismay.

"And you're a man of reputation," Palli went on persuasively.

Cazaril jerked. "No good one, surely . . . !"

"What, everyone knows of Royesse Iselle's clever secretary, the man who keeps his own counsel—and hers—the Bastion of Gotorget—utterly indifferent to wealth—"

"No, I'm not," Cazaril assured him earnestly. "I just dress badly. I quite like wealth."

"And possessing the royesse's total confidence. And don't pretend a courtier's greed to me—with my own eyes I saw you turn down three rich Roknari bribes to betray Gotorget, the last while you were starving near to death, and I can produce living witnesses to back me."

"Well, of *course* I didn't—"

"Your voice would be listened to in council, Caz!"

Cazaril sighed. "I . . . I'll think about it. I have nearer duties. Say that I'll speak in the sealed session if and only if you think my testimony would be truly needed. Temple internal politics are no business of mine." A twinge in his gut made him regret that word choice. *I fear I am afflicted with the goddess's own internal politics, just now.*

Palli's happy nod claimed this as a firmer assent than Cazaril quite wished. He rose, thanked Cazaril, and took his leave.

16

Two afternoons later, Cazaril was sitting unguardedly at his work-table mending his pens when a page of the Zangre entered his antechamber and announced, "Here is Dedicat Rojeras, in obedience to the order of the Royesse Iselle, m'lord."

Rojeras was a man of about forty, with sandy red hair receding a little from his forehead, freckles, and keen blue eyes. The man's trade was recognizable by the green robes of a lay dedicat of Cardegoss's Temple Hospital of the Mother's Mercy that swung at his brisk step, and his rank by the master's braid sewn over his shoulder. Cazaril knew at once that none of his ladies could be the quarry, or the Mother's Order would have sent a woman physician. He stiffened in alarm, but nodded politely. He rose and turned to convey the message to the inner chambers only to find Lady Betriz and the royesse already at the door, smiling unsurprised greetings to the man.

Betriz dropped a half curtsey in exchange for the dedicat's deep bow, and said, "This is the man I told you about, Royesse. The Mother's senior divine says he has made a special study of wasting diseases, and has apprentices who've traveled from all over Chalion to be taught by him!"

So, Lady Betriz's excursion to the temple yesterday had included more than prayers and charity offerings. Iselle had less to learn about court conspiracies than Cazaril had thought. She'd certainly smuggled this past *him* smoothly enough. He was ambushed, and by his own ladies. He smiled tightly, swallowing his fear. The man had none of the luminous signs of second sight about him; what could he tell from Cazaril's mere body?

Iselle looked the physician over and nodded satisfaction. "Dedicat Rojeras, please examine my secretary and report back to me."

"Royesse, I don't need to see a physician!" *And I most especially don't need a physician to see me.*

"Then all we shall waste is a trifle of time," Iselle countered, "which the gods give us each day all the same. Upon pain of my displeasure, I order you to go with him, Cazaril." There was no mistaking the determination in her voice.

Damn Palli, for not only putting this into her head, but teaching her how to block his escape. Iselle was too quick a study. Still . . . the physician would either diagnose a miracle, or he would not. If he did, Cazaril could call for Umegat, and let the saint, with his undoubted high connections to the Temple, deal with it. And if not, what harm was in it?

Cazaril bowed obedient, if stiffly offended, assent, and led his unwelcome visitor downstairs to his bedchamber. Lady Betriz followed, to see that her royal mistress's orders were carried out. She offered him a quick apologetic smile, but her eyes were apprehensive as Cazaril closed his door upon her.

Shut in with Cazaril, the physician made him sit by the window while he felt his pulse and peered into his eyes, ears, and throat. He bade Cazaril make water, which he sniffed and studied in a glass tube held up to the light. He inquired after Cazaril's bowels, and Cazaril reluctantly admitted to the blood. Then Cazaril was required to undress and lie down, and suffer to have his heart and breathing listened to by the man's ear pressed to his chest, and be poked and prodded all over his body by the cool, quick fingers. Cazaril had to explain how he came by his flogging scars; Rojeras's comments upon them were limited to some hair-raising suggestions of how he might rid Cazaril of his remaining adhesions, should Cazaril desire it and gather the nerve. Withal, Cazaril thought he would prefer to wait and fall off another horse, and said so, which only made Rojeras chuckle.

Rojeras's smile faded as he returned to a more careful, and

deeper, probing of Cazaril's belly, feeling and leaning this way and that. "Pain here?"

Cazaril, determined to pass this off, said firmly, "No."

"How about when I do this?"

Cazaril yelped.

"Ah. Some pain, then." More poking. More wincing. Rojeras paused for a time, his fingertips just resting on Cazaril's belly, his gaze abstracted. Then he seemed to shake himself awake. He reminded Cazaril of Umegat.

Rojeras still smiled as Cazaril dressed himself again, but his eyes were shadowed with thought.

Cazaril offered encouragingly, "Speak, Dedicat. I am a man of reason, and will not fall to pieces."

"Is it so? Good." Rojeras took a breath and said plainly, "My lord, you have a most palpable tumor."

"Is . . . that it," said Cazaril, gingerly seating himself again in his chair.

Rojeras looked up swiftly. "This does not surprise you?"

Not as much as my last diagnosis did. Cazaril thought longingly of what a relief it would be to learn that his recurring belly cramp was such a natural, normal lethality. Alas, he was quite certain that most people's tumors didn't scream obscenities at them in the middle of the night. "I have had reasons to think something was not right. But what does this mean? What do you think will happen?" He kept his voice as neutral as possible.

"Well . . ." Rojeras sat on the edge of Cazaril's vacated bed and laced his fingers together. "There are so many kinds of these growths. Some are diffuse, some knotted or encapsulated, some kill swiftly, some sit there for years and hardly seem to give trouble at all. Yours seems to be encapsulated, which is hopeful. There is one common sort, a kind of cyst that fills with liquid, that one woman I cared for held for over twelve years."

"Oh," said Cazaril, and produced a heartened smile.

"It grew to over a hundred pounds by the time she died," the physician went on. Cazaril recoiled, but Rojeras continued blithely, "And there is another, a most interesting one that I have only seen twice in my years of study—a round mass that, when opened, proved to contain knots of flesh with hair and teeth and bones. One was in a woman's belly, which almost made sense, but another was in a man's leg. I theorize that they were engendered by an escaped demon, trying to grow to human form. If the demon had succeeded, I posit that it might have chewed its way out and entered the world in fleshly form, which would surely have been an abomination. I have for long wished to find such another one in a patient who was still alive, that I might study it and see if my theory is so." He eyed Cazaril in speculation.

With the greatest effort, Cazaril kept himself from jolting up and screaming. He glanced down at his swollen belly in terror, and carefully away. He had thought his affliction spiritual, not physical. It had not occurred to him that it could be both at once. *This* was an intrusion of the supernatural into the solid that seemed all too plausible, given his case. He choked out, "Do *they* grow to a hundred pounds, too?"

"The two I excised were much smaller," Rojeras assured him.

Cazaril looked up in sudden hope. "You can cut them out, then?"

"Oh—only from dead persons," said the physician apologetically.

"But, but . . . might it be done?" If a man were brave enough to lie down and offer himself in cold blood to razor-edged steel . . . if the abomination could be carved out with the brutal speed of an amputation . . . Was it possible to physically excise a miracle, if that miracle were in fact made flesh?

Rojeras shook his head. "On an arm or a leg, maybe. But this . . . You were a soldier—you've surely seen what happens with dirty belly wounds. Even if you chanced to survive the shock and pain of the cutting, the fever would kill you within a few days." His voice grew more earnest. "I have tried it three times, and only because my patients threatened to kill themselves if I would not try. They all died. I don't care to kill any more good people that way. Do not tease and torment yourself with such desperate impossibilities. Take what you can of life meantime, and pray."

It was praying that got me into this—or this into me . . . "Do not tell the royesse!"

"My lord," said the physician gravely, "I must."

"But I must not—not *now*—she must not dismiss me to my bed! I cannot leave her side!" Cazaril's voice rose in panic.

Rojeras's brows rose. "Your loyalty commends you, Lord

Cazaril. Calm yourself! There is no need for you to take to your bed before you feel the need. Indeed, such light duties as may come your way in her service may occupy your mind and help you to compose your soul."

Cazaril breathed deeply, and decided not to disabuse Rojeras of his pleasant illusions about service to the House of Chalion. "As long as you make it clear that I am not to be exiled from my post."

"As long as you grasp that this is not a license to exert yourself unduly," Rojeras returned sternly. "You are plainly in need of more rest than you have allowed yourself."

Cazaril nodded hasty agreement, trying to look at once biddable and energetic.

"There is one other important thing," Rojeras added, stirring as if to take his leave but not yet rising. "I only ask this because, as you say, you are a man of reason, and I think you might understand."

"Yes?" said Cazaril warily.

"Upon your death—long delayed, we must pray—may I have your note of hand saying I might cut out your tumor for my collection?"

"You *collect* such horrors?" Cazaril grimaced. "Most men content themselves with paintings, or old swords, or ivory carvings." Offense struggled with curiosity, and lost. "Um . . . how do you keep them?"

"In jars of wine spirits." Rojeras smiled, a faint embarrassed flush coloring his fair skin. "I know it sounds gruesome, but I keep hoping . . . if only I learn *enough*, someday I will understand, someday I will be able to find some way to keep these things from killing people."

"Surely they are the gods' dark gifts, and we cannot in piety resist them?"

"We resist gangrene, by amputation, sometimes. We resist the infection of the jaw, by drawing out the bad tooth. We resist fevers, by applications of heat and cold, and good care. For every cure, there must have been a first time." Rojeras fell silent. After a moment he said, "It is clear that the Royesse Iselle holds you in much affection and esteem."

Cazaril, not knowing quite how to respond to this, replied, "I have served her since last spring, in Valenda. I had formerly served in her grandmother's household."

"She is not given to hysterics, is she? Highborn women are sometimes . . ." Rojeras gave a little shrug, in place of saying something rude.

"No," Cazaril had to admit. "None of her household are. Quite the reverse." He added, "But surely you don't have to tell the ladies, and distress them, so . . . so soon?"

"Of course I do," said the physician, although in a gentled tone. He rose to his feet. "How can the royesse choose good actions without good knowledge?"

An all too cogent point. Cazaril chewed on it in embarrassment as he followed the dedicat back upstairs.

Betriz leaned out onto the corridor at the sound of their approaching steps. "Is he going to be all right?" she demanded of Rojeras.

Rojeras held up a hand. "A moment, my lady."

They made their way into the royesse's sitting chamber, where Iselle waited bolt upright on the carved chair, her hands tight in her lap. She accepted Rojeras's bow with a nod. Cazaril didn't want to watch, but he did want to know what was said, and so sank into the chair Betriz anxiously dragged up for him, and to which Iselle pointed. Rojeras remained standing in the presence of the royesse.

"My lady," Rojeras said to Iselle, bowing again as if in apology for his bluntness, "your secretary is afflicted with a tumor in his gut."

Iselle stared at him in shock. Betriz's face drained of all expression. Iselle swallowed, and said, "He's not . . . not *dying*, surely?" She glanced fearfully at Cazaril.

Rojeras, losing his grip on his stated principles of forthrightness in the face of this, retreated briefly into courtly dissimulation. "Death comes to all men, variously. It is beyond my skills to say how long Lord Cazaril may yet live." His glance aside caught Cazaril's hard, pleading stare, and he added faithfully, "There is no reason he may not continue in his secretarial duties as long as he feels well enough. You should not permit him to overtax himself, however. By your leave, I should like to return each week to reexamine him."

"Of course," said Iselle faintly.

After a few more words on the subject of Cazaril's diet and duties, Rojeras made a courteous departure.

Betriz, tears blurring her velvety brown eyes, choked, "I didn't think it was going to be—had you guessed this when—Cazaril, I don't want you to die!"

Cazaril replied ruefully, "Well, I don't want me to die either, so that makes two of us."

"Three," said Iselle. "Cazaril—what can we *do* for you?"

Cazaril, about to reply, *nothing*, seized this opportunity instead to rap out firmly, "This above all—kindly do not discuss this with every castle gossiper. It is my earnest desire that this stay private information for—for as long as may be." For one thing, the news that Cazaril was dying might give dy Jironal some fresh ideas about his brother's death. The chancellor had to return to Cardegoss soon, possibly frustrated enough to start rethinking his missing corpse problem.

Iselle accepted this with a slow nod, and Cazaril was permitted to return to his antechamber, where he failed to concentrate upon his account books. After the third time Lady Betriz tiptoed out to inquire if he wanted anything, once at the royesse's instigation and twice on her own, Cazaril counterattacked by declaring it was time for some long-neglected grammar lessons. If they weren't going to leave him alone, he might as well make use of their company. His two pupils were very subdued, ladylike, and submissive this afternoon. Even though this meek studious virtue was something he'd long wished for, he found himself hoping it wouldn't last.

Still, they brushed through the lessons pretty well, even the long drill on court Roknari grammatical modes. His prickly demeanor did not invite consolation. The ladies, bless their steadfast wits, did not attempt to inflict any on him. By the end the two young women were treating him almost normally again, as he plainly desired, though around Betriz's grave mouth no dimples solaced him.

Iselle rose to shake out her knots by pacing about the chamber; she stopped to stare out the window at the chill winter mist that filled the ravine below the Zangre's walls. She rubbed absently at her sleeve, and remarked querulously, "Lavender is not my color. It's like wearing a bruise. There is too much death in Cardegoss. I wish we'd never come here."

Considering it impolitic to agree, Cazaril merely bowed, and withdrew to make himself ready to go down to dinner.

*　　*　　*

❧THE FIRST FLAKES OF WINTER SNOW POWDERED THE streets and walls of Cardegoss that week, but melted off in the afternoons. Palli kept Cazaril informed of the arrival of his fellow lord dedicats, filtering in to the capital one by one, and in turn decanted Zangre gossip from his friend. Mutual aid and trust, Cazaril reflected, but also a dual breach of the walls that each of them, in theory, helped to man. Yet if it ever came down to choosing sides between the Temple and the Zangre, Chalion would already have lost.

Dy Jironal, Royse Teidez in tow, returned as if blown in by the cold southeast wind that also dumped an unwelcome gift of sleet on the town in passing. To Cazaril's relief, the chancellor was empty-handed, balked of quarry in his quest for justice and revenge. No telling from dy Jironal's set face if he had despaired of his hunt, or had just been drawn back by spies, riding hard and fast, to tell him of the forces gathering in Cardegoss that were not of his own summoning.

Teidez dragged back to his quarters in the castle looking tired, sullen, and unhappy. Cazaril was not surprised. Chasing down every death for three provinces around that had occurred during the night of Dondo's taking-off had surely been gruesome enough even without the vile weather.

During his bedazzlement by Dondo's practiced sycophancy, Teidez had neglected his elder sister's company. When he came to visit Iselle's chambers that afternoon, he both accepted and returned a sisterly embrace, seeming more eager to talk to her than he had for a long time. Cazaril withdrew discreetly to his antechamber and sat with his account books open, fiddling with his drying quill. Since Orico had for a betrothal gift assigned the rents of six towns to the support of his sister's household, and not taken them back when funeral had replaced wedding, Cazaril's accounts and correspondence had grown more complex.

He listened meditatively through the open door to the rise and fall of the young voices. Teidez detailed his trip to his sister's eager ears: the muddy roads and floundering horses, the tense and cranky men, indifferent food and chilly quarters. Iselle, in a voice that betrayed more envy than sympathy, pointed out how good a practice it was for his future winter campaigns. The cause of the journey was scarcely touched upon between them, Teidez still baffled and offended by his sister's rejection of his late hero, and Iselle apparently unwilling to burden him with knowledge of the more grotesque causes of her antipathy.

Besides being shocked by the sudden and dreadful nature of Lord Dondo's murder, Teidez must be one of the few who'd known the man who genuinely mourned him. And why not? Dondo had flattered and cajoled and made much of Teidez. He'd showered the boy with gifts and treats, some toxically inappropriate for his age, and how was Teidez to grasp that grown men's vices were not the same as grown men's honors?

The elder dy Jironal must seem a cold and unresponsive companion by comparison. The expedition had apparently left a trail of disruption behind as its inquiries grew rough and ready in dy Jironal's frustration. Worse, dy Jironal, who needed Teidez desperately, was insufficiently adept at concealing how little he liked him, and had left him to his handlers—secretary-tutor, guards, and servants—treating him as tailpiece rather than lieutenant. But if, as his surly words hinted, Teidez had begun to reciprocate his chief guardian's dislike, it was surely for all the wrong reasons. And if his new secretary was taking up any of the abandoned load of his noble education, nothing in Teidez's tale gave hint of it.

At length, Nan dy Vrit bade the young people prepare for dinner, and drew the visit to a close. Teidez walked slowly out through Cazaril's antechamber, frowning at his boots. The boy was grown almost as tall as his half brother Orico, his round face hinting that in future he might grow as broad as well, though for now he kept youth's muscular fitness. Cazaril turned a leaf in his account book at random, dipped his pen again, and glanced up with a tentative smile. "How do you fare, my lord?"

Teidez shrugged, but then, halfway across the room, wheeled back, and came to Cazaril's table. His expression was not miffed—or not merely miffed—but tired and troubled as well. He drummed his finger briefly on the wood, and stared down over the pile of books and papers. Cazaril folded his hands and cast him an encouraging look of inquiry.

Teidez said abruptly, "There's something wrong in Cardegoss. Isn't there."

There were so many things wrong in Cardegoss, Cazaril

scarcely knew how to take Teidez's words. He said cautiously, "What makes you think that?"

Teidez made a little gesture, pulled short. "Orico is sickly, and does not rule as he should. He sleeps so much, like an old man, but he's not *that* old. And everyone says he's lost his"—Teidez colored slightly, and his gesture grew vaguer—"you know . . . cannot act as a man is supposed to, with a woman. Has it never struck you that there is something *uncanny* about his strange illness?"

After a slight hesitation, Cazaril temporized, "Your observations are shrewd, Royse."

"Lord Dondo's death was uncanny, too. *I* think it's all of a piece!"

The boy was thinking; good! "You should take your thoughts to . . ." not dy Jironal, "your brother Orico. He is the most proper authority to address them." Cazaril tried to imagine Teidez getting a straight answer out of Orico, and sighed. If Iselle could not draw sense from the man, with all her passionate persuasion, what hope had the much less articulate Teidez? Orico would evade answer unless stiffened to it in advance.

Should Cazaril take this tutelage into his own hands? Not only had he not been given authority to disclose the state secret, he wasn't even supposed to know it himself. And . . . the knowledge of the Golden General's curse *needed* to come straight to Teidez from the roya, not around him or despite him, lest it take up a suspicious tinge of conspiracy.

He'd been silent too long. Teidez leaned forward across the table, eyes narrowing, and hissed, "Lord Cazaril, *what do you know?*"

I know we dare not leave you in ignorance much longer. Nor Iselle either. "Royse, I shall talk to you of this later. I cannot answer you tonight."

Teidez's lips tightened. He swiped a hand through his dark amber curls in a gesture of impatience. His eyes were uncertain, untrusting, and, Cazaril thought, strangely lonely. "I see," he said in a bleak tone, and turned on his heel to march out. His low-voiced mutter carried back from the corridor, "I must do it myself . . ."

If he meant, talk to Orico, good. Cazaril would go to Orico first, though, yes, and if that proved insufficient, return with Umegat to back him up. He set his pens in their jar, closed his books, took a breath to steel himself against the twinges that stabbed him with sudden movement, and pushed to his feet.

❧AN INTERVIEW WITH ORICO WAS EASIER RESOLVED upon than accomplished. Taking him as still an ambassador for Iselle's Ibran proposal, the roya ducked away from Cazaril on sight, and set the master of his chamber to offer up a dozen excuses for his indisposition. The matter was made more difficult by the need for this conversation to take place in private, just between the two of them, and uninterrupted. Cazaril was walking down the corridor from the banqueting hall after supper, head down and considering how best to corner his royal quarry, when a thump on his shoulder half spun him around.

He looked up, and an apology for his clumsy abstraction died on his lips. The man he'd run into was Ser dy Joal, one of Dondo's now-unemployed bravos—and what were all those ripe souls doing for pocket money these days? Had they been inherited by Dondo's brother?—flanked by one of his comrades, half-grinning, and Ser dy Maroc, who frowned uneasily. The man who'd run into him, Cazaril corrected himself. The candlelight from the mirrored wall sconces made bright sparks in the younger man's alert eyes.

"Clumsy oaf!" roared dy Joal, sounding just a trifle rehearsed. "How dare you crowd me from the door?"

"I beg your pardon, Ser dy Joal," said Cazaril. "My mind was elsewhere." He made a half bow, and began to go around.

Dy Joal dodged sideways, blocking him, and swung back his vest-cloak to reveal the hilt of his sword. "I say you crowded me. Do you give me the lie, as well?"

This is an ambush. Ah. Cazaril stopped, his mouth tightening. Wearily, he said, "What do you want, dy Joal?"

"Bear witness!" Dy Joal motioned to his comrade and dy Maroc. "He crowded me."

His comrade obediently replied, "Aye, I saw," though dy Maroc looked much less certain.

"I seek a touch with you for this, Lord Cazaril!" said dy Joal.

"I see that you do," said Cazaril dryly. But was this drunken stupidity, or the world's simplest form of assassination? A duel to first blood, approved practice and outlet for high spirits among young courtly hotheads, followed by *The sword slipped, upon my honor! He ran upon it!* and whatever number of paid witnesses one could afford to confirm it.

"I say I will have three drops of your blood, to clear this slight." It was the customary challenge.

"*I* say you should go dip your head in a bucket of water until you sober up, boy. I do not duel. Eh?" Cazaril lifted his arms briefly, hands out, flipping his own vest-cloak open to show he'd borne no sword in to dinner. "Let me pass."

"Urrac, lend the coward your sword! We have our two witnesses. We'll have this outside, now." Dy Joal jerked his head toward the doors at the corridor's end that led out into the main courtyard.

The comrade unbuckled his sword, grinned, and tossed it to Cazaril. Cazaril lifted an eyebrow, but not his hand, and let the sheathed weapon clatter, uncaught, to his feet. He kicked it back to its owner. "I do not duel."

"Shall I call you coward direct?" demanded Joal. His lips were parted, and his breath already rushing in his elation, anticipating battle. Cazaril saw out of the corner of his eye a couple of other men, attracted by the raised voices, advance curiously down the corridor toward this knot of altercation.

"Call me anything you please, depending on how much of a fool you want to sound. Your mouthings are naught to me," sighed Cazaril. He did his best to project languid boredom, but his blood was pulsing faster in his ears. Fear? No. *Fury* . . .

"You have a lord's name. Have you no lord's honor?"

One corner of Cazaril's mouth turned up, not at all humorously. "The confusion of mind you dub honor is a disease, for which the Roknari galley-masters have the cure."

"So much for your honor, then. You shall not refuse me three drops for mine!"

"That's right." Cazaril's voice went oddly calm; his heart, which had sped, slowed. His lips drew back in a strange grin. "That's right," he breathed again.

Cazaril held up his left hand, palm out, and with his right jerked out his belt knife, last used for cutting bread at supper. Dy Joal's hand spasmed on his sword hilt, and he half drew.

"Not within the roya's hall!" cried dy Maroc anxiously. "You know you must take it outside, dy Joal! By the Brother, he has no sword, you cannot!"

Dy Joal hesitated; Cazaril, instead of advancing toward him, shook back his left sleeve—and drew his knife blade shallowly across his own wrist. Cazaril felt no pain, none. Blood welled, gleaming dark carmine in the candlelight, though not spurting dangerously. A kind of haze clouded his vision, blocking out everyone but himself and the now uncertainly grinning young fool who'd hustled him for a touch. *I'll give you touch.* He spun his knife back into its belt sheath. Dy Joal, not yet wary enough, let his sword slide back and lifted his hand from it. Smiling, Cazaril held up his hands, one arm bleeding, the other bare. Then he lunged.

He caught up the shocked dy Joal and bore him backward to the wall, where he landed with a thump that reverberated down the corridor, one arm trapped behind him. Cazaril's right hand pressed under dy Joal's chin, lifting him from his feet and pinning him to the wall by his neck. Cazaril's right knee ground into dy Joal's groin. He kept up the pressure, to deny dy Joal his trapped arm; the other clawed at him, and he pinned it, too, to the wall. Dy Joal's wrist twisted in the slippery blood of his grip, but could not break free. The purpling young man did not, of course, cry out, though his eyes rolled whitely, and a grunting gargle broke from his lips. His heels hammered the wall. The bravos knew Cazaril's crooked hands had held a pen; they'd forgotten he'd held an oar. Dy Joal wasn't going anywhere now.

Cazaril snarled in his ear, low-voiced but audible to all, "I don't duel, boy. I kill as a soldier kills, which is as a butcher kills, as quickly, efficiently, and with as least risk to myself as I can arrange. If I decide you die, you will die when I choose, where I choose, by what means I choose, and you will never see the blow coming." He released dy Joal's now-enfeebled arm and brought his left wrist up, and pressed the bloody cut to his terrified victim's half-open, trembling mouth. "You want three drops of my blood, for your honor? You shall drink them." Blood and spittle spurted around dy Joal's chattering teeth, but the bravo didn't even dare try to bite, now. "Drink, damn you!" Cazaril pressed harder, smearing blood all over dy Joal's face, fascinated with the vividness of it, red streaks on livid skin, the catch of rough beard stubble against his wrist, the bright blur of the candlelight reflected in the welling tears spilling from the staring eyes. He stared into them, watching them cloud.

"Cazaril, for the gods' sake let him *breathe*." Dy Maroc's distressed cry broke through Cazaril's red fog.

Cazaril reduced the pressure of his grip, and dy Joal inhaled, shuddering. Keeping his knee in place, Cazaril drew back his bloodied left hand in a fist, and placed, very precisely, a hard blow to the bravo's stomach that shook the air again; dy Joal's knees jerked up with it. Only then did Cazaril step back and release the man.

Dy Joal fell to the floor and bent over himself, gasping and choking, weeping, not even trying to get up. After a moment, he vomited.

Cazaril stepped across the mess of food and wine and bile toward Urrac, who lurched backward until stopped by the far wall. Cazaril leaned into his face and repeated softly, "I don't duel. But if you seek to die like a bludgeoned steer, cross me again."

He turned on his heel; dy Maroc's face, drained white, wavered past his vision, hissing, "Cazaril, have you gone *mad*?"

"Try me." Cazaril grinned fiercely at him. Dy Maroc fell back. Cazaril strode down the corridor past a blur of men, blood drops still spattering off his fingers as he swung his arms, and out into the chill shock of the night. The closing door cut off a rising babble of voices.

He almost ran across the icy cobbles of the courtyard toward the main block and refuge, both his steps and his breath growing faster and less even as something—sanity, delayed terror?—-seeped back into his mind. His belly cramped violently as he mounted the stone stairs. His fingers shook so badly as he fumbled out his key to let himself into his bedchamber that he dropped it twice and had to use both hands, braced against the door, to finally guide it into the lock. He locked the door again behind him, and fell, wheezing and groaning, across his bed. His attendant ghosts had fled into hiding during the confrontation, their desertion unnoticed by him at the time. He rolled onto his side, and curled around his aching stomach. Now, at last, his cut wrist began to throb. So did his head.

He'd seen men go berserk a few times, in the madness of battle. He'd just never imagined what it must feel like from the inside, before. No one had mentioned the floating exhilaration, intoxicating as wine or sex. An unusual, but natural, result of nerves, mortality, and fright, jammed together in too small a space, too short a time. Not unnatural. Not . . . the thing in his belly reaching out to twist and taunt and trick him into death, and its own release. . . .

Oh.

You know what you did to Dondo. Now you know what Dondo is doing to you.

17

It was by chance, late the following morning, that Cazaril spied Orico ambling out the Zangre gates toward the menagerie with only a page at his heels. Cazaril tucked the letters he'd been carrying to the Chancellery office into the inner pocket of his vest-cloak, turned from the door of Ias's Tower, and followed. The roya's master of the chamber had earlier refused to disturb his lord's after-breakfast nap; clearly, Orico had finally roused himself and now sought comfort and solace among his animals. Cazaril wondered if the roya had awoken with as bad a headache as he had.

As he strode across the cobbles, Cazaril marshaled his arguments. If the roya feared action, Cazaril would point out that inaction was equally likely to be bent to ill by the curse's malign influence. If the roya insisted that the children were too young, he would note that they should not then have been ordered to Cardegoss in the first place. But now that they were here, if Orico could not protect them then he had an obligation to both Chalion and the children to tell them of their danger. Cazaril would call on Umegat to confirm that the roya could not, did not, in fact, hold the curse all to himself. *Do not send them blindfolded into battle* he would plead, and hope Palli's cry would strike Orico as much to the heart as it had him. And if it didn't . . .

If he took this into his own hands, should he first tell Teidez, as Heir of Chalion, and appeal for his aid in protecting his sister? Or

Iselle, and enlist her help in managing the more difficult Teidez? The second choice would better allow him to hide his complicity behind the royesse's skirts, but only if the secret of his guilt survived her shrewd cross-examination.

A scraping of hooves broke into his self-absorption. He looked up just in time to dodge from the path of the cavalcade starting out from the stables. Royse Teidez, mounted on his fine black horse, led a party of his Baocian guards, their captain and two men. The royse's black-and-lavender mourning garb made his round face appear drawn and pale in the winter sunlight. Dondo's green stone glinted on the guard captain's hand, raised to return Cazaril's polite salute.

"Where away, Royse?" Cazaril called. "Do you hunt?" The party was armed for it, with spears and crossbows, swords and cudgels.

Teidez drew up his fretting horse and stared briefly down at Cazaril. "No, just a gallop along the river. The Zangre is . . . stuffy, this morning."

Indeed. And if they just happened to flush a deer or two, well, they were prepared to accept the gods' largesse. But not really hunting while in mourning, no. "I understand," said Cazaril, and suppressed a smile. "It will be good for the horses." Teidez lifted his reins again. Cazaril stepped back, but then added suddenly, "I would speak to you later, Royse, on the matter that concerned you yesterday."

Teidez gave him a vague wave, and a frown—not exactly assent, but it would do. Cazaril bowed farewell as they clattered out of the stable yard.

And remained bent over, as the worst cramp yet kicked him in the belly with the power of a horse's hind hooves. His breathing stopped. Waves of pain seemed to surge through his whole body from this central source, even to burning spasms in the palms of his hands and the soles of his feet. A hideous vision shook him of Rojeras's postulated demon-monster preparing to bloodily claw its way out of him into the light. One creature, or two? With no bodies to keep their spirits apart, bottled under the pressure of the Lady's miracle, might Dondo and the demon have begun to blend together into one dreadful being? It was true that he'd distinguished only one voice, not a duet, baying at him from his belly in the night. His knees sank helplessly to the cold cobbles. He drew in a shuddering breath. The world seemed to churn around his head in short, dizzy jerks.

After a few minutes, a shadow trailing a powerful aroma of horses loomed at his shoulder. A gruff voice muttered in his ear, "M'lord? You all right?"

Cazaril blinked up to see one of the stable grooms, a middle-aged fellow with bad teeth, bending over him. "Not . . . really," he managed to reply.

"Ought you go indoors, sir?"

"Yes . . . I suppose . . ."

The groom helped him to his feet with a hand under his elbow, and steadied him back through the gates to the main block. At the bottom of the stairs Cazaril gasped, "Wait. Not yet," and sat heavily upon the steps.

After an awkward minute the groom asked, "Should I get someone for you, m'lord? I should return to my duties."

"It's . . . just a spasm. It will pass off in a few minutes. I'm all right now. Go on." The pain was dwindling, leaving him feeling flushed and strange.

The groom frowned uncertainly, staring down at Cazaril, but then ducked his head and departed.

Slowly, as he sat quietly on the stair, he began to regain his breath and balance, and was able to straighten his back again. The world stopped pulsing. Even the couple of ghost-blotches that had crept out of the walls to cluster at his feet grew quiescent. Cazaril eyed them in the shadows of the stairwell, considering what a cold and lonely damnation was their slow erosion, loss of all that had made them individual men and women. What must it be like, to feel one's very spirit slowly rot away around one, as flesh rotted from dead limbs? Did the ghosts sense their own diminishment, or did that self-perception, too, mercifully, wear away in time? The Bastard's legendary hell, with all its supposed torments, seemed a sort of heaven by comparison.

"Ah! Cazaril!" A surprised voice made him look up. Palli stood with one booted foot on the first step, flanked by two young men also wearing the blue and white of the Daughter's Order beneath gray wool riding cloaks. "I was just coming to find you." Palli's dark brows drew down. "What are you doing sitting on the stairs?"

"Just resting a moment." Cazaril produced a quick, concealing smile, and levered himself up, though he kept a hand on the wall, as if casually, for balance. "What's afoot?"

"I hoped you would have time to take a stroll down to the temple with me. And talk to some men about that"—Palli made a circling gesture with his finger—"little matter of Gotorget."

"Already?"

"Dy Yarrin came in last night. We are now a sufficient assembly to make binding decisions. And with dy Jironal also arrived back in town, it's as well we chart our course without further delay."

Indeed. Cazaril would search out Orico immediately upon his return, then. He glanced at the two companions and back at Palli, as if seeking introduction, but with the hidden question in his glance, *Are these safe ears?*

"Ah," said Palli cheerfully. "Permit me to make known to you my cousins, Ferda and Foix dy Gura. They rode with me from Palliar. Ferda is lieutenant to my master of horse, and his younger brother Foix—well, we keep him for the heavy lifting. Make your bow to the castillar, boys."

The shorter, stouter of the two grinned sheepishly, and they both managed reasonably graceful courtesies. They bore a faint family resemblance to Palli in the strong lines of jaw and the bright brown eyes. Ferda was of middle height and wiry, an obvious rider, his legs already a little bowed, while his brother was broad and muscular. They seemed a pleasant enough pair of country lordlings, healthy, cheerful, and unscarred. And appallingly young. But Palli's faint emphasis on the word *cousins* answered Cazaril's silent question.

The two brothers fell in behind as Cazaril and Palli walked out the gates and down into Cardegoss. Young they might be, but their eyes were alert, looking all around, and they casually kept their sword hilts free of entanglement with cloak and vest-cloak. Cazaril was glad to know Palli did not go about the streets of Cardegoss unattended even in this bright gray winter noon. Cazaril tensed as they passed under the dressed-stone walls of Jironal Palace, but no armed bravos issued from its ironbound doors to molest them. They arrived in the Temple Square having encountered no one more daunting than a trio of maidservants. They smiled at the men in the colors of the Daughter's Order and giggled among themselves after passing, which slightly alarmed the dy Gura brothers, or at least made them stride out more stiffly.

The great compound of the Daughter's house made a wall along one whole side of the temple's five-sided square. The main gate was devoted to the women and girls who were the house's more usual dedicats, acolytes, and divines. The men of its holy military order had their own separate entrance, building, and stable for couriers' horses. The hallways of the military headquarters were chilly despite a sufficiency of lit sconces and the abundance of beautiful tapestries and hangings, woven and embroidered by pious ladies all over Chalion, blanketing its walls. Cazaril started toward the main hall, but Palli drew him down another corridor and up a staircase.

"You do not meet in the Hall of the Lord Dedicats?" Cazaril inquired, looking over his shoulder.

Palli shook his head. "Too cold, too large, and too empty. We felt excessively exposed there. For these sealed debates and depositions, we've taken a chamber where we can feel a majority, and not freeze our feet."

Palli left the dy Gura brothers in the corridor to contemplate a brightly colored quilted rendering of the legend of the virgin and the water jar, featuring an especially voluptuous virgin and goddess. He ushered Cazaril past a pair of Daughter's guardsmen, who looked closely at their faces and returned Palli's salute, and through a set of double doors carved with interlaced vines. The chamber beyond held a long trestle table and two dozen men, crowded but warm—and above all, Cazaril noted, private. In addition to the good wax candles, a window of colored glass depicting the Lady's favorite spring flowers fought the winter gloom.

Palli's fellow lord dedicats sat at attention, young men and graybeards, in blue-and-white garb bright and expensive or faded and shabby, but all alike in the grim seriousness of their faces. The provincar of Yarrin, ranking lord of Chalion present, held down the head of the table beneath the window. Cazaril wondered how many here were spies, or at least careless mouths. The group seemed already too large and diverse for successful conspiracy, despite their outward precautions to seal their conclave. *Lady, guide them to wisdom.*

Palli bowed, and said, "My lords, here is the Castillar dy Cazaril, who was my commander at the siege of Gotorget, to testify before you."

Palli took an empty seat halfway around the table and left Cazaril standing at its foot. Another lord dedicat had him swear an oath of truth in the goddess's name. Cazaril had no trouble re-peating with sincerity and fervor the part about, *May Her hands hold me, and not release me.*

Dy Yarrin led the questioning. He was shrewd and clearly well primed by Palli, for he had the whole tale of the aftermath of Go-torget out of Cazaril in a very few minutes. Cazaril added no col-oring details. For some here, he didn't need to; he could mark by the tightening of their lips how much of what was unspoken they understood. Inevitably, someone wanted to know how he had first come to such enmity with Lord Dondo, and he was reluctantly compelled to repeat the story of his near beheading in Prince Olus's tent. It was normally considered bad manners to denigrate the dead, on the theory that they could not defend themselves. In Dondo's case, Cazaril wasn't so sure. But he kept that account, too, as brief and bald as possible. Despite his succinctness, by the time he was done he was leaning on his hands on the table, feeling dan-gerously light-headed.

A brief debate followed on the problem of obtaining corrobo-rating evidence, which Cazaril had thought insurmountable; dy Yarrin, it seemed, did not find it so. But then, Cazaril had never thought to try to obtain testimony from surviving Roknari, or via sister chapters of the Daughter's Order across the borders in the princedoms.

"But my lords," Cazaril said diffidently into one of the few brief pauses in the flow of suggestion and objection, "even if my words were proved a dozen times over, mine is no great matter by which to bring down a great man. Not like the treason of Lord dy Lutez."

"*That* was never well proved, even at the time," murmured dy Yarrin in a dry tone.

Palli put in, "What is a great matter? I think the gods do not cal-culate greatness as men do. I for one find a casual destruction of a man's life even more repugnant than a determined one."

Cazaril leaned more heavily on the table, in the interests of not collapsing in an illustrative way at this dramatic moment. Palli had insisted his voice would be listened to in council; very well, let it be a voice of caution. "Choosing your own holy general is surely within your mandate, lords. Orico may well even accede to your selection, if you make it easy for him. Challenging the chancellor of Chalion and holy general of your brother order is reaching beyond, and it is my considered opinion that Orico will never be persuaded to support it. I recommend against it."

"It is all or nothing," broke in one man, and "Never again will we endure another Dondo," began another.

Dy Yarrin held up his hand, stemming the tide of hot comment. "I thank you, Lord Cazaril, for both your testimony and your opinion." His choice of words invited his fellows to note which was which. "We must continue this debate in private conclave."

It was a dismissal. Palli pushed back his chair and rose to his feet. They collected the dy Guras from the corridor; Cazaril was a little surprised when Palli's escort did not stop at the house's gates. "Should you not return to your council?" he asked, as they turned into the street.

"Dy Yarrin will tell me of it, when I get back. I mean to see you safe to the Zangre's gates. I've not forgotten your tale of poor Ser dy Sanda."

Cazaril glanced over his shoulder at the two young officers pacing behind as they crossed over to the temple plaza. *Oh.* The armed escort was for *him.* He decided not to complain, asking Palli instead, "Who looks like your prime candidate for holy general, then, to present to Orico? Dy Yarrin?"

"He would be my choice," said Palli.

"He does seem a force in your council. Has he a little self-interest, there?"

"Perhaps. But he means to hand the provincarship of Yarrin down to his eldest son, and devote his whole attention to the order, if he is chosen."

"Ah. Would that Martou dy Jironal had done likewise for the Son's Order."

"Aye. So many posts, how is he serving any of them rightly?"

They climbed uphill, threading their way through the stone-paved town, stepping carefully across central gutters well rinsed by the recent cold rains. Narrow streets of shops gave way to wider squares of fine houses. Cazaril considered dy Jironal, as his palace loomed once more on their route. If the curse worked by distorting and betraying virtues, what good thing had it corrupted in Martou dy Jironal? Love of family, perhaps, turning it into mistrust of all that was not family? His excessive reliance on his brother Dondo was surely turning to weakness and downfall. Maybe. "Well . . . I hope that level heads prevail."

Palli grimaced. "Court life is turning you into a diplomat, Caz."

Cazaril returned a bleak smile. "I can't even begin to tell you what court life is turning me—ah!" He ducked as one of Fonsa's crows popped over a nearby housetop and came hurtling down at his head, screaming hoarsely. The bird almost tumbled out of the air at his feet, and hopped across the pavement, cawing and flapping. It was followed by two more. One landed on Cazaril's outflung arm and clung there, shrieking and whistling, its claws digging in. A few black feathers spiraled wildly in the air. "Blast these birds!" He'd thought they had lost interest in him, and here they were back, in all their embarrassing enthusiasm.

Palli, who had jumped back laughing, glanced up over the roof tiles and said, "Five gods, something has stirred them up! The whole flock is in the air above the Zangre. Look at them circle about!"

Ferda dy Gura shielded his eyes and stared where Palli pointed at the distant whirl of dark shapes, like black leaves in a cyclone, dipping and swooping. His brother Foix pressed his hands to his ears as the crows continued to shriek around their feet, and shouted over the din, "Noisy, too!"

These birds were not entranced, Cazaril realized; they were hysterical. His heart turned cold in his chest. "There's something very wrong. Come on!"

He was not in the best shape for running uphill. He had his hand pressed hard to the violent stitch in his side as they approached the stable block at the Zangre's outskirts. His courier birds flapped above his head in escort. By that time, men's shouts could be heard beneath the crows' continued screaming, and Palli and his cousins needed no urging to keep pace with him.

A groom in the royal tabard of the menagerie was staggering in circles before its open doors, screaming and crying, blood running down his face. Two of Teidez's green-and-black-clad Baocian guards stood before the doors with swords drawn, holding off three Zangre guards who hovered apprehensively before them, also with blades out, seeming not to dare to strike. The crows lacked no such courage. They stooped awkwardly at the Baocians, trying to claw with their talons and stab with their beaks. The Baocians cursed and beat them off. Two bundles of black feathers lay on the cobbles already, one still, one twitching.

Cazaril strode up to the menagerie doors, roaring, "What in the Bastard's name is going on here? How dare you slay the sacred crows?"

One of the Baocians pointed his sword toward him. "Stay back, Lord Cazaril! You may not pass! We have strict orders from the royse!"

Lips drawn back in fury, Cazaril knocked the sword aside with his cloaked arm, lunged forward, and wrenched it from the guardsman's grasp. "Give me that, you fool!" He flung it to the stones in the general direction of the Zangre guards, and Palli, who had drawn in a panic when the unarmed Cazaril had waded into the fray. The sword clanged and spun across the cobbles, till Foix stopped it with a booted foot stamped down upon it, and held it with a challenging weight and stare.

Cazaril turned on the second Baocian, whose blade drooped abruptly. Recoiling from Cazaril's step, the guardsman cried hastily, "Castillar, we do this to preserve the life of Roya Orico!"

"Do what? Is Orico in there? *What are you about?*"

A feline snarl, rising to a yowl, from inside whirled Cazaril around, and he left the daunted Baocian to the Zangre guards, now encouraged to advance. He strode into the shadowed aisle of the menagerie.

The old tongueless groom was on his knees on the tiles, bent over, making choked weeping sounds. His thumbless hands were pressed to his face, and a little blood ran between his fingers; he looked up at the sound of Cazaril's step, his quavering wet mouth ravaged with woe. As he ran past the bears' stalls, Cazaril glimpsed two inert black heaps studded with crossbow bolts, fur wet and matted with blood. The vellas' stall door was open, and they lay on their sides in the bright straw, eyes open and fixed, throats slashed.

At the far end of the aisle, Royse Teidez was rising to his feet from the limp body of the spotted cat. He pushed himself up with his bloodied sword, and leaned upon it, panting, his face wild and exultant. His shadow roiled around him like thunderclouds at midnight. He looked up at Cazaril and grinned fiercely. "Ha!" he cried.

The Baocian guard captain, a twisted little bird still in his hand, plunged out of the aviary into Cazaril's path. Bundles of colored feathers, dead and dying birds of all sizes, littered the aviary floor, some still fluttering helplessly. "Hold, Castillar—" he began. His words were whipped away as Cazaril grasped him by the tunic and spun him around, throwing him to the floor into the path of Palli, who was following on his heels muttering in astonished dismay, "Bastard weeps. Bastard weeps . . ." That had been Palli's battle-mumble at Gotorget, when his sword had risen and fallen endlessly on men coming up over the ladders, and he'd had no breath for cries.

"Hold him," Cazaril snarled over his shoulder, and strode on toward Teidez.

Teidez threw back his head and met Cazaril's eyes square-on. "You can't stop me—I've done it! I have saved the roya!"

"What—what—what—" Cazaril was so frightened and furious, his lips and mind could scarcely form coherent words. "Fool boy! What destructive madness is this, this . . . ?" His hands opened, shaking, and jerked about.

Teidez leaned toward him, his teeth glinting in his drawn-back lips. "I've broken the curse, the black magic that has been making Orico sick. It was coming from these evil animals. They were a secret gift from the Roknari, meant to slowly poison him. And we've slain the Roknari spy—I think . . ." Teidez glanced somewhat doubtfully over his shoulder.

Only then did Cazaril notice the last body on the floor at the far end of the aisle. Umegat lay on his side in a heap, as unmoving as the birds or the vellas. The carcasses of the sand foxes lay tumbled nearby. Cazaril had not seen him at first, because his clear white glow was extinguished. *Dead?* Cazaril moaned, lurched toward him, and fell to his knees. The left side of Umegat's head was lacerated, the gray-bronze braid disheveled and soaked with gore. His skin was as gray as an old rag. But his scalp was still sluggishly bleeding, therefore . . .

"Does he still breathe?" asked Teidez, advancing to peer over Cazaril's shoulder. "The captain hit him with his sword pommel, when he would not give way . . ."

"Fool, fool, *fool* boy!"

"No fool I! *He* was behind it all." Teidez nodded toward Umegat. "A Roknari wizard, sent to drain and kill Orico."

Cazaril ground his teeth. "Umegat is a Temple divine. Sent by the Bastard's Order to care for the sacred animals, who were given by the god to *preserve* Orico. And if you have not slain him, it is the only good luck here." Umegat's breath came shallow and odd, his hands were cold as a corpse's, but he did breathe.

"No . . ." Teidez shook his head. "No, you're wrong, that can't be . . ." For the first time, the heroic elation wobbled in his face.

Cazaril uncoiled and rose to his feet, and Teidez stepped back a trifle. Cazaril turned to find Palli, blessedly, at his back, and Ferda at Palli's shoulder, staring around at it all in horrified amazement. Palli, at least, Cazaril could trust to know field aid.

"Palli," he rasped out, "take over here. See to the wounded grooms, this one especially. His skull may be broken." He pointed down to Umegat's darkened body. "Ferda."

"My lord?"

Ferda's badge and colors would gain him admittance anywhere in the sacred precincts. "Run to the temple. Find Archdivine Mendenal. Let no one and nothing keep you from coming instantly to him. Tell him what has transpired here, and have him send Temple physicians—tell him, Umegat needs the Mother's midwife, the special one. He'll know what you mean. Hurry!"

Palli, already kneeling beside Umegat, added, "Give me your cloak. And run, boy!"

Ferda tossed his cloak at his commander, whirled, and was gone before Palli drew a second breath. Palli began to wrap the gray wool around the unconscious Roknari.

Cazaril turned back to Teidez, whose eyes were darting this way and that in growing uncertainty. The royse retreated to the life-emptied husk of the leopard, six feet from nose to tail tip lying limply on the tiles. Its beautiful spotted fur hid the mouths of its wounds, marked by matted blood on its sides. Cazaril thought of dy Sanda's pierced corpse.

"I slew it with my sword, because it was a royal symbol of my House even if it was ensorcelled," Teidez offered. "And to test my courage. It clawed my leg." He bent and rubbed awkwardly at his right shin, where his black trousers were indeed ripped and hanging in blood-wet ribbons.

Teidez was the Heir of Chalion, and Iselle's brother. Cazaril could not wish the beast had bitten out his throat. Should not, anyway. "Five gods, how did you come by this black nonsense?"

"It is not nonsense! You knew Orico's illness was uncanny! I saw it in your face—Bastard's demons, anyone could see it. Lord Dondo told me the secret, before he died. Was murdered—murdered to keep the secret, *I* think, but it was too late."

"Did you come up with this . . . plan of attack, on your own?"

Teidez's head came up, proudly. "No, but when I was the only one left, I carried it through all by myself! We had been going to do it together, after Dondo married Iselle—destroy the curse, and free the House of Chalion from its evil influence. But then it was left to me. So I made myself his banner-carrier, his arm to reach from beyond the grave and strike one last blow for Chalion!"

"Ah! Ah!" Cazaril was so overcome, he stamped in a circle. But had Dondo believed his own rubbish, or had this been a clever plan to use Teidez, obliquely and unprovably, to disable or assassinate Orico? Malice, or stupidity? With Dondo, who could tell? "No!"

"Lord Cazaril, what should we do with these Baocians?" Foix's voice inquired diffidently.

Cazaril looked up to find the disarmed Baocian guard captain held between Foix and one of the Zangre guards. "And you!" snarled Cazaril at him. "You tool, you fool, you lent yourself to this, this stupid sacrilege, and told no one? Or are you Dondo's creature still? Ah! Take him and his men and lock them in a cell, until . . ." Cazaril hesitated. Dondo was behind this, oh yes, reaching out to wreak chaos and disaster, it bore his stamp—but for once, Cazaril suspected, Martou was not behind Dondo. Quite the opposite, unless he missed his guess. "Until the chancellor is notified," Cazaril continued. "You there—" A downward sweep of his arm commanded another Zangre guard's attention. "Run to the Chancellery, or Jironal Palace or wherever he may be found, and tell him what has happened here. Beg him to wait upon me before he goes to Orico."

"Lord Cazaril, you cannot order my guards arrested!" cried Teidez.

Cazaril was the only one here with the air, if not the fact, of authority needed to carry out this next step. "*You* are going straight to your chamber, until your brother orders otherwise. *I* will escort you there."

"Take your hand off me!" Teidez yelped, as Cazaril's iron grip closed around his upper arm. But he did not quite dare to struggle against whatever he was seeing in Cazaril's face.

Cazaril said through his teeth, in a voice dripping false cordiality, "No, indeed. You are wounded, young lord, and I have a duty to help you to a physician." He added under his breath, to Teidez's ear alone, "And I will knock you flat and drag you, if I have to."

Teidez, recovering what dignity he could, grumbled to his guard captain, "Go quietly with them, then. I'll send for you later, when I have proved Lord Cazaril's error." Since his two captors had already spun the captain around and were marching him out, this ended up addressed to the Baocian's back, and fell a little flat. The injured grooms had crept up to Palli's side, and were trying to help him with Umegat. Palli glanced over his shoulder and gave Cazaril a quick, reassuring wave.

Cazaril nodded back, and, under the guise of lending support, strong-armed the royse out of the nightmarish abattoir he had made of the roya's menagerie. *Too late, too late, too late . . .* beat in his brain with every stride. Outside, the crows were no longer whirling and screaming in the air. They hopped about in agitation upon the cobbles, seeming as bewildered and directionless as Cazaril's own thoughts.

Still keeping a grip on Teidez, Cazaril marched him through the Zangre's gates, where, *now*, more guards had appeared. Teidez closed his lips on further protest, though his sullen, angry, and insulted expression boded no good for Cazaril later on. The royse scorned to favor his wounded leg, though it left a trail of bloodied footprints across the cobbles of the main courtyard.

Cazaril's attention was jerked leftward when one of Sara's waiting women and a page appeared in the doorway to Ias's Tower. "Hurry, hurry!" the woman urged the boy, who dashed toward the gates, white-faced. He nearly caromed off Cazaril in his haste.

"Where away, boy?" Cazaril called after him.

He turned and danced backward for a moment. "Temple, lord. Dare not stay—Royina Sara—the roya has collapsed!" He turned and sprinted in earnest through the gates; the guards stared at him, and, uneasily, back toward Ias's Tower.

Teidez's arm, beneath Cazaril's hand, lost its stiff resistance. Beneath his scowl, a scared look crept into his eyes, and he glanced aside warily at his self-appointed detainer.

After a moment's indecision, Cazaril, not letting go of Teidez, wheeled around and started for Ias's Tower instead. He hurried to catch up with the waiting woman, who had ducked back inside, and called after her, but she seemed not to hear him as she scurried up the end stairs. He was wheezing as he reached the third floor, where Orico kept his chambers. He stared in apprehension down its central corridor.

Royina Sara, her white shawl bundled about her and a woman at her heels, was hurrying up the hall. Cazaril bowed anxiously as she came to the staircase.

"My lady, what has happened? Can I help?"

She touched her hand to her frightened face. "I scarcely know yet, Castillar. Orico—he was reading aloud to me in my chambers while I stitched, as he sometimes does, for my solace, when suddenly he stopped, and blinked and rubbed his eyes, and said he could not see the words anymore, and that the room was all dark. But it wasn't! Then he fell from his chair. I cried for my ladies, and we put him in his bed, and have sent for a Temple physician."

"We saw the roya's page," Cazaril assured her. "He was running as fast as he could."

"Oh, good . . ."

"Was it an apoplexy, do you think?"

"I don't think . . . I don't know. He speaks a little, and his breath is not very labored . . . What was all that shouting, down by the stables, earlier?" Distractedly, not waiting for an answer, she passed him and mounted the stairs.

Teidez, his face gone leaden, licked his lips but said no more as Cazaril turned him around and led him down to the courtyard.

The royse did not find his voice again till they were mounting the stairs in the main block, where he repeated breathlessly, "It cannot be. Dondo told me the menagerie was black sorcery, a Roknari curse to keep Orico sick and weak. And I could *see* that it was so."

"A Roknari curse, there truly is, but the menagerie is a white miracle that keeps Orico alive despite it. Was. Till now," Cazaril added bitterly.

"No . . . no . . . it's all wrong. Dondo told me—"

"Dondo was mistaken." Cazaril hesitated briefly. "Or else Dondo wished to hurry the replacement of a roya who favored his elder brother with one who favored himself."

Teidez's lips parted in protest, but no sound came from them. Cazaril didn't think the royse could be feigning the shocked look in his eyes. The only mercy in this day, if mercy it was—Dondo might have misled Teidez, but he seemed not to have corrupted him, not to that extent. Teidez was tool, not co-conspirator, not a willing fratricide. Unfortunately, he was a tool that had kept on functioning after the workman's hand had fallen away. *And whose fault was it that the boy swallowed down lies, when no one would feed him the truth?*

The sallow fellow who was the royse's secretary-tutor looked up in surprise from his writing desk as Cazaril swung the boy into his chambers.

"Look to your master," Cazaril told him shortly. "He's injured. He is not to quit this building until Chancellor dy Jironal is informed what has occurred, and gives him leave." He added, with a little sour satisfaction, "If you knew of this outrage, and did nothing to prevent it, the chancellor will be furious with you."

The man paled in confusion; Cazaril turned his back on him. Now to go see what was happening with Umegat . . .

"But Lord Cazaril," Teidez's voice quavered. "What should I do?"

Cazaril spat over his shoulder, as he strode out again, "Pray."

18

As he turned onto the end stairs, Cazaril heard a woman's slippers scuffing rapidly on the steps. He looked up to find Lady Betriz, her lavender skirts trailing, hurrying down toward him.

"Lord Cazaril! What's going on? We heard shouting—one of the maids cried Royse Teidez has run mad, and tried to slay the roya's animals!"

"Not mad—misled. I think. And not tried—succeeded." In a few brief, bitter words, Cazaril described the horror in the stable block.

"But *why?*" Her voice was husky with shock.

Cazaril shook his head. "A lie of Lord Dondo's, nearly as I can tell. He convinced the royse that Umegat was a Roknari wizard using the animals to somehow poison the roya. Which turned the truth exactly backwards; the animals sustained Orico, and now he has collapsed. Five gods, I cannot explain it all here upon the stairs. Tell Royesse Iselle I will attend upon her soon, but first I must see to the injured grooms. Stay away—keep Iselle away from the menagerie." And if he didn't give Iselle action, she'd surely take it for herself . . . "Wait upon Sara, both of you; she's half-distracted."

Cazaril continued on down the stairs, past the place where he had been—deliberately?—decoyed away by his own pain, earlier. Dondo's demonic ghost made no move to grip him *now*.

Back at the menagerie, Cazaril found that the excellent Palli and his men had already carried off Umegat and the more seriously injured of the undergrooms to the Mother's hospital. The remaining groom was stumbling around trying to catch a hysterical little blue-and-yellow bird that had somehow escaped the Baocian guard captain and taken refuge in the upper cornices. Some servants from the stable had come over and were making awkward attempts to help; one had taken off his tabard and was sweeping it up, trying to knock the bird out of the air.

"Stop!" Cazaril choked back panic. For all he knew, the little feathered creature was the last thread by which Orico clung to life. He directed the would-be helpers instead to the task of collecting the bodies of the slain animals, laying them out in the stable courtyard, and cleaning up the bloody mess on the tiles inside. He scooped up a handful of grains from the vellas' stall, remains of their last interrupted dinner, and coaxed the little bird down to his own hand, chirping as he'd seen Umegat do. Rather to his surprise, the bird came to him and suffered itself to be put back into its cage.

"Guard it with your life," he told the groom. Then added, scowling for effect, "If it dies, you die." An empty threat, though it must do for now; the grooms, at least, looked impressed. *If it dies, Orico dies?* That suddenly seemed frighteningly plausible. He turned to lend a hand in dragging out the heavy bodies of the bears.

"Should we skin them, lord?" one of the stable hands inquired, staring at the results of Teidez's hellish hunt piled up outside on the paving stones.

"No!" said Cazaril. Even the few of Fonsa's crows still lingering about the stable yard, though they regarded the bloody carcasses with wary interest, made no move toward them. "Treat them . . . as you would the roya's soldiers who had died in battle. Burned or buried. Not skinned. Nor eaten, for the gods' sakes." Swallowing, Cazaril bent and added the bodies of the two dead crows to the row. "There has been sacrilege enough this day." And the gods forfend Teidez had not slain a holy saint as well as the sacred animals.

A clatter of hooves heralded the arrival of Martou dy Jironal, fetched, presumably, from Jironal Palace; he was followed up the hill by four retainers on foot, gasping for breath. The chancellor swung down from his snorting, sidling horse, handed it off to a bowing groom, and advanced to stare at the row of dead animals.

The bears' dark fur riffled in the cold wind, the only movement. Dy Jironal's lips spasmed on unvoiced curses. "What is this madness?" He looked up at Cazaril, and his eyes narrowed in bewildered suspicion. "Did *you* set Teidez onto this?" Dy Jironal was not, Cazaril judged, dissimulating; he was as off-balance as Cazaril himself.

"I? No! I do not control Teidez." Cazaril added sourly, "And neither, it appears, do you. He was in your constant company for the past two weeks; had you no hint of this?"

Dy Jironal shook his head.

"In his defense, Teidez seems to have had some garbled notion that this act would somehow help the roya. That he'd no better sense is a fault of his age; that he had no better knowledge . . . well, you and Orico between you have served him ill. If he'd been more filled with truth, he'd have had less room for lies. I've had his Baocian guard locked up, and taken him to his chambers, to await . . ." *the roya's orders* would not be forthcoming now. Cazaril finished, "your orders."

Dy Jironal's hand made a constricted gesture. "Wait. The royesse—he was closeted with his sister yesterday. Could she have set him on?"

"Five witnesses will say no. Including Teidez himself. He gave no sign yesterday that this was in his mind." Almost no sign. *Should have, should have, should have . . .*

"You control the Royesse Iselle closely enough," snapped dy Jironal bitterly. "Do you think I don't know who encouraged her in her defiance? I fail to see the secret of her pernicious attachment to you, but I mean to cut that connection."

"Yes." Cazaril bared his teeth. "Dy Joal tried to wield your knife last night. He'll know to charge you more for his services next time. Hazard pay." Dy Jironal's eyes glittered with understanding; Cazaril took a breath, for self-control. This was bringing their hostilities much too close to the surface. The last thing he desired was dy Jironal's full attention. "In any case, there is no mystery. Teidez says your amiable brother Dondo plotted this with him, before he died."

Dy Jironal stepped back a pace, eyes widening, but his teeth clenched on any other reaction.

Cazaril continued, "Now, what *I* should dearly like to know is—and you are in a better position to guess the answer than I am—did *Dondo* know what this menagerie really did for Orico?"

Dy Jironal's gaze flew to his face. "Do you?"

"All the Zangre knows by now: Orico was stricken blind, and fell from his chair, during the very moments his creatures were dying. Sara and her ladies brought him to his bed, and have sent for the Temple physicians." This answer both evaded the question and abruptly redirected dy Jironal's attention; the chancellor paled, whirled away, and made for the Zangre gates. He did not, Cazaril noted, stay to inquire after Umegat. Clearly, dy Jironal knew what the menagerie did; did he understand how?

Do you?

Cazaril shook his head and turned the other way, for yet another weary march down into town.

Cardegoss's Temple Hospital of the Mother's Mercy was a rambling old converted mansion, bequeathed to the order by a pious widow, on the street beyond the Mother's house from the Temple Square. Cazaril tracked Palli and Umegat through its maze to a second-floor gallery above an inner courtyard. He spotted the chamber readily by the reunited dy Gura brothers standing guard outside its closed door. They saluted and passed him through.

He entered to find Umegat laid out unconscious upon a bed. A white-haired woman in a Temple physician's green robes bent over him stitching up the lacerated flap of his scalp. She was assisted by a familiar, dumpy middle-aged woman whose viridescent tinge owed nothing to her green dress. Cazaril could still see her faint effulgence with his eyes closed. The archdivine of Cardegoss himself, in his five-colored vestment, hovered anxiously. Palli leaned against a wall with his arms crossed; his face lightened, and he pushed to his feet when he saw Cazaril.

"How goes it?" Cazaril asked Palli in a low voice.

"Poor fellow's still out cold," Palli murmured back. "I think he must have taken a mighty whack. And you?"

Cazaril repeated the tale of Orico's sudden collapse. Archdivine Mendenal stepped closer to listen, and the physician glanced over her shoulder. "Had they told you of this turn, Archdivine?" Cazaril added.

"Oh, aye. I will follow Orico's physicians to the Zangre as soon as I may."

If the white-haired physician wondered why an injured groom should claim more of the archdivine's attention than the stricken roya, she gave no more sign than a slight lifting of her eyebrows. She finished her last neat stitch and dipped a cloth in a basin to wash the crusting gore from the shaved scalp around the wound. She dried her hands, checked the rolled-back eyes under Umegat's lids, and straightened. The Mother's midwife gathered up Umegat's cut-away left braid and the rest of the medical mess, and made all tidy.

Archdivine Mendenal clutched his fingers together, and asked the physician, "Well?"

"Well, his skull is not broken, that I can feel. I shall leave the wound uncovered to better mark bleeding or swelling. I can tell nothing more until he wakes. There's naught to do now but keep him warm and watch him till he stirs."

"When will that be?"

The physician stared down dubiously at her patient. Cazaril did, too. The fastidious Umegat would have hated his present crumpled, half-shorn, desperately limp appearance. Umegat's flesh was still that deathly gray, making his golden Roknari skin look like a dirty rag. His breath rasped. *Not good.* Cazaril had seen men who looked like that go on to recover; he'd also seen them sink and die.

"I cannot say," the physician replied at last, echoing Cazaril's own mental diagnosis.

"Leave us, then. The acolyte will watch him for now."

"Yes, Your Reverence." The physician bowed, and instructed the midwife, "Send for me at once if he either wakes, or takes a fever, or starts to convulse." She gathered up her instruments.

"Lord dy Palliar, I thank you for your aid," the archdivine said. He added, "Lord Cazaril, please stay."

Palli said merely, "You're entirely welcome, Your Reverence," then after a heartbeat, as the hint penetrated, "Oh. Ah. If you're all right, Caz . . . ?"

"For now."

"Then I should perhaps return to the Daughter's house. If you need anything, at any time, send for me there, or at Yarrin Palace, and I'll 'tend upon you at once. You should not go about alone." He gave Cazaril a stern look, to be sure this was understood as command and not parting pleasantry. He, too, then bowed, and, opening the door for the physician, followed in her wake.

As the door closed, Mendenal turned to Cazaril, his hands outstretched in pleading. "Lord Cazaril, what should we do?"

Cazaril recoiled. "Five gods, *you're* asking *me*?"

The man's lips twisted ruefully. "Lord Cazaril, I've only been the archdivine of Cardegoss for two years. I was chosen because I was a good administrator, I fancy, and to please my family, because my brother and my father before him were powerful provincars. I was dedicated to the Bastard's Order at age fourteen, with a good dower from my father to assure my care and advancement. I have served the gods faithfully all my life, but . . . they do not speak to me." He stared at Cazaril, and glanced aside to the Mother's midwife, with an odd hopeless envy in his eyes, devoid of hostility. "When a pious ordinary man finds himself in a room with three working saints—if he has any wits left—he seeks instruction, he does not feign to instruct."

"*I* am not . . ." Cazaril bit back the denial. He had more urgent concerns than arguing over the theological definition of his current condition, though if this was sainthood, the gods must *exceed* themselves for damnation. "Honorable Acolyte—I'm sorry, I have forgotten your name?"

"I am Clara, Lord Cazaril."

Cazaril gave her a little bow. "Acolyte Clara. Do you see—do you *not* see—Umegat's glow? I've never seen him when—is it supposed to go out when a man is asleep or unconscious?"

She shook her head. "The gods are with us waking and sleeping, Lord Cazaril. I'm sure I don't have the strength of sight you do, but indeed, the Bastard has withdrawn his presence from Learned Umegat."

"Oh, no," breathed Mendenal.

"Are you sure?" said Cazaril. "It could not be a defect in my—in your second sight?"

She glanced at him, wincing a little. "No. For I can see you plainly enough. I could see you before you came in the door. It is almost painful to be in the same room with you."

"Does this mean the miracle of the menagerie is broken?" asked Mendenal anxiously, gesturing at the unconscious groom. "We have no dike now against the tide of this black curse?"

She hesitated. "Umegat no longer hosts the miracle. I do not know if the Bastard has transferred it to another's will."

Mendenal wheeled to stare hopefully at Cazaril. "His, perhaps?"

She frowned at Cazaril, absently holding her hand to her brow as if to shade her eyes. "If I am a saint, as Learned Umegat has named me, I am only a small domestic one. If Umegat's tutelage had not sharpened my perceptions over the years, I should merely have thought myself unusually lucky in my profession."

Luck, Cazaril couldn't help reflecting, had not been *his* most salient experience since he'd stumbled into the gods' maze.

"And yet the Mother only reaches through me from time to time, then passes on. Lord Cazaril . . . blazes. From the day I first saw him at Lord Dondo's funeral. The white light of the Bastard and the blue clarity of the Lady of Spring, both at once, the constant living presence of two gods, all mixed with some other dark thing I cannot make out. Umegat could see more clearly. If the Bastard has added more to the roil already there, I cannot tell."

The archdivine touched brow, lips, navel, groin, and heart, fingers spread wide, and stared hungrily at Cazaril. "Two gods, two gods at once, and in this room!"

Cazaril bent forward, hands clenching, hideously reminded by the pressure of his belt of the terrifying distention beneath it. "Did Umegat not make known to you what I did to Lord Dondo? Did you not talk to Rojeras?"

"Yes, yes, and I spoke to Rojeras too, good man, but of course he could not understand—"

"He understood better than you seem to. I bear death and murder in my gut. An abomination, for all I know taking physical and not just psychic form, engendered by a demon and Dondo dy Jironal's accursed ghost. Which screams at me nightly, by the way, in Dondo's voice, with all his vilest vocabulary, and Dondo had a mouth like the Cardegoss main sewer. With no way out but to tear me open. It is not holy, it is *disgusting*!"

Mendenal stepped back, blinking.

Cazaril clutched his head. "I have terrible dreams. And pains in my belly. And rages. And I'm afraid Dondo is leaking."

"Oh, dear," said Mendenal faintly. "I had no idea, Lord Cazaril. Umegat said only that you were skittish, and it was best to leave you in his hands."

"Skittish," Cazaril repeated hollowly. "And oh, did I mention the ghosts?" It was surely a measure of . . . something, that they seemed the least of his worries.

"Ghosts?"

"All the ghosts of the Zangre follow me about the castle and cluster around my bed at night."

"Oh," said Mendenal, looking suddenly worried. "Ah."

"Ah?"

"Did Umegat warn you about the ghosts?"

"No . . . he said they could do me no harm."

"Well, yes and no. They can do you no harm while you live. But as Umegat explained it to me, the Lady's miracle has delayed the working out of the Bastard's miracle, not reversed it. It follows that, hm, should Her hand open, and the demon fly away with your soul—and Dondo's, of course—it will leave your husk with a certain, um, dangerous theological emptiness which is not quite like natural death. And the ghosts of the excluded damned will attempt to, er, move in."

After a short, fraught silence, Cazaril inquired, "Do they ever succeed?"

"Sometimes. I saw a case once, when I was a young divine. The degraded spirits are shambling stupid things, but it's so very awkward to get them out again once they take possession. They must be burned . . . well, *alive* is not quite the right term. Very ugly scene, especially if the relatives don't understand, because, of course, being your body, it screams in your voice. . . . It would not, in the event, be *your* problem, of course, you would be, um, elsewhere by then, but it might save, hm, others some painful troubles, if you make sure you always have someone by you who would understand the necessity of burning your body before sunset . . ." Mendenal trailed off apologetically.

"Thank you, Your Reverence," said Cazaril, with awful politeness. "I shall add that to Rojeras's theory of the demon growing itself a new body in my tumor and gnawing its way out, should I ever again be in danger of getting a night's sleep. Although I suppose there's no reason *both* could not occur. Sequentially."

Mendenal cleared his throat. "Sorry, my lord. I thought you should know."

Cazaril sighed. "Yes . . . I suppose I should." He looked up, remembering last night's scene with dy Joal. "Is it possible . . . suppose the Lady's grip loosened just a little. Is it possible for Dondo's soul to leak into mine?"

Mendenal's brows rose. "I don't . . . Umegat would know. Oh, how I wish he would wake up! I suppose it would be a faster way for Dondo's ghost to get a body than to grow one in a tumor. You would think it would be too small." He made an uncertain measuring gesture with his hands.

"Not according to Rojeras," said Cazaril dryly.

Mendenal rubbed his forehead. "Ah, poor Rojeras. He thought I had taken a sudden interest in his specialty when I asked about you, and of course, I did not correct his misapprehension. I thought he was going to talk for half the night. I finally had to promise him a purse for his ward, to escape the tour of his collection."

"I'd pay money to escape that, too," Cazaril allowed. After a moment he asked curiously, "Your Reverence . . . why was I not arrested for Dondo's murder? How did Umegat finesse that?"

"Murder? There was no murder."

"Excuse me, the man is dead, and by my hand, by death magic, which is a capital crime."

"Oh. Yes, I see. The ignorant are full of errors about death magic, well, even the name is wrong. It's a nice theological point, d'you see. *Attempting* death magic is a crime of intent, of conspiracy. *Successful* death magic is not death magic at all, but a miracle of justice, and cannot be a crime, because it is the hand of the god that carries off the victim—victims—I mean, it's not as if the roya can send his officers to arrest the Bastard, eh?"

"Do you think the present chancellor of Chalion will appreciate the distinction?"

"Ah . . . no. Which is why Umegat advised that the Temple prefer a discreet approach to this . . . this very complicated issue." Mendenal scratched his cheek in new worry. "Not that the supplicant of such justice has ever lived through it, before . . . the distinction was clearer when it was all theoretical. *Two* miracles. I never thought of two miracles. Unprecedented. The Lady of Spring must love you dearly."

"As a teamster loves his mule that carries his baggage," said Cazaril bitterly, "whipping it over the high passes."

The archdivine looked a little distraught; only Acolyte Clara's lips twisted in appreciation. Umegat would have snorted, Cazaril thought. He began to understand why the Roknari saint had been so fond of talking shop with him. Only the saints would joke so about the gods, because it was either joke or scream, and they alone knew it was all the same to the gods.

"Yes, but," said Mendenal. "Umegat concurred—so extraordinary a preservation must surely be for an extraordinary purpose. Have you . . . have you no guess at all?"

"Archdivine, I know naught." Cazaril's voice shook. "And I am . . ." he broke off.

"Yes?" encouraged Mendenal.

If I say it aloud, I will fall to pieces right here. He licked his lips, and swallowed. When he forced the words from his tongue at last, they came out a hoarse whisper. "I am very frightened."

"Oh," said the archdivine after a long moment. "Ah. Yes, I . . . I see that it would be . . . Oh, if only Umegat would wake up!"

The Mother's midwife cleared her throat, diffidently. "My lord dy Cazaril?"

"Yes, Acolyte Clara?"

"I think I have a message for you."

"What?"

"The Mother spoke to me in a dream last night. I was not altogether sure, for my sleeping brain spins fancies out of whatever is common in my thoughts, and I think often of Her. So I had meant to take it to Umegat today, and be guided by his good advice. But She said to me, She said"—Clara took a breath, and steadied her voice, her expression growing calmer—" 'Tell my Daughter's faithful courier to beware despair above all.'"

"Yes?" said Cazaril after a moment. "And . . . ?" Blast it, if the gods were going to trouble to send him messages in other people's dreams, he'd prefer something less cryptic. And more practical.

"That was all."

"Are you sure?" asked Mendenal.

"Well . . . She might have said, her Daughter's faithful courtier. Or castle-warder. Or captain. Or all four of them—that part's blurred in my memory."

"If it is so, who are the other three men?" asked Mendenal, puzzled.

The unknowing echo of the Provincara's words to him in Valenda chilled Cazaril to the pit of his aching belly. "I . . . I am, Arch-divine. I am." He bowed to the acolyte, and said through stiff lips, "Thank you, Clara. Pray to your Lady for me."

She gave him a silent, understanding smile, and a little nod.

Leaving the Mother's acolyte to keep close watch over Umegat, the archdivine excused himself to go attend upon Roya Orico, and with a shy diffidence invited Cazaril to accompany him to the Zangre gates. Cazaril found himself grateful for the offer and followed him out. His earlier towering rage and terror had long since passed, leaving him limp and weak. His knees buckled on the gallery stairs; but for catching the railing he would have tumbled down half a flight. To his embarrassment, the solicitous Mendenal insisted Cazaril be carried up the hill in his own sedan chair, hoisted by four stout dedicats, with Mendenal walking beside. Cazaril felt a fool, and conspicuous. But, he had to admit, vastly obliged.

❧THE INTERVIEW CAZARIL HAD BEEN DREADING DID not take place until after supper. Summoned by a page, he climbed reluctantly to the royesse's sitting room. Iselle, looking strained, awaited him attended by Betriz; the royesse waved him to a stool. Candles burning brightly in all the mirrored wall sconces did not drive away the shadow that clung about her.

"How does Orico go on?" he asked the ladies anxiously. They had neither of them come to supper in the banqueting hall, instead remaining with the royina and the stricken roya above stairs.

Betriz answered, "He seemed calmer this evening, when he found he was not completely blind—he can see a candle flame with his right eye. But he is not passing water properly, and his physician thinks he is in danger of growing dropsical. He does look terribly swollen." She bit her lip in worry.

Cazaril ducked his head at the royesse. "And were you able to see Teidez?"

Iselle sighed. "Yes, right after Chancellor dy Jironal dressed him down. He was too distraught to be sensible. If he were younger, I would name it one of his tantrums. I'm sorry he is grown too big to slap. He takes no food, and throws things at his servants, and now he's freed from his chambers, is refusing to come out. There's nothing to do when he gets like this but to leave him alone. He'll be better tomorrow." Her eyes narrowed at Cazaril, and her lips compressed. "And so, my lord. Just how long have you known of this black curse that hangs over Orico?"

"Sara finally talked to you . . . did she?"

"Yes."

"What exactly did she say?"

Iselle gave a tolerably accurate summation of the story of Fonsa and the Golden General, and the descent of the legacy of ill fortune through Ias to Orico. She did not mention herself or Teidez.

Cazaril chewed on a knuckle. "You have about half the facts, then."

"I do not like this half portion, Cazaril. The world demands I make good choices on no information, and then blames my maidenhood for my mistakes, as if my maidenhood were responsible for my ignorance. Ignorance is not stupidity, but it might as well be. And I *do not like* feeling stupid." Steel rang in these last words, unmistakably.

He bowed his head in apology. He wanted to weep for what he was about to lose. It was not to shield her maiden innocence, nor Betriz's, that he had kept silent for too long, nor even dread of arrest. He had feared to lose the paradise of their regard, been sickened with the horror of becoming hideous in their eyes. *Coward. Speak, and be done.*

"I first learned of the curse the night after Dondo's death, from the groom Umegat—who is no groom, by the way, but a divine of the Bastard, and the saint who hosted the miracle of the menagerie for Orico."

Betriz's eyes widened. "Oh. I . . . I liked him. How does he go on?"

Cazaril made a little balancing gesture with one hand. "Badly. Still unconscious. And worse, he's"—he swallowed, *Here we go*—"stopped glowing."

"Stopped glowing?" said Iselle. "I didn't know he'd started."

"Yes. I know. You cannot see it. There's . . . something I haven't told you about Dondo's murder." He took a breath. "It was me who sacrificed crow and rat, and prayed to the Bastard for Dondo's death."

"Ah! I'd suspected as much," said Betriz, sitting straighter.

"Yes, but—what you don't know is, I was granted it. I should have died that night, in Fonsa's tower. But another's prayers intervened. Iselle's, I think." He nodded to the royesse.

Her lips parted, and her hand went to her breast. "I prayed that the Daughter spare me from Dondo!"

"You prayed—and the Daughter spared *me*." He added ruefully, "But not, as it turned out, from Dondo. You saw how at his funeral all the gods refused to sign that his soul was taken up?"

"Yes, and so he was excluded, damned, trapped in this world," said Iselle. "Half the court feared he was loose in Cardegoss, and festooned themselves with charms against him."

"In Cardegoss, yes. Loose . . . no. Most lost ghosts are bound to the place where they died. Dondo's is bound to the person who killed him." He shut his eyes, unable to bear looking at their draining faces. "You know my tumor? It's not a tumor. Or not only a tumor. Dondo's soul is trapped inside of me. Along with the death demon, apparently, but the demon, at least, is blessedly quiet about it all. It's Dondo who won't shut up. He screams at me, at night. Anyway." He opened his eyes again, though he still did not dare look up. "All this . . . divine activity has given me a sort of second sight. Umegat has it—there is a little saint of the Mother in town who has it—and I have it. Umegat has—had—a white glow. The Mother Clara shines a faint green. They have both told me I am mostly blue and white, all roiling and blazing." At last, he forced himself to look up and meet Iselle's eyes. "And I can see Orico's curse as a dark shadow. Iselle, listen, this is important. I don't think Sara knows this. It's not just a shadow on Orico. It's on you and Teidez, too. All the descendants of Fonsa seem to be smeared by this black thing."

After a little silence, sitting stiff and still, Iselle said only, "That makes a sort of sense."

Betriz was eyeing him sideways. By the testimony of his belt, his tumor was not grown more gross than before, but her gaze made him feel monstrous. He bent a little over his belly and managed a weak, unfelt grin in her direction.

"But how do you get rid of this . . . haunting?" Betriz asked slowly.

"Um . . . as I understand it, if I am killed, my soul will lose its anchor in my body, and the death demon will be released to finish its job. I think. I'm a little afraid the demon will try to trick or betray me to my death, if it can; it seems a trifle single-minded. It wants to go home. Or, if the Lady's hand opens, the demon will be released, and wrench my soul from my body, and off we all go together again the same." He decided not to burden her with Rojeras's other theory.

"No, Lord Caz, you don't understand. I want to know how you can get rid of it *without* dying."

"I'd like to know that, too," Cazaril sighed. With an effort, he straightened his spine and managed a better smile. "It doesn't matter. I traded my life for Dondo's death of my own free will, and I've received my due. Payment of my debt is merely delayed, not rescinded. The Lady apparently keeps me alive for some service I have yet to perform. Or else I would slay myself in disgust and end it."

Iselle, eyes narrowing at this, sat up and said sharply, "Well, I do not release you from *my* service! Do you hear me, Cazaril?"

His smile grew more genuine, for an instant. "Ah."

"Yes," said Betriz, "and you can't expect *us* to get all squeamish just because you're . . . inhabited. I mean . . . *we're* expected to share our bodies someday. Doesn't make *us* horrible, does it?" She hesitated at where this metaphor was taking her.

Cazaril, whose mind had been shying from just that parallel for some time, said mildly, "Yes, but with Dondo? *You* both drew the line at Dondo." In truth, every man he'd ever killed had traveled back up the shock of his sword arm into his memory, and rode with him still, in a sense. *And so we bear our sins.*

Iselle put her hand to her lips in sudden alarm. "Cazaril—he can't get *out*, can he?"

"I pray to the Lady he may not. The idea of him seeping into my mind is . . . is the worst of all. Worse even than . . . never mind. Oh. That reminds me, I should warn you about the ghosts." Briefly, he repeated what the archdivine had told him about making sure his body was burned, and why. It afforded him an odd relief, to have that out. They were dismayed, but attentive; he thought he might trust them to have the courage for the task. And then was ashamed to have not trusted their courage earlier.

"But listen, Royesse," he went on. "The Golden General's curse has followed Fonsa's get, but Sara is shadowed, too. Umegat and I both think she married into it."

"Her life has certainly been made miserable enough by it," agreed Iselle.

"It therefore follows logically, that you might marry *out* of it. It is a hope, anyway, a great hope. I think we should turn our minds to the matter—I would have you out of Cardegoss, out of the curse, out of Chalion altogether, as soon as may be arranged."

"With the court in this uproar, marriage arrangements are out of—" Iselle paused abruptly. "But . . . what about Teidez? And Orico? And Chalion itself? Am I to abandon them, like a general running away from a losing battle?"

"The highest commanders have wider responsibilities than a single battle. If a battle may not be won—if the general cannot save that day, at least such a retreat saves the good of another day."

She frowned doubtfully, taking this in. Her brows lowered. "Cazaril . . . do you think my mother and grandmother knew of this dark thing that hangs over us?"

"Your grandmother, I don't know. Your mother . . ." If Ista had seen the ghosts of the Zangre for herself, she must have been lent the second sight for a time. What did this imply? Cazaril's imagination foundered. "Your mother knew something, but I don't know how much. Enough to be terrified when you were called to Cardegoss, anyway."

"I'd thought her overfussy." Iselle's voice lowered. "I'd thought her mad, as the servants whispered." Her frown deepened. "I have a lot to think about."

As her silence lengthened, Cazaril rose, and bade both ladies a polite good night. The royesse acknowledged him with an absent nod. Betriz clasped her hands together, staring at him in agonized searching, and dipped a half curtsey.

"Wait!" Iselle called suddenly as he reached the door. He wheeled around; she sprang from her chair, strode up to him, and gripped both his hands. "You are too tall. Bend your head," she commanded.

Obligingly, he ducked his head; she stood on tiptoe. He blinked in surprise as her young lips planted a firm and formal kiss upon his brow, and then upon the back of each hand, lifted to her mouth. And then she sank to the floor in a rustle of perfumed silk, and as his mouth opened in inarticulate protest, she kissed each booted foot with the same unhesitating firmness.

"There," said Iselle, rising. Her chin came up. "Now you may be dismissed."

Tears were running down Betriz's face. Too shaken for words, Cazaril bowed deeply and fled to his unquiet bed.

19

Cazaril found the Zangre
eerily quiet the following day. After
Dondo's death the court had been
alarmed, yes, but excited and given over to gossip and whispering.
Now even the whispering was stilled. All who had no direct duties
stayed away, and those who had inescapable tasks went about them
in a hurried, apprehensive silence.

Iselle and Betriz spent the day in Ias's tower, waiting upon Sara
and Orico. At dawn, Cazaril and the grim castle warder oversaw
the cremation and burial of the remains of the animals. For the rest
of the day, Cazaril alternated feeble attempts to attend to the mess
on his desk with trudges down to the temple hospital. Umegat lay
unchanged, gray and rasping. After his second visit, Cazaril stopped
in at the temple itself and prayed, prostrate and whispering, before
all five altars in turn. If he was in truth infected with this saint-disease,
dammit, shouldn't it be good for something?

The gods do not grant miracles for our purposes, but for theirs,
Umegat had said. Yes? It seemed to Cazaril that this bargain ought
to run two ways. If people stopped lending the gods their wills by
which to do miracles, eh, what would the gods do about it then?
Well, the first thing to happen would be that I'd drop dead. There was
that. Cazaril lay a long time before the altar of the Lady of Spring,
but here found himself mute, not even his lips moving. Abashed,
ashamed, despairing? But wordy or wordless, the gods returned
him only the same blank silence, five times over.

He was reminded of Palli's insistence that he not go about alone when, slogging back up the hill, he passed dy Joal and another of dy Jironal's retainers entering Jironal Palace. Dy Joal's hand curled on his sword hilt, but he did not draw; with polite, wary nods, they walked wide about each other.

Back in his office, Cazaril rubbed his aching brow and turned his thoughts to Iselle's marriage. Royse Bergon of Ibra, eh. The boy would do as well as any and better than most, Cazaril supposed. But this turmoil in the court of Chalion made open negotiations impossible to carry out; it would have to be a secret envoy, and soon. Running down the list in his mind of courtiers capable of such a diplomatic mission turned up none Cazaril would trust. Running down the much shorter list of men he could trust turned up no experienced diplomats. Umegat was laid low. The archdivine could not leave in secret. Palli? March dy Palliar had the rank, at least, to demand Ibra's respect. He tried to imagine honest Palli negotiating the subtleties of Iselle's marriage contract with the Fox of Ibra, and groaned. Maybe . . . maybe if Palli were sent with an extremely detailed and explicit list of instructions . . . ?

Needs must drive. He would broach it to Palli tomorrow.

❧CAZARIL PRAYED ON HIS KNEES BEFORE BED TO BE spared from the nightmare that had recurred three nights running, where Dondo grew back to life size within his swelling stomach and then, somehow dressed in his funeral robes and armed with his sword, carved his way out. Perhaps the Lady heard his plea; at any rate, he woke at dawn, his head and heart pounding, from a new nightmare. In this one, Dondo somehow sucked Cazaril's soul into his own belly in his place, and escaped to take over Cazaril's body. And then embarked on a career of rapine in the women's quarters while Cazaril, helpless to stop him, watched. To his dismay, as he panted in the gray light and regained his grip on reality, Cazaril realized his body was painfully aroused.

So, *was* Dondo plunged into a lightless prison, sealed from sound, deprived of sensation? Or did he ride along as the ultimate spy and voyeur? Cazaril had not imagined making love to Be—to any lady since this damned affliction had been visited upon him;

he imagined it now, a crowded quartet between the sheets, and shuddered.

Briefly, Cazaril envisioned escaping by the window. He might squeeze his shoulders through, and dive; the drop would be stupendous, the crunch at the end . . . quick. Or with his knife, taken to wrists or throat or belly or all three . . . He sat up, blinking, to find a half a dozen phantasms gathered avidly around him, crowding each other like vultures around a dead horse. He hissed, lurched, and swiped his arm through the air to scatter them. Could a body with its head smashed in be animated by one of them? The archdivine's words implied so. Escape through suicide was blocked by this ghastly patrol, it seemed. Dreading sleep, he stumbled from bed and went to wash and dress.

Coming back from a perfunctory breakfast in the banqueting hall, Cazaril encountered a breathless Nan dy Vrit upon the stairs. "My lady begs you 'tend upon her at once," Nan told him, and Cazaril nodded and pushed up the steps. "Not in her chambers," Nan added, as he started past the third floor. "In Royse Teidez's."

"Oh." Cazaril's brows rose, and he turned instead to pass his own chamber and go down the hall to Teidez's, Nan at his heels.

As he entered the office antechamber, twin to Iselle's above, he heard voices from the rooms opening beyond; Iselle's murmur, and Teidez's, raised: "I don't want anything to eat. I don't want to see anyone! Go away!"

The sitting room was cluttered with weapons, clothes, and gifts, strewn about haphazardly. Cazaril picked his way across to the bedchamber.

Teidez lay back on his pillows, still in his nightgown. The close, moist air of the room smelled of boy sweat, and another tang. Teidez's secretary-tutor hovered anxiously on one side of the bed; Iselle stood with her hands on her hips on the other. Teidez said, "I want to go back to sleep. Get out." He glanced up at Cazaril, cringed, and pointed. "I especially don't want him in here!"

Nan dy Vrit said, in a very domestic voice, "Now, none of that, young lord. You know better than to talk to old Nan that way."

Teidez, cowed by some ancient habit, went from surly to whiney. "I have a headache."

Iselle said firmly, "Nan, bring a light. Cazaril, I want you to look at Teidez's leg. It looks very odd to me."

Nan held a brace of candles high, supplementing the wan gray daylight from the window. Teidez at first clutched his blankets to his chest, but didn't quite dare fight his older sister's glare; she twitched them out of his hands and folded them aside.

Three scabbed, parallel grooves ran in a spiral partway around the boy's right leg. In themselves, they did not appear deep or dangerous, but the flesh around them was so swollen that the skin was shiny and silvery. Translucent pink drainage and yellow pus oozed from their edges. Cazaril forced himself to keep his expression even as he studied the hot red streaks climbing past the boy's knee and winding up the inside of his thigh. Teidez's eyes were glazed. He jerked back his head as Cazaril reached for him. "Don't touch me!"

"Be still!" Cazaril commanded in a low voice. Teidez's forehead, beneath Cazaril's wrist, was scorching.

He glanced up at the sallow-faced secretary, watching with a frown. "How long has he been feverish?"

"Just this morning, I believe."

"When did his physician last see this?"

"He would not have a physician, Lord Cazaril. He threw a chair at me when I tried to help him, and bandaged it himself."

"*And you let him?*" Cazaril's voice made the secretary jump.

The man shrugged uneasily. "He would have it so."

Teidez grumbled, "*Some* people obey me. I'll remember who, too, later." He glowered up at Cazaril through half-lowered lashes, and stuck out his lower lip at his sister.

"He's taken an infection. I'll see that a Temple physician is sent in to him at once."

Teidez, disgruntled, wriggled back down under his covers. "Can I go back to sleep now? *If* you don't mind. And draw the curtain, the light hurts my eyes."

"Yes, stay abed," Cazaril told him, and withdrew.

Iselle followed him into the antechamber, lowering her voice. "It's not right, is it?"

"No. It's not. Good observation, Royesse. Your judgment was correct."

She gave him a satisfied nod, and he bowed himself out and made for the end stairs. By Nan dy Vrit's shadowed face, she at least understood just how not-right it was. All Cazaril could think of, as he hastened down the stairs and back across the stones of the courtyard toward Ias's Tower, was how very seldom he'd seen any man, no matter how young or strong, survive an amputation that high upon the thigh. His stride lengthened.

By good luck, Cazaril found dy Jironal at once, in the Chancellery. He was just sealing a saddlebag and dispatching a courier with it.

"How are the roads?" dy Jironal asked the fellow, who was typically lean and wiry and wore the Chancellery's tabard over an odd assortment of winter woolens.

"Muddy, m'lord. It will be dangerous to ride after dark."

"Well, do your best," dy Jironal sighed, and clapped him on the shoulder. The man saluted and made his way out past Cazaril.

Dy Jironal scowled at his new visitor. "Cazaril."

"My lord." Cazaril offered a fractional bow and entered.

Dy Jironal seated himself on the edge of his desk, and folded his arms. "Your attempt to hide behind the Daughter's Order in its plot to unseat me is doomed to fail, you know," he said conversationally. "I intend to see that its failure will be miserable."

Impatiently, Cazaril waved this aside. He'd have been more surprised had dy Jironal *not* had an ear in the order's councils. "You have much worse troubles this morning than anything I can offer you, my lord."

Dy Jironal's eyes widened in surprise; his head tilted in an attitude of sudden attention. "Oh?"

"What did Teidez's wound look like when you saw it?"

"What wound? He showed me no wound."

"On his right leg—he was scratched by Orico's leopard, apparently, while he was killing the poor beast. In truth, the marks didn't look deep, but they've taken an infection. His skin burns. And you know how a poisoned wound sometimes throws out feverish marks upon the skin?"

"Aye," said dy Jironal uneasily.

"Teidez's run from ankle to groin. They look like a bloody conflagration."

Dy Jironal swore.

"I advise you pull that troop of useless physicians off of Orico for a moment and send them across to Teidez's chambers. Or you could lose two royal puppets in one week."

Dy Jironal's glare met Cazaril's like flint on steel, but after one fierce inhalation he nodded and shifted to his feet. Cazaril followed him out. Corrupted with greed and familial pride dy Jironal might be, but he wasn't incompetent. Cazaril could see why Orico might have chosen to endure much, in exchange for that.

After assuring himself that dy Jironal was climbing the stairs to Orico's chambers with due haste, Cazaril turned back down them. He'd had no word from the temple hospital since last night; he wanted to check again on Umegat. He made his way out the Zangre gates past the ill-fated stable block. A little to his surprise, he spotted Umegat's tongueless undergroom climbing the hill toward him. The man waved his thumbless hand when he saw Cazaril, and hurried his step.

He arrived breathless and smiling. His face was marked with livid bruises, red-purple around one eye, from the futile fight in the menagerie, and his broken nose was still swollen, its lacerated edge dark and scabbed. But his eyes were shining in their wrecked matrix; he almost danced up to Cazaril.

Cazaril's brows rose. "You look happy—what, man, is Umegat awake?"

He nodded vigorously.

Cazaril grinned back at him, faint with relief.

He spoke a mumbled sort of gargle, of which Cazaril made out perhaps one word in four, but enough to gather he was on some urgent errand. He motioned Cazaril to wait outside the silent, dark menagerie, and returned in a few minutes with a sack tied to his belt and clutching a book, which he brandished happily. By which Cazaril understood Umegat was not only awake, but well enough to want his favorite book—Ordol, Cazaril noted with bemusement. Glad of the stout little man's company, Cazaril walked beside him down into town.

Cazaril reflected on the fellow's stigmata of martyrdom, displayed with such seeming indifference. It was silent testimony of horrendous torment, endured in the name of his god. Had his terror lasted an hour, a day, months? It was not quite possible to be sure whether the softened roundness of his appearance was the result of castration or just old age. Cazaril couldn't very well ask him his story. Just attempting to listen to his badly mouthed ordinary exchanges was a painful strain upon the ears and attention. He didn't even know if the fellow was Chalionese or Ibran, Brajaran or Roknari, or how he had come to Cardegoss, or how long he had served with Umegat. Doing his daily duties as they came to him. He stumped along now with the book under his arm, eyes bright. So, this was what a faithful servant of the gods, heroic and beloved, ended up looking like.

They arrived at Umegat's chamber to find him sitting up in bed against some pillows. He was pale and washed-out, his prickly scalp puckered along its stitches, remaining hair a tumbled rat's nest, lips crusted, his face unshaved. The tongueless groom rummaged in his sack, pulled out some shaving gear, and waved it triumphantly in the air; Umegat smiled wanly. He stared at Cazaril, not lifting his head from the pillow. He rubbed his eyes, and squinted uncertainly.

Cazaril swallowed. "How do you feel?"

"Headache," Umegat managed. He snorted softly. Finally, he said, "Are *all* my beautiful creatures dead?" His tongue was thick, his voice low and a little slurred, but he seemed coherent enough.

"Nearly all. There was one little blue-and-yellow bird got away. It's back safely in its cage now. I let no one make trophies of them. I saw them cremated like fallen soldiers yesterday. Archdivine Mendenal has undertaken to find their ashes a place of honor."

Umegat nodded, then winced. His crusted lips tightened.

Cazaril glanced at the undergroom—yes, this man had to be one of those who knew the truth—and back to Umegat, and said hesitantly, "Do you know you've stopped glowing?"

Umegat blinked rapidly at him. "I . . . suspected it. At least *you* are much less disturbing to look upon, this way."

"Your second sight is taken from you?"

"Mm. Second sight is redundant to reason anyway. You live, therefore I know perfectly well the Lady's hand still grips you." He added after a moment, "I always knew it was only lent to me for a time. Well, it was quite a ride while it lasted." His voice fell to a whisper. "Quite a ride." He turned his face away. "I could have borne it being taken back. To have it knocked from my hands . . . I should have seen it coming."

The gods should have warned you . . .

The little elderly undergroom, whose face had drooped at the pain in Umegat's voice, picked up the book and held it out consolingly.

Umegat smiled weakly and took it tenderly from him. "At least I have my old profession to fall back on, eh?" His hands smoothed the pages open to some familiar spot, and he glanced down. His smile faded. His voice sharpened. "Is this a joke?"

"Is what a joke, Umegat? It is your book, I saw him bring it from the menagerie."

Umegat struggled awkwardly to sit upright. "What *language* is this?"

Cazaril advanced and glanced over his shoulder. "Ibran, of course."

Umegat paged through the book, fingers shaking, his eyes twitching over the pages, his breath coming faster through lips open in something like terror. "It is . . . it is *gibberish*. It's just, just . . . little blotches of *ink. Cazaril!*"

"It is Ibran, Umegat. It's just Ibran."

"It is my eyes. It is something in me . . ." He clutched his face, rubbed his eyes, and cried suddenly, "Oh, gods!" and burst into tears. The tears became wracking sobs on the third breath. "I am punished!"

"Get the physician, fetch the physician," Cazaril cried to the frightened-looking undergroom, and the man nodded and sped away. Umegat's clutching fingers were tearing the pages in his blind grip. Awkwardly, Cazaril tried to help him, patting his shoulder, straightening the book and then taking it away altogether. The coolly resisted breakdown, having breached Umegat's walls in this unguarded spot, poured through, and the man wept—*not* like a child. No child's sobs were ever this terrifying.

After agonizing minutes, the white-haired physician arrived and soothed the distraught divine; he seized upon her in hope, and would scarcely let her hands go free to carry out her business. Her explanation that many men and women taken with a palsy-stroke improved in a few days, people carried in by anxious relatives even walking out on their own a few days later, did the most to help him regain his shattered self-control. It took all his strength of mind, for her further tests, conducted after sending a passing dedicat running to the order's library, revealed he could not read Roknari nor Darthacan either, and furthermore, his hands had lost the ability to wield a pen to make any kind of letters.

The quill fell from his awkward grip, trailing ink across the linens, and he buried his face in his hands, groaning again, "I am punished. My joy and my refuge, taken from me . . ."

"Sometimes, people can relearn things they have forgotten," the physician said tentatively. "And your understanding of the words in your ears has not been taken, nor your recognition of the people you know. I have seen that happen, with some afflicted people. Someone could still read books aloud to you . . ."

Umegat's eyes met those of the tongueless groom, who was standing to one side still holding the Ordol. The old man scrubbed his fist across his mouth and made an odd noise down in his throat, a whimper of pure despair. Tears were running from the corners of his eyes down his seamed face.

Umegat's breath puffed from his lips, and he shook his head; drawn from his trouble by its reflection in that aged face, he reached across to grip the undergroom's hand. "Sh. Sh. Aren't we a pair, now." He sighed, and sank back on his pillows. "Never say the Bastard has no sense of humor." After a moment his eyes closed. Exhausted, or shutting it all out, Cazaril was not sure which.

He choked down his own terrified demand of, *Umegat, what should we do now?* Umegat was in no condition to do anything, even give direction. Even pray? Cazaril hardly dared ask him to pray for Teidez, under the circumstances.

Umegat's breath thickened, and he dropped into an uneasy doze. Softly, careful to make no sound, the undergroom laid out his shaving gear on a side table and sat patiently to await his wakening again. The physician made notes and left quietly. Cazaril followed her out to the gallery overlooking the courtyard. Its central fountain was not playing in this chill, and the water in it was dark and scummy in the gray winter light.

"*Is* he punished?" he asked her.

She rubbed the back of her neck in a weary gesture. "How do I know? Head injuries are the strangest of all. I once saw a woman whose eyes appeared wholly undamaged go blind from a blow to the *back* of her head. I've seen people lose speech, lose control of half their body but not the other half. Are they punished? If so, the gods are evil, and that I do not believe. I think it is chance."

I think the gods load the dice. He wanted to urge her to take good care of Umegat, but clearly she already was doing so, and he didn't want to sound frantic, or as though he doubted her skill or dedication. He bade her a polite good morning instead, and took himself off to track down the archdivine and apprise him of the ugly turn of Teidez's wound.

He found Archdivine Mendenal in the temple at the Mother's altar, celebrating a ceremony of blessing upon a rich leather merchant's wife and newborn daughter. Cazaril perforce waited until the family had laid their thanksgiving offerings and filed out again before approaching him and murmuring his news. Mendenal turned pale, and hurried off to the Zangre at once.

Cazaril had developed unsettling new views of the efficacy and safety of prayer, but laid himself down on the cold pavement before the Mother's altar anyway, thinking of Ista. If there was little hope of mercy for Teidez's own sake, lured into violent sacrilege and left there by Dondo, surely the Mother might spare some pity for his mother Ista? The goddess's message to him via Her acolyte's dream the other day had sounded merciful. In a way. Though it might prove to be merely brutally practical. Prone on the polished patterned slates, he could feel the lethal lump in his belly, an uncomfortable mass seeming the size of his doubled fists.

He rose at length and sought out Palli at Provincar dy Yarrin's narrow old stone palace. Cazaril was conducted by a servant to a guest chamber at the back of the house. Palli was seated at a small table, writing in a ledger, but laid his quill aside when Cazaril entered and motioned his visitor to a chair across from him.

As soon as the servant had shut the door behind him Cazaril leaned forward and said, "Palli, could you, at need, ride courier to Ibra in secret for the Royesse Iselle?"

Palli's brows climbed. "When?"

"Soon."

He shook his head. "If by soon you mean now, I think not. I am much taken up with my duties as a lord dedicat—I have promised dy Yarrin my voice and my vote in the Council."

"You could leave a proxy with dy Yarrin, or some other trusted comrade."

Palli rubbed his shaven chin, and vented a dubious, "Hm."

Cazaril considered claiming to be a saint of the Daughter, and pulling rank on Palli, dy Yarrin, and their entire military order. It would require complicated explanations. It would require divulging the secret of Fonsa's curse. It would entail not merely admitting, but asserting, his . . . peculiar disorder. God-touched. God-*ravished*. And sounding as mad or madder than Ista ever had. He compromised. "I think this may *be* the Daughter's business."

Palli's lips screwed up. "How can you tell?"

"I just can."

"Well, I can't."

"Wait, I know. Before you go to sleep tonight, pray for guidance."

"Me? Why don't you?"

"My nights are . . . full."

"And since when did you believe in prophetic dreams? I thought you always claimed it was nonsense, people fooling themselves, or pretending to an importance they could otherwise never claim."

"It's a . . . recent conversion. Look, Palli. Just do it for, for the experiment. To please me, if you will."

Palli made a surrendering gesture. "For you, yes. For the rest of it . . ." His black brows lowered. "Ibra . . . ? Just who would I be riding in secret from?"

"Dy Jironal. Mostly."

"Oh? Dy Yarrin might be interested in that. Something in it for him?"

"Not in any direct way, I don't think." Cazaril added reluctantly, "And likewise secret from Orico."

Palli sat back, his head tilting. His voice lowered. "Coy, Caz. Just what kind of noose are you offering to put round my neck, here? Is this treason?"

"Worse," Cazaril sighed. "Theology."

"Eh?"

"Oh, that reminds me." Cazaril pinched the bridge of his nose, trying to decide if his headache was getting worse. "Tell dy Yarrin his councils are being reported by some spy to dy Jironal. Though he may be canny enough to realize it already, I don't know."

"Worse and worse. Are you getting enough sleep, Caz?"

A bark of bitter laughter broke from Cazaril's lips. "No."

"You always did go strangely fey when you were overtired, y'know. Well, I'm not riding anywhere on the basis of a bunch of dark hints."

"In the event, you'd be given full knowledge."

"When I am given full knowledge, then I'll decide."

"Fair enough," Cazaril sighed. "I will discuss it with the royesse. But I didn't want to propose to her a man who would fail her."

"Hey!" said Palli indignantly. "When have I failed?"

"Never, Palli. That's why I thought of you." Cazaril grinned and, with a little grunt of pain, pushed to his feet. "I must return to the Zangre." Briefly, he described the unpleasant progression of Teidez's claw mark.

Palli's face grew very sober indeed. "Just how bad is it?"

"I don't . . ." Caution tempered Cazaril's frankness. "Teidez is young, strong, well fed. I see no reason why he cannot throw off this infection."

"Five gods, Caz, he's the hope of his House. What will Chalion do if he doesn't? And Orico laid low as well!"

Cazaril hesitated. "Orico . . . hasn't been well for some time, but I'm sure dy Jironal never imagined them both becoming so sick at once. You might note to dy Yarrin that our dear chancellor is going to be fairly distracted for the next few days. If the lord dedicats want to get past him to Orico's bed and get anything signed, now might be their best chance."

He extracted himself from Palli's cascade of second thoughts, although not from Palli's insistence that he take the dy Gura brothers for escort. Climbing the hill once more, his circling calculations of how to effect Iselle's escape from the wreck of her cursed House spiraled inward on a much simpler grim determination not to fall down in front of these earnest young men, to be hauled home stumbling with his arms across their shoulders.

🐦CAZARIL FOUND THE THIRD-FLOOR CORRIDOR OF THE main block promisingly crowded upon his return. Green-robed physicians and their acolyte assistants scurried in and out. Servants hurried with water, linens, blankets, strange drinks in silver ewers. As Cazaril lingered, wondering what assistance he might offer, the archdivine emerged from the antechamber and started down the corridor, his face set and introspective.

"Your Reverence?" Cazaril touched his five-colored sleeve in passing. "How goes the boy?"

"Ah, Lord Cazaril." Mendenal turned aside briefly. "The chancellor and the royesse have given me purses for prayers on his behalf. I go to set them in motion."

"Do you think . . . prayers will do any good?" *Do you think any prayers will do good?*

"Prayer is always good."

No, it's not, Cazaril wanted to reply, but held his tongue.

Mendenal added suggestively, lowering his voice, "Yours might be especially efficacious. At this time."

Not so far as Cazaril had noticed. "Your Reverence, I do not hate any man in this world enough to inflict the results of *my* prayers upon him."

"Ah," said Mendenal uneasily. He managed a smile, and took polite leave.

Royesse Iselle stepped into the corridor and glanced up and down it. She spied Cazaril and motioned him to her.

He bowed. "Royesse?"

She, too, lowered her voice; everyone here seemed to speak in hushed tones. "There is talk of an amputation. Can you—would you be willing—to help hold him down, if it chances so? I think you are familiar with the procedure?"

"Indeed, Royesse." Cazaril swallowed. Nightmare memories of bad moments in field hospitals flitted through his mind. He had never been able to decide if the men who tried to take it bravely or the men whose minds broke in terror were the hardest for their helpers to endure. Better by far the men who were unconscious to start with. "Tell the physicians I am at their service, and Lord Teidez's."

Cazaril could hear from the antechamber where he leaned against the wall to wait just when the proposal was floated to Teidez. The boy was going to be of the second category, it seemed. He cried, and bellowed that he would not be made a cripple by traitors and idiots, and threw things. His rising hysteria was only calmed when a second physician opined that the infection was not gangrene after all—Cazaril's nose agreed—but rather, blood poisoning, and that amputation would do more harm than good now. Treatment was reduced to a mere lancing, although from Teidez's yells and struggles it might as well have been an amputation. Despite the draining of the wound, Teidez's fever soared; servants brought buckets of cold water to make him a bath in a copper tub in the sitting room, then the physicians had to wrestle him into it.

Between physicians, acolytes, and servants, they seemed to have enough hands for these practical tasks, and Cazaril withdrew for a time to his own office on the floor above. There he diverted his mind by writing tart letters to those town councils late with their royally mandated payments to the royesse's household, which was all of them. They had sent letters of excuse claiming poor crops, banditry, plague, evil weather, and cheating tax gatherers. Six towns' worth of troubles; Cazaril wondered if Orico had pulled a fast one with his betrothal gift and dumped the six worst towns on his rent rolls onto his sister and Dondo, or whether all of Chalion was in such disarray.

Iselle and Betriz came in, looking weary and strained.

"My brother is more ill than I have ever seen him," Iselle confided to Cazaril. "We are going to set up my private altar and pray before dinner. I'm wondering if we should perhaps fast as well."

"I think what may be needed here are not others' prayers, but Teidez's himself; and not for health, but for forgiveness."

Iselle shook her head. "He refuses to pray at all. He says it's not his fault, but Dondo's, which is certainly true up to a point. . . . He cries he never intended to hurt Orico, and they are slanderers who say so."

"Is anyone saying so?"

Betriz put in, "No one says it to the royesse's face. But there are strange rumors among the servants, Nan says."

Iselle's frown deepened. "Cazaril . . . could it be?"

Cazaril leaned his elbows on his table and rubbed the ache between his brows. "I think . . . not on Teidez's part. I believe him when he says it was Dondo's idea. Dondo, now, of him I would believe anything. Think it through from his point of view. He marries Teidez's sister, then arranges for Teidez to ascend the throne while still a minor. He knew from watching his brother Martou just how much power a man may wield sitting in a roya's pocket. Grant you, I don't know how he intended to rid himself of Martou, but I am certain Dondo meant to be the next chancellor, perhaps regent, of Chalion. Maybe even roya of Chalion, depending on what evil chances he could arrange for Teidez."

Iselle caught her lower lip in her teeth. "And here I thought you had only saved *me*." She touched Cazaril briefly on the shoulder and passed on into her chambers.

Cazaril accompanied Iselle and Betriz on their predinner visit to Orico. Orico, though no better, was no worse. They found him arrayed in fresh linens, sitting up in bed, and being read to by Sara. The roya spoke hopefully of an improvement in his right eye, for he thought he could now see shapes moving. Cazaril thought the physician's diagnosis of dropsy all too likely, for Orico's gross flesh was swollen even more grossly; the roya's thumbprint, placed upon the tight fat of his face, stayed pale and visible for a long time. Iselle downplayed the alarming reports of Teidez's infection to Orico, but in the antechamber on the way out spoke frankly to Sara. Sara's lips tightened; she made little comment to Teidez's sister, but Cazaril thought that here at least was one who did not pray for the bewildered brutal boy.

After supper, Teidez's fever rose even higher. He stopped fighting and complaining, and fell into lassitude. A couple of hours before midnight, he seemed to fall to sleep. Iselle and Betriz at last left the royse's antechamber and climbed to their own rooms for some rest.

Close to midnight, unable to sleep for sake of his usual anticipations, Cazaril again went down the corridor to Teidez's chambers. The chief physician, going to wake the boy to administer some fever-reducing syrup, fresh-concocted and delivered by a panting acolyte, found that Teidez could not be roused.

Cazaril trudged up the stairs to report this to a sleepy Nan dy Vrit.

"Well, there's naught Iselle can do about it," opined Nan. "She's just dropped off, poor girl. Can we not let her sleep?"

Cazaril hesitated, then said, "No."

So the two tired, worried young women dressed themselves again and trooped back down to Teidez's crowded sitting room. Chancellor dy Jironal arrived, fetched from Jironal Palace.

Dy Jironal frowned at Cazaril, and bowed to Iselle. "Royesse. This sickroom is no place for you." His sour glance back to Cazaril silently added, *Or you.*

Iselle's eyes narrowed, but she replied in a quiet, dignified voice, "None here has a better right. Or a greater duty." After a brief pause, she added, "And I must bear witness on my mother's behalf."

Dy Jironal inhaled, then apparently thought better of whatever he'd been about to say. He might profitably save the clash of wills for some other time and place, Cazaril thought. There would be opportunities enough.

Cold compresses failed to lower Teidez's fever, and needle pricks failed to rouse him. His anxious attendants were thrown into a flurry when he had a brief seizure. His breathing became even more rasping and labored than the unconscious Umegat's had been. Out in the corridor, a quintet of cantors, one voice from each of the five orders, sang prayers; their voices blended and echoed, a heartbreakingly beautiful background of sound to these dreadful doings.

The harmonies paused. In that moment, Cazaril realized the labored breathing from the bedchamber beyond had stopped. Everyone fell silent in the face of that silence. One of the several attendant physicians, his face drained and wet with tears, came to the antechamber and called in dy Jironal and Iselle for witnesses. Voices rose and fell, very soft and low, from Teidez's bedchamber for a moment or two.

Both were pale when they came out again. Dy Jironal was pale and shocked; even to the last, Cazaril realized, the man had been expecting Teidez to pull through and recover. Iselle was pale and nearly expressionless. The black shadow boiled thickly about her.

Every face in the antechamber turned toward her, like compass needles swinging. The royacy of Chalion had a new Heiress.

20

Iselle's eyes, though reddened with fatigue and grief, were dry. Betriz, going to support her, dashed tears from the corners of hers. It was a little hard to tell which young woman leaned upon the other.

Chancellor dy Jironal cleared his throat. "I will take word of this bereavement to Orico." Belatedly, he added, "Allow me to serve you in this, Royesse."

"Yes . . ." Iselle looked around the chamber a little blindly. "Let all these good people go about their tasks."

Dy Jironal's brows drew down, as though a hundred thoughts flitted behind his eyes, and he scarcely knew which to grasp first. He glanced at Betriz, and at Cazaril. "Your household . . . your household must be increased to match your new dignity. I shall see to it."

"I cannot think about all these things now. Tomorrow will be soon enough. For tonight, my lord Chancellor, please leave me to my sorrow."

"Of course, Royesse." Dy Jironal bowed, and made to depart.

"Oh," Iselle added, "pray do not dispatch any courier to my mother until I can write a letter to include."

In the doorway, dy Jironal paused and gave another half bow in acknowledgment. "Certainly."

As Betriz escorted Iselle out, the royesse murmured to Cazaril in passing, "Cazaril, 'tend on me in half an hour. I must think."

Cazaril bent his head.

The crowd of courtiers in the antechamber and sitting room dispersed, but for Teidez's secretary, who stood looking bereft and useless. Only the acolytes and servants whose task it now was to wash and prepare the royse's body remained. The stunned and distraught chorus of cantors sang one last prayer, this time a threnody for the passage of the dead, their voices choked and wavering, and then they, too, turned to make their way out.

Cazaril was not sure if his head or his belly ached more. He fled into his own chamber at the end of the hallway, shut the door behind him, and braced himself for Dondo's nightly onslaught, not, his knotting stomach told him, to be any further delayed.

His familiar cramps doubled him over as usual, but to his surprise, Dondo was silent tonight. Was he, too, daunted by Teidez's death? If Dondo had intended the boy's destruction to follow from Orico's, he had it now—too late to serve any purpose he'd pursued in life.

Cazaril did not find the silence a respite. His heightened sensitivity to that malevolent presence assured him Dondo was still trapped within him. Hungry. Angry. Thinking? Intelligence had not been a notable characteristic of Dondo's spewing before now. Perhaps the shock of his death was passing off. Leaving . . . what? A waiting. A stalking? Dondo had been a competent hunter, once.

It occurred to Cazaril that while the demon might seek only to fill its two soul-buckets and return to its master, Dondo likely did not share that desire. The belly of his best enemy was a hateful prison to him, but neither the Bastard's purging hell nor the chilled forgetfulness of a gods-rejected ghost was a very satisfactory alternative fate. Exactly what else might be possible Cazaril could scarcely imagine, but he was intensely aware that if Dondo sought a physical form through which to reenter the world, his own was closest to hand. One way or another. His hands kneaded his belly, and he tried to decide, for the hundredth time, how fast his tumor was really growing.

The cramps and the wracking quarter hour of terror passed. Iselle's request returned to his mind. Composing the necessary letter to Ista informing her of her son's death would be excruciating; little wonder Iselle should desire assistance. Unequal to the task though Cazaril felt himself to be, whatever she asked of him in her grief and devastation he must undertake to supply. He uncurled himself, heaved out of bed, and climbed the stairs.

He found Iselle already seated at his antechamber desk, his best parchment, pens, and sealing wax laid out before her. Extra candles were lit all around the chamber, driving back the dark. Upon a square of silk, Betriz was just laying out and counting over an odd little pile of ornaments: brooches, rings, and the pale glowing heap of Dondo's rope of pearls that Cazaril had not yet had opportunity to deliver to the Temple.

Iselle was frowning down at the blank page and turning her seal ring round and round on her thumb. She glanced up, and said in a low voice, "Good, you're here. Close the door."

He shut it quietly behind him. "At your service, Royesse."

"I pray so, Cazaril: I pray so." Her eyes searched him.

Betriz said, in a worried voice, "He is so sick, Iselle. Are you sure?"

"I am sure of nothing but that I have no time left. And no other choices." She drew a long breath. "Cazaril, tomorrow morning I want you to ride to Ibra as my envoy to arrange my marriage to Royse Bergon."

Cazaril blinked, laboring to catch up with a baggage train of thought evidently already far down the road. "Chancellor dy Jironal will never let me leave."

"Of *course* it can't be openly." Iselle made an impatient gesture. "So you will ride first to Valenda, which is nearly on the way, as my personal courier to take the news of my brother's death to my mother. Dy Jironal will agree, delighted, he'll think, to see the back of you—he'll doubtless even lend you a courier's baton by which to commandeer horses from the Chancellery's posting houses. You know by noon tomorrow he'll have stuffed my household with his spies."

"That was very clear."

"But after you stop in Valenda, you'll ride not back to Cardegoss, but on to Zagosur, or wherever Royse Bergon is to be found. In the meantime, I will insist that Teidez be buried in Valenda, his beloved home."

"Teidez couldn't wait to get out of Valenda," Cazaril pointed out, beginning to feel dizzy.

"Yes, well, dy Jironal doesn't know that, does he? The chancellor would not let me out of Cardegoss and his eye for any other reason, but he cannot deny the demands of family piety. I will enlist Sara's support in the project, too, first thing tomorrow morning."

"You are doubly in mourning now, for your brother and his. He cannot foist another fiancé upon you for months yet."

She shook her head. "An hour ago, I became the future of Chalion. Dy Jironal must take and keep hold of me if he means to control that future. The critical moment is not the beginning of my mourning for Teidez, but of the beginning of my mourning for Orico. At which time—and not before—I pass into dy Jironal's control absolutely. Unless I am married first.

"Once I'm out of Cardegoss, I mean not to go back. In this weather, Teidez's cortege could be weeks on the road. And if the weather doesn't cooperate, I'll find other delays. By the time you return with Royse Bergon, I should still be safe in Valenda."

"Wait, what—*return* with Royse Bergon?"

"Yes, of *course* you must bring him to me. Think it through. If I leave Chalion to be wed in Ibra, dy Jironal will declare me in rebellion, forcing me to return at the head of a column of foreign troops. But if I seize my ground from the very first instant, I will never have to wrest it back. *You* taught me that!"

I did . . . ?

She leaned forward, growing more intent. "I will have Royse Bergon, yes, but I will not give up Chalion to get him, no, not one yard of soil. Not to dy Jironal, and not to the Fox either. These are my terms. Bergon and I will each of us inherit our respective crowns to ourselves. Bergon will hold authority in Chalion as roya-consort, and I will hold authority in Ibra as royina-consort, each through the other, reciprocally and equally. Our future son—the Mother and Father willing—to inherit and join them into one crown thereafter. But my future authority in Chalion is to be *mine*, not made over as dowry to my spouse. I will not be turned into a Sara, a mere and disregarded wife, silenced in my own councils!"

"The Fox will be greedy for more."

Her chin came up. "This is why I must have you as my envoy and no other. If you cannot get me Royse Bergon on terms that do not violate my future sovereignty, then turn around and ride home. And upon Orico's death, I will raise my banner against dy Jironal myself." Her mouth set in a grim line; her black shadow roiled. "Curse or no curse, I will not be Martou dy Jironal's bridled mare to ride to his spurring."

Yes—Iselle had the nerve, the will, and the wit to resist dy Jironal as Orico did not; as Teidez would never have. Cazaril could see it in her eyes, could see armies with pennoned lances writhing in the black dark hanging around her like a pall of smoke from a burning town. This was the form that the curse of her House would take in the next generation: not personal sorrow, but civil war between royal and noble faction, tearing the country apart from end to end.

Unless she could shrug off House and curse both, and pass into the protection of Bergon . . .

"I will ride for you, Royesse."

"Good." She sat back and swept her hand over the blank parchments. "Now we must make several letters. The first shall be your letter of authority to the Fox, and I think it should be in my own hand. You've read and written treaties. You must tell me all the right phrases, so I do not sound like an ignorant girl."

"I'll do my best, but am no lawyer, Iselle."

She shrugged. "If we succeed, I will have swords to back my words. And if we do not, no legal niceties will make them stand. Let them be plain and clear. Begin . . ."

A grueling three-quarters of an hour of lip-biting concentration resulted in a clean draft, which Iselle signed with a flourish and sealed with her seal ring. Betriz, meanwhile, had finished collecting and inventorying the little pile of coins and jewelry.

"Is that all the coin we have?" asked Iselle.

"Unfortunately, yes," sighed Betriz.

"Well, he'll just have to pawn the jewelry when he gets to Valenda, or some other safe place." Iselle wrapped the silk around the gauds and shoved them across the table to Cazaril. "Your purse, my lord. Daughter grant it is enough to get you there and back."

"More than enough, if I am not cheated."

"Mind you, this is to spend, not save. You are to put on a good show as my representative in Ibra. Remember to dress. And Royse Bergon is to travel in a style befitting his rank and mine, and no shame to Chalion."

"That could be tricky. I mean, without the army. I will bend my thoughts to it. Much will depend on, well, a number of unsettled things. Which reminds me. We must have a secure means of communication. Dy Jironal or his spies will surely be making all efforts to intercept any letters you receive."

"Ah."

"There is a very simple cipher that is nonetheless nearly impossible to break. It depends upon having two copies of the same printing of some book. One goes with me, one stays with you two. Three-number sequences pick out words—page number, line number, and rank in the line—which the recipient then works backward to find the word again. You do not always use the same numberings for the same words, but find them on another page, if you can. There are better ciphers, but there is no time to teach them to you. I, uh . . . have not two of any book, though."

"I will find two such books before you leave tomorrow," said Betriz sturdily.

"Thank you." Cazaril rubbed his forehead. It was madness to undertake to ride, sick and maybe bleeding, over the mountains in midwinter. He would fall off his horse into the snows and freeze, and he and his horse *and* his letters of authorization would all be eaten by the wolves.

"Iselle. My heart is willing. But my body is occupied territory, half–laid waste. I am afraid I will fail in the journey. My friend March dy Palliar is a good rider and a strong sword arm. May I offer him as your envoy instead?"

Iselle frowned in thought. "I think it will be a duel of wits with the Fox for the hand of Bergon, not a duel of steel. Better to send the wits to Ibra and keep the sword in Chalion."

Beguiling thought, to leave Iselle and Betriz not unguarded after all, but with a strong friend to call upon . . . a friend with friends, aye. "In either case, may I bring him into our councils tomorrow?"

Iselle glanced across at Betriz; Cazaril did not see any clear signal pass between them, but Iselle nodded decisively. "Yes. Bring him to me at the earliest possible instant."

The royesse pulled another piece of paper toward her and picked up a fresh quill. "Now I shall write a personal letter to the Royse Bergon, which you shall take sealed and pass to him unopened. And after that"—she sighed—"the letter to my mother. I think you cannot help me with either of these. Go get some sleep, while you can."

Dismissed, he rose and bowed.

As he reached the door, she added softly, "I'm glad it shall be you to tell her the news, Cazaril, and not some random Chancellery courier. Though it will be hard." She drew a deep breath and bent to the paper. The candlelight made her amber hair glow in an aureole about her abstracted face. Cazaril left her in the pool of light, and stepped into the darkness of the cold corridor.

❧CAZARIL WAS AWAKENED AT DAWN BY INSISTENT KNOCKING at his chamber door. When he stumbled out of bed and went to unlock it he found not the page with some summons that he'd expected, but Palli.

The normally neat Palli looked as though he had dressed in the dark, by guess; his hair was bent with sleep and sticking out in odd directions. His eyes were wide and dark. The yawning dy Gura brothers, looking sleepy but cheerful, smiled at Cazaril from their station in the corridor as Palli shouldered within. Cazaril handed out his bedside candle for the taller of them, Ferda, to light from the wall sconce; he handed it back to his lord and commander Palli, who took it with hands that shook slightly. Palli didn't speak till the door closed behind him and Cazaril.

"Bastard's demons, Caz! What is all this about?"

"Which what?" asked Cazaril in some confusion.

Palli lit another brace of candles on Cazaril's washstand and whirled about. "Pray for guidance, you said. In my sleep, if you please. I was killed five times in my dreams last night, I'll have you know. Riding somewhere. Each time more horribly. In the last dream, my horses ate me. I don't want to put my leg across anything, horse, mule, or sawhorse, for a week at least!"

"Oh." Cazaril blinked, taking this in. It seemed clear enough. "In that case, I don't want you to ride anywhere."

"That's a relief."

"I must go myself."

"Go where? In this weather? It's snowing now, you know."

"Ah, it wanted only that. Hasn't anyone told you yet? Royse Teidez died about midnight last night, of his infected wound."

Palli's face abruptly sobered; his mouth formed a silent "O." "That changes things in Chalion."

"Indeed. Let me dress, and then come upstairs with me." Hastily, Cazaril splashed chill water on his face and shrugged into yesterday's clothes.

In the chambers above, Cazaril found Betriz also still dressed in last night's black-and-lavender court mourning. It was plain she had not yet slept. Cazaril drew the dy Gura brothers out of sight of the corridor and closed them in his office antechamber. He and Palli entered the sitting room.

Betriz's hand touched a sealed packet waiting on a small table. "All the letters are ready to go to"—she glanced at Palli and hesitated—"Valenda."

"Is Iselle asleep?" Cazaril asked quietly.

"Resting only. She'll want to see you. Both." Betriz disappeared into the bedchambers for a moment, from which floated low murmuring, then returned with a pair of books under her arm. "I sneaked down to the roya's library and found two identical volumes. There weren't many true duplicates. I thought I'd better take the biggest, so as to have more words to choose from."

"Good," said Cazaril, and took one from her. He glanced at it, and choked back a black laugh. *Ordol*, read the gold letters on the spine. *The Fivefold Pathway*. "Perfect. I need to brush up on my theology." He laid it down with the packet of letters.

Iselle emerged, wrapped in a heavy blue velvet dressing gown from which the white lace of her nightgown peeped. Her amber hair cascaded down across her shoulders. Her face was as pale and puffy with lack of sleep as Betriz's. She nodded to Cazaril and to Palli. "My lord dy Palliar. Thank you for coming to my aid."

"I, uh . . ." said Palli. He cast a rather desperate glance at Cazaril, *What am I agreeing to?*

"Will he ride for you?" Betriz asked Cazaril anxiously. "You should not attempt this, you know you should not."

"Ah . . . no. Palli, instead I'm asking you to swear service and protection to the Royesse Iselle, personally, in the names of the gods, and especially the Lady of Spring. There is no treason in this;

she is the rightful Heiress of Chalion. And you will thus have the honor of being the first of her courtiers to do so."

"I, I, I . . . I can swear my fealty in addition to what I have sworn to your brother Orico, lady. I cannot swear to you instead of to him."

"I do not ask for your service before what you give to Orico. I only ask for your service before what you give to Orico's chancellor."

"Now, that I can do," said Palli, brightening. "And with a will." He kissed Iselle's forehead, hands, and slippers, and, still kneeling before her skirts, swore the oaths of a lord of Chalion, witnessed by Betriz and Cazaril. He added, still on his knees, "What would you think, Royesse, of Lord dy Yarrin as the next holy general of the Daughter's Order?"

"I think . . . such great preferences are not yet mine to give. But he would certainly be more acceptable to me than any candidate from dy Jironal's clan."

Palli nodded slow approval of her measured words and rose to his feet. "I'll let him know."

"Iselle will need all the practical support you can give her, all through the funeral for Teidez," said Cazaril to Palli. "He is to be buried in Valenda. Might I suggest she select your troop from Palliar to be part of the roysc's cortege? It will give you good excuse to confer often, and will assure that you are by her side when she rides out of Cardegoss."

"Oh, quick thinking," said Iselle.

Cazaril didn't feel quick. He felt his wits were laboring along after Iselle's as though in boots coated with twenty pounds of mud. Each. The authority that had fallen to her last night seemed to have released some coiled energy within her; she burned with it, inside her cocoon of darkness. He was afraid to close his eyes, lest he see it blazing in there still.

"But must you ride alone, Cazaril?" asked Betriz unhappily. "I don't like that."

Iselle pursed her lips. "As far as Valenda, I think he must. There is scarcely anyone in Cardegoss I would trust to dispatch with him." She studied Cazaril in doubt. "In Valenda, perhaps my grandmother may supply men. In truth, you should not arrive at the Fox's court alone and unattended. I don't want us to appear desperate to him." She added a trifle bitterly, "Although we are."

Betriz plucked at her black velvets. "But what if you fall ill on the road? Suppose your tumor grows worse? And who would know to burn your body if you die?"

Palli's head swiveled round. "Tumor? Cazaril! What is this, now?"

"Cazaril, didn't you tell him? I thought he was your friend!" Betriz turned to Palli. "He means to jump on a horse and ride—ride!—off to Ibra with a great uncanny murderous tumor in his gut, and no help on the road. I don't think that's brave, I think it's *stupid*. To Ibra he must go, for want of any other equal to the deed, but not alone like this!"

Palli sat back, his thumb across his lips, and studied Cazaril through narrowing eyes. He said at last, "I thought you looked sick."

"Yes, well, there's nothing to be done about it."

"Um . . . just how bad . . . I mean, um, are you . . ."

"Am I dying? Yes. How soon? No one knows. Which makes my life different from yours, as Learned Umegat points out, not at all. Well, who wants to die in bed?"

"You did, you always said. Of extreme old age, in bed, with somebody's wife."

"Mine, by preference," Cazaril sighed. "Ah, well." He managed not to look at Betriz. "My death is the gods' problem. For me, I ride as soon as a horse can be saddled." He grunted to his feet, and collected the book and the packet.

Palli glanced at Betriz, who clenched her hands together and stared beseechingly at him. He muttered an oath under his breath, stood, and strode abruptly to the door to the antechamber, which he jerked open. Foix dy Gura, his ear to the other side, staggered upright, and blinked and smiled at his commander. His brother Ferda, leaning on the opposite wall, snorted.

"Hello, boys," said Palli smoothly. "I have a little task for you."

CAZARIL, PALLI AT HIS HEELS, STRODE OUT THE ZAN-gre gates dressed for winter riding, the saddlebag slung over his shoulder heavy with a change of clothes, a small fortune, theology, and arguable treason.

He found the dy Gura brothers already in the stable yard before him. Sped back to Yarrin Palace by Palli's urgent orders, they had also changed out of their blue-and-white court dress into garb more practical for riding, with tall and well-worn boots.

Betriz was with them, wrapped in a white wool cloak. They had their heads close together, and Betriz was gesticulating emphatically. Foix glanced up to see Cazaril approaching; his broad face set in a sober and rather intimidated expression. He made a motion, and said something; Betriz glanced over her shoulder, and the conversation abruptly ceased. The brothers turned around and made small bows to Cazaril. Betriz stared at him steadily, as if his face were some lesson he'd set her to memorize.

"Ferda!" said Palli. The horse-master came to attention before him. Palli withdrew two letters from his vest-cloak, one sealed, one merely folded. "This"—he handed the folded paper to Ferda—"is a letter of authorization from me, as a lord dedicat of the Daughter's Order, entitling you to whatever assistance you may need to draft from our sister chapters on your journey. Any costs to be settled up with me at Palliar. This other"—he handed across the sealed letter—"is for you to open in Valenda."

Ferda nodded, and tucked them both away. The second letter of hand put the dy Gura brothers under Cazaril's command in the name of the Daughter, with no other details. Their trip to Ibra was going to make an interesting surprise for them.

Palli walked about them, inspecting with a commander's eye. "You have enough warm clothes? Armed for bandits?" They displayed polished swords and readied crossbows—bowstrings protected from dampness, with a sufficiency of quarrels—gear all in good condition. Only a few flakes of snow now spun through the moist air to land on wool and leather and hair, there to melt to small droplets. The dawn snowfall had proved a mere dusting, here in town. In the hills it would likely be heavier.

From beneath her cloak, Betriz produced a fluffy white object. Cazaril blinked it into focus as a fur hat in the style of Chalion's hardy southern mountaineers, with flaps meant to be folded down over the ears with the fur inward and tied under the chin. While both men and women wore similar styles, this one was clearly meant for a lady, in white rabbit skin with flowers brocaded in gold thread over the crown. "Cazaril, I thought you might need this in the high passes."

Foix raised his brows and grinned, and Ferda snickered behind his hand. "Fetching," he said.

Betriz reddened. "It was the only thing I could find in the time I had," she said defensively. "Better than having your ears freeze!"

"Indeed," said Cazaril gravely. "I do not have so good a hat. I shall be very grateful." Ignoring the grinning youths, he took it from her and knelt to pack it carefully in his saddlebag. It wasn't just a gesture to gratify Betriz, though he smiled inwardly at her sniff in Ferda's direction; when the brothers met the winter wind in the border mountains, those grins would vanish soon enough.

Iselle appeared through the gates, in a velvet cloak so dark a purple as to be almost black, attended by a shivering Chancellery clerk who handed over a numbered courier's baton in exchange for Cazaril's signature in his ledger. He clapped the ledger shut and scurried back over the drawbridge and out of the cold.

"You were able to get dy Jironal's order?" Cazaril inquired, tucking the baton into a secure inner pocket of his coat. The baton would command its bearer fresh horses, food, and clean, if hard and narrow, beds in any Chancellery posting house on the main roads across Chalion.

"Not dy Jironal's. Orico's. Orico is still roya in Chalion, though even the Chancellery clerk had to be reminded of the fact." Iselle snorted softly. "The gods go with you, Cazaril."

"Alas, yes," he sighed, then realized that had been not an observation, but a farewell. He bowed his head to kiss her chilled hands. Betriz eyed him sideways. He hesitated, then cleared his throat and took her hands as well. Her fingers spasmed around his at the touch of his lips, and her breath drew in, but her eyes stared away over his head. He straightened to see the dy Gura brothers shrinking under her glower.

A Zangre groom led out three saddled courier horses. Palli clasped hands with his cousins. Ferda took the reins of what proved to be Cazaril's horse, a rangy roan that matched his height. The muscular Foix hastened to give him a leg up, and as he settled in the saddle with a faint grunt inquired anxiously, "Are you all right, sir?"

They hadn't even started yet; *what* had Betriz been telling them? "Yes, it's all fine," Cazaril assured him. "Thank you." Ferda presented him with his reins, and Foix assisted him in tying on his precious saddlebags. Ferda leapt lightly aboard his horse, his brother climbed more heavily onto his, and they started out of the stable yard. Cazaril turned in his saddle to watch Iselle and Betriz making their way back across the drawbridge and through the Zangre's great gate. Betriz looked back, and raised her hand high; Cazaril returned the salute. Then the horses rounded the first corner, and the buildings of Cardegoss hid the gate from his view. A single crow followed them, swooping from gutter to cornice.

On the first street, they met Chancellor dy Jironal riding slowly up from Jironal Palace, flanked by two armed retainers on foot. He'd obviously been home to wash and eat and change his clothes, and attend to his more urgent correspondence. Judging from his gray face and bloodshot eyes, he'd had no more sleep than Iselle the night past.

Dy Jironal reined in, and gave Cazaril an odd little salute. "Where away, Lord Cazaril"—his eye took in the light courier saddles, stamped with the castle-and-leopard of Chalion—"upon my Chancellery's horses?"

Cazaril returned a half bow from his saddle. "Valenda, my lord. The Royesse Iselle decided she did not want some stranger bearing the bad news to her mother and grandmother, and has dispatched me as her courier."

"Mad Ista, eh?" Dy Jironal's lips screwed up. "I do not envy you that task."

"Indeed." Cazaril let his voice go hopeful. "Order me back to Iselle's side, and I shall obey you at once."

"No, no." Dy Jironal's lip curled just slightly in satisfaction. "I can think of no man more fitted for this sad duty. Ride on. Oh— when do you mean to return?"

"I'm not yet sure. Iselle desired me to be sure her mother was going to be all right before I returned. I do not expect Ista to take the news well."

"Truly. Well, we'll watch for you."

I wager you will. He and dy Jironal exchanged guarded nods, and the two parties rode on in their opposite directions. Cazaril glanced back to catch dy Jironal glancing back, just before he turned the corner toward the Zangre's gates. Dy Jironal would know no ambush could now catch Cazaril's start on the courier horses. The return was another opportunity. *Except that I won't be coming back on this road.*

Or at all? He'd turned over in his mind all the disasters that might follow failure; what would be his fate if he succeeded? What did the gods do with used saints? He'd never to his knowledge met one, save perhaps, now, Umegat . . . a thought that was not, upon consideration, very reassuring.

They reached the city gate and crossed over the bridge to the river road. Fonsa's crow did not follow farther, but perched upon the gate's high crenellations and vented a few sad caws, which echoed as they descended into the ravine. The Zangre's cliff wall, naked of verdure in the winter, rose high and stark across the dark, rapid water of the river. Cazaril wondered if Betriz would watch from one of the castle's high windows as they passed along the road. He wouldn't be able to see her up there, so high and shadowed.

His bleak thoughts were scattered by the thud and splash of hooves. An inbound courier flashed past them, galloping horse lathered and blowing. He—no, she—waved at them in passing. Female couriers were much favored by some of the Chancellery's horse-masters, at least on the safer routes, for they claimed their light weight and light hands spared the animals. Foix waved back, and turned in his saddle to watch her flying black braids. Cazaril didn't think he was just admiring her horsemanship.

Ferda nudged his mount up next to Cazaril's. "May we gallop now, my lord?" he asked hopefully. "Daylight is dear, and these beasts are fresh."

But five gods, I'm not. Cazaril took a breath of grim anticipation. "Yes."

He clapped his booted heels to the roan's side, and the animal bounded into a long-strided canter. The road opened before them across the snow-streaked dun landscape, winding into gray mists heavy with the faint sweet rot of winter vegetation. Vanishing into uncertainty.

21

They came to Valenda at dusk
on the following day. The town bulked
black against a pewter sky, its deepen-
ing shadows relieved here and there by the orange flare of some
torch or candle, faint sparks of light and life. They'd had no remounts on the branch road to Valenda, courier stations being reserved for the route to the Baocian provincial seat of Taryoon, so
the last leg had been a long one for the horses. Cazaril was content
to let the tired beasts walk, heads down on a long rein, the remaining stretch through the city and up the hill. He wished he
could stop here, stop, and sink down by the side of the road, and
not move for days. In minutes, it would be his task to tell a mother
that her son was dead. Of all the trials he expected to face on this
journey, this was the worst.

Too soon, they reached the Provincara's castle gates. The
guards recognized him at once and ran shouting for the servants;
the groom Demi held his horse, and was the first to ask, *Why are
you here, my lord?* The first, but not the last.

"I bear messages to the Provincara and the Lady Ista," Cazaril
replied shortly, bent over his pommel. Foix popped up at his
horse's shoulder, staring up expectantly; Cazaril heaved his off leg
up over the horse's haunches, kicked free of the other stirrup, and
dropped to his feet. His knees buckled, and he would have fallen
then, but for the strong hand that caught his elbow. They'd made
good time. He wondered dizzily how dearly he would pay for it.

He stood a moment, trembling, till his balance returned to him. "Is Ser dy Ferrej here?"

"He has escorted the Provincara to a wedding feast in town," Demi told him. "I don't know when they mean to return."

"Oh," said Cazaril. He was almost too tired to think. He'd been so exhausted last night, he'd fallen asleep in the posting-house bunk within minutes of being steered to it by his helpers, and slept even through Dondo. Wait for the Provincara? He'd meant to report to her first, and let her determine how to tell her daughter. *No. This is unbearable. Get it over with.* "In that case, I will see the Lady Ista first."

He added, "The horses need to be rubbed down and watered and fed. These are Ferda and Foix dy Gura, men of good family in Palliar. Please see that they are given . . . everything. We've not eaten." Nor washed, but that was obvious; everyone's sweat-soaked woolens were splashed with winter road mud, hands grimed, faces streaked with dirt. They were all three blinking and weary in the torchlight of the courtyard. Cazaril's fingers, stiff from clutching his reins in the cold since dawn, plucked at the ties of his saddlebags. Foix took that task from him, too, and pulled the bags off the horse. Cazaril rather determinedly took them back from him, folded them over his arm, and turned. "Take me to Ista now, please," he said faintly. "I have letters for her from the Royesse Iselle."

A house servant led him within, and up the stairs in the new building. The man had to wait for Cazaril to climb slowly after him. His legs felt like lead. Murmurs rose and fell between the man and the royina's attendants, as he negotiated Cazaril's entry to her chambers. The air within was perfumed with bowls of dried flower petals and aglow with candlelight and warmth from the corner fireplace. Cazaril felt huge and awkward and filthy in this dainty sitting room.

Ista sat on a cushioned bench, dressed in warm wraps, her dun hair bound in a thick rope down her back. Like Sara, the inky shadow of the curse hung about her. *So. I was right in that guess.*

Ista turned toward him; her eyes widened, and her face stiffened. She surely knew something was terribly wrong just by his sudden presence here. The hundred ways to break the news to her gently that he'd rehearsed during the long hours of riding seemed to fall through his fingers, under the pressure of those dark, dilated eyes. Any delay now would be cruel beyond measure. He fell to one knee before her, and cleared his throat.

"First. Iselle is well. Hold to that." He inhaled. "Second. Teidez died two nights ago, from an infected wound."

The two women attending upon Ista cried out, and clutched each other. Ista barely moved, but for a little flinch, as if an invisible arrow had struck her. She vented a long, wordless exhalation.

"You understand my words, Royina?" Cazaril said hesitantly.

"Oh, yes," she breathed. One corner of her mouth turned up; Cazaril could not call it a smile. It was nothing like a smile, that black irony. "When it is too-long-anticipated, a blow falls as a relief, you see. The waiting is over. I can stop fearing, now. Can you understand that?"

Cazaril nodded.

After a moment of silence, broken only by the sobbing of one of her women, she added quietly, "How came he by this wound? Hunting? Or something . . . else?"

"Not . . . hunting exactly. In a way it was . . ." Cazaril licked his lips, chapped with the cold. "Lady, do you see anything *odd* about me?"

"I see only with my eyes, now. I've been blind for years, you see. *You* see?"

Her emphasis made her meaning very plain, Cazaril thought. "Yes."

She nodded and sat back. "I thought so. There is a look about one who sees with *those* eyes."

A trembling attendant crept up to Ista, and said in an overly light voice, "Lady, perhaps you should come away to bed, now. Your lady mother will surely be back soon . . ." She shot Cazaril a meaningful look over her shoulder; clearly, the woman thought Ista was going into one of her mad fugues. Into what everyone thought was one of her fugues. Had Ista ever been mad?

Cazaril sat back on his heels. "Please leave us now. I must have some private speech with the royina on matters of some urgency."

"Sir, my lord . . ." The woman managed a false smile, and whispered in his ear, "We dare not leave her in this stricken hour—she might do herself some harm."

Cazaril climbed to his full height, and took both ladies by the arms, and steered them gently but inexorably out the door. "I will undertake to guard her. Here, you may wait in this chamber across the hall, and if I need you, I will call out, all right?" He shut both doors upon their protests.

Ista waited unmoving, but for her hands. She held a fine lace handkerchief, which she commenced to folding, over and over, into smaller and smaller squares. Cazaril grunted down to sit cross-legged on the floor at her feet and stare up into that wide-eyed, chalky face.

"I have seen the Zangre's ghosts," he said.

"Yes."

"More. I have seen the dark cloud that hangs over your House. The Golden General's curse, the bane of Fonsa's heirs."

"Yes."

"You know of it, then?"

"Oh, yes."

"It hangs about you now."

"Yes."

"It hung about Orico, and Sara. Iselle—and Teidez."

"Yes." She tilted her head and stared away.

Cazaril thought about a state of shock he had seen sometimes come upon men in battle, between the moment a blow fell, and the time their bodies fell; men who should have been unconscious, should have been dead, staggering about yet for a time, accomplishing, sometimes, extraordinary acts. Was this quiet coherence such a shock, soon to melt—should he seize it? Or had Ista ever really been incoherent? *Or did we just not understand her?*

"Orico has become very ill. How I came by my second sight is all of a piece with this black tangle. But please, please, lady, tell me how you came to know. What did you see, and when, and how? I *must* understand. Because I think—I fear—it has been given to me, it has *fallen* to me, to act. Yet nothing has told me what that action must be. Even second sight cannot pierce this dark."

Her brows went up. "I can tell you truths. I cannot give you understanding. For how can one give what one does not possess? I have always told the truth."

"Yes. I see that now." He took a daring breath. "But have you ever told all of it?"

She sucked on her lower lip a moment, studying him. Her

trembling hands, seeming to belong to some other Ista than the one of this carven face, began unfolding the tight knot of the handkerchief again upon her knee. Slowly, she nodded. Her voice was so low, Cazaril had to tilt his head to be sure of catching all her words.

"It began when I became pregnant with Iselle. The visions. The second sight came and went. I thought it was an effect of my pregnancy—bearing turns some women's brains. The physicians convinced me of that, for a time. I saw the blind ghosts drifting. I saw the dark cloud hanging upon Ias, and young Orico. I heard voices. I dreamed of the gods, of the Golden General, of Fonsa and his two faithful companions burning in his tower. Of Chalion burning like the tower.

"After Iselle was born, the visions ceased. I thought I had been mad, and then got well again."

The eye could not see itself, not even the inner eye. *He* had been granted Umegat, been granted knowledge bought at others' cost and handed to him as a gift. How frightened would he be by now, if he were still groping for explanations of the inexplicable?

"Then I became pregnant again, with Teidez. And the visions began again, twice as bad as before. It was unbearable to think myself mad. Only when I threatened to kill myself did Ias confess to me that it was the curse, and that he knew it. Had always known of it."

And how betrayed, to find that those who'd known the truth hadn't told him, had left him to stagger about in isolated terror?

"I was horrified that I had brought my two children into this dire danger. I prayed and prayed to the gods that it might be lifted, or that they would tell me how it might be lifted, that they would spare the innocent.

"Then the Mother of Summer came to me, when I was round to bursting with Teidez. Not in a dream, not while I was sleeping, but when I was awake and sober, in the broad day. She stood as close to me as you are now, and I fell to my knees. I could have touched her robe, if I'd dared. Her breath was a perfume, like wildflowers in the summer grasses. Her face was too beautiful for my eyes to comprehend, it was like staring into the sun. Her voice was music."

Ista's lips softened; even now, the peace of that vision echoed briefly in her face, a flash of beauty like the reflection of sunlight on dark waters. But her brows tightened again, and she spoke on, bending forward, growing, if possible, more shadowed, more intent.

"She said that the gods sought to take the curse back, that it did not belong in this world, that it was a gift to the Golden General that he had spilt improperly. She said that the gods might draw the curse back to them only through the will of a man who would lay down his life three times for the House of Chalion."

Cazaril hesitated. The sound of his own breath in his nostrils seemed enough to drown out that quiet voice. But the question rose helplessly to his lips, though he cursed himself for sounding a fool. "Um . . . I don't suppose that three men could lay down their lives once each, instead?"

"No." Her lips curved in that weird ironic not-smile. "You see the problem."

"I . . . I . . . I don't see the solution, though. Was it a trick, this . . . prophecy?"

Her hands opened briefly, ambiguously, then began folding the handkerchief again. "I told Ias. He told Lord dy Lutez, of course; Ias kept nothing from dy Lutez, except for me. Except for me."

Historical curiosity overcame Cazaril. Now that they were comrades in . . . sainthood, or something like it, it seemed easy to talk to Ista. The ease was lunatic, tilted, fragile, if he blinked it would be gone beyond recall, and yet . . . saint to saint and soul to soul, for this floating moment it was an intimacy stranger and more soaring than lover to lover. He began to understand why Umegat had fallen upon him with such hunger. "What *was* their relationship, really?"

She shrugged. "They were lovers since before I was born. Who was I to judge them? Dy Lutez loved Ias; I loved Ias. Ias loved us both. He tried so hard, cared so much, trying to bear the weight of all his dead brothers and his father Fonsa, too. He'd worn himself near to death with the caring, and yet it all went wrong, and wrong again."

She hesitated for a time, and Cazaril was terrified for an instant that he had inadvertently done something to bring this flow of confidences to an end. But apparently she was marshaling . . . not her thoughts, but her heart: for she went on, even more slowly. "I don't remember now whose idea it first was. We sat in a night council, the three of us, after Teidez was born. I still had the sight. We knew both of our children were drawn into this dark thing, and poor Orico, too. 'Save my children,' Ias cried, laying his forehead down upon the table, weeping. 'Save my children.' And Lord dy Lutez said, 'For the love I bear you, I will try; I will dare this sacrifice.' "

He scarcely dared whisper it. "But five gods, how?"

Her head jerked. "We discussed a hundred schemes; how might one kill a man, and yet bring him back to die again? Impossible, and yet not quite. We finally settled on drowning as the best to try. It would occasion the least physical injury, and there were many stories of people who'd been brought back from drowning. Dy Lutez rode out to investigate some of them, to try to determine the trick of it."

Cazaril's breath huffed out. *Drowning, oh, gods.* And in the coldest of cold blood . . . his hands were shaking, too, now. Her voice went on, quiet and relentless.

"We swore a physician to secrecy, and descended to the dungeons of the Zangre. Dy Lutez let himself be stripped and bound, arms and legs tight to his body, and hung upside down over the tank. We lowered him down headfirst. And raised him again, when he stopped struggling at last . . ."

"And he'd died?" said Cazaril softly. "Then the treason charge was . . ."

"Died indeed, but not for the last time. We revived him, just barely."

"Oh."

"Oh, it was working, though!" Her hands clenched. "I could feel it, I could see it, the crack in the curse! But dy Lutez—his nerve broke. The next night, he would not undertake the second immersion. He cried I was trying to assassinate him, for jealousy's sake. Then Ias and I . . . made a mistake."

Cazaril could see where this was going, now. Closing his eyes would not spare him from seeing. He forced them to stay open, and on her face.

"We seized him, and made the second trial by force. He screamed and wept . . . Ias wavered, I cried, 'But we have to! Think of the children!' But this time when we drew him out, he was drowned dead, and not all our tears and prayers revived him then.

"Ias was shattered. I was distraught. My inner vision was stripped from my eyes. The gods turned their faces from me . . ."

"Then the treason charge was false." *Profoundly false.*

"Yes. A lie, to hide our sins. To explain the body." Her breath drew in. "But his family was allowed to inherit his estate—nothing was attaindered."

"Except his reputation. His public honor." An honor that had been all in all to proud dy Lutez; who had valued all his wealth and glory but as outward signs of it.

"It was done in the panic of the moment, and then we could not draw back from it. Of all our regrets, I think that one gnawed Ias the most, in the months after.

"Ias would not try again, would not try to find another volunteer. It had to be a willing sacrifice, you see; no struggling murder would have done it, but only a man stepping forth of his own volition, with eyes wide-open. Ias turned his face to the wall and died of grief and guilt"—her hands stretched the scrap of lace almost to tearing—"leaving me alone with two little children and no way to protect or save them from this . . . black . . . *thing* . . ." She drew breath, her chest heaving. But she did not spiral into hysteria, as Cazaril, tensing to spring up and call for her attendants, feared. As her breathing slowed, he let his muscles slacken again. "But you," she said at last. "The gods have touched you?"

"Yes."

"I am sorry."

An unsteady laugh left his lips. "Aye." He rubbed the back of his neck. It was his turn for confession, now. He might shade the truth with others, for expediency's sake. Not with Ista. He owed her weight for weight and value for value. Wound for wound. "How much news had you from Cardegoss of Iselle's brief betrothal, and Lord Dondo dy Jironal's fate?"

"One messenger followed atop another before we could celebrate—we could not tell what to make of it."

"Celebrate? A forty-year-old matched to a sixteen-year-old?"

Her chin came up, for a moment so like Iselle that Cazaril caught his breath. "Ias and I were further apart in age than that."

Ah. Yes. That would tend to give her a different view of such things. "Dondo was no Ias, my lady. He was corrupt—debauched—impious, an embezzler—and I am almost certain he had Ser dy Sanda murdered. Maybe even by his own hand. He was colluding with his brother Martou to gain complete control of the House of Chalion, through Orico, Teidez—and Iselle."

Ista's hand touched her throat. "I met Martou, years ago, at court. He already aspired then to be the next Lord dy Lutez. Dy Lutez, the brightest, noblest star ever to shine in the court of Chalion—Martou might have studied to clean his boots, barely. Dondo, I never met."

"Dondo was a disaster. I first encountered him years ago, and he had no character then. He grew worse with age. Iselle was distraught, and furious to have him forced upon her. She prayed to the gods to release her from this abominable match, but the gods . . . didn't answer. So I did.

"I stalked him for a day, intending to assassinate him for her, but I couldn't get near him. So I prayed to the Bastard for a miracle of death magic. And I was granted it."

After a moment, Ista's eyebrows went up. "Why aren't you dead?"

"I thought I was dying. When I awoke to find Dondo dead without me, I didn't know what to think. But Umegat determined Iselle's prayers had brought down a second miracle, and the Lady of Spring had spared my life from the Bastard's demon, but only temporarily. Saint Umegat—I thought he was a groom—" His story was growing hopelessly tangled. He took a deep breath, and backed up and explained about Umegat and the miracle of the menagerie, and how it had preserved poor Orico in the teeth of the curse.

"Except that Dondo, before he died, when he still thought he was about to be married to Iselle, told Teidez it was the other way around—that the menagerie was an evil Roknari sorcery set up to sicken Orico. And Teidez believed him. Five days ago, he took his Baocian guard and slew nearly every sacred animal in it, and only by chance failed to slay the saint as well. He took a scratch from Orico's dying leopard—I swear, it was only a scratch! If I had realized . . . The wound became poisoned. His end was . . ." Cazaril remembered who he was talking to. ". . . was very quick."

"Poor Teidez," whispered Ista, staring away. "My poor Teidez. You were born to be betrayed, I think."

"Anyway," finished Cazaril, "because of this strange concatenation of miracles, the death demon and the ghost of Dondo were bound in my belly. Encapsulated in some kind of tumor, evidently. When they are released, I will die."

Ista's grieving face went still. Her eyes rose to search Cazaril's face. "That would be twice," she said.

"Ah . . . eh?"

Her hands abandoned the tortured handkerchief, and went out to grip Cazaril's collar. Her gaze became scorching, almost painful in its intensity. Her breath came faster. "Are you Iselle's dy Lutez?"

"I, I, I," stammered Cazaril; his stomach sank.

"Twice. Twice. But how to accomplish the third? Oh. Oh. Oh . . ." Her eyes were dilated, the pupils pulsing. Her lips shivered with hope. "*What are you?*"

"I, I, I'm only Cazaril, my lady! I am no dy Lutez, I am sure. I am not brilliant, or rich, or strong. Or beautiful, the gods know. Or brave, though I fight when I'm trapped, I suppose."

She made an impatient gesture. "Take away all those ornaments—stripped, naked, upside down, the man still shone. Faithful. Unto death. Only . . . not unto two deaths. Or three."

"I—this *is* madness, now. This is not the way I intend to break the curse, I promise you." Five gods, not *drowning*. "I have another plan to rescue Iselle from it."

Her eyes probed him, still with that frightening wildness. "Have the gods spoken to you, then?"

"No. I go by my reason."

She sat back, to his relief releasing him, and her brows crimped in puzzlement. "Reason? In this?"

"Sara—and you—married into the House and the curse of Chalion. I think Iselle can marry out of it. This escape could not have been available to Teidez, but now . . . I am on my way to Ibra, to try to arrange Iselle's marriage with Ibra's new Heir, Royse Bergon. Dy Jironal will seek to prevent this, because it will spell the end of his power in Chalion. Iselle means to slip away from him by bringing Teidez's body back here to Valenda to be buried." Cazaril detailed Iselle's plan to ride with the cortege, then rendezvous with Bergon in Valenda.

"Maybe," breathed Ista. "Maybe . . ."

He was unsure what she was referring to. She was still giving him an extremely unsettling look.

"Your mother," he said. "Does she know of all this? The curse, the true tale of dy Lutez?"

"I tried to tell her, once. She decided I was truly mad. It's not a bad life, being mad, you know. It has its advantages. You don't have to make any decisions. What to eat, what to wear, where to go . . .

who lives, who dies . . . You can try it yourself, if you like. Just tell the truth. Tell people you are pregnant with a demon and a ghost, and you have a tumor that talks vilely to you, and the gods guard your steps, and see what happens next." Her throaty laugh did not incline Cazaril to smile along. Her lips twisted. "Don't look so alarmed, Lord Cazaril. If I repeat your story, you have only to deny me, and I will be thought mad, not you."

"I . . . think you have been denied enough. Lady."

She bit her lip and looked away; her body trembled.

Cazaril shifted, and was reminded of his saddlebag, leaning against his hip. "Iselle wrote you a letter, and one to her grandmother, and charged me to deliver them to you." He burrowed into the bag, found his packet of correspondence, and handed Ista her letter. His hands were shaking from fatigue and hunger. Among other things. "I should go get rid of this dirt and eat something. By the time the Provincara returns, perhaps I can make myself fit for her company."

Ista held the letter to her breast. "Call my ladies to me, then. I shall retire now, I think. No reason more to wake . . ."

Cazaril glanced up sharply. "Iselle. Iselle is a reason to wake."

"Ah. Yes. One more hostage to go. Then I can sleep forever." She leaned forward and patted his shoulder in an odd reassurance. "But for now I will just sleep tonight. I'm so tired. I think I must have done all my mourning and wailing in advance, and there is none left in me now. All emptied out."

"I understand, lady."

"Yes, you do. How strange."

Cazaril reached gingerly out to the bench, pushed himself up, and went to let the weepy attendants back in. Ista set her teeth and suffered them to descend upon her. Cazaril hoisted his saddlebags and bowed himself out.

❧A WASH, A CHANGE OF CLOTHES, AND A HOT MEAL did much to restore Cazaril physically, though his mind still reeled from his conversation with Ista. When the servants set him to await the Provincara's return in her quiet little parlor in the new building, he was grateful for the chance to marshal his thoughts. A cheerful fire was set for him in the chamber's excellent fireplace. Aching in every bone, he sat in her cushioned chair, sipped well-watered wine, and tried not to nod off. The old lady was not likely to stay out very late.

Indeed, she soon appeared, flanked by her cousin-companion Lady dy Hueltar and the grave Ser dy Ferrej. She was dressed in gala splendor in green satins and velvets, glittering with jewels, but one look at her ashen face told Cazaril that the bad news had already been blurted to her by some excited servant. Cazaril lurched to his feet, and bowed.

She gripped his hands, searching his face. "Cazaril, is it true?"

"Teidez has died, suddenly, of an infection. Iselle is well"—he took a breath—"and Heiress of Chalion."

"Poor boy! Poor boy! Have you told Ista yet?"

"Yes."

"Oh, dear. How did she take it?"

Well did not describe it. Cazaril chose, "Calmly, Your Grace. At least, she did not fly into any sort of wild pelter, as I'd feared. I think the blows her life has dealt her have left her numb. I don't know how she'll be tomorrow. Her attendants have put her to bed."

The Provincara vented a sigh and blinked back tears.

Cazaril knelt to his saddlebags. "Iselle entrusted me with a letter for you. And there is a note for you, Ser dy Ferrej, from Betriz. She did not have time to write much." He handed out the two sealed missives. "They will both be coming here. Iselle means to have Teidez buried in Valenda."

"Oh," said the Provincara, cracking the cold wax of the letter's seal, careless of where the sprinkles fell. "Oh, how I long to see her." Her eyes devoured the penned lines. "Short," she complained. Her gray eyebrows went up. "*Cazaril will explain everything to you,* she says."

"Yes, Your Grace. I have much to tell you, some of it in confidence."

She waved out her companions. "Go, I will call you back." Dy Ferrej was breaking open his letter by the time he reached the door.

She sat with a rustle of fabric, still clutching the paper, and gestured Cazaril to another chair, which he pulled up to her knee. "I must see to Ista before she sleeps."

"I'll try to be succinct, Your Grace. This is what I have learned this season in Cardegoss. What I went through to learn it . . ." That cost, the cracking open of his world, Ista had understood at once; he was not sure the Provincara would grasp it. "Doesn't matter now. But Archdivine Mendenal in Cardegoss can confirm the truth of it all, if you get a chance at him. Tell him I sent you, and he will deny you nothing."

Her brows went up. "How is it you bend an archdivine?"

Cazaril snorted softly. "I pull rank."

She sat up, her lips thinning. "Cazaril, don't make stupid jokes with me. You grow as cryptic as Ista."

Yes, Ista's self-protective sense of—not humor, irony—likely *was* irritating, at close quarters. Ista. Who spoke for Ista? "Provincara . . . your daughter is heartbroken, ravaged in will. She longs for the release of death. But she is not mad. The gods are not so merciful."

The old woman hunched, as though his words grated over a raw spot. "Her grief is extravagant. Was no woman ever widowed before? Has none lost a child? I've suffered both, but I did not moan and mope and carry on so, not for years. I cried my hour, yes, but then I continued about my duties. If she is not broken in reason, then she is vastly self-indulgent."

Could he make her understand Ista's differences without violating Ista's tacit confidences? Well, even a partial truth might help. He bent his head to hers. "It all goes back to the great war of Fonsa the Fairly-Wise with the Golden General . . ." In the plainest possible terms, he detailed the inner workings of the curse upon the history of the House of Chalion. There were enough other disasters in Ias's reign that he scarcely needed to touch on the fall of dy Lutez. Orico's impotence, the slow corruption of his advisors, the failure of both his policies and his health brought the tale to the present.

The Provincara scowled. "Is all this vile luck a work of Roknari black magic, then?"

"Not . . . as I understand it. It is a spillage, a perversion of some ineffable divinity, lost from its proper place."

She shrugged. "Close enough. If it acts like black magic, then black magic it is. The practical question is, how to counter it?"

Cazaril wasn't sure about that close enough. Surely only correct understanding could lead to correct action. Ista and Ias had tried to force a solution, as though the curse were magic, to be countered by magic. A rite done by rote.

She added, "And does this link to this wild tale we heard of Dondo dy Jironal being murdered by death magic?"

That, at least, he could answer, none better. He had already decided to strip out as much of the unnatural detail as possible from her version of events. He did not think her confidence in him would be augmented by his babbling of demons, ghosts, saints, second sight, and even more grotesque things. More than enough remained to astound her. He began with the tale of Iselle's disastrous betrothal, although he did not attribute the source of Dondo's death miracle, concealing his act of murder as he'd concealed Ista's.

The Provincara was not so squeamish. "If Lord Dondo was as bad as you say," she sniffed, "I shall say prayers for that unknown benefactor!"

"Indeed, Your Grace. I pray for him daily."

"And Dondo a mere younger son—for Iselle! What was that fool Orico thinking?"

Abandoning the ineffable, he presented the menagerie to her as a marvel devised by the Temple to preserve Orico's failing health, true enough as far as it went. She grasped instantly the secret political purpose of Dondo's setting Teidez to its—and Orico's—destruction, and ground her teeth. She moaned for Teidez's betrayal. But the news that Valenda must now prepare for a funeral, a wedding, and a war, possibly simultaneously, revitalized her.

"Can Iselle count on her uncle dy Baocia's support?" Cazaril asked her. "How many others can he and you bring in against dy Jironal's faction?"

The Provincara made rapid inventory of the lords she might draw in to Valenda, ostensibly for Teidez's funeral, in fact to pry Iselle from dy Jironal's hands. The list impressed him. After all her decades of political observation in Chalion, the Provincara didn't even need to look at a map to plan her tactics.

"Have them ride in for Teidez's funeral with every man they can muster," said Cazaril. "Especially, we must control the roads between here and Ibra, to guarantee the safety of Royse Bergon."

"Difficult," said the Provincara, sitting back with her lips pursing. "Some of dy Jironal's own lands, and those of his brothers-in-law, lie between here and the border. You should have a troop to ride with you. I will strip Valenda to give you the men."

"No," said Cazaril slowly. "You'll need all your men when Iselle arrives, which may well be before I can return. And if I take a troop to Ibra, our speed will be limited. We cannot hope to obtain remounts on the road for so large a company, and maintaining secrecy would become impossible. Better we should travel outward light and fast and unmarked. Save the troop to meet us coming back. Oh, and beware, your Baocian captain you sent with Teidez sold himself to Dondo—he cannot be trusted. You'll have to find some way to replace him when he returns."

The Provincara swore. "Bastard's demons, I'll have his ears."

They made plans to pass his ciphered letters to Iselle, and hers to him, through Valenda, making it appear to dy Jironal's spies that Cazaril still was in her grandmother's company. The Provincara undertook to pawn some of Iselle's jewelry for him on the morrow, at the best rate, to raise the coin he'd need for the next part of his journey. They settled a dozen other practical details in as many minutes. Her very determination made her god-proof, Cazaril imagined; for all her attention to pious ceremony, no god was going to slip into that iron will even edgewise. The gods had given her less perilous gifts, and he was grateful enough for them.

"You understand," he said at last, "I think this marriage scheme may rescue Iselle. I don't know that it will also save Ista." Neither Ista, drifting sadly about the castle of Valenda, nor Orico, lying blind and bloated in the Zangre. And no exhortation of the Provincara to Ista to bestir herself would be of any use, while this black thing still choked her like a poisoned fog.

"If it only rescues Iselle from the clutches of Chancellor dy Jironal, it will satisfy me. I can't believe Orico made such vile provisions in his will." That legal note had exercised her almost more than the supernatural matters. "Taking my granddaughter from me without even consulting me!"

Cazaril fingered his beard. "You realize, if all this succeeds, your granddaughter will become your liege lord. Royina in her own right of all Chalion, and royina-consort of Ibra."

Her lips screwed up. "That's the maddest part of all. She's just a girl! Not but that she always had more wits than poor Teidez. What can all the gods of Chalion be thinking, to place such a child on the throne at Cardegoss!"

Cazaril said mildly, "Perhaps that the restoration of Chalion is the work of a very long lifetime, and that no one so old as you or I could live to see it through."

She snorted. "You're barely more than a child yourself. Children in charge of the whole world these days, no wonder it's all gone mad. Well . . . well. We must bustle about tomorrow. Five gods, Cazaril, go sleep, though I doubt I shall. You look like death warmed over, and you haven't my years to excuse you."

Creakily, he clambered to his feet and bowed himself out. The Provincara's bursts of irate energy were fragile. It would take all her retainers' aid to prevent her from exhausting herself dangerously. He found the anxiously waiting Lady dy Hueltar in the next room, and sent her in to attend upon her lady cousin.

❧THEY GAVE CAZARIL BACK HIS CHILLY, HONORABLE, customary chamber in the main keep. He slid gratefully between heated sheets. It was as much like coming home as anything he'd experienced for years. Yet his new eyes rendered familiar places strange again; the world made strange as he was remade, over and over, and no place to rest at last.

Dondo, in all his motley ghostly glory, scarcely kept Cazaril awake that night. He had become a danger almost too routine to be dreaded. Fresh fears assailed Cazaril now.

Memory of the terrible hope in Ista's eyes unnerved him. And the reflection that tomorrow, he would mount a horse whose every stride would carry him closer to the sea.

22

Cazaril regretfully gave up use of the Chancellery's courier remounts when they left Valenda, in favor of secrecy. No merit in handing dy Jironal a signed record of their route and destination. Armed with Palli's letter of recommendation, they instead arranged exchanges for fresh horses at local town chapters of the Daughter's Order. At the foot of the mountains on the western frontier, they were obliged to deal with a local horse trader for the sturdy and surefooted mules to carry them over the heights.

The man had clearly been making a fine living for years skinning desperate travelers. Ferda looked over the beasts offered them, and said indignantly, "This one has heaves. And if that one isn't throwing out a splint, my lord, I'll eat your hat!" The horse trader and he fell at once into acrimonious argument.

Cazaril, leaning in exhaustion on the corral rail and thinking only of how much he didn't want to throw a leg over any animal, spavined or not, for the next thousand years, at last straightened and let himself through the gate. He walked out into the herd of milling horses and mules, stirred up by the rough-and-ready capture of their rejected comrades, spread his hands, and closed his eyes. "If it please you, Lady, give us three good mules."

At a nudge at his side, he opened them again. A curious mule, its brown eyes limpid, stared at him. Two more muscled in, their long ears waggling; the tallest one, dark brown with a creamy nose, rested its chin on his shoulder and breathed out a contented-sounding snort, spraying the environs.

"Thank you, Lady," muttered Cazaril. And more loudly, "All right. Follow me." He plodded back through the hoof-pocked muck to the gate. The three mules fell in behind, snuffling with interest.

"We'll take these three," he told the horse trader, who, along with Ferda, had fallen silent and was staring openmouthed.

The horse trader found his voice first. "But—but those are my three best animals!"

"Yes. I know." He let himself back out, leaving the horse trader to hold the gate against the three mules who still tried to follow him, shouldering up heavily against the boards and making anxious mulish noises. "Ferda, come to a price. I'm going to go lie down in that lovely straw stack. Wake me when we're saddled up . . ."

His mule proved healthy, steady, and bored. There was nothing better, in Cazaril's view, on these treacherous mountain trails than a bored mule. The fiery steeds Ferda favored for making time over the flats could have climbed no faster on these breath-stealing slopes, besides making a menace of themselves with their nervous sidling on the narrow places. And the mule's gentle amble didn't churn his guts. Although if the goddess granted Her saint mules, he didn't know why She didn't also give him better weather.

The dy Gura brothers stopped laughing at Cazaril's hat about halfway up the pass over the Bastard's Teeth range. He folded the fine fur flaps down over his ears and tied their strings under his chin before the sleet, driven by the tumbling updrafts, started stinging their faces. He squinted into the wind between the laid-back ears of his laboring mule at the track winding up through rocks and ice, and mentally measured out the daylight left to them.

After a time, Ferda reined back beside him. "My lord, should we take shelter from this blizzard?"

"Blizzard?" Cazaril brushed ice spicules from his beard, and blinked. Oh. Palliar's winters were mild, sodden rather than snowy, and the brothers had never been out of their province before. "If this were a blizzard, you wouldn't be able to see your mule's ears from where you sit. This isn't unsafe. Merely unpleasant."

Ferda made a face of dismay, but pulled his hood strings tighter and bent into the wind. Indeed, in a few more minutes they broke out of the squall, and visibility returned; the high vale opened out before their eyes. A few fingers of pale sunlight poked down through silvery clouds to dapple the long slopes—falling away downward.

Cazaril pointed, and shouted encouragingly, "Ibra!"

❧THE WEATHER MODERATED AS THEY STARTED THE long descent toward the coast, though the grunting mules shuffled no faster. The rugged border mountains gave way to less daunting hills, humped and brown, with broad valleys winding between. When they left the snow behind Cazaril reluctantly permitted Ferda to trade in their excellent mules for swifter horses. A succession of improving roads and increasingly civilized inns brought them in just two more days to the river course that ran down to Zagosur. They passed through outlying farms, and over bridges across irrigation canals swollen with the winter rains.

They debouched from the river valley to find the city rising up before them: gray walls, a blocky jumble of whitewashed houses with roofs of the distinctive green tile of this region, the fortress at its crown, the famous harbor at its feet. The sea stretched out beyond, steel gray, the endless level horizon of it streaked with aqua light. The salt-and-sea-wrack smell of low tide, wafting inland on a cold breeze, made Cazaril's head jerk back. Foix inhaled deeply, his eyes alight with fascination as he drank in his first sight of the sea.

Palli's letter and the dy Gura brothers' rank secured them shelter at the Daughter's house off Zagosur's main Temple plaza. Cazaril sent the boys to buy, beg, or borrow formal dress of their order, while he took himself off to a tailor. The news that the tailor might name his price so long as he produced something swiftly launched a flurry of activity that resulted in Cazaril emerging, little more than an hour later, with a tolerable version of Chalionese court mourning garb under his arm.

After a chilly sponge bath, Cazaril quickly slipped into a heavy lavender-gray brocade tunic, very high-necked, thick dark purple wool trousers, and his cleaned and polished boots. He adjusted the sword belt and sword Ser dy Ferrej had lent him so long ago, rather worn but looking more honorable thereby, and swung the satisfying weight of a black silk-velvet vest-cloak over the whole. One of Iselle's remaining rings, a square-cut amethyst, just fit over Cazaril's little finger, its isolated heavy gold suggesting restraint rather than poverty. Between the court mourning and the gray streaks in his beard, he fancied the result was as grave and dignified as could be wished. Serious. He packaged up his precious diplomatic letters and tucked them under his arm, collected his outriders, who had refurbished themselves in neat blue and white, and led the way through the narrow, winding streets up the hill to the Great Fox's lair.

Cazaril's appearance and bearing brought him before the Roya of Ibra's castle warder. Showing his letters and their seals to this official sped him in turn to the roya's own secretary, who met them standing in a bare whitewashed antechamber, chilly with Zagosur's perpetual winter damp.

The secretary was spare, middle-aged, and harried. Cazaril favored him with a half bow, equal to equal.

"I am the Castillar dy Cazaril, and I come from Cardegoss on a diplomatic mission of some urgency. I bear letters of introduction to the roya and Royse Bergon dy Ibra from the Royesse Iselle dy Chalion." He displayed their seals, but folded them back to his chest when the secretary reached for them. "I received these from the royesse's own hand. She bade me deliver them into the roya's own hand."

The secretary's head tilted judiciously. "I'll see what I can do for you, my lord, but the roya is very plagued with petitioners, mostly relatives of former rebels attempting to intercede for the roya's mercy, which is stretched thin at present." He looked Cazaril up and down. "I think perhaps no one has warned you—the roya has forbid the court to wear mourning for the late Heir of Ibra, as he died in a state of unreconciled rebellion. Only those who wish to cast their defiance in the roya's teeth are wearing that sad garb, and most of them have the presence of mind to do it in, ah, absence. If you do not intend the insult, I suggest you go change before you beg an audience."

Cazaril's brows went up. "Is no one here before me with the news? We rode fast, but I didn't think we had outdistanced it. I do not wear these bruised colors for the Heir of Ibra, but for the Heir of Chalion. Royse Teidez died barely a week ago, suddenly, of an infection."

"Oh," said the secretary, startled. "Oh." He regained his balance smoothly. "My condolences indeed to the House of Chalion, to lose so bright a hope." He hesitated. "Letters from the *Royesse Iselle*, do you say?"

"Aye." Cazaril added, for good measure, "Roya Orico lies gravely ill, and does not do business, or so it was when we left Cardegoss in haste."

The secretary's mouth opened, and closed. He finally said, "Come with me," and led them to a more comfortable chamber, with a small fire in a corner fireplace. "I'll go see what I can do."

Cazaril lowered himself into a cushioned chair near the gentle glow. Foix took a bench, though Ferda prowled about, frowning in an unfocused fashion at the wall hangings.

"Will they see us, sir?" asked Ferda. "To have ridden all this way, only to be kept waiting on the doorstep like some peddler . . ."

"Oh, yes. They'll see us." Cazaril smiled slightly, as a breathless servant arrived to offer the travelers wine and the little spiced shortbread cakes, stamped with an Ibran seal, which were a Zagosur specialty.

"Why does this dog have no legs?" Foix inquired, staring a trifle cross-eyed at the indented creature before biting into his cake.

"It is a sea dog. It has paddles in place of paws, and chases fish. They make colonies upon the shore, here and there down the coast toward Darthaca." Cazaril allowed the servant to pour him but a swallow of wine, partly for sobriety, partly to avoid waste; as he'd anticipated, he'd barely wet his lips before the secretary returned.

The man bowed lower than before. "Come this way, if it please you, my lord, gentlemen."

Ferda gulped down his glassful of dark Ibran wine, and Foix brushed crumbs from his white wool vest-cloak. They hastily followed Cazaril and the secretary, who led them up some stairs and across a little arched stone bridge to a newer part of the fortress. After more turnings, they came to a pair of double doors carved with sea creatures in the Roknari style.

These swung open to emit a well-dressed lord, arm in arm with another courtier, complaining, "But I waited five days for this audience! What is this foolery—!"

"You'll just have to wait a little longer, my lord," said the courtier, guiding him off with a firm hand under his elbow.

The secretary bowed Cazaril and the dy Gura brothers inside, and announced their names and ranks.

It was not a throne room, but a less formal receiving chamber, set up for conference, not ceremony. A broad table, roomy enough to spread out maps and documents, occupied one end. The long far wall was pierced with a row of doors with square windowpanes set top to bottom, giving onto a balcony-cum-battlement that in turn overlooked the harbor and shipyard that were the heart of Zagosur's wealth and power. The silvery sea light, diffuse and pale, illuminated the chamber through the generous glass, making the candle flames in the sconces seem wan.

Half a dozen men were present, but Cazaril's eye had no trouble picking out the Fox and his son. At seventy-odd, the roya of Ibra was stringy, balding, the russet hair of his younger days reduced to a wispy fringe of white around his pate. But he remained vigorous, not fragile with his years, alert and relaxed in his cushioned chair. The tall youth standing at his side had the straight brown Darthacan hair of his late mother, though tinged with reddish highlights, worn just long enough to cushion a helmet, cut bluntly. *He looks healthy, at least. Good . . .* His sea-green vest-cloak was set with hundreds of pearls in patterns of curling surf, which made it swing in elegant, weighty ripples when he turned toward these new visitors.

The man standing on the Fox's other side was proclaimed by his chain of office to be the chancellor of Ibra. A wary and intimidated-looking fellow, he was the—from all reports, overworked—servant of the Fox, not a rival for his power. Another man's badges marked him as a sea lord, an admiral of Ibra's fleet.

Cazaril went to one knee before the Fox, not too ungracefully despite his saddle-stiffness and aches, and bowed his head. "My lord, I bring sad news from Ibra of the death of Royse Teidez, and urgent letters from his sister the Royesse Iselle." He proffered Iselle's letter of his authority.

The Fox cracked the seal, and scanned rapidly down the simple penned lines. His brows climbed, and he glanced back keenly at Cazaril. "Most interesting. Rise, my lord Ambassador," he murmured.

Cazaril took a breath, and managed to surge back to his feet without having either to push off the floor with his hand or, worse, catch himself on the roya's chair. He looked up to find Royse Bergon staring hard at him, his lips parted in a frown. Cazaril blinked, and favored him with a tentative nod and smile. He was quite a well-made young man, withal, even-featured, perhaps handsome when he wasn't scowling so. No squint, no hanging lip— a little stocky, but fit, not fat. And not forty. Young, clean-shaven, but with a vigor in the shadow on his chin that promised he was grown to virility. Cazaril thought Iselle should be pleased.

Bergon's stare intensified. "Speak again!" he said.

"Excuse me, my lord?" Cazaril stepped back, startled, as the royse stepped forward and circled him, his eyes searching him up and down, his breath coming faster.

"Take off your shirt!" Bergon demanded suddenly.

"What?"

"Take off your shirt, take off your shirt!"

"My lord—Royse Bergon—" Cazaril was thrown back in memory to the ghastly scene engineered by dy Jironal to slander him to Orico. But there were no sacred crows here in Zagosur to rescue him. He lowered his voice. "I beg you, my lord, do not shame me in this company."

"Please, sir, a year and more ago, in the fall, were you not rescued from a Roknari galley off the coast of Ibra?"

"Oh. Yes . . . ?"

"Take off your shirt!" The royse was practically dancing, circling around him again; Cazaril felt dizzy. He glanced at the Fox, who looked as baffled as everyone else, but waved his hand curiously, endorsing the royse's peculiar demand. Confused and frightened, Cazaril complied, popping the frogs of his tunic and slipping it off together with his vest-cloak, and folding the garments over his arm. He set his jaw, trying to stand with dignity, to bear whatever humiliation came next.

"You're *Caz*! You're *Caz*!" Bergon cried. His frown had changed to a demented grin. Ye gods, the royse was mad, and after all this pelting gallop over plain and mountain, unfit for Iselle after all—

"Why, yes, so my friends call me—" Cazaril's words were choked off as the royse abruptly flung his arms around him, and nearly lifted him off his feet.

"Father," Bergon cried joyously, "this is the man! This is the man!"

"*What*," Cazaril began, and then, by some trick of angle and shift of voice, he knew. Cazaril's own gape turned to grin. *The boy has grown!* Roll him back a year in time and four inches in height, erase the beard-shadow, shave the head, add a peck of puppy fat and a blistering sunburn . . . "Five gods," he breathed. "Danni? Danni!"

The royse grabbed his hands and kissed them. "Where did you go? I fell sick for a week after I was brought home, and when I finally set men to look for you, you'd disappeared. I found other men from the ship, but not you, and none knew where you'd gone."

"I was ill also, in the Mother's hospital here in Zagosur. Then I, um, walked home to Chalion."

"Here! Right here all the time! I shall burst. Ah! But I sent men to the hospitals—oh, how did they miss you there? I thought you must have died of your injuries, they were so fearsome."

"I was sure he must have died," said the Fox slowly, watching this play with unreadable eyes. "Not to have come to collect the very great debt my House owed to him."

"I did not know . . . who you were, Royse Bergon."

The Fox's gray eyebrows shot up. "Truly?"

"No, Father," Bergon confirmed eagerly. "I told no one who I was. I used the nickname Mama used to call me by when I was little. It seemed to me more unsafe to claim my rank than to pass anonymously." He added to Cazaril, "When my late brother's bravos kidnapped me, they did not tell the Roknari captain who I was. They meant me to die on the galley, I think."

"The secrecy was foolish, Royse," chided Cazaril. "The Roknari would surely have set you aside for ransom."

"Yes, a great ransom, and political concessions wrung from my father, too, no doubt, if I'd allowed myself to be made hostage in my own name." Bergon's jaw tightened. "No. I would not hand myself to them to play that game."

"So," said the Fox in an odd voice, staring up at Cazaril, "you did not interpose your body to save the royse of Ibra from defilement, but merely to save some random boy."

"Random slave boy. My lord." Cazaril's lips twisted, as he watched the Fox trying to work out just what this made Cazaril, hero or fool.

"I wonder at your wits."

"I'm sure I was half-witted by then," Cazaril conceded amiably.

"I'd been on the galleys since I was sold as a prisoner of war after the fall of Gotorget."

The Fox's eyes narrowed. "Oh. So you're *that* Cazaril, eh?"

Cazaril essayed him a small bow, wondering what he had heard of that fruitless campaign, and shook out his tunic. Bergon hastened to help him don it again. Cazaril found himself the object of stunned stares from every man in the room, including Ferda and Foix. His tilted grin barely kept back bubbling laughter, though underneath the laughter seethed a new terror that he could scarcely name. *How long have I been walking down this road?*

He pulled out the last letter in his packet, and swept a deeper bow to Royse Bergon. "As the document your respected father holds attests, I come as spokesman for a proud and beautiful lady, and I come not just to him, but to you. The Heiress of Chalion begs your hand in marriage." He handed the sealed missive to the startled Bergon. "In this, I will let the Royesse Iselle speak for herself, which she is most fit to do by virtue of her singular intellect, her natural right, and her holy purpose. After that, I will have much else to tell you, Royse."

"I'm eager to hear you, Lord Cazaril." Bergon, after a taut glance around the chamber, took himself off to a window-door, where he popped the letter's seal and read it at once, his lips softening with wonder.

Amazement, too, touched the Fox's lips, though it rendered them anything but soft. Cazaril had no doubt he'd put the man's wits to the gallop. For his own wits he now prayed for wings.

❧CAZARIL AND HIS COMPANIONS WERE, OF COURSE, invited to dine that night in the roya's hall. Near sunset, Cazaril and Bergon went walking together along the sea strand below the fortress. It was as close to private speech as he was likely to obtain, Cazaril thought, waving the dy Guras back to trail along through the sand out of earshot. The growl of the surf cloaked the sound of their voices. A few white gulls swooped and cried, as piercing as any crow, or pecked at the smelly sea wrack on the wet sand, and Cazaril was reminded that these scavengers with their cold golden eyes were sacred to the Bastard in Ibra.

Bergon bade his own heavily armed guard walk at a distance, too, though he did not seek to dispense with them. The silent routine of his precautions reminded Cazaril once more that civil war in this country was but lately ended, and Bergon had been both piece and player in that vicious game already. A piece that had played himself, it seemed.

"I'll never forget the first time I met you," said Bergon, "when they dropped me down beside you on the galley bench. For a moment you frightened me more than the Roknari did."

Cazaril grinned. "What, just because I was a scaly, scabbed, burnt scarecrow, hairy and stinking?"

Bergon grinned back. "Something like that," he admitted sheepishly. "But then you smiled, and said *Good evening, young sir*, for all the world as if you were inviting me to share a tavern bench and not a rowing bench."

"Well, you were a novelty, of which we didn't get many."

"I thought about it a lot, later. I'm sure I wasn't thinking too clearly at the time—"

"Naturally not. You arrived well roughed-up."

"Truly. Kidnapped, frightened—I'd just collected my first real beating—but you helped me. Told me how to go on, what to expect, taught me how to survive. You gave me extra water twice from your own portion—"

"Eh, only when you really needed it. I was already used to the heat, as desiccated as I was like to get. After a time one can tell the difference between mere discomfort and the feverish look of a man skirting collapse. It was very important that you not faint at your oar, you see."

"You were kind."

Cazaril shrugged. "Why not? What could it cost me, after all?"

Bergon shook his head. "Any man can be kind when he is comfortable. I'd always thought kindness a trivial virtue, therefore. But when we were hungry, thirsty, sick, frightened, with our deaths shouting at us, in the heart of horror, you were still as unfailingly courteous as a gentleman at his ease before his own hearth."

"*Events* may be horrible or inescapable. *Men* have always a choice—if not whether, then how, they may endure."

"Yes, but . . . I hadn't known that before I saw it. That was when

I began to believe it was possible to survive. And I don't mean just my body."

Cazaril smiled wryly. "I was taken for half-cracked by then, you know."

Bergon shook his head again, and kicked up a little silver sand with his boot as they paced along. The westering sun picked out the foxy copper highlights in his dark Darthacan hair.

Bergon's late mother had been perceived in Chalion as a virago, a Darthacan interloper suspected of fomenting her husband's strife with his Heir on her son's behalf. But Bergon seemed to remember her fondly; as a child he'd been through two sieges with her, cut off from his father's forces in the intermittent war with his half brother. He was clearly accustomed to strong-minded women with a voice in men's councils. When he and Cazaril had shared the oar bench he had spoken of his dead mother, although in disguised terms, when he'd been trying to encourage himself. Not of his live father. Bergon's precocious wit and self-control as demonstrated in the dire days on the galley weren't, Cazaril reflected, entirely the legacy of the Fox.

Cazaril's smile broadened. "So let me tell you," he began, "all about the Royesse Iselle dy Chalion . . ."

Bergon hung on Cazaril's words as he described Iselle's winding amber hair and her bright gray eyes, her wide and laughing mouth, her horsemanship and her scholarship. Her undaunted, steady nerve, her rapid assessment of emergencies. Selling Iselle to Bergon seemed approximately as difficult as selling food to starving men, water to the parched, or cloaks to the naked in a blizzard, and he hadn't even touched yet on the part about her being due to inherit a royacy. The boy seemed half in love already. The Fox would be a greater challenge; the Fox would suspect a catch. Cazaril had no intention of confiding the catch to the Fox. Bergon was another matter. *For you, the truth.*

"There is a darker urgency to Royesse Iselle's plea," Cazaril continued, as they reached the end of the crescent of beach and turned about again. "This is in the deepest confidence, as she prays to have safe confidence in you as her husband. For your ear alone." He drew in sea air, and all his courage. "It all goes back to the war of Fonsa the Fairly-Wise and the Golden General . . ."

They made two more turns along the stretch of sand, crossing back over their own tracks, before Cazaril's tale was told. The sun, going down in a red ball, was nearly touching the flat sea horizon, and the breaking waves shimmered in dark and wondrous colors, gnawing their way up the beach as the tide turned. Cazaril was as frank and full with Bergon as he'd been with Ista, keeping nothing back save Ista's confession, not even his own personal haunting by Dondo. Bergon's face, made ruddy by the light, was set in profound thought when he finished.

"Lord Cazaril, if this came from any man's lips but yours, I doubt I would believe it. I'd think him mad."

"Although madness may be an effect of these events, Royse, it is not the cause. It's all real. I've seen it. I half think I am drowning in it." An unfortunate turn of phrase, but the sea growling so close at hand was making Cazaril nervous. He wondered if Bergon had noticed Cazaril always turned so as to put the royse between him and the surf.

"You would make me like the hero of some nursemaid's tale, rescuing the fair lady from enchantment with a kiss."

Cazaril cleared his throat. "Well, rather more than a kiss, I think. A marriage must be consummated to be legally binding. Theologically binding, likewise, I would assume."

The royse gave him an indecipherable glance. He didn't speak for a few more paces. Then he said, "I've seen your integrity in action. It . . . widened my world. I'd been raised by my father, who is a prudent, cautious man, always looking for men's hidden, selfish motivations. No one can cheat him. But I've seen him cheat himself. If you understand what I mean."

"Yes."

"It was very foolish of you, to attack that vile Roknari galley-man."

"Yes."

"And yet, I think, given the same circumstances, you would do it again."

"Knowing what I know now . . . it would be harder. But I would hope . . . I would pray, Royse, that the gods would still lend me such foolishness in my need."

"What is this astonishing foolishness, that shines brighter than all my father's gold? Can you teach me to be such a fool too, Caz?"

"Oh," breathed Cazaril, "I'm sure of it."

*   *   *

❧CAZARIL MET WITH THE FOX IN THE COOL OF THE following morning. He was escorted again to the high, bright chamber overlooking the sea, but this time for a more private conference, just himself, the roya, and the roya's secretary. The secretary sat at the end of the table, along with a pile of paper, new quills, and a ready supply of ink. The Fox sat on the long side, fiddling with a game of castles and riders, its pieces exquisitely carved of coral and jade, the board fashioned of polished malachite, onyx, and white marble. Cazaril bowed, and, at the roya's wave of invitation, seated himself across from him.

"Do you play?" the Fox inquired.

"No, my lord," said Cazaril regretfully. "Or only very indifferently."

"Ah. Pity." The Fox pushed the board a little to one side. "Bergon is very warmed with your description of this paragon of Chalion. You do your job well, Ambassador."

"That is all my hope."

The roya touched Iselle's letter of credential, lying on the glossy wood. "Extraordinary document. You know it binds the royesse to whatever you sign in her name."

"Yes, sir."

"Her authority to charge you so is questionable, you know. There is the matter of her age, for one thing."

"Well, sir, if you do not recognize her right to make her own marriage treaty, I suppose there's nothing for me to do but mount my horse and ride back to Chalion."

"No, no, I didn't say I questioned it!" A slight panic tinged the old roya's voice.

Cazaril suppressed a smile. "Indeed, sir, to treat with us is public acknowledgment of her authority."

"Hm. Indeed, indeed. Young people, so trusting. It's why we old people must guard their interests." He picked up the other list Cazaril had given him last night. "I've studied your suggested clauses for the marriage contract. We have much to discuss."

"Excuse me, sir. Those are not suggested. Those are required. If you wish to propose additional items, I will hear you."

The roya arched his brows at him. "Surely not. Just taking one—this matter of inheritance during the minority of their heir, if they are so blessed. One accident with a horse, and the royina of

Chalion becomes regent of Ibra! It won't do. Bergon bears the risks of the battlefield, which his wife will not."

"Well, which we hope she will not. Or else I am curiously poorly informed of the history of Ibra, my lord. I thought the royse's mother won two sieges?"

The Fox cleared his throat.

"In any case," Cazaril continued, "we maintain that the risk is reciprocal, and so must be the clause. Iselle bears the risks of childbirth, which Bergon never will. One breech birth, and he could become regent of Chalion. How many of your wives have outlived you, sir?"

The Fox took a breath, paused, and went on, "And then there's this naming clause!"

A few minutes of gentle argument determined that Bergon dy Ibra-Chalion was no more euphonious than Bergon dy Chalion-Ibra, and that clause, too, was allowed to stand.

The Fox pursed his lips and frowned thoughtfully. "I understand you are a landless man, Lord Cazaril. How is it that the royesse does not reward you as befits your rank?"

"She rewards me as befits hers. Iselle is not royina of Chalion—yet."

"Huh. I, on the other hand, am the present roya of Ibra, and have the power to dispense . . . much."

Cazaril merely smiled.

Encouraged, the Fox spoke of an elegant villa overlooking the sea, and placed a coral castle piece upon the table between them. Fascinated to see where this was going, Cazaril refrained from observing how little he cared for the sight of the sea. The Fox spoke of fine horses, and an estate to graze them upon, and how inappropriate he found Clause Three. Some riders were added. Cazaril made neutral noises. The Fox breathed delicately of the money whereby a man might dress himself as befit an Ibran rank rather higher than castillar, and how Clause Six might profitably be rewritten. A jade castle piece joined the growing set. The secretary made notes. With each wordless murmur from Cazaril, both respect and contempt grew in the Fox's eyes, though as the pile grew he remarked in a tone of some pain, "You play better than I expected, Castillar."

At last the Fox sat back and waved at his little pile of offering symbols. "How does it suit you, Cazaril? What do you think this girl can give you that I cannot better, eh?"

Cazaril's smile broadened to a cheerful grin. "Why, sir. I believe she will give me an estate in Chalion that will suit me perfectly. One pace wide and two paces long, to be mine in perpetuity." Gently, so as not to imply an insult either given or taken, he stretched out his hand and pushed the pieces back toward the Fox. "I should probably explain, I bear a tumor in my gut, that I expect to kill me shortly. These prizes are for living men, I think. Not dying ones."

The Fox's lips moved; astonishment and dismay flickered in his face, and the faintest flash of unaccustomed shame, quickly suppressed. A brief bark of laughter escaped him. "Five gods! The girl has wit and ruthlessness enough to teach me my trade! No wonder she gave you such powers. By the Bastard's balls, she's sent me an unbribeable ambassador!"

Three thoughts marched across Cazaril's mind: first, that Iselle had no such crafty plan, second, that were it to be pointed out to her, she would say *Hm!* and file the notion away against some future need, and third, that the Fox did not need to know about the first.

The Fox sobered, staring more closely at Cazaril. "I am sorry for your affliction, Castillar. It is no laughing matter. Bergon's mother died of a tumor in her breast, taken untimely young—just thirty-six, she was. All the grief she married in me could not daunt her, but at the end . . . ah, well."

"I'm thirty-six," Cazaril couldn't help observing rather sadly.

The Fox blinked. "You *don't* look well, then."

"No," Cazaril agreed. He picked up the list of clauses. "Now, sir, about this marriage contract . . ."

In the end, Cazaril gave away nothing on his list, and obtained agreement to it all. The Fox, rueful and reeling, offered some intelligent additions to the contingency clauses to which Cazaril happily agreed. The Fox whined a little, for form's sake, and made frequent reference to the submission due a husband from a wife—also not a prominent feature of recent Ibran history, Cazaril diplomatically did not point out—and to the unnatural strong-mindedness of women who rode too much.

"Take heart, sir," Cazaril consoled him. "It is not your destiny today to win a royacy for your son. It is to win an *empire* for your grandson."

The Fox brightened. Even his secretary smiled.

Finally, the Fox offered him the castles and riders set, for a personal memento.

"For myself, I think I shall decline," said Cazaril, eyeing the elegant pieces regretfully. A better thought struck him. "But if you care to have them packaged up, I should be pleased to carry them back to Chalion as your personal betrothal gift to your future daughter-in-law."

The Fox laughed and shook his head. "Would that I had a courtier who offered me so much loyalty for so little reward. Do you truly want nothing for yourself, Cazaril?"

"I want time."

The Fox snorted regretfully. "Don't we all. For that, you must apply to the gods, not the roya of Ibra."

Cazaril let this one pass, though his lips twitched. "I'd at least like to live to see Iselle safely wed. This is a gift you can indeed give me, sir, by hastening these matters along." He added, "And it is truly urgent that Bergon become royse-consort of Chalion before Martou dy Jironal can become regent of Chalion."

Even the Fox was forced to nod judiciously at this.

🐟THAT NIGHT AFTER THE ROYA'S CUSTOMARY BANquet, and after he'd shaken off Bergon who, if he could not stuff him with the honors Cazaril steadfastly declined, seemed to want to stuff him at least with food, Cazaril stopped in at the temple. Its high round halls were quiet and somber at this hour, nearly empty of worshippers, though the wall lights as well as the central fire burned steadily, and a couple of acolytes kept night watch. He returned their cordial good evenings, and walked through the tile-decorated archway into the Daughter's court.

Beautiful prayer rugs were woven by the maidens and ladies of Ibra, who donated them to the temples as a pious act, saving the knees and bodies of petitioners from the marble chill of the floors. Cazaril thought that if the custom were imported to Chalion along with Bergon, it could well improve the rate of winter worship there. Mats of all sizes, colors, and designs were ranged around the Lady's altar. Cazaril chose a broad thick one, dense with wool and slightly blurry representations of spring flowers, and laid himself down upon it. Prayer, not drunken sleep, he reminded himself, was his purpose here . . .

On the way to Ibra, he'd seized the chance at every rural rudimentary Daughter's house, while Ferda saw to the horses, to pray: for Orico's preservation, for Iselle's and Betriz's safety, for Ista's solace. Above all, intimidated by the Fox's reputation, he'd begged for the success of his mission. That prayer, it seemed, had been answered in advance. How far in advance? His outflung hands traced over the threads of his rug, passed loop by loop through some patient woman's hands. Or maybe she hadn't been patient. Maybe she'd been tired, or irritated, or distracted, or hungry, or angry. Maybe she had been dying. But her hands had kept moving, all the same.

How long have I been walking down this road?

Once, he would have traced his allegiance to the Lady's affairs to a coin dropped in the Baocian winter mud by a clumsy soldier. Now he was by no means so sure, and by no means sure he liked the new answer.

The nightmare of the galleys came before the coin in the mud. Had all his pain and fear and agony there been manipulated by the gods to their ends? Was he nothing but a puppet on a string? Or was that, a mule on a rope, balky and stubborn, to be whipped along? He scarcely knew whether he felt wonder or rage. He considered Umegat's insistence that gods could not seize a man's will, but only wait for it to be offered. When had he signed up for *that*?

Oh.

Then.

One starving, cold, desperate night at Gotorget, he'd walked his commander's rounds upon the battlements. On the highest tower, he'd dismissed the famished, fainting boy on guard to go below for a time and get what refreshment he could, and stood the watch himself. He'd stared out at the enemy's campfires, glowing mockingly in the ruined village, in the valley, on the ridges all around, speaking of abundant warmth, and cooking food, and confidence, and all the things his company lacked within the walls. And thought of how he'd schemed, and temporized, and exhorted his men to faithfulness, plugged holes fought sorties scraped for unclean food bloodied his sword at the scaling ladders and above all, prayed. Till he'd come to the end of prayers.

In his youth at Cazaril, he'd followed the common path of most highborn young men, and become a lay dedicat of the Brother's Order, with its military promises and aspirations. He'd sent up his prayers, when he'd bothered to pray at all, by rote to the god assigned to him by his sex, his age, and his rank. On the tower in the dark, it seemed to him that following that unquestioned path had brought him, step by step, into this impossible snare, abandoned by his own side and his god both.

He'd worn his Brother's medal inside his shirt since the ceremony of his dedication at age thirteen, just before he'd left Cazaril to be apprenticed as a page in the old provincar's household. That night on the tower, tears of fatigue and despair—and yes, rage—running down his face, he'd torn it off and flung it over the battlement, denying the god who'd denied him. The spinning slip of gold had disappeared into the darkness without a sound. And he'd flung himself prone on the stones, as he lay now, and sworn that any other god could pick him up who willed, or none, so long as the men who had trusted him were let out of this trap. As for himself, he was done. Done.

Nothing, of course, happened.

Well, eventually it started to rain.

In time, he'd picked himself back up off the pavement, ashamed of his tantrum, grateful that none of his men had witnessed the performance. The next watch came on, and he'd gone down in silence. Where nothing more happened for some weeks, till the arrival of that well-fed courier with the news that it had all been in vain, and all their blood and sacrifice was to be sold for gold to go into dy Jironal's coffers.

And his men were marched to safety.

And his feet alone went down another road . . .

What was it that Ista had said? *The gods' most savage curses come to us as answers to our own prayers. Prayer is a dangerous business.*

So, in choosing to share one's will with the gods, was it enough to choose once, like signing up to a military company with an oath? Or did one have to choose and choose and choose again, every day? Or was it both? Could he step off this road anytime, get on a horse, and ride to, say, Darthaca, to a new name, a new life? Just like Umegat's postulated hundred other Cazarils, who'd not even shown up for duty. Abandoning, of course, all who'd trusted him, Iselle and Ista and the Provincara, Palli and Betriz . . .

But not, alas, Dondo.

He squirmed a little on the mat, uncomfortably aware of the pressure in his belly, trying to convince himself it was just the Fox's banquet, and not his tumor creeping to hideous new growth. Racing to some grotesque completion, waiting only for the Lady's hand to falter. Maybe the gods had learned from Ista's mistake, from dy Lutez's failure of nerve, as well? Maybe they were making sure their mule couldn't desert in the middle like dy Lutez this time . . . ?

Except into death. That door was always ajar. What waited him on the other side? The Bastard's hell? Ghostly dissolution? Peace?
Bah.

On the other side of the Temple plaza, in the Daughter's house, what waited him was a nice soft bed. That his brain had reached this feverish spin was a good sign he ought to go get in it. This wasn't prayer anyway, it was just argument with the gods.

Prayer, he suspected as he hoisted himself up and turned for the door, was putting one foot in front of the other. Moving all the same.

At the last moment, with principles agreed upon, treaties written out in multiple copies in a fair court hand, signed by all parties and their witnesses, and sealed, practicalities nearly brought all to a halt. The Fox, not without reason in Cazaril's view, balked at sending his son into Chalion with so little guarantee of his personal safety. But the roya had neither the men nor the money in his war-weary royacy to raise a large force to guard Bergon, and Cazaril was fearful of the effect upon Chalion of taking arms across the border, even in so fair a cause. Their debate grew heated; the Fox, shamed by the reminder that he owed Bergon's very life to Cazaril, took to avoiding Cazaril's petitions in a way that reminded Cazaril forcibly of Orico.

Cazaril received Iselle's first ciphered letter, via the relay of couriers from the Daughter's Order that he had set up on their outbound route. It had been penned just four days after he had left Cardegoss, and was brief, simply confirming that Teidez's funeral rites had taken place without incident, and that Iselle would leave the capital that afternoon with his cortege for Valenda and the interment. She noted, with obvious relief, *Our prayers were answered—the sacred animals showed the Son of Autumn has taken him up after all. I pray he will find ease in the god's good company.* She added, *My eldest brother lives, and has back sight in one eye. But he remains very swollen. He stays at home, abed.* More chillingly, she reported: *Our enemy has set two of his nieces as ladies-in-waiting in my household. I will not be able to write often. The Lady speed your embassy.*

He looked in vain for a postscript from Betriz, nearly missing it till he turned the paper over. Minute numbers in her distinctive hand lay half-hidden beneath the cracked wax of the seal itself. He scraped at the residue with his thumbnail. The brief notation thus revealed led him to a page toward the back of the book, one of Ordol's most lyrical prayers: a passionate plea for the safety of a beloved one who traveled far from home. How many years—decades—had it been since someone far away had prayed just for him? Cazaril wasn't even sure if this had been meant for his eyes, or only for those of the gods, but he touched the tiny cipher secretly to the five sacred points, lingering a little on his lips, before leaving his chamber to seek Bergon.

He shared the other side of the letter with the royse, who studied it, and the code system, with fascination. Cazaril composed a brief note telling of the success of his mission, and Bergon, his tongue clamped between his teeth, laboriously ciphered out a letter in his own hand to go to his new betrothed along with it.

Cazaril counted days in his head. It was impossible that dy Jironal not have spies in the court of Ibra. Sooner or later, Cazaril's appearance there must be reported back to Cardegoss. How soon? Would dy Jironal guess that Cazaril's negotiations on Iselle's behalf had prospered so stunningly? Would he seize the royesse's person, would he calculate Cazaril's next move, would he try to intercept Bergon in Chalion?

After several days of the deadlock over the royse's safety, Cazaril, in a burst of genius, sent Bergon in to argue his own case. This was an envoy the Fox could not evade, not even in his private chambers. Bergon was young and energetic, his imagination passionately engaged, and the Fox was old and tired. Worse, or perhaps, from Cazaril's point of view, better, a town in South Ibra of the late Heir's party rose in arms about some failure of treaty, and the Fox was forced to muster men to ride out to pacify it again. Frenzied with the dilemma, torn between his great hopes and his icy fears for his sole surviving son, the Fox threw the resolution back upon Bergon and his coterie.

Resolution, Cazaril was discovering, was one thing Bergon did not lack. The royse quickly endorsed Cazaril's scheme to travel lightly and in disguise across the hostile country between the Ibran border and Valenda. For escort Bergon chose, besides Cazaril and the dy Guras, only three close companions: two young Ibran lords, dy Tagille and dy Cembuer, and the only slightly older March dy Sould.

The enthusiastic dy Tagille proposed that they travel as a party of Ibran merchants bound for Cardegoss. Cazaril did insist that all the men, noble or humble, who rode with the royse be experienced in arms. The group assembled within a day of Bergon's decision, in what Cazaril prayed was secrecy, at one of dy Tagille's manors outside Zagosur. It was not, Cazaril discovered, so small a company as all that; with servants, it came to over a dozen mounted men and a baggage train of half a dozen mules. In addition the servants led four fine matched white Ibran mountain ponies meant as a gift for Bergon's betrothed, in the meantime doubling as spare mounts.

They started off in high spirits; the companions obviously thought it a high and noble adventure. Bergon was more sober and thoughtful, which pleased Cazaril, who felt as though he were leading a party of children into caverns of madness. But at least in Bergon's case, not blindly. Which was better than the gods had done for *him*, Cazaril reflected darkly. He wondered if the curse could be tricking him, leading them all into war and not out of it. Dy Jironal hadn't started out so corrupt, either.

Being limited to the speed of the slowest pack mule, the pace was not so painful as the race to Zagosur had been. The climb up from the coast to the base of the Bastard's Teeth took four full days. Another letter from Iselle caught up with Cazaril there, this one written some fourteen days after he'd departed Cardegoss. She reported Teidez buried with due ceremony in Valenda, and her success in her ploy of remaining there, extending her visit to her bereaved mother and grandmother. Dy Jironal had been forced to return to Cardegoss by reports of Orico's worsening ill health. Unfortunately, he had left behind not only his female spies, but also several companies of soldiers to guard Chalion's new Heiress. *I'm taking thought what to do about them*, Iselle reported, a turn of phrase that brought up the hairs on the back of Cazaril's neck. She also included a private letter to Bergon, which Cazaril passed along unopened. Bergon didn't share its contents, but he smiled frequently over Ordol's pages as he deciphered it, head bent close to the candles in their stuffy inn chamber.

More encouragingly, the Provincara had included a letter of her own, declaring that Iselle had received private promises of support for the Ibran marriage not only from her uncle the provincar of Baocia, but three other provincars as well. Bergon would have defenders, when he arrived.

When Cazaril showed this note to Bergon, the royse nodded decisively. "Good. We go on."

They suffered a check nonetheless here, when discouraged travelers coming back down the road to their inn that night reported the pass blocked with new snow. Consulting the map and his memory, Cazaril led the company instead a day's ride to the north, to a higher and less frequented pass still reported clear. The reports proved correct, but two horses strained their hocks on the climb. As they neared the divide, the March dy Sould, who claimed himself more comfortable on the deck of a ship than the back of a horse, and who had been growing quieter and quieter all morning, suddenly leaned over the side of his saddle and vomited.

The company bunched to a wheezing halt on the trail, while Cazaril, Bergon, and Ferda consulted, and the usually witty dy Sould mumbled embarrassed and disturbingly muddled apologies and protests.

"Should we stop and build a fire, and try to warm him?" the royse asked in worry, staring around the desolate slopes.

Cazaril, himself standing half-bent-over, replied, "He's dazed as a man in a high fever, but he's not hot. He's seacoast-bred. I think this is not an infection, but rather a sickness that sometimes overcomes lowlanders in the heights. In either case, it will be better to care for him down out of this miserable rocky wilderness."

Ferda, eyeing him sideways, asked, "How are *you* doing, my lord?"

Bergon, too, frowned at him in concern.

"Nothing that stopping and sitting down here will improve. Let's push on."

They mounted again, Bergon riding near to dy Sould when the trail permitted. The sick man clung to his saddle with grim determination. Within half an hour, Foix gave a thin and breathless whoop, and pointed to the cairn of rocks that marked the Ibra-

Chalion border. The company cheered, and paused briefly to add their stones. They began the descent, steeper even than the climb. Dy Sould grew no worse, reassuring Cazaril of his diagnosis. Cazaril grew no better, but then, he didn't expect to.

In the afternoon, they came over the lower lip of a barren vale and dropped into a thick pine wood. The air seemed richer here, even if only with the sharp delicious scent of the pines, and the bed of needles underfoot cushioned the horses' sore feet. The sighing trees sheltered them all from the wind's prying fingers. As they rounded a curve, Cazaril's ears picked up the muffled thump of trotting hooves from the path ahead, the first fellow traveler they had encountered all day; just one rider, though, so no danger to their number.

The rider was a grizzled man with fierce bushy eyebrows and beard, dressed in stained leathers. He hailed them and, a little to Cazaril's surprise, pulled up his shaggy horse across their path.

"I am castle warder to the Castillar dy Zavar. We saw your company coming down the vale, when the clouds broke. My lord sends me to warn you, there is a storm blowing up the valley. He invites you to shelter with him till the worst is past."

Dy Tagille greeted this offer of hospitality with delight. Bergon dropped back and lowered his voice to Cazaril. "Do you think we ought, Caz?"

"I'm not sure . . ." He tried to think if he'd ever heard of a Castillar dy Zavar.

Bergon glanced at his friend dy Sould, drooping over his pommel. "I'd give much to get him indoors. We are many, and armed."

Cazaril allowed, "We'd not make good speed in a blizzard, besides the risk of losing the trail."

The grizzled castle warder called out, "Suit yourselves, gentlemen, but since it's my job to collect the bodies from the ditches in this district come spring, I'd take it as a personal favor if you'd accept. The storm will blow through before morning, I'd guess."

"Well, I'm glad we at least got over the pass before this broke. Yes," decided Bergon. He raised his voice. "We thank you, sir, and do accept your lord's kind offer!"

The grizzled man saluted, and nudged his horse back down the road. A mile farther on, he wheeled to the left and led them up a fainter trail through the tall, dark pines. The path dropped, then rose steeply for a time, zigzagging. The horses' haunches bunched and surged, pushing them uphill. Away through the trees, Cazaril could hear the distant squabbling and cawing of a flock of crows, and was comforted in memory.

They broke out into the gray light upon a rocky spur. Perched on the outcrop rose a small and rather dilapidated fortress built of undressed native stone. An encouraging curl of smoke rose from its chimney.

They passed under a fieldstone arch into a courtyard paved with slates; a stable opened directly onto it, as well as a broad wooden portico over the doors leading into the main hall. Its margins were cluttered with tools, barrels, and odd trash. Curing deer hides were nailed up to the stable wall. Some tough-looking men, servants or grooms or guards or all three in this rough rural household, moved from the portico to help with the party's horses and mules. But it was the nearly half dozen new ghosts, whirling frantically about the courtyard, that opened Cazaril's eyes wide and stopped the breath in his throat.

That they were fresh, he could tell by their crisp gray outlines, still holding the forms they'd had in life: three men, a woman, and a weeping boy. The woman-shape pointed to the grizzled man. White fire streamed from her mouth, silent screams.

Cazaril jerked his horse back beside Bergon's, leaned over, and muttered, "This is a trap. Look to your weapons. Pass the word." Bergon fell back beside dy Tagille, who in turn bent to speak quietly to a pair of the party's grooms. Cazaril smiled in dissimulation, and sidled his horse over to Foix's, where he held up his hand before his mouth as if sharing a jest, and repeated the warning. Foix smiled blandly and nodded. His eyes darted around the courtyard, counting up the odds, as he leaned toward his brother.

The odds did not seem ill, but for that rangy lout up on the wooden perch beside the gate, leaning against the inner wall, a crossbow dangling, as if casually, from his hand. Except that it was cocked. Cazaril maneuvered back by Bergon, putting himself and his horse between the royse and the gate. " 'Ware bowman," he breathed. "Duck under a mule."

The ghosts were darting from place to place about the yard, pointing out concealed men behind the barrels and tools, shadowed in the stalls, and, apparently, waiting just inside the main

door. Cazaril revised his opinion of the odds. The grizzled man motioned to one of his men, and the gate swung shut behind the
party. Cazaril twisted in his saddle and dug his hand into his saddlebag. His fingers touched silk, then the smooth coolness of round
beads; he had not pawned Dondo's pearls in Zagosur because the
price was disadvantageous there, so close to the source. He swept
his hand up, drawing out the glistening rope of them in a grand gesture. As he swung the string around his head, he popped the cord
with his thumb. Pearls spewed off the end of the line and bounced
about the slate-paved court. The startled toughs laughed, and
began to dive for them.

Cazaril dropped his arm, and shouted, "Now!"

The grizzled commander, who had apparently been just about
to shout a similar order, was taken aback. Cazaril's men drew steel
first, falling upon the distracted enemy. Cazaril half fell out of his
saddle just before a crossbow bolt thunked into it. His horse reared
and bolted, and he scrambled to pull his own sword out of its scabbard.

Foix, bless the boy, had managed to get his own crossbow quietly unshipped before the chaos of shouting men and plunging
horses struck. One of the male ghosts streaked past Cazaril's inner
eye, and pointed at an obscured shape dodging along the top of the
portico. Cazaril tapped Foix's arm, and shouted, "Up there!" Foix
cocked and whirled just as a second bowman popped up; Cazaril
could swear the frantic ghost tried to guide the quarrel. It entered
the bowman's right eye and dropped him instantly. Foix ducked
and began recocking; the ratcheting mechanism whirred.

Cazaril, turning to seek an enemy, found one seeking him.
From the main door, steel drawn, barged a startlingly familiar form:
Ser dy Joal, dy Jironal's stirrup-man, whom Cazaril had last seen in
Cardegoss. Cazaril raised his sword just in time to deflect dy Joal's
first furious blow. His belly twinged, cramped, then knotted ago-
nizingly as they circled briefly for advantage, and then dy Joal bore
in.

The excruciating belly pain drained the strength from Cazaril's
arm, almost doubling him over; he barely beat off the next attack,
and counterattack was suddenly out of the question. Out of the
corner of his eye, he saw the female ghost curl tightly in upon herself. She—or was that a pearl?—or both united, somehow slid

under dy Joal's boot. Dy Joal skidded violently and unexpectedly forward, flailing for balance. Cazaril's point rammed through his throat and lodged briefly in the bones of his neck.

A hideous shock ran up Cazaril's arm. Not just his belly but his whole body seemed to cramp, and his vision blurred and darkened. Within him, Dondo screamed in triumph. The death demon surged up like a whirling fire behind his eyes, eager and implacable. Cazaril convulsed, vomiting. In Cazaril's uncontrolled recoil, his sword ripped out sideways; vessels spurted, and dy Joal collapsed at his feet in a welter of blood.

Cazaril found himself on his hands and knees on the icy slates, his sword, dropped from his nerveless hand, still ringing faintly. He was trembling all over so badly he could not stand up again. He spat bile from his watering mouth. On his sword's point, as it lay on the stone, dy Joal's wet blood steamed and smoked, blackening. Surges of nausea swept through his swollen and pulsing abdomen.

Inside him, Dondo wailed and howled in frustrated rage, slowly smothered again to silence. The demon settled back like a stalking cat on its belly, watchful and tense. Cazaril clenched and unclenched his hand, just to be sure he was still in possession of his own body.

So. The death demon wasn't fussy whose souls filled its buckets, so long as there were two of them. Cazaril's and Dondo's, Cazaril's and some other killer's—or victim's—he wasn't just sure which, or if it even mattered, under the circumstances. Dondo clearly had hoped to cling to his body, and let Cazaril's soul be ripped away. Leaving Dondo in, so to speak, possession. Dondo's goals and those of the demon were, it seemed, slightly divergent. The demon would be happy if Cazaril died in any way at all. Dondo wanted a murder, or a murdering.

Sunk strengthless to the stones, tears leaking between his eyelids, Cazaril became aware that the noise had died down. A hand touched his elbow, and he flinched. Foix's distressed voice came to his ear, "My lord? My lord, are you wounded?"

"Not . . . not stabbed," Cazaril got out. He blinked, wheezing. He reached out for his blade, then jerked his hand back, fingertips stinging. The steel was hot to the touch. Ferda appeared on his other side, and the two brothers drew him to his feet. He stood shivering with reaction.

"Are you sure you're all right?" said Ferda. "That dark-haired lady in Cardegoss promised us the royesse would have our ears if we did not bring you back to her alive."

"Yes," put in Foix, "and that *she* would have the rest of our skins for a drum head, thereafter."

"Your skins are safe, for now." Cazaril rubbed his watering eyes and straightened a little, staring around. A sergeantly-looking groom, sword out, had half a dozen of the toughs lying facedown on the slates in surrender. Three more bandits sat leaning against the stable wall, moaning and bleeding. Another servant was dragging up the body of the dead crossbowman.

Cazaril scowled down at dy Joal, lying sprawled before him. They hadn't exchanged a single word in their brief encounter. He was deeply sorry he'd torn out the bravo's lying throat. His presence here implied much, but confirmed nothing. Was he dy Jironal's agent or acting on his own?

"The leader—where is he? I want to put him to the question."

"Over there, my lord"—Foix pointed—"but I'm afraid he won't be answering."

Bergon was just rising from the examination of an unmoving body; the grizzled man, alas.

Ferda said uneasily, in a tone of apology, "He fought fiercely and wouldn't surrender. He had wounded two of our grooms, so Foix finally downed him with a crossbow bolt."

"Do you think he really was the castle warder here, my lord?" Foix added.

"No."

Bergon picked his way over to him, sword in hand, and looked him up and down in worry. "What do we do now, Caz?"

The female ghost, grown somewhat less agitated, was beckoning him toward the gate. One of the male ghosts, equally urgent, was beckoning him toward the main door. "I . . . I follow, momentarily."

"What?" said Bergon.

Cazaril tore his gaze away from what only his inner eye saw. "Lock them"—he nodded toward their surrendered foes—"up in a stall, and set a guard. Whole and wounded together for now. We'll tend to them after our own. Then send a body of able men to search the premises, see if there are any more hiding. Or . . . or anybody else. Hiding. Or . . . whatever." His eye returned to the gate, where the streaming woman beckoned again. "Foix, bring your bow and sword and come with me."

"Should we not take more men, lord?"

"No, I don't think so . . ."

Leaving Bergon and Ferda to direct the mopping-up, Cazaril at last headed for the gate. Foix followed, staring as Cazaril turned without hesitation down a path into the pines. As they walked along it, the cries of the crows grew louder. Cazaril braced himself. The path opened out onto the edge of a steep ravine.

"Bastard's hell," whispered Foix. He lowered his bow and touched the five theological points, forehead-lip-navel-groin-heart, in a warding gesture.

They'd found the bodies.

They were thrown upon the midden, tumbled down the edge of the crevasse atop years of kitchen and stable yard waste. One younger man, two older; in this rural place it was not possible to distinguish certainly master from man by dress, as all wore practical working leathers and woolens. The woman, plump and homely and middle-aged, was stripped naked, as was the boy, who appeared to have been about five. Both mutilated according to a cruel humor. Violated, too, probably. Dead about a day, Cazaril judged by the progress the crows had made. The woman-ghost was weeping silently, and the child-ghost clung to her and wailed. They were not god-rejected souls, then, just sundered, still dizzied from their deaths and unable to find their way without proper ceremonies.

Cazaril fell to his knees, and whispered, "Lady. If I am alive in this place, you must be, too. If it please you, give these poor spirits ease."

The ghostly faces changed, rippling from woe to wonder; the insubstantial bodies blurred like sun diffractions in a high, feathered cloud, then vanished.

After about a minute Cazaril said muzzily, "Help me up, please."

The bewildered Foix levered him up with a hand under his elbow. Cazaril staggered around and started back up the path.

"My lord, should we not look around for others?"

"No, that's all."

Foix followed him without another word.

In the slate-paved courtyard, they found Ferda and an armed groom just emerging again from the main doorway.

"Did you find anyone else?" Cazaril asked him.

"No, my lord."

Beside the door, only the young male ghost still lingered, although its luminescent body seemed to be ribboning away like smoke in a wind. It writhed in a kind of agony, gesturing Cazaril on. What dire urgency was it that turned it from the open arms of the goddess to cling to this wounded world? "Yes, yes, I'm coming," Cazaril told it.

It slipped inside; Cazaril motioned Foix and Ferda, looking uneasily at him, to follow on. They passed through the main hall and under a gallery, back through the kitchens, and down some wooden stairs to a dark, stone-walled storeroom.

"Did you search in here?" Cazaril called over his shoulder.

"Yes, my lord," said Ferda.

"Get more light." He stared intently at the ghost, which was now circling the room in agitation, whirling in a tightening spiral. Cazaril pointed. "Move those barrels."

Foix rolled them aside. Ferda clattered back down from the kitchen with a brace of tallow candles, their flames yellow and smoky but bright in the gloom. Concealed beneath the barrels they found a stone slab in the floor with an iron ring set in it. Cazaril motioned to Foix again; the boy grabbed the ring and strained, and shifted the slab up and aside, revealing narrow steps descending into utter blackness.

From below, a faint voice cried out.

The ghost bent to Cazaril, seeming to kiss his forehead, hands, and feet, and then streamed away into eternity. A faint blue sparkle, like a chord of music made visible, glittered for a moment in Cazaril's second sight, and was gone. Ferda, the candles in one hand and his drawn sword in the other, cautiously descended the stone steps.

Clamor and babble wafted back up through the dank slot. In a few moments, Ferda appeared again, supporting up the stairs a disheveled stout old man, his face bruised and battered, his legs shaking. Following in his wake, weeping for gladness, a dozen other equally shattered people climbed one by one.

The freed prisoners all fell upon Ferda and Foix with questions and tales at once, inundating them; Cazaril leaned unobtrusively upon a barrel and pieced together the picture. The stout man proved the real Castillar dy Zavar, a distraught middle-aged woman his castillara, and two young people a son and a—in Cazaril's view, miraculously spared—daughter. The rest were servants and dependents of this rural household.

Dy Joal and his troop had descended upon them yesterday, at first seeming merely rough travelers. Only when a couple of the bravos had made to molest the castillar's cook, and her husband and the real castle warder had gone to her defense and attempted to eject the unwelcome visitors, had steel been drawn. It truly was the house's custom to take in benighted or storm-threatened wayfarers from the road over the pass. No one here had known or recognized dy Joal or any of his men.

The old castillar gripped Ferda's cloak anxiously. "My elder son, does he live? Have you seen him? He went to my castle warder's aid . . ."

"Was he a young man of about these men's age"—Cazaril nodded to the dy Gura brothers—"dressed in wool and leathers like your own?"

"Aye . . ." The old man's face drained in anticipation.

"He is in the care of the gods, and much comforted there," Cazaril reported factually.

Cries of grief greeted this news; wearily, Cazaril mounted the stairs to the kitchen in the mob's wake, as they spread out to regain their house, recover their dead, and care for the wounded.

"My lord," Ferda murmured to him, as Cazaril paused briefly to warm himself by the kitchen fire, "had you ever been to this house before?"

"No."

"Then how did you—I heard nothing, when I looked in that cellar. I would have left those poor people to die of thirst and hunger and madness in the dark."

"I think dy Joal's men would have confessed to them, before the night was done." Cazaril frowned grimly. "Among the many other things I intend to learn from them."

The captured bravos, under a duress Cazaril was happy to allow and the freed housemen eager to supply, told their half of the tale soon enough. They were a mixed lot, including some lawless and impoverished discharged soldiers who had followed the griz-zled man, and a few local hirelings, one of whom had led them to dy Zavar's holding for sake of its amazing vantage of the road from its highest tower. Dy Joal, riding to the Ibran border alone and in a hurry, had picked them all up from a town at the foot of these mountains, where they had formerly eked out a living alternating between guarding travelers and robbing them.

The bravos knew only that dy Joal had come there looking to waylay a man expected to be riding over the passes from Ibra. They did not know who their new employer really was, although they'd despised his courtier's clothes and mannerisms. It was abundantly clear to Cazaril that dy Joal had not been in control of the men he'd hastily hired. When the altercation about the cook had tipped over into violence, he'd not had either the nerve or the muscle to stop it, administer discipline, or restore order before events had run their ugly course.

Bergon, disturbed, drew Cazaril aside in the flickering torch-light of the courtyard where this rough-and-ready interrogation was taking place. "Caz, did I bring this wretched chance down upon poor dy Zavar's good people?"

"No, Royse. It's clear dy Joal was expecting only me, riding back as Iselle's courier. Chancellor dy Jironal has sought to tear me from her service for some time—secretly assassinate me, if there proved no other way. How I wish I hadn't killed that fool! I'd give my teeth to know how much dy Jironal knows by now."

"Are you sure the chancellor set this trap?"

Cazaril hesitated. "Dy Joal had a personal grudge against me, but . . . the world knew merely that I'd ridden to Valenda. Dy Joal could only have had surmise of my true route from dy Jironal. Therefore, we may be certain dy Jironal had some report of me from his spies in Ibra. His knowledge of our real aim lags—but not, I think, by much. Dy Joal was a stopgap, hurriedly dispatched. And certainly not the only such agent. Something else must follow."

"How soon?"

"I don't know. Dy Jironal commands the Order of the Son; he can draw on its men as soon as he can evolve a plausible enough lie by which to move them."

Bergon tapped his sheathed sword against his leather-clad thigh, and frowned up at the sky, which was clearing as evening fell. The mountain spines to the west were black silhouettes against a lingering green glow, and the first stars shone overhead. The grizzled man's tale of an approaching blizzard had proved a mere decoy, although a light snow squall that had blown through earlier might have been the seed of the idea. "The moon is nearly full, and will be well up by midnight. If we ride both night and day, perchance we can push across this disturbed country before dy Jironal can bring up any more reinforcements."

Cazaril nodded. "Let him rush his men to patrol a border that we're already across? Good. I like it."

Bergon studied him in doubt. "But . . . will you be able to ride, Caz?"

"I'd rather ride than fight."

Bergon sighed agreement. "Yes."

❧THE GRATEFUL, GRIEVING CASTILLAR DY ZAVAR pressed all the refreshment his disrupted household could spare upon them. Bergon decided to leave the mules, injured grooms, and lamed horses in his care, to follow on when they could, and lighten his own party thereby. Ferda selected the fastest, soundest horses, and made sure they were rubbed down well and fed and rested until time to start. March dy Sould had recovered after a few hours of rest in this more nourishing air, and insisted on accompanying the royse. Dy Cembuer, who had suffered a broken arm and some freely bleeding cuts in the courtyard fight, undertook to stay with the grooms and baggage and assist dy Zavar until all were ready to travel.

The problem of justice upon the brigands, Cazaril was relieved to leave to their victims. Bergon's midnight departure would spare them having to witness the hangings at dawn. He left the scattered portion of Dondo's pearls for the stricken household to collect, and tucked the remains of the rope back in his saddlebag.

The royse's cavalcade took to the road again when the moon rose over the hills before them, filling the snowy vales with liquid light. There would be no turning aside now before Valenda.

24

They retraced Cazaril's outbound route across western Chalion, changing horses at obscure rural posts of the Daughter's Order. At every stop he inquired anxiously for any further ciphered messages from Iselle or news from Valenda that might reveal the tactical situation into which they rushed. He grew increasingly uneasy at the absence of letters. In the original plan, they had envisioned Iselle waiting with her grandmother and mother, guarded by her uncle dy Baocia's troops. Cazaril feared this ideal condition no longer held.

They checked at midevening twenty-five miles short of Valenda at the village of Palma. The region around Palma was noted for its fine pasturage; a post of the Daughter's Order there devoted itself to raising and training remounts for the Temple. Cazaril was certain of obtaining fresh horses in Palma. He prayed for fresh intelligence as well.

Cazaril did not so much dismount from his blown horse as fall slowly, all in a piece, as if his body were carved from a single block of wood. Both Ferda and Foix had to support him through the order's sprawling compound. They brought him into a shabbily comfortable chamber, where a bright fire burned in a fieldstone fireplace. A plain pine table had been hastily cleared of someone's card game. The dedicat-commander of the post hurried in to wait upon them. The man glanced uncertainly from dy Tagille to dy Sould; his gaze passed over Bergon, who'd dressed as a groom since the border for caution's sake. The commander fell into apologetic confusion when the royse was introduced, and sent his lieutenant scurrying for food and drink to offer his distinguished company.

Cazaril sat by the table in a cushioned chair, wonderfully unlike a saddle even if the room did still seem to be rocking around him. He was beginning to dislike horses almost as much as he disliked boats. His head felt stuffed with wool, and his body didn't bear thinking about. He broke into the exchange of courtly amenities to croak, "What word have you from Valenda? Do you hold any new messages from the Royesse Iselle?" Ferda pressed a glass of watered wine into his hand, and he gulped half of it at once.

The dedicat-commander gave him a little understanding headshake, his lips tightening. "Chancellor dy Jironal marched a thousand more of his men into the town last week. He has another thousand bivouacked along the river. They patrol the countryside, looking for you. Searchers have stopped here twice. He holds Valenda tight in his grip."

"Didn't Provincar dy Baocia have any men there?"

"Yes, two companies, but they were badly outnumbered. No one would start the fight at Royse Teidez's interment, and after that they dared not."

"Have you heard from March dy Palliar?"

"He used to bring the letters. We've had no direct word from the royesse for five days. It's rumored that she is very ill and sees no one."

Bergon's eyes widened in alarm. Cazaril squinted and rubbed his aching head. "Ill? Iselle? Well . . . maybe. Or else held close-confined by dy Jironal, and the illness a tale put about." Had one of Cazaril's letters fallen into the wrong hands? He had feared they might have to either spirit the royesse out of Valenda, or break her free by force of arms, preferably the former. He hadn't planned what to do if she had fallen, perhaps, too sick to ride at this critical moment.

His muzzy brain evolved a mad vision of somehow sneaking Bergon in to her, over the rooftops and balconies like a lover in a poem. No. A night of secret love between them might break the curse, channel it back somehow to the gods who had spilled it, but he couldn't see how it would miraculously make away with two thousand or so very fleshly soldiers.

"Does Orico still live?" he asked at last.

"As far as we've heard."

"We can do nothing more tonight." He wouldn't trust any plan that came out of his tired brain tonight. "Tomorrow, Foix and Ferda and I will go into Valenda on foot, in disguise, and reconnoiter. I promise you I can pass for a road vagabond. If we can't see our way clear, then fall back to Provincar dy Baocia's people in Taryoon, and plan again."

"*Can* you walk, my lord?" asked Foix in a dubious voice.

Right now, he wasn't sure if he could stand up. He glowered helplessly at Foix, who was tired but resilient, pink rather than gray after days in the saddle. Youth. Eh. "By tomorrow, I will." He rubbed his face. "Do dy Jironal's men realize they are not guardians but prison-keepers? That they are being led into possible treason against the rightful Heiress?"

The dedicat-commander sat back, and opened his hands. "Such charges are being flung about like snowballs from both parties right now. Rumors that the royesse has sent agents into Ibra to contract a marriage with the new Heir are flying everywhere." He gave Royse Bergon an apologetic nod.

So much for the secrecy of his mission. He considered the pitfalls of potential party lines in Chalion. Iselle and Orico versus dy Jironal, all right. Iselle versus Orico and Dy Jironal . . . hideously dangerous.

"The news has had a mixed reception," the commander continued. "The ladies look on Bergon with approval and want to make a romance of it all, because it's said that he is brave and well-favored. Soberer heads worry that Iselle may sell Chalion to the Fox, because she is, ah, young and inexperienced."

In other words, *foolish and flighty*. Sober heads had much to learn. Cazaril's lips drew back on a dry grin. "No," he mumbled. "We have not done that." He realized that he was speaking to his knees, his forehead having unaccountably sunk to the table and anchored there.

After about a minute Bergon's voice murmured gently in his ear, "Caz? Are you awake?"

"Mm."

"Would you like to go to bed, my lord?" the dedicat-commander inquired after another pause.

"Mm."

He whimpered a little as strong hands under each arm forced him to his feet. Ferda and Foix, leading him off somewhere, cruelly. The table had been soft enough . . . He didn't even remember falling into the bed.

❧SOMEONE WAS SHAKING HIS SHOULDER.

A hideously cheerful voice bellowed in his ear, "Rise and ride, Captain Sunshine!"

He spasmed and clawed at his covers, tried to sit up, and thought better of the effort. He pulled open his glued-shut eyelids, blinking in the candlelight. The identity of the voice finally penetrated. "Palli! You're alive!" He meant to shout joyfully. At least it came out audibly. "What time is it?" He struggled again to sit up, making it onto one elbow. He seemed to be in some evicted officer-dedicat's plainly furnished bedchamber.

"About an hour before dawn. We've been riding all night. Iselle sent me to find you." He raised his brace of candles higher. Bergon was standing anxiously at his shoulder, and Foix too. "Bastard's demons, Caz, you look like death on a trencher."

"That . . . has been observed." He lay back down. Palli was here. Palli was here, and all was well. He could shove Bergon and all his burdens off onto him, lie here, and not get up. Die alone and in peace, taking Dondo out of the world with him. "Take Royse Bergon and his company to Iselle. Leave me—"

"What, for dy Jironal's patrols to find? Not if I value my future fortune as a courtier! Iselle wants you safe with her in Taryoon."

"Taryoon? Not Valenda?" He blinked. "Safe?" This time he did struggle up, and all the way to his feet, where he passed out.

The black fog lifted, and he found Bergon, round-eyed, holding him slumped on the edge of the bed.

"Sit a minute with your head down," Palli advised.

Cazaril obediently bent over his aching belly. If Dondo had visited him last night, he'd not been home. The ghost had kicked him a few times in his sleep, though, it felt like. From the inside out.

Bergon said softly, "He ate nothing when we came in last night. He collapsed straightaway, and we put him to bed."

"Right," said Palli, and jerked his thumb at the hovering Foix, who nodded and slipped out of the room.

"Taryoon?" Cazaril mumbled from the vicinity of his knees.

"Aye. She gave all two thousand of dy Jironal's men the slip, she did. Well, first of all, before that, her uncle dy Baocia pulled his men out and went home. The fools let him go; thought it was a danger removed from their midst. Yes, and made free to move at will! Then Iselle rode out five days running, always with a troop of dy Jironal's cavalry for escort, and gave them more exercise than they cared for. Had 'em absolutely convinced she meant to escape while riding. So when she and Lady Betriz went walking out one day with old Lady dy Hueltar, they let her go by. I was waiting with two saddled horses, and two women to change cloaks with 'em and go back with the old lady. We were gone down that ravine so fast . . . The old Provincara undertook to conceal she'd flown for as long as possible, pass it off that she was ill in her mother's chambers. They've doubtless tumbled to it by now, but I'll wager she was safe with her uncle in Taryoon before Valenda knew she was gone. Five gods, those girls can ride! Sixty miles cross-country between dusk and dawn under a full moon, and only one change of horses."

"Girls?" said Cazaril. "Is Lady Betriz safe, too?"

"Oh, aye. Both of 'em chipper as songbirds, when I left 'em. Made me feel old."

Cazaril squinted up at Palli, five years his junior, but let this pass. "Ser dy Ferrej . . . the Provincara, Lady Ista?"

Palli's face sobered. "Still hostages in Valenda. They all told the girls to go on, you know."

"Ah."

Foix brought him a bowl of bean porridge, hot and aromatic, on a tray, and Bergon himself arranged his pillows and helped him sit up to eat it. Cazaril had thought he was ravenous, yet found himself unable to force down more than a few bites. Palli was keen to get away while the darkness still cloaked their numbers. Cazaril struggled to oblige, letting Foix help him back into his clothes. He dreaded the attempt to ride again.

In the post's stable yard, he found that their escort, a dozen men of the Daughter's Order who'd followed Palli from Taryoon, waited with a horse litter slung between two mounts. Indignant at first, he let Bergon persuade him into it, and the cavalcade swung away into the graying dark. The rough back roads and trails they took made the litter jounce and sway nauseatingly. After half an hour of this, he cried for mercy, and undertook to climb on a horse. Someone had thought to bring along a smooth-paced ambler for this very purpose, and he clung to the saddle and endured its rippling gait while they swung wide around Valenda and its occupiers' patrols.

In the afternoon, they dropped down from some wooded slopes onto a wider road, and Palli rode alongside him. Palli eyed him curiously, a little sideways.

"I hear you do miracles with mules."

"Not me. The goddess." Cazaril's smile twisted. "She has a way with mules, it seems."

"I'm also told you're strangely hard on brigands."

"We were a strong company, well armed. If the brigands hadn't been set onto us by dy Joal, they would never have attempted us."

"Dy Joal was one of dy Jironal's best swords. Foix says you took him down in seconds."

"That was a mistake. Besides, his foot slipped."

Palli's lips twitched. "You don't have to go around telling people that, you know." He stared ahead between his horse's bobbing ears for a time. "So, the boy you defended on the Roknari galley was Bergon himself."

"Yes. Kidnapped by his brother's bravos, it turned out. Now I know why the Ibran fleet rowed so hard after us."

"Did you never guess who he really was? Then or later?"

"No. He had . . . he had a deal more self-control than even I realized at the time. *That* one will make a roya worth following, when he comes into his own."

Palli glanced ahead to where Bergon rode with dy Sould, and signed himself in wonder. "The gods are on our side, right enough. Can we fail?"

Cazaril snorted bitterly. "Yes." He thought of Ista, Umegat, the tongueless groom. Of the deathly straits he was in. "And when we fail, the gods do, too." He didn't think he'd ever quite realized that before, not in those terms.

At least Iselle was safe for now behind the shield of her uncle; as Heiress, she would attract other ambitious men to her side. She would have many, not least Bergon himself, to protect her from her enemies, although advisors wise enough to also protect her from her friends might be harder for her to come by. . . . But what provision against the looming hazards could he effect for Betriz?

"Did you get the chance to know Lady Betriz better while you escorted the cortege to Valenda, and after?" he asked Palli.

"Oh, aye."

"Beautiful girl, don't you think? Did you get much conversation with her father, Ser dy Ferrej?"

"Yes. A most honorable man."

"So I thought, too."

"She's very worried for him right now," Palli added.

"I can imagine. And him for her, both now and later. If . . . if all goes well, she will be a favorite of the future royina. That kind of political influence could be worth far more to a shrewd man than a mere material dowry. If the man had the wit to see it."

"No question of it."

"She's intelligent, energetic . . ."

"Rides well, too." Palli's tone was oddly dry.

Cazaril swallowed, and with an effort at a casual tone got out, "Couldn't you just see her as the future Marchess dy Palliar?"

Palli's mouth turned up on one side. "I fear my suit would be hopeless. I believe she has another man in her eye. Judging from all the questions she's asked me about him, anyway."

"Oh? Who?" He tried, briefly and without success, to convince himself Betriz dreamed of, say, dy Rinal, or one of the other courtiers of Cardegoss . . . eh. Lightweights, the lot of them. Few of the younger men had the wealth or influence, and none the wit, to make her a good match. In fact, now Cazaril came to consider the matter, none of them was good enough for her.

"It was in confidence. But I definitely think you should ask her all about it, when we get to Taryoon." Palli smiled, and urged his horse forward.

Cazaril considered the implications of Palli's smile, and of the white fur hat still tucked into his saddlebags. *The woman you love, loves you?* Had he any real doubt of it? There was, alas, more than enough impediment to twist this joyous suspicion into sorrow. *Too late, too late, too late.* For her fidelity he could return her only grief; his bier would be too hard and narrow to offer as a wedding bed.

It was a grace note in this lethal tangle nonetheless, like finding a survivor in a shipwreck or a flower blooming in a burned-over field. Well . . . well, she must simply get over her ill-fated attachment to him. And he must exert the utmost self-control not to encourage it in her. He wondered if he could promote Palli to her if he put it as the last request of a dying man.

Fifteen miles out from Taryoon, they were met by a large Baocian guard company. *They* had a hand litter, and relays of men to carry it aloft; too far gone by now to be anything but grateful, Cazaril let himself be loaded into it without protest. He even slept for a couple of hours, lumping along wrapped in a feather quilt, his aching head cushioned by pillows. He woke at length and watched the dreary darkening winter landscape wobble past him like a dream.

So, this was dying. It didn't seem as bad, lying down. *But please, just let me live to see this curse lifted from Iselle.* It was a great work, one any man might look back on and say, *That was my life; it was enough.* He asked nothing more now but to be permitted to finish what he'd started. Iselle's wedding, and Betriz made safe—if the gods would but give him those two gifts, he thought he could go in quiet content. *I'm tired.*

❧THEY ENTERED THE GATES OF THE BAOCIAN PROVINcial capital of Taryoon an hour after sunset. Curious citizens collected in the path of their little procession, or marched beside it with torches to light the way, or hurried out to watch from balconies as they passed. On three occasions, women tossed down flowers, which after their first uncertain flinch, Bergon's Ibran companions caught; it helped that the ladies had good aim. The young lords sent hopeful and enthusiastic kisses through the air in return. They left interested murmurs in their wake, especially up on the balconies. Near the city center Bergon and his friends, escorted by Palli, were diverted to the town palace of the wealthy March dy Huesta, one of the provincar's chief supporters and, not coincidentally, his brother-in-law. The Baocian guard carried Cazaril's litter on at a smart pace to the provincar's own new palace, down the street from the cramped and lowering old fortress.

Clutching his precious saddlebags containing the future of two countries, Cazaril was brought by dy Baocia's castle warder to a fire-warmed bedchamber. Numerous wax lights revealed two waiting man-servants with a hip bath, extra hot water, soap, scissors, scents, and towels. A third man bore in a tray of mild white cheese, fruit cakes, and quantities of hot herb tea. Someone was taking no chances with Cazaril's wardrobe, and had laid out a change of clothing on the bed, court mourning complete from fresh undergarments through brocades and velvets out to a silver and amethyst belt. The transformation from road wreckage to courtier took barely twenty minutes.

From his filthy saddlebags Cazaril drew his packet of documents, wrapped in oilcloth around silk, and checked them for dirt and bloodstains. Nothing untoward had leaked in. He discarded the grubby oilcloth and tucked the offerings under his arm. The castle warder guided Cazaril through a courtyard where workmen labored by torchlight to lay down the last paving stones, and into an adjoining building. They passed through a series of rooms to a spacious tiled chamber softened with rugs and wall hangings. Man-high iron candelabras holding five lights each, intricately wrought, shed a warming glow. Iselle sat in a large carved chair by the far wall, attended by Betriz and the provincar, also all in court mourning.

They looked up as he entered, the women eagerly, the middle-aged dy Baocia's expression tempered with caution. Iselle's uncle bore only a slight resemblance to his younger sister Ista, being solid rather than frail, though he was not overtall either, and he shared Ista's dun hair color, gone grizzled. Dy Baocia was attended in turn by a stout man Cazaril took for his secretary, and an elderly fellow in the five-colored robes of the archdivine of Taryoon. Cazaril eyed him hopefully for any flicker of god light, but he was only a plain devout.

The dark cloud still hung thickly about Iselle in Cazaril's second sight, though, roiling in a sluggish and sullen fashion. *But not for much longer, by the Lady's grace.*

"Welcome home, Castillar," said Iselle. The warmth of her voice was like a caress on his brow, her use of his title a covert warning.

Cazaril signed himself. "Five gods, Royesse, all is well."

"You have the treaties?" dy Baocia asked, his gaze fixing on the packets under Cazaril's arm. He held out an anxious hand. "There has been much concern over them in our councils."

Cazaril smiled slightly and walked past him to kneel at Iselle's feet, managing with careful effort not to grunt with pain, or pitch over in unseemly clumsiness. He brushed his lips across the backs of the hands she held out to him, and pressed the packet of documents in them, and them alone, as they turned palm up. "All is as you commanded."

Her eyes were bright with appreciation. "I thank you, Cazaril." She glanced up at her uncle's secretary. "Fetch a chair for my ambassador, please. He has ridden long and hard, with little rest." She began folding back the silk.

The secretary brought up a chair with a wool-stuffed cushion. Cazaril smiled rather fixedly in thanks and considered the problem of getting up again gracefully. Rather to his embarrassment, Betriz knelt to his side, and after a second more, the archdivine to his other, and both contrived to hoist him up. Betriz's dark eyes searched him, lingering briefly and fearfully on his tumor-distended midsection, but she could do no more here than smile in encouragement.

Iselle was reading the marriage contract, though she spared a moment as Cazaril seated himself to cast a small smile in his direction. Cazaril watched and waited. As she finished each page she handed the rectangle of calligraphed and ink-stamped parchment up to her hovering uncle, who had them fairly snatched in turn by the archdivine. The secretary was last in line, but no less intent in his perusal. He collected the pages reverently back into order as they came to him.

Dy Baocia clutched his hands together and watched as the archdivine's eyes sped down the last page. He held the parchment out silently to the stout secretary.

"Well?" said the provincar.

"She hasn't sold Chalion." The archdivine signed himself and opened both hands palm out in thanks to the gods. "She's bought Ibra! My congratulations, Royesse, to your ambassador—and to you."

"To us all," said dy Baocia. All three men were looking vastly more cheerful.

Cazaril cleared his throat. "Indeed, but I trust you will not say as much to Royse Bergon. The treaties are potentially advantageous to both sides, after all." He glanced at dy Baocia's secretary. "Though perhaps it would allay people's fears to have the articles copied out in a large fair hand and posted on the wall beside your palace doors, for everyone to read."

Dy Baocia frowned uncertainly, but the archdivine nodded, and said, "A very wise suggestion, Castillar."

"It would please me very much," said Iselle in a soft voice. "I pray you, Uncle, have it seen to."

A breathless page burst into the chamber, to skid to a stop before dy Baocia and blurt, "Your lady says Royse Bergon's party 'proaches at the gate, and you are to 'tend on her at once to welcome him."

"I'm on my way." The provincar took a breath and smiled at his niece. "And so we bring your lover to you. Remember now, you must demand all the kisses of submission, brow, hands, and feet. Chalion must be seen to rule Ibra. Guard the pride and honor of your House. We must not let him put himself above you, or he will quickly become overweening. You must start as you mean to go on."

Iselle's eyes narrowed. Around her, the shadow darkened, seeming to tighten its grip.

Cazaril sat up, and shot her a look of alarm and a tiny headshake. "Royse Bergon has pride also, no less honorable than your own, Royesse. And he will stand before his own lords here, too."

She hesitated; then her lips firmed. "I *shall* start as I mean to go on." Her voice was suddenly not soft at all, but steel-edged. She gestured at the contract. "The substance of our equality is there, Uncle. My pride demands no greater show. We shall exchange the kisses of welcome, each to each, upon our hands alone." The darkness uncurled a little; Cazaril felt an odd shiver, as though some predatory shadow had passed over his head and flown on, thwarted.

"An admirable discretion," Cazaril endorsed this in relief.

The page, dancing from foot to foot, held open the door for the provincar, who swept out in haste.

"Lord Cazaril, how was your journey?" Betriz taxed him in this interlude. "You look so . . . tired."

"A weary lot of riding, but it all went well enough." He shifted in his seat and smiled up at her.

Her dark brows arched. "I think we must have Ferda and Foix in, to tell us more. Surely it was not so plain and dull as that."

"Well, we had a little trouble with brigands in the mountains. Dy Jironal's doing, I'm fairly sure. Bergon acquitted himself very well. The Fox . . . went easier than I expected, for a reason I didn't." He leaned forward, and lowered his voice to them both. "You remember my benchmate on the galleys I told of, Danni, the boy of good family?"

Betriz nodded, and Iselle said, "I am not likely to forget."

"I didn't guess how good a family. Danni was an alias Bergon gave, to keep himself secret from his captors. It seems his kidnapping was a ploy of Ibra's late Heir. Bergon recognized me when I stood before the Ibran court—*he* had changed and grown almost out of reckoning."

Iselle's lips parted in astonishment. After a moment she breathed, "*Surely* the goddess gave you to me."

"Yes," he admitted reluctantly. "I've come to that conclusion myself."

Her eyes turned toward the double doors on the opposite side of the chamber. Her hands twisted in her lap in a sudden flush of nerves. "How shall I recognize him? Is he—is he well-favored?"

"I don't know how ladies judge such things—"

The doors swung wide. A great mob of persons surged through: pages, hangers-on, dy Baocia and his wife, Bergon and dy Sould and dy Tagille, and Palli bringing up the rear. The Ibrans had been treated to baths as well, and wore the best clothes they'd managed to pack in their meager bags, supplemented, Cazaril was fairly sure, with some judicious emergency borrowings. Bergon's eyes flicked in a smiling panic from Betriz to Iselle, and settled on Iselle. Iselle gazed from face to face among the three strange Ibrans in a momentary terror.

Tall Palli, standing behind Bergon, pointed at the royse and mouthed, *This one!* Iselle's gray eyes brightened, and her pale cheeks flooded with color.

Iselle held out her hands. "My lord Bergon dy Ibra," she said in a voice that only quavered a little. "Welcome to Chalion."

"My lady Iselle dy Chalion," Bergon, striding up to her, returned breathlessly. "Dy Ibra thanks you." He knelt to one knee, and kissed her hands. She bent her head, and kissed his.

Bergon rose again and introduced his companions, who bowed properly. With a slight scrape, the provincar and the archdivine, with their own hands, brought up a chair for Bergon and set it by Iselle's on the other side from Cazaril. From a leather pouch dy Tagille held out, Bergon produced his royal greeting-gift, a necklace of fine emeralds—one of the last of his mother's pieces not pawned by the Fox to buy arms. The white horses unfortunately were still back on the road somewhere. Bergon had been going to bring a rope of new Ibran pearls, but had made the substitution on Cazaril's most earnest advice.

Dy Baocia made a little speech of welcome, which would have been rather longer if Iselle's aunt, catching her niece's eye, had not seized a pause in his periods to invite the assembled company into the next room to partake of refreshments. The young couple was left to have some private speech, and bent their heads together, largely inaudible to the eager eavesdroppers who lingered by the open doors and frequently peeked in to see how they were getting along.

Cazaril was not least forward among this number, craning his neck anxiously from his repositioned chair and alternating between nibbling on little cakes and biting his knuckles. Their voices grew sometimes louder, sometimes softer; Bergon gestured, and Iselle twice laughed out loud, and three times drew in her breath, her hands going to her lips, eyes widening. Iselle lowered her voice and spoke earnestly; Bergon tilted his head and listened intently, and never took his eyes from her face, except twice to glance out at Cazaril, after which they lowered their voices still further.

Lady Betriz brought him a glass of watered wine, nodding at his grateful thanks. Cazaril felt he could guess who had taken the thought to have the hot water and servants and food and clothes waiting ready for him. Her fresh skin glowed golden in the candlelight, smooth and youthful, but her somber dress and pulled-back hair lent her an unexpectedly mature elegance. An ardent energy, on the verge of moving into power and wisdom . . .

"How did you leave things in Valenda, do you think?" Cazaril asked her.

Her smile sobered. "Tense. But we hope with Iselle drawn out, it will grow less so. Surely dy Jironal will not dare offer violence to the widow and mother-in-law of Roya Ias?"

"Mm, not as his first move. In desperation, anything becomes possible."

"That's true. Or at least, people stop arguing with you about what's possible and what's not."

Cazaril considered the young women's wild night ride that had flipped their tactical situation so abruptly topside-to. "How did you get away?"

"Well, dy Jironal had apparently expected us all to cower in the castle, intimidated by his show of arms. You can imagine how that sat with the old Provincara. His women spies watched Iselle all the time, but not me. I took Nan and we went about the town, doing little domestic errands for the household, and observing. His men's defenses all faced outward, prepared to repel would-be rescuers. And no one could keep us from going to the temple, where Lord dy Palliar stayed, to pray for Orico's health." Her smile dimpled. "We became very pious, for a time." The dimple faded. "Then the Provincara got word, I don't know through what source, that the chancellor had dispatched his younger son with a troop of his House cavalry to secure Iselle and bring her in haste back to Cardegoss, because Orico was dying. Which may be true, for all we know, but all the better reason not to place herself in dy Jironal's hands. So escape became urgent, and it was done."

Palli had drifted over to listen; dy Baocia strolled up to join them.

Cazaril gave dy Baocia a nod. "Your lady mother wrote me of promises of support from your fellow provincars. Have you gained any more assurances?"

Dy Baocia rattled off a list of names of men he had written to, or heard from. It was not as long as Cazaril would have liked.

"Thus words. What of troops?"

Dy Baocia shrugged. "Two of my neighbors have promised more material support to Iselle, at need. They don't relish the sight of the chancellor's personal troops occupying one of my towns any more than I do. The third—well, he's married to one of dy Jironal's daughters. He sits tight for the moment, saying as little as possible to anyone."

"Understandable. Where is dy Jironal now, does anyone know?"

"In Cardegoss, we think," said Palli. "The Daughter's military order still remains without a holy general. Dy Jironal feared to absent himself for long from Orico's side lest dy Yarrin get in and persuade Orico to his party. Orico himself is hanging by a thread, dy Yarrin reports secretly to me. Sick, but not, I think, witless; the roya seems to be using his own illness to delay decision, trying to offend no one."

"Sounds very like him." Cazaril fingered his beard and glanced up at dy Baocia. "Speaking of the Temple's soldiers, how large a force of the Brother's Order is stationed in Taryoon?"

"Just a company, about two hundred men," the provincar answered. "We are not garrisoned heavily like Guarida or other of the provinces bordering the Roknari princedoms."

That was two hundred men inside Taryoon's walls, Cazaril reflected.

Dy Baocia read his look. "The archdivine will have speech with their commander later tonight. I think the marriage treaty will do much to persuade him that the new Heiress is loyal to, ah, the future of Chalion."

"Still, they do have their oaths of obedience," murmured Palli. "It would be preferable not to strain them to breaking."

Cazaril considered riding times and distances. "Word of Iselle's flight from Valenda will surely have reached Cardegoss by now. News of Bergon's arrival must follow on its heels. At that point dy Jironal will see the regency he counted upon slipping through his fingers."

Dy Baocia smiled in elation. "At that point, it will be over. Events are moving much faster than he—or indeed, anyone—could have anticipated." The sidelong look he cast Cazaril tinged respect with awe.

"Better that way," said Cazaril. "He must not be pricked into making moves he cannot later back away from." If two sides, both cursed, struck against each other in civil war, it was perfectly possible for both sides to lose. It would be the perfect culmination of the Golden General's death gift for all of Chalion to collapse in upon itself in such agony. *Winning* consisted of finessing the struggle so as to avert bloodshed. Although when Bergon moved Iselle out of the shadow, it would presumably leave poor Orico still in it, and dy Jironal sharing his nominal master's fate . . . *And what of Ista, then?* "Bluntly, much depends upon when the roya dies. He could linger, you know." The curse would surely twist Orico toward whatever fate was most ghastly. This would seem a more reliable guide if there were not so very many ways disasters could play out. Umegat's menagerie had been averting, Cazaril realized, a deal more evil than just ill health. "Looking ahead, we must consider what sops to offer to Chancellor dy Jironal's pride—both before Iselle's ascent to the royacy, and after."

"I don't think he'll be content with sops, Caz," Palli objected. "He's been roya of Chalion in all but name for over a decade."

"Then surely he must be getting *tired*," sighed Cazaril. "Some plums to his sons would soften him. Family loyalty is his weakness, his blind side." Or so the curse suggested, which deformed all virtue to an obverse vice. "Ease him out, but show favor to his clan . . . pull his teeth slowly and gently, and it's done." He glanced up at Betriz, listening intently; yes, she could be counted on to report this debate to Iselle, later.

In the other chamber, Iselle and Bergon rose. She laid her hand on his proffered arm, and they both stole shy glances at their partner; two persons looking more pleased with each other, Cazaril was hard put to imagine. Although when Iselle entered the reception room with her fiancé and glanced around triumphantly at the assembled company, she looked quite as pleased with herself. Bergon's pride had a slightly more dazzled air, though he spared Cazaril, scrambling up from his seat, a reassuringly determined nod.

"The Heiress of Chalion," said Iselle, and paused.

"And the Heir of Ibra," Bergon put in.

"Are pleased to announce that we will take our marriage oaths," Iselle continued, "before the gods, our noble Ibran guests, and the people of this town . . ."

"In the temple of Taryoon at noon upon the day after tomorrow," Bergon finished.

The little crowd broke into cheers and congratulations. And, Cazaril had no doubt, calculations of the speed at which a column of enemy troops might ride; to which the answer worked out, *Not that fast.* United and mutually strengthened, the two young lead-ers could move at need thereafter in close coordination. Once Iselle was married out from under the curse, time was on their side. Every day would gain them more support. Unstrung by the most profound relief, Cazaril sank back into his chair, grinning with the pain of the anguished cramp in his gut.

25

In a palace frantic with prepa-
rations, Cazaril found himself the next
day the only man with nothing to do.
Iselle had arrived in Taryoon with little more than the clothes she
rode in; all of Cazaril's correspondence and books of her chambers
were still in Cardegoss. When he attempted to wait upon her and
inquire what duties she desired of him, he found her rooms
crammed with mildly hysterical tire-women being directed by her
Aunt dy Baocia, all charging in and out with piles of garments in
their arms.

Iselle fought her head out through a swaddling of silks to gasp,
"You've just ridden over eight hundred miles on my behalf. Go *rest*,
Cazaril." She held her arm out obediently while a woman tried a
sleeve upon it. "No, better—compose two letters for my uncle's
clerk to copy out, one to all the provincars of Chalion, and one to
every Temple archdivine, announcing my marriage. Something
they can read out to the people. That should be a nice, quiet task.
When you have all seventeen—no, sixteen—"

"Seventeen," put in her aunt, from the vicinity of her hem.
"Your uncle will want one for his chancellery records. Stand
straight."

"When all are made ready, set them aside for me and Bergon to
sign tomorrow after the wedding, and then see that they are sent
out." She nodded firmly, to the annoyance of the tire-woman trying to adjust her neckline.

Cazaril bowed himself out before he was stuck with a pin, and leaned a moment over the gallery railing.

The day was exquisitely fair, promising spring. The sky was a pale-washed blue, and mild sunlight flooded the newly paved courtyard, where gardeners were carting in orange trees in full flower in tubs, rolling them out to stand around the now-bubbling fountain. He diverted a passing servant and had a writing table brought out and set in the sun for himself. And a chair with a thick, soft cushion, because while a lot of those eight hundred miles were now a blur in his mind, his backside seemed to remember them all. He leaned back with the warm light falling on his face, and his eyes closed, composing his periods, then bent forward to scribble. Dy Baocia's clerk carried off the results for copying out in a much fairer hand than Cazaril's soon enough, and then he just leaned back with his eyes closed, period.

He didn't even open them for the approaching footsteps, till a clank on his table surprised him. He looked up to find a servant, directed by Lady Betriz, setting down a tray with tea, a jug of milk, a dish of dried fruit, and bread glazed with nuts and honey. She dismissed the servant and poured the tea herself, and pressed the bread upon him, sitting on the edge of the fountain to watch him eat it.

"Your face looks very gaunt again. Haven't you been eating properly?" she inquired severely.

"I have no idea. What lovely sunshine this is! I hope it holds through tomorrow."

"Lady dy Baocia thinks it will, though she said we might have rain again by the Daughter's Day."

The scent of the orange blossoms pooled in the shelter of the court, seeming to mix with the honey in his mouth. He swallowed tea to chase the bread and observed in idle wonder, "In three days' time it will be exactly a year since I walked into the castle of Valenda. I wanted to be a scullion."

Her dimple flashed. "I remember. It was last Daughter's Day eve that we first met each other, at the Provincara's table."

"Oh, I saw you before that. Riding into the courtyard with Iselle and . . . and Teidez." *And poor dy Sanda.*

She looked stricken. "You did? Where were you? I didn't see you."

"Sitting on the bench by the wall. You were too busy being scolded by your father for galloping to notice me."

"Oh." She sighed, and trailed her hand through the fountain's little pool, then shook off the cold drops with a frown. The Daughter of Spring might have breathed out today's air, but it was still Old Winter's water. "It seems a hundred years ago, not just one."

"To me, it seems an eye blink. Time . . . outruns me now. Which explains why I wheeze so, no doubt." He added quietly after a moment, "Has Iselle confided to her uncle about the curse we seek to break tomorrow?"

"No, of course not." At his raised brows, she added, "Iselle is Ista's daughter. She cannot speak of it, lest men say she is mad, too. And use it as an excuse to seize . . . everything. Dy Jironal thought of it. At Teidez's interment, he never missed a chance to pass some little comment on Iselle to any lord or provincar in earshot. If she wept, wasn't it too extravagant; if she laughed, how odd that she should do so at her brother's funeral; if she spoke, he whispered that she was frenetic; if she fell silent, wasn't she grown strangely gloomy? And you could just *watch* men begin to see what he told them they were seeing, whether it was there or not. Toward the end of his visit there, he even said such things in her hearing, to see if he could frighten and enrage her, and then accuse her of becoming an unbalanced virago. And he circulated outright lies, as well. But I and Nan and the Provincara were onto his little game by then, and we warned Iselle, and she kept her temper in his company."

"Ah. Excellent girl."

She nodded. "But as soon as we heard the chancellor's men were coming to fetch her back to Cardegoss, Iselle was frantic to escape Valenda. Because once he'd got her close-confined, he could put about any story he pleased of her behavior, and who would there be to deny it? He might get the provincars of Chalion to approve the extension of his regency for the poor mad girl for as long as he pleased, without ever having to raise a sword." She took a breath. "And so she dares not mention the curse."

"I see. She is wise to be wary. Well, the gods willing it will soon be over."

"The gods and the Castillar dy Cazaril."

He made a little warding gesture and took another sip of tea. "When did dy Jironal learn I was gone to Ibra?"

"I don't think he guessed anything till after the cortege reached Valenda, and you weren't to be found there. The old Provincara said he received some reports from his Ibran spies—I think that's partly why, anxious as he was to get back and block dy Yarrin from Orico, he would not leave Valenda till he had his own household troops installed there."

"He sent assassins to intercept me at the border. I wonder if he thought I would just be returning alone, with the next round of negotiations? I don't think he expected Royse Bergon so soon."

"No one did. Except Iselle." She rubbed her fingers across the fine black wool of her vest-cloak lying over her knee. Her next glance up at him was uncomfortably penetrating. "While you have spent yourself trying to save Iselle . . . have you discovered how to save yourself?"

He was silent a moment, then said simply, "No."

"It's . . . it's not right."

He glanced vaguely around the deliciously sunny court, avoiding her eyes. "I like this nice new building. It has no ghosts in it at all, do you know?"

"You're changing the subject." Her frown deepened. "You do that a lot when you don't want to talk about something. I just realized."

"Betriz . . ." He softened his voice. "Our feet were set on different paths from the night I called down death upon Dondo. I can't go back. You are going to be living, and I am not. We can't go on together, even if . . . well, we just can't."

"You don't know how much time you're given. It could be weeks. Months. But if an hour is all the gift the gods give us, all the more insult to the gods to scorn it."

"It's not the shortage of time." He shifted miserably. "It's the abundance of company. Think of us alone together—you, me, Dondo, the death demon . . . am I not a horror to you?" His tone grew almost pleading. "I assure you I'm a horror to me!"

She glanced at his gut, then stared off across the courtyard, her jaw set mulishly. "I do not believe that being haunted is catching. Do you think I lack the courage?"

"Never that," he breathed.

She addressed her feet in a growl. "I'd storm heaven for you, if I knew where it was."

"What, didn't you read old Ordol's book while you were helping Iselle cipher those letters? He claims that the gods, and we, are
both right here all the time, a shadow's thickness apart. We've no
distance to cross at all to get to each other." *I can see their world
from where I sit, in fact.* So Ordol was right. "But you cannot force
the gods. It's only fair, I suppose. They cannot force us, either."

"You're doing it *again*. Twisting the topic."

"What are you planning to wear tomorrow? Shall it be pretty?
You're not allowed to outshine the bride, you know."

She glared at him.

Up on the gallery, Lady dy Baocia popped out of Iselle's chambers and called down to Betriz a complicated question involving
what seemed to Cazaril a great many different fabrics. Betriz
waved back and rose reluctantly to her feet. She flung rather
sharply over her shoulder, as she made for the staircase, "Well, that
may all be so, and you as doomed as you please, but if I'm thrown
from a horse tomorrow and break my neck, I hope you feel a fool!"

"More of a fool," he murmured to the swish of her retreating
skirts. The bright courtyard was a blur in his disobedient eyes, and
he rubbed thcm clear with a hard, surreptitious swipe of his sleeve.

❧THE WEDDING DAY DAWNED AS FAIR AS HOPED. THE
orange-blossom-scented courtyard was crowded as it could hold
when Iselle, attended by her aunt and Betriz, appeared at the top
of the gallery stairs. Cazaril tilted his face up and squinted happily.
The tire-women had performed heroic feats with silks and satins,
garbing her in all the shades of blue proper for a bride. Her blue
vest-cloak was trimmed with as many Ibran pearls as could be
found in Taryoon, patterned as a frieze of stylized leopards. A smattering of applause broke out as, moving a little stiffly in all her fin-
ery, she smiled and descended the steps. Her hair gleamed like a
river of treasure in the sunlight. Two dy Baocia girl-cousins managed her train, under the sporadic direction of their mother. Even
the curse seemed to wrap about her like some trailing sable robe.
But not for much longer . . .

Cazaril obediently fell in beside Provincar dy Baocia, and so
found himself helping to lead the parade afoot through twisting

streets to Taryoon's nearby temple. Through a wonder of coordination, Bergon's procession from March dy Huesta's palace arrived
at the temple portico simultaneously with Iselle's. The royse wore
the reds and oranges of his age and sex, and an expression of determined bravery that would not have been out of place on a man
storming a bastion. Palli and his dozen soldier-brothers in court
dress of their order had joined the royse's party along with Foix
and Ferda, so as not to let the Ibrans look, and perhaps feel, so outnumbered. Despite the short notice, Cazaril calculated that over a
thousand persons of rank crowded into the temple's round center
court; and what seemed the entire citizenry of Taryoon lined the
routes of the royesse and royse. A festival mood had clearly seized
the city.

The two processions coalesced in a swirl of color and entered
the sacred precincts. Taryoon had good temple singers, and the enthusiastic choir made the walls fairly ring with their songs. The
young couple, led by the archdivine, entered each of the temple's lobes in turn. They knelt and prayed upon new carpets for
the blessing of each god: to the Daughter and the Son, in thanks
for their protection in life's journey so far; and to the Mother
and the Father, in hopes of passing into their company in due
course.

By theology and tradition, the Bastard had no official place in
a ceremony of marriage, but all prudent couples sent a placating
gift anyway. Cazaril and dy Tagille had been commissioned to play
holy couriers today. They received the offerings from Bergon and
Iselle and, along with a small but earnestly loud detachment of
singing children, marched around the outside of the main building
to the Bastard's tower. A smiling, white-robed divine stood ready
to receive them inside at the altar.

The royal couple had been forced to borrow clothes, money,
food, and housing for this day, but Bergon did not shortchange the
god; dy Tagille laid down a fat purse of Ibran gold along with his
prayers. Iselle sent a promise, written in her own hand, to undertake payment of roof repairs upon the Bastard's tower in
Cardegoss when she became royina there. Cazaril added a gift of
his own—the blood-tainted rope of pearls, all the residue of
Dondo's broken string that had not fallen to the brigands. Such a
difficult and cursed item was, absolutely without question, the

god's just affair, and Cazaril breathed a sigh of relief when it was off his hands at last.

Proceeding back along the walkway from the Bastard's tower behind the slightly wobbly choir of urchins, Cazaril glanced at the crowd and caught his breath. A man, middle-aged—around him hung a subdued gray light like a winter's day. When Cazaril closed his eyes, the faint light still glowed there. He looked again with his first sight. The man wore the black-and-gray robes and red shoulder braid of an officer of the Taryoon Municipal Court—probably a petty judge. And petty saint of the Father, as Clara had been of the Mother in Cardegoss . . . ?

The man was staring back at Cazaril in openmouthed astonishment, his face drained. There was no chance for them to exchange any word here, as Cazaril was drawn back into the ceremonies inside the high, echoing court of the temple, but Cazaril resolved to ask the archdivine about him at the first opportunity.

At the central fire, the newly married royse and royesse each made a short speech, then the archdivine, Cazaril, and everyone else paraded back through the banner-hung streets to dy Baocia's new palace. There, a grand feast was laid on to fill the afternoon and the celebrators to happy repletion. The food was all the more amazing for having been assembled in just two days; Cazaril suspected supplies had been robbed from the Daughter's Day festival, coming up. But he didn't think the goddess would begrudge them. As principal guests, both Cazaril and the archdivine had places to hold, so he didn't get a chance for private speech until the after-dinner music and dancing drew the younger people off to the courtyards. At that point, the two men he sought found him.

The petty judge stood at the archdivine's shoulder looking unnerved. Cazaril and he exchanged a sidelong look as the archdivine performed a hasty introduction.

"My lord dy Cazaril—may I present to you the Honorable Paginine. He serves the municipality of Taryoon . . ." The archdivine lowered his voice. "He says you are god-touched. Is this so?"

"Alas, yes," sighed Cazaril. Paginine nodded in an *I thought so* sort of way. Cazaril glanced around and drew the pair aside. It was hard to find a private spot; they ended up in a tiny inner court off one of the palace's side entrances. Music and laughter carried through the darkening air. A servant lit torches in wall brackets and returned inside. Overhead, high clouds moved across the first stars.

"Your colleague the archdivine of Cardegoss knows all about me," Cazaril told the archdivine of Taryoon.

"Oh." The archdivine blinked and looked vastly relieved. Cazaril thought it was a misplaced confidence, but he elected not to rob it from him. "Mendenal is an excellent fellow."

"The Father of Winter has given you some gift, I see," Cazaril said to the petty judge. "What is it?"

Paginine ducked his head nervously. "Sometimes—not every time—He permits me to know who is lying in my justiciar's chamber, and who is telling the truth." Paginine hesitated. "It doesn't always do as much good as you'd think."

Cazaril vented a short laugh.

Paginine brightened visibly to both Cazaril's inner and outer eye, and smiled dryly. "Ah, you understand."

"Oh, yes."

"But you, sir . . ." Paginine turned to the archdivine with a troubled look. "I said god-touched, but that hardly describes what I'm seeing. It . . . it almost *hurts* to look at him. Three times since I was given the sight I have met others who are also god-afflicted, but I've never seen anything like him."

"Saint Umegat in Cardegoss said I looked like a burning city," Cazaril admitted.

"That's . . ." Paginine eyed him sidewise. "That's well put."

"He was a man of words." *Once.*

"What is your gift?"

"I, uh . . . I think I *am* the gift, actually. To the Royesse Iselle."

The archdivine touched his hand to his lips, then hastily signed himself. "So that explains the stories circulating about you!"

"What stories?" said Cazaril in bewilderment.

"But Lord Cazaril," the judge broke in, "what is that terrible shadow hanging about Royesse Iselle? That is no godly thing! Do you see it, too?"

"I'm . . . working on it. Getting rid of that ugly thing seems to be my god-given task. I think I'm almost done."

"Oh, that's a relief." Paginine looked much happier.

Cazaril realized he wanted nothing so much as to take Paginine aside to talk shop. *How do you deal with these matters?* The archdivine might be pious, perhaps a good administrator, possibly a learned theologian, but Cazaril suspected he didn't understand the discomforts of the saint trade. Paginine's bitter smile told all. Cazaril wanted to go get drunk with him, and compare complaints.

To Cazaril's embarrassment, the archdivine bowed low to him, and said in an awed, hushed voice, "Blessed Sir, is there anything I can do for you?"

Betriz's question echoed in his mind, *Have you discovered how to save yourself?* Maybe you couldn't save yourself. Maybe you had to take turns saving each other . . . "Tonight, no. Tomorrow . . . later in the week, there is a personal matter I should like to wait upon you about. If I may."

"Certainly, Blessed Sir. I am at your service."

They returned to the party. Cazaril was exhausted, and longed for bed, but the courtyard below his chamber door was full of noisy revelers. A breathless Betriz asked him once to dance, from which exercise he smilingly excused himself; she didn't lack for partners. Her gaze checked him often, as he sat watching from the wall and nursing his watered wine. He did not lack for company, as a string of men and women struck up friendly conversations with him, angling for employment in the future royina's court. To all of them he returned courteous but noncommittal replies.

The Ibran lords were collecting Chalionese ladies rather as spilled honey collected ants, and looking very happy indeed. Halfway through the evening, Lord dy Cembuer arrived, completing their company and their delight. The Ibrans exchanged tales of their respective journeys, to the awe and fascination of their eager Chalionese listeners. To Cazaril's intense political pleasure, Bergon was cast as the hero of this romantic adventure, with Iselle no less as heroine for her night ride from Valenda. As appealing unifying myths went, this one was going to beat dy Jironal's feeble fable of Poor Mad Iselle all hollow, Cazaril rather thought. *And* our *tale is true!*

At last came the hour and the ceremony Cazaril had been breathlessly awaiting, where Bergon and Iselle were conducted up to their bedchamber. Neither, Cazaril was pleased to note, had drunk enough to become inebriated. Since his own wine had somehow grown less watered as the evening progressed, he found himself a little tongue-tied when the royse and royesse called him up to the foot of the staircase to give and receive ceremonial kisses of thanks upon their hands. Moved, he signed himself and called down hopeful blessings on their heads. The solemn grateful intensity of their return gazes discomfited him.

Lady dy Baocia had arranged a small choir to sing prayers to waft the couple on their way upstairs; the crystal voices served to suppress the ribaldry to manageable proportions. Iselle was no more than beautifully blushing and starry-eyed when she and Bergon leaned over the railing to give smiling thanks to all, and throw down flowers.

They disappeared into the candlelit glow of their suite, and the doors swung shut behind them. Two of dy Baocia's officers took up station on the gallery to guard their repose. In a little while, most of the tire-women and attendants emerged, including Lady Betriz. She was instantly carried off by Palli and dy Tagille for more dancing.

The revels looked to continue till dawn, but to Cazaril's relief a misty rain began to sift down out of the chilling sky, driving the musicians and dancers out of his courtyard and indoors to the adjoining building. Slowly, his hand heavy on the railing, Cazaril climbed the stairs to his own chamber, around the gallery corner from the royse and royesse's. *My duty is done. Now what?*

He scarcely knew. A vast moral terror seemed lifted from his shoulders. Only he would live and die by his choices—and mistakes—now. *I refuse to regret. I will not look back.* A moment of balance, on the cusp of past and future.

He rather thought he would look up the little judge again tomorrow. The man's company might well relieve his loneliness.

❦ACTUALLY, I'M NOT NEARLY LONELY ENOUGH, HE thought not much later as Dondo's incoherent obscene bellows, released by their hour of ascendance, came roaring up to his inward ear. The sundered ghost was more wild with fury tonight than Cazaril had ever experienced it, its last vestiges of intelligence and sanity shredding away in its rage. Cazaril could imagine why, and grinned through his agony as he rolled on his bed, curled around the ghastly pulsing pain in his belly.

He almost blacked out, then forced himself up, and to consciousness, horrified by the possibility that the fiendishly aroused Dondo might try to take over his body while he was still alive in it and use it for some vile assault upon Iselle and Bergon. He writhed on the floor in something resembling convulsions, choking back the screams and filth that tried to fly from his mouth, no longer sure *whose* words they were.

When the attack passed, he lay panting on the cold boards, his nightgown rucked up around himself, his fingernails torn and bloody. He had vomited, and lay in it. He touched his wet beard to find spittle flayed to foam hanging around his lips. His stomach—or had that grotesque out-bulging been a dream?—had returned to its former mild distension, though his whole abdominal sheet still ached and quivered like torn muscles after some overtorqued exertion.

I can't go on like this much longer. Something had to give way—his body, his sanity, his breath. His faith. Something.

He rose, and cleaned up the floor, and washed himself at his basin and found a clean dry shirt for a nightdress, then straightened his sweat-stained twisted sheets, lit all the candles in the room, and crawled back into bed. He lay eyes wide, devouring the light.

❦AT LENGTH, THE SOUNDS OF SERVANTS' MURMURS and quiet footsteps along the gallery told him the palace was awakening. He must have dozed, for his candles were burned out, and he didn't remember them guttering. Gray light seeped in under his door and through his shutters.

There would be morning prayers. Morning prayers seemed a good plan, even if the idea of attempting to move was daunting. Cazaril rose. Slowly. Well, his wasn't going to be the only hangover in Taryoon this morning. Even if *he* hadn't been drunk. The household had put off court mourning for the wedding; he selected among the garments that had been bestowed upon him, achieving what he hoped was a sober yet cheerful result.

He went down to the courtyard to await the sun and the young people. No sun was to be had yet; the rain had stopped, but the sky was clouded and chill. Cazaril used his handkerchief to dry the stone edge of the fountain and seated himself. He exchanged a smile and a *good morning* with an old servingwoman who passed by with linens. A crow stalked about on the far end of the courtyard, looking for dropped scraps of food. Cazaril exchanged a tilted stare with it, but the bird evinced no special fascination with him. Upon consideration, he was more relieved than otherwise at its avian indifference.

At last, up on the gallery, the doors Cazaril was waiting for swung open. The sleepy Baocian guards bracketing them stood to attention. Women's voices sounded, and one man's, low and cheerful. Bergon and Iselle appeared, dressed for morning prayers, her hand set lightly upon his proffered arm. They swung about to descend the stairs side by side, and stepped out of the gallery's shadow.

No . . . the shadow followed them.

Cazaril squeezed his eyes shut and open again. His breath stopped.

The choking cloud that wrapped Iselle, now wrapped Bergon, too.

Iselle smiled across at her husband, and Bergon smiled back at her; last night, they had looked excited and tired and a little scared. This morning, they looked like two people in love. With blackness boiling up around them both like the smoke from a burning ship.

As they approached, Iselle sang him a cheerful, "Good morning, Lord Caz!"

Bergon grinned, and said, "Will you not join us, sir? We have much to give thanks together for this morning, do we not?"

Cazaril's lips drew back on the travesty of a smile. "I . . . I . . . a little later. I left something in my room."

He heaved himself up and rushed past them up the stairs. He turned and looked again from the gallery as they passed out of the courtyard. Still trailing shadows.

He slammed the door of his chamber behind himself and stood gasping, almost weeping. *Gods. Gods. What have I done?*

I haven't freed Iselle. I've cursed Bergon.

26

Distraught, Cazaril kept to his chamber all morning. In the afternoon a page knocked, with the unwelcome news that the royse and royesse desired him to attend upon them in their rooms. Cazaril considered feigning illness, though he hardly need feign. No, for Iselle would surely bring physicians down upon him, probably in packs—he remembered the last time, with Rojeras, and shuddered. With a boundless reluctance, he straightened his garments, making himself presentable, and walked out around the gallery to the royal suite.

The sitting room's high casement windows were open to the cool spring light. Iselle and Bergon, still in festive dress from the noon banquet at the March dy Huesta's palace, awaited him. They sat around the corner from each other at a table that bore paper, parchment, and new pens, with a third chair pulled invitingly to the other side. Their heads, amber and brown, were bent together in low-voiced conversation. The shadow still boiled slowly around them, viscous as hot tar. At Cazaril's step, they both looked up at him and smiled. He moistened his lips and bowed, his face stiff.

Iselle gestured at the papers. "Our next most urgent task is to compose a letter to my brother Orico, to acquaint him of the steps we have taken, and assure him of our most loyal submission. I think we should include extracts of all the articles of our marriage most favorable to Chalion, to help reconcile him to it, don't you think?"

Cazaril cleared his throat and swallowed.

Bergon's brows drew inward. "Caz, you look as pale as a . . . um. Are you all right? Please, sit down!"

Cazaril managed a tiny headshake. Again he was tempted to flee into some malingering lie—or half-truth, now, for he was feeling sick enough. "Nothing is all right," he whispered. He sank to one knee before the royse. "I have made a vast mistake. I'm sorry. I'm sorry."

Iselle's wary, startled face blurred in his vision. "Lord Caz . . . ?"

"Your marriage"—he swallowed again, and forced his numb lips to speak on—"has not lifted the curse from Iselle as I'd hoped. Instead, it has spread it to you both."

"*What?*" breathed Bergon.

Tears clogged Cazaril's voice. "And now I know not what to do . . ."

"How do you know this?" Iselle asked urgently.

"I can see it. I can see it on you both now. If anything, it's even darker and thicker. More grasping."

Bergon's lips parted in dismay. "Did I . . . did we do something wrong? Somehow?"

"No, no! But both Sara and Ista married into the House of Chalion, and into the curse. I thought it was because men and women were different, that it somehow followed the male line of Fonsa's heirs along with the name."

"But I am Fonsa's heir, too," said Iselle slowly. "And flesh and blood are more than just names. When two become wed, it doesn't mean that one disappears and only the other remains. We are joined, not subsumed. Oh, is there nothing we can do? There must be something!"

"Ista said," Cazaril began, and stopped. He was not at all sure he wanted to tell these two decisive young people what Ista had said. Iselle might take thought again . . .

Ignorance is not stupidity, but it might as well be, Iselle had cried. It was much too late to shelter her now. By the wrath of the gods, she was to be the next royina of Chalion. With the right to rule came the duty to protect—the privilege of receiving protection had to be left behind with childhood's other toys. Even protection from bitter knowledge. *Especially from knowledge.*

Cazaril swallowed to unlock his throat. "Ista said there was another way."

He climbed into the chair and sat heavily. In a broken voice, in terms so plain as to be almost brutal, Cazaril repeated the tale Ista had told him of Lord dy Lutez, Roya Ias, and her vision of the goddess. Of the two dark hellish nights in the Zangre's dungeons with the bound man and the vat of icy water. When he finished, both his listeners were pale and staring.

"I thought—I feared—I might be the one," Cazaril said. "Because of the night I tried to barter my life for Dondo's death. I was *terrified* that I might be the one. *Iselle's dy Lutez*, as Ista named me. But I swear before all the gods, if I thought it would work, I'd have you take me outside right now and drown me in the courtyard fountain. Twice. But I cannot become the sacrifice now. My second death must be my last, for the death demon will fly away with my soul and Dondo's, and I don't see how there can be any getting it back into my body then." He rubbed his wet eyes with the back of his hand.

Bergon gazed at his new wife as if his eyes could swallow her. He finally said huskily, "What about me?"

"What?" said Iselle.

"I undertook to come here to save you from this thing. So, the method's just got a little harder, that's all. I'm not afraid of the water. What if you drowned me?"

Cazaril's and Iselle's instant protests tumbled out together; Cazaril gave way with a little wave of his hand. Iselle repeated, "It was tried once. It was tried, and it didn't work. I'm not about to drown either one of you, thank you very much! No, nor hang you either, nor any other horrid thing you can think of. No!"

"Besides," Cazaril put in, "the goddess's words were, a man must lay down his life three times *for* the House of Chalion. Not *of* the House of Chalion." At least, according to Ista. Had she repeated her vision verbatim? Or did her words embed some treacherous error? Never mind, so long as they deterred Bergon from his horrifying suggestion. "I don't think you can break the curse from the inside, or it would have been Ias, not dy Lutez, who put himself into the barrel. And, five gods forgive me, Bergon, you are now inside this thing."

"It feels wrong anyway," said Iselle, her eyes narrowing. "Some kind of cheat. What was that thing you told me Saint Umegat said, when you'd asked him what you should do? About daily duties?"

"He said I should do my daily duties as they came to me."

"Well, and so. Surely the gods are not done with us." She drummed her fingers on the tabletop. "It occurs to me . . . my mother lay down twice in childbed for the House of Chalion. She never had the chance for a third such trial. *That* is certainly a duty that the gods give to one."

Cazaril considered the havoc that the curse might wreak, intersecting with the hazards of pregnancy and childbirth as it had intersected with the chances of Ias's and Orico's battles, and shivered. Barrenness like Sara's was the least of the potential disasters. "Five gods, Iselle, I think we'd do better to put me into the barrel."

"And besides," said Bergon, "the goddess said a man. She did say a man, didn't She, Caz?"

"Uh . . . that was Lady Ista's account of the words, yes."

"The divines say, when the gods instruct men in their pious duties, they mean women, too," Iselle growled. "You can't have it both ways. Anyway, I lived under the curse for sixteen years, unknowing. I survived somehow."

But it's getting worse now. Stronger. Teidez's death seemed a fair example to Cazaril of its working out—the boy's special strengths and virtues, few as they had been, all twisted to a dire ill. Iselle and Bergon between them had many strengths and virtues. The scope for the curse's distortions was immense.

Iselle and Bergon were gripping hands across the tabletop. Iselle knuckled her eyes with her free hand, pinched the bridge of her nose, and sniffed deeply.

"Curse or no curse," she said, "we must make dutiful submission to Orico, and at once. So that dy Jironal cannot declare me to be in revolt. If only I were by Orico, I know I could persuade him of the benefit of this marriage to Chalion!"

"Orico is very persuadable," Cazaril admitted dryly. "It's making him *stay* persuaded that's the difficult part."

"Yes, and I don't forget for a moment that dy Jironal is with Orico in Cardegoss. My greatest fear is that the chancellor may, upon hearing this news, somehow persuade Orico to again change the terms of his will."

"Attach enough of the provincars of Chalion to your party, Royesse, and they may be willing to help you resist any such late codicils."

Iselle frowned deeply. "I wish we might go up to Cardegoss. I should be by Orico, if this proves to be his deathbed. We should be in the capital when events unfold."

Cazaril paused, then said, "Difficult. You must not put yourself in dy Jironal's hands."

"I had not planned to go unattended." Her smile flashed darkly, like the moon on a knife blade. "But we should seize every legal nicety as well as every tactical advantage. It would be well to remind the lords of Chalion that all the chancellor's legal power flows to him through the roya. Only."

Bergon said uneasily, "You know the man better than I do. Do you think dy Jironal will just sit still at this news?"

"The longer he can be induced to sit, the better. We gain support daily."

"*Have* you heard anything of dy Jironal's response?" Cazaril asked.

"Not yet," said Bergon.

The time lag ran both ways, alas. "Let me know at once if you do." Cazaril drew a long breath, flattened out a clean sheet of paper, and picked up a quill. "Now. How do you two wish to style yourselves . . . ?"

❧THE PROBLEM OF HOW TO DELIVER THIS POLITICALLY vital missive was a trifle delicate, Cazaril reflected, crossing the courtyard below the royal chambers with the signed and sealed document in his hands. It would not do to toss it into a courier bag for delivery at the gallop to the Zangre Chancellery. The article needed a delegation of men of rank not only to give it, and Iselle and Bergon, the proper weight, but also to assure that it was delivered to Orico and not dy Jironal. Trustworthy men must read the letter out accurately to the dying roya in his blindness, and give politic answers to any questions Orico might have about his sister's precipitate nuptials. Lords and divines—some of each, Cazaril decided. Iselle's uncle was fitted to recommend suitable men who might ride out fast, and tonight. His stride lengthened, as he started in search of a page or servant to tell him dy Baocia's whereabouts.

Under the tiled archway into the court, he met Palli and dy

Baocia himself, hurrying in. They, too, both still wore their banquet garb.

"Caz!" Palli hailed him. "Where were you at dinner?"

"Resting. I . . . had a bad night."

"What, and here I'd have sworn you were the only one of us who went to bed sober."

Cazaril let this one pass. "What's this?"

Palli held up a sheaf of opened letters. "News from dy Yarrin in Cardegoss, sent in haste by Temple courier. I thought the royse and royesse should know at once. Dy Jironal rode out of the Zangre before midmorning yesterday, none knows where."

"Did he take troops—no, tell it once. Come on." Cazaril turned on his heel and led the way back up the gallery stairs to the royal chambers. One of Iselle's servants admitted them, and went to bring the young couple out to the sitting room again. While they were waiting Cazaril showed them the letter to Orico and explained its contents. The provincar nodded judiciously, and named some likely lords for the task of carrying it to Cardegoss.

Iselle and Bergon entered, Iselle still patting her braided hair into place, and the three men bowed to them. Royse Bergon, at once alert to the papers in Palli's hand, bade them be seated around the table.

Palli repeated his news of dy Jironal. "The chancellor took only a light force of his household cavalry. It seemed to dy Yarrin that he meant to ride either a short way, or very fast."

"What news of my brother Orico?" asked Iselle.

"Well, here . . ." Palli passed the letter to her for examination. "With dy Jironal out of the way, dy Yarrin tried at once to get in to see the roya, but Royina Sara said he was asleep, and refused to disturb his rest for any supplication. Since she had undertaken to smuggle in dy Yarrin before despite dy Jironal, he fears the roya may have taken a turn for the worse."

"What's the other letter?" asked Bergon.

"Old news, but interesting all the same," said Palli. "Cazaril, what in the world is the old archdivine saying about you? The commander of the Taryoon troop of the Order of the Son came to me, all a-tremble—he seems to think you're god-touched and dares not approach you. He wanted to talk to a man who bore Temple oaths like himself. He'd received a copy of an order that had gone out from the Chancellery to all the military posts of the Order of the Son in western Chalion—for your arrest, if it please you, for treason. You are slandered—"

"Again?" murmured Cazaril, taking the letter.

"And accused of sneaking into Ibra to sell Chalion to the Fox. Which, since all the world now knows the real case, falls a trifle flat."

Cazaril scanned down the order. "I see. This was his net to catch me if his assassins failed at the border. He set it out a bit too late, I'm afraid. As you say, old news."

"Yes, but it has a sequel. This obedient fool of a troop commander sent a letter in turn to dy Jironal, admitting he'd seen you but excusing himself from arresting you. He protested that the arrest order was clearly a misapprehension. That you had acted under the Royesse Iselle's orders, and had done great good for Chalion, and no treason; that the marriage was immensely popular with the people of Taryoon. And that everyone thinks the royesse is extremely beautiful, too. That the new Heiress was seen by everyone as wise and good, and a great relief and hope after the disasters of Orico's reign."

Dy Baocia snorted. "Which, as they are concomitantly the disasters of dy Jironal's reign, works out to an unintended insult. Or was it unintended?"

"I rather think so. The man is, um, plain-minded and plain-spoken. He says he meant it to help persuade dy Jironal to turn to the royesse's support."

"It's more likely to effect the opposite," said Cazaril slowly. "It would persuade dy Jironal that his own support is failing rapidly and that he had better take action at once to shore it up. When would dy Jironal have received this sage advice from his subordinate?"

Palli's lips twisted. "Early yesterday morning."

"Well . . . there's nothing in it that he would not have received from other sources by then, I suppose." Cazaril passed the order over to Bergon, waiting with keen interest.

"So, dy Jironal's out of Cardegoss," said Iselle thoughtfully.

"Yes, but gone where?" asked Palli.

Dy Baocia pulled his lip. "If he left with so few men, it has to be to somewhere that his forces are mustered. Somewhere within striking distance of Taryoon. That means either to his son-in-law the provincar of Thistan, to our east, or to Valenda, to our north-west."

"Thistan is actually closer to us," said Cazaril.

"But in Valenda, he holds my mother and sister hostage," said dy Baocia grimly.

"No more now than before," said Iselle, her voice stiff with sup-pressed worry. "They bade me go, Uncle . . ."

Bergon was listening with close attention. The Ibran royse had grown up with civil war, Cazaril was reminded; he might be dis-turbed, but he showed no signs of panic.

"I think we should ride straight for Cardegoss while dy Jironal is out of it, and take possession," said Iselle.

"If we are to mount such a foray," her uncle demurred, "we should take Valenda first, free our family, and secure our base. But if dy Jironal is mustering men to attack Taryoon, I do not wish to strip it of defenses."

Iselle gestured urgently. "But if Bergon and I are out of Taryoon, dy Jironal will have no reason to attack it. Nor Valenda either. It's me he wants—*must* have."

"The vision of dy Jironal ambushing your column on the road, where you are out in the open and vulnerable, doesn't appeal to me much either," said Cazaril.

"How many men could you spare to escort us to Cardegoss, Uncle?" Iselle asked. "Mounted. The foot soldiers to follow at their best speed. And how soon could they be mustered?"

"I could have five hundred of horse by tomorrow night, and a thousand of foot the day after," dy Baocia admitted rather reluc-tantly. "My two good neighbors could send as many, but not as soon."

Dy Baocia could pull out double that number from his hat, Cazaril thought, if he weren't hedging. Too great a care could be as fatal as too great a carelessness when the moment came to hazard all.

Iselle folded her hands in her lap and frowned fiercely. "Then have them make ready. We will keep the predawn vigil of prayers for the Daughter's Day and attend the procession as we had planned. Uncle, Lord dy Palliar, if it please you send out what men you can find to ride in all directions for news of dy Jironal's movements. And then we'll see what new information we have by to-morrow night, and take a final decision then."

The two men bowed, and hurried out; Iselle bade Cazaril stay a moment.

"I did not wish to argue with my uncle," she said to him in a tone of doubt, "but I think Valenda is a distraction. What do you think, Cazaril?"

"From the point of view of the roya and royina of Chalion-Ibra . . . it does not command a position of geographic importance. Whoever may hold it."

"Then let it be a sink for dy Jironal's forces instead of our own. But I suspect my uncle will be difficult about it."

Bergon cleared his throat. "The road to Valenda and the road to Cardegoss run together for the first stage. We could put it about that we were making for Valenda, but then strike for Cardegoss instead at the fork."

"Put it about to who?"

"Everyone. Pretty nearly. Then whatever spies dy Jironal has among us will send him haring off in the wrong direction."

Yes, actually, this *was* the son of the Fox of Ibra . . . Cazaril's brows twitched up in approval.

Iselle thought it over, then frowned. "It works only if my uncle's men will follow us."

"If we lead, they'll have no choice but to follow us, I think."

"My hope is to avoid a war, not start one," said Iselle.

"Then *not* marching up to a town full of the chancellor's forces makes sense, don't you think?" said Bergon.

Iselle smiled mistily, leaned over, and kissed him on the cheek; he touched the spot in mild wonder. "We shall *both* take thought until tomorrow," she announced. "Cazaril, start that letter toward my brother Orico all the same, as if we meant to sit tight here in Taryoon. Perchance we shall overtake it on the road and deliver it ourselves."

🐦WITH DY BAOCIA'S AND THE ARCHDIVINE'S GUIDANCE, Cazaril found no lack of eager volunteers in town or temple to take the royesse's letter to Cardegoss. Men seemed to be flocking to the royal couple's side. Those who'd missed the wedding itself were now pouring into town for the Daughter's Day celebration tomorrow. All that youth and beauty acted as a powerful talisman upon men's hearts; the Lady of Spring's season of renewal was being strongly identified with Iselle's impending reign. The trick would be to get the governance of Chalion on a more even footing while the mood held, so that it might still stand strong in less happy hours. Surely no witness here in Taryoon would ever quite forget this time of hope; it would still linger in their eyes when they looked at an older Iselle and Bergon.

Thus Cazaril oversaw a party of a dozen grave men climb into their saddles at a time of night when most men were climbing into their beds. He gave the official documents into the hands of a senior divine, a sober lord who had risen high in the Order of the Father. The March dy Sould rode with them, as Bergon's witness and spokesman. The earnest ambassadors clattered out of the temple plaza, and Palli walked Cazaril back to dy Baocia's palace and wished him good night.

The little distracting flurry of action fading in his mind, Cazaril's steps grew heavy again as he climbed the stairs of his courtyard gallery. The weight of the curse was a secret burden dragging down all bright hopes. A younger Orico had started out his reign just as eager and willing as Iselle, a dozen years ago. As if he'd believed then that if only he applied *enough* effort, goodwill, steady virtue, he could overcome the black blight. But it had all gone wrong. . . .

There were worse fates than becoming Iselle's dy Lutez, Cazaril reflected. He might become Iselle's *dy Jironal*. How much frustration, how much corrosion could a loyal man endure before going mad, watching such a long slow drain of youth and hope into age and despair? And yet, whatever Orico had been, he had held on long enough for the next generation to gain its chance. Like some doomed little hero holding back a dike of woe, and drowning while the others escaped the tide.

Cazaril readied himself for bed, and his nightly attack, but Dondo was surprisingly quiescent. Exhausted? Recouping his forces? Waiting . . . Despite that malevolent presence and promise, Cazaril slept at last.

*   *   *

🦎A SERVANT WOKE HIM AN HOUR BEFORE DAWN AND led him by candlelight down into the courtyard, where the royal couple's inner household was to have its holy vigil. The air was chill and foggy, but a few faint stars directly overhead promised a fair dawning soon. Ibran-style prayer mats had been arranged around the central fountain, and each person took their station upon them, on knees or prone as they were so moved; Iselle and Bergon knelt side by side. Lady Betriz placed herself between the royesse and Cazaril. Dy Tagille and dy Cembuer, yawning, hurried in to join them on the outer ring of rugs, with some half a dozen other persons of lesser rank. A divine from the temple led a short prayer aloud, then invited all to meditate upon the blessings of the turning season. All over Taryoon, winter's fires were being extinguished. When all was in readiness, the last candles were blown out. A profound darkness and silence descended.

Quietly, Cazaril laid himself prone upon his rug, arms outstretched. He told over the couple of spring prayers he knew three times each, but then gave up trying to fill his mind with rote words to keep his thoughts out. If he let his thoughts run their course, perhaps some silence would follow. And in it he might hear . . . what?

He changed the subject, Betriz had charged, when the answers were too difficult for him. He'd tried to do so to the gods. He hadn't fooled them either, apparently.

Ista had been given her chance to lift the curse, and failed; and had failed, it seemed, for her generation. If he failed, he suspected he would not be allowed to go around to try again. So would Iselle or Bergon or both get to be the new Orico, holding back the tide until they foundered, to create the next chance?

They will be vastly unlucky in their children. He knew it, suddenly, with a cold clarity. The whole of their scheme for peace and order rode upon the hope of a strong, bright heir to follow them both. They would pour themselves until empty into children miscarried, dead, mad, exiled, betrayed . . .

I'd storm heaven for you, if I knew where it was.

He knew where it was. It was on the other side of every living person, every living creature, as close as the other side of a coin, the other side of a door. Every soul was a potential portal to the gods. *I wonder what would happen if we all opened up at once?* Would it flood the world with miracle, drain heaven? He had a sudden vision of saints as the gods' irrigation system, like the one around Zagosur; a rational and careful opening and closing of sluice gates to deliver each little soul-farm its just portion of benison. Except that this felt more like floodwaters backed up behind a cracking dam.

Ghosts were exiles upon the wrong border, people turned inside out. Why didn't it work the other way around? What would it be like to be an anti-ghost of flesh let loose in a world of spirit? Would one be frustratingly invisible to most spirits, impotent there, as ghosts were invisible to most men?

And if I can see ghosts sundered from their bodies, why I can't see them when they're still in their bodies? Had he ever tried? How many people were ranged around him right now? He closed his eyes and tried to see them in the dark with his inner sight. His senses were still confused by matter; somewhere in the outer rank of prayer rugs, someone started to snore, and was nudged awake with a startled grunt by a snickering companion. If only it worked that way, it would be like seeing through a window into heaven.

If the gods saw people's souls but not their bodies, in mirror to the way people saw bodies but not souls, it might explain why the gods were so careless of such things as appearance, or other bodily functions. Such as pain? Was pain an illusion, from the gods' point of view? Perhaps heaven was not a place, but merely an angle of view, a vantage, a perspective.

And at the moment of death, we slide through altogether. Losing our anchor in matter, gaining . . . what? Death ripped a hole between the worlds.

And if one death ripped a little hole in the world, quickly healed, what would it take to rip a bigger hole? Not a mere postern gate to slip out of, but a wide breach, mined and sapped, one that holy armies might pour in through?

If a god died, what kind of hole would it rip between earth and heaven? What was the Golden General's blessing-curse anyway, this exiled *thing* from the other side? What kind of portal had the Roknari genius opened for himself, what kind of channel had he been . . . ?

Cazaril's swollen belly cramped, and he rolled a little sideways to give it ease. *I am a most peculiar locus at present.* Two exiles from the world of spirit were trapped inside his flesh. The demon, which did not belong here at all, and Dondo, who should have left but was anchored by his unrelinquished sins. Dondo did not desire the gods. Dondo was a clot of self-will, a leaden plug, digging into his body with claws like grappling hooks. If not for Dondo, he could run away.

Could I?

He imagined it . . . suppose this lethal anchor were suddenly and—ha—miraculously removed. He could run away . . . but then he'd never know how it might have worked out. *That Cazaril. If only he'd hung on another day, another mile, he might have saved the world. But he quit just an hour too soon* . . . Now, *there* was a damnation to make the sundered ghosts seem a faint quaint amusement. A lifetime—an eternity?—of second-guessing himself.

But the only way ever to know for *certain* was to ride it out all the way to his destruction.

Five gods, I am surely mad. I believe I would limp all the way to the Bastard's hell for that frightful curiosity's sake.

Around him, he could hear the others breathing, the occasional little rustle of fabric. The fountain burbled gently. The sounds comforted him. He felt very alone, but at least it was in good company.

Welcome to sainthood, Cazaril. By the gods' blessings, you get to host miracles! The catch is, you don't get to choose what they are. . . .

Betriz had it exactly backward. It wasn't a case of storming heaven. It was a case of letting heaven storm you. Could an old siege-master learn to surrender, to open his gates?

Into your hands, O lords of light, I commend my soul. Do what you must to mend the world. I am at your service.

The sky was brightening, turning from Father Winter's gray to the Daughter's own fine blue. In the shadowed court, Cazaril could see the shapes of his companions begin to shade and fill with the light's gift of color. The scent of the orange blossoms hung heavily in the dawn damp, and more faintly, the perfume of Betriz's hair. Cazaril pushed back up onto his knees, stiff and cold.

From somewhere in the palace, a man's bellow split the air, and was abruptly cut off. A woman shrieked.

27

Cazaril put a hand to the pavement, shoving himself to his feet, and
pushed back his vest-cloak from his
sword hilt. All around him, the others were rising and looking
about in alarm.

"Dy Tagille." Bergon motioned to his Ibran companion. "Go
see."

Dy Tagille nodded and departed at a run.

Dy Cembuer, his right arm still in a sling, clenched and unclenched his left hand, awkwardly freed his sword hilt, and began
striding after him. "We should bar the gate."

Cazaril glanced around the courtyard, and at the tiled archway.
Its decorative wrought-iron gate swung wide after dy Tagille. Was
there another entrance? "Royesse, Royse, Betriz, you must not get
trapped in here." He ran after dy Cembuer, his heart already
pounding. If he could get them out before the—

A frantic page pelted through as dy Cembuer reached the
archway. "My lords, help, armed men have broken into the palace!"
He looked wildly over his shoulder.

And here they are. Two men, swords out, ran in the page's track.
Dy Cembuer, trying to push the gate shut with his sword in his left
hand, barely ducked the first blow. Then Cazaril was upon them.
His first swing was wild, and his target parried it with a clang that
echoed around the court.

"Get out!" he screamed over his shoulder. "Over the roofs if you have to!" Could Iselle climb in her court dress? He could not look to see if he was obeyed, for his opponent recovered and bore in hard. The bravos, soldiers, whatever they were, wore ordinary street clothes, no identifying colors or badges—the better to infiltrate the city in little groups, mixed in with the festival crowd, no doubt.

Dy Cembuer slashed his man. A heavy return blow landed on his broken arm, and he whitened and fell back with a muffled cry. Another soldier appeared around the corner and ran toward the archway, wearing the Baocian colors of green and black, and for a moment Cazaril's heart lifted in hope. Until he recognized him as Teidez's suborned guard captain—growing ever more expert in betrayal, apparently.

The Baocian captain's lips drew back as he saw Cazaril, and he gripped his sword grimly, moving in beside his comrade. Cazaril had neither breathing space nor a hand free to try to close the gate on them again, and besides, dy Cembuer's opponent had fallen in the path. Cazaril did not dare fall back. This narrow choke point forced them to come at him one at a time, the best odds he was likely to get today. His hand was growing numb from the ringing blows transmitted up his blade into his hilt, and his gut was cramping. But his every gasping breath bought another stride of running time for Bergon and Iselle and Betriz. One step, two steps, five steps . . . Where was dy Tagille? Nine steps, eleven, fifteen . . . How many men were coming up after these? His blade hacked a piece out of his first attacker's jaw, and the man reeled back with a bloody cry, but it only left the guard captain with a better angle for attack. The man still wore Dondo's green ring. It flashed as his sword darted and parried. Forty steps. Fifty . . .

Cazaril fought in an exaltation of terror, so hard-pressed to defend himself that the supernatural dangers of a successful thrust of his own, of the death demon tearing his soul out of his body along with his dying victim's, scarcely seemed to apply. Cazaril's world narrowed; he no longer sought to win the day, or this fight, or his life, but merely another stride. Each stride a little victory. Sixty . . . something . . . he was losing count. Begin again. *One. Two. Three . . .*

I am probably going to die now. Twice was no charm. He howled inside with the waste of it, mad with regret that he could not die *enough.* His arm was shaking with fatigue. This gate wanted a swordsman, not a secretary, but the royesse's private holy vigil had included only the few nobles. Was no one coming up behind him in support? Surely even the old servants could grab something and throw it . . . *Twenty-two* . . .

Could he fall back across the courtyard to the stairs? Was the royal party gone up the stairs yet? He threw a frantic glance backward, a mistake, for he lost his rhythm; with a *scree* of metal, the captain's sword snaked his from his tingling grip. His blade clattered across the stone, spinning. The Baocian bore Cazaril violently backward through the archway and knocked him to the pavement. Half a dozen attackers surged through the gate after the captain and spread out across the courtyard; a couple of them, prudent and experienced, kicked him in passing to keep him down. He still didn't know who they were, but he had no doubt *whose* they were.

Coughing, he rolled on his side in time to see dy Jironal, swearing, stride through the gate in the wake of another half dozen men. Dy Cembuer was still down, bent in on himself, teeth clenched in agony. Were Iselle and Bergon safe away? Down a servants' stair, over the roof tiles? Pray the gods they had not panicked and barricaded themselves in their chambers . . . Dy Jironal headed toward the stairs to the gallery, where a little knot of his men waited to make a concerted rush.

"Martou!" Cazaril bellowed, wrenching over and up onto his knees.

Dy Jironal swung round as though spun on the end of a rope. "You!" At his motion, the Baocian guard captain and another soldier grasped Cazaril by the arms, bending them up behind him, and dragged him to his feet.

"You are too late!" Cazaril called. "She's wed and bedded, and there's no way you can undo it now. Chalion owns Ibra at the fairest price ever paid, and all the country celebrates its good fortune. She is the Child of Spring and the delight of the gods. You can't win against her. Give over! Save your life, and the lives of your men."

"Wed?" snarled dy Jironal. "Widowed, if needs be. She is a mad traitor and the whore of Ibra and accursed, and I'll not have it!" He whirled again toward the stairs.

"You're the whore, Martou! You sold Gotorget for Roknari money that I refused, and you sold me to the galleys to stop my mouth!" Cazaril glared around frantically at the hesitating troop. *Fifty-five, fifty-six, fifty-seven* . . . "This liar sells his own men. Follow him, and you risk betrayal the first moment he smells profit!"

Dy Jironal turned again, drawing his sword. "I'll stop your mouth, you miserable fool! Hold him *up*."

Wait, no—

The two men holding Cazaril jerked a little apart, their eyes widening, as dy Jironal began to stride forward, twisting for a mighty two-handed swing. "My lord, it's murder," faltered the man holding Cazaril's left arm. The beheading arc was blocked by Cazaril's captors, and dy Jironal changed in mid-career to a violent low thrust, lunging forward with all the weight of his fury behind his arm.

The steel pierced silk brocade and skin and muscle and drove through Cazaril's gut, and Cazaril was nearly jerked off his feet with the force of it.

Sound ceased. The sword was sliding through him as slowly as a pearl dropped in honey, and as painlessly. Dy Jironal's red face was frozen in a rictus of rage. On either side of Cazaril, his captors bent and leaned away, mouths creeping open on startled cries that never emerged.

With a yowl of triumph that only Cazaril heard, the death demon coursed up the sword blade, leaving it red-hot in its wake, and into dy Jironal's hand. With a scream of anguish, a black syrup that was Dondo poured after. Crackling blue-white sparks grew around dy Jironal's sword arm like ivy twining, and then spiraled around his whole body. Slowly, dy Jironal's head tilted back, and white fire came from his mouth as his soul was uprooted from him. His hair stood on end, and his eyes widened and boiled white. The driven sword still moved with his falling weight, and Cazaril's flesh sizzled around it. White and black and red whirled together, braided round each other, and flowed away in no direction. Cazaril's perception was drawn into the twisting cyclone's wake, up out of his body like a rising column of smoke. Three deaths and a demon all bound together. They flowed into a blue *Presence* . . .

Cazaril's mind exploded.

He opened outward, and outward, and outward still, till all the world lay below him as if seen from a high mountain. But not the realm of matter. This was a landscape of soul-stuff; colors he could not name, of a shattering brilliance, bore him up upon a glorious turbulence. He could hear all the minds of the world whispering, a sighing like wind in a forest—if one could but distinguish, simultaneously and separately, the song of each leaf. And all the world's cries of pain and woe. And shame and joy. And hope and despair and aspiration . . . A thousand thousand moments from a thousand thousand lives poured through his distending spirit.

From the surface below him, little bubbles of soul-color were boiling up one by one and floating into a turning dance, hundreds, thousands, like great raindrops falling upward . . . *It is the dying, pouring in through the rents of the worlds into this place.* Souls gestated by matter in the world, dying into this strange new birth. *Too much, too much, too much* . . . His mind could not hold it all, and the visions burst from him like water falling through his fingers.

He'd once thought of the Lady of Spring as a sort of pleasant, gentle young woman, in his vague and youthful conceptualizations. The divines and Ordol had honed it scarcely further than to a mental picture of a nice immortal lady. This overwhelming Mind listened to every cry or song in the world at once. She watched the souls spiral up in all their terrible complex beauty with the delight of a gardener inhaling the scent of Her flowers. And now this Mind turned Her attention fully upon Cazaril.

Cazaril melted, and was cupped in Her hands. He thought She drank him, siphoning him out of the violent concatenation of the dy Jironal brothers and the demon, who shot away *elsewhere.* He was blown from Her lips again, back down in a tightening spiral through the great slash in the world that was his death, and once again into his body. Dy Jironal's sword blade was just emerging from his back. Blood bloomed around the metal point like a rose.

And now to work, the Lady whispered. *Open to me, sweet Cazaril.*

Can I watch? he asked tremulously.

Whatever you can bear, is permitted.

He sank back in a languid ease, as the goddess flowed through him into the world. His lips curved up in a smile, or started to; his fleshly body was as sluggish as those of the men around him in the courtyard. He seemed to be sinking to his knees. Dy Jironal's corpse had not yet finished falling to the pavement, although his dead hand had spasmed from his sword hilt. Dy Cembuer was lifting himself upon his good arm, his mouth opening upon a cry that was going to eventually become, *Cazaril!* Some men were throwing themselves prone. Some were starting to run.

The goddess drew the curse of Chalion like thick black wool into Her hands. Lifting it from Iselle and Bergon, somewhere in the streets of Taryoon. From Ista in Valenda. From Sara in Cardegoss. From all the land of Chalion, mountain to mountain, river to plain. Cazaril could not sense Orico in the dark fog. The Lady spun it out again through Cazaril. As it twisted through him into the other realm, its darkness fell away, and then he wasn't sure if it was a thread or a stream of bright clean water, or wine, or something even more wonderful.

Another Presence, solemn and gray, waited there, and took it up. And took it in. And sighed in something like relief, or completion, or balance. *I think it was the blood of a god.* Spilled, soiled, drawn up again, cleaned, and returned at last . . .

I don't understand. Was Ista mistaken? Did I miscount my deaths?

The goddess laughed. *Think it through . . .*

Then the vast blue Presence poured out of the world through him like a river thundering over a waterfall. The beauty of a triumphal music he knew he would never quite remember, till he came to Her realm again, cracked his heart. The great rent drew closed. Healed. Sealed.

And, abruptly as that, it all was gone.

❧THE CRACK OF THE STONE PAVEMENT HITTING HIS knees was his first returning sensation. Desperately, he held himself upright, sitting on his heels, so as not to wrench the sword blade around in his flesh. The hilt and a handspan of bright blade hung below his downward-turning gaze, driven at a crooked upward angle into his stomach just below and to the left of his navel. The point seemed to come out somewhere to the right of his spine, and higher. *Now* came the pain. As he drew his first shuddering breath, the weapon bobbed a trifle. The stink of cauterized flesh assailed his nostrils, mixed with a celestial perfume like spring flowers. He trembled with shock and cold. He tried to hold very still.

He had a distressing urge to giggle. That would hurt. More . . .

Not all the scorched-meat smell was from him. Dy Jironal lay before him. Cazaril had seen corpses burned from the outside in— never before from the inside out. The chancellor's hair and clothes smoked a little, but then went out without catching to flame.

Cazaril's attention was arrested by a pebble that lay on the pavement near his knee. It was so *dense*. So *persistent*. The gods could not lift so much as a feather, but he, a mere human, might pick up this ancient unchanging object and place it wherever he wished, even into his pocket. He wondered why he had never appreciated the stubborn fidelity of matter. A dried leaf lay nearby, even more stunning in its complexity. Matter invented so many *forms*, and then went on to generate beauty beyond itself, minds and souls rising up out of it like melody from an instrument . . . matter was an amazement to the gods. Matter remembered itself so very clearly. He could not think why he had failed to notice it before. His own shaking hand was a miracle, as was the fine metal sword in his belly, and the orange trees in the tubs—one was tipped over now, wonderfully fractured and spilling—and the tubs, and the birdsong starting in the morning, and the water—water! Five gods, water!— in the fountain, and the morning light filtering into the sky . . .

"Lord Cazaril?" came a faint voice from his elbow.

He glanced aside to find that dy Cembuer had crept up to him.

"*What was that?*" Dy Cembuer sounded very close to tears.

"Some miracles." Too many in one place at one time. He was overwhelmed with miracles. They filled his eyes in every direction.

Speaking was a mistake, for the vibration stirred the pain in his gut. Though he *could* speak; the sword did not appear to have pierced his lung. He imagined how much it would hurt to cough blood, just now. *Gut wound, then. I will be dead again in three days.* He could smell a faint scent of shit, mixed with the scorched meat and the goddess's perfume. And sobbing . . . no, wait, the deadly fecal smell was not coming from him, yet. The Baocian captain was curled up in a tight ball on his side a little way off, his arms locked around his head, weeping. He did not seem to have any wound. Ah. Yes. He had been the nearest living witness. The goddess must have brushed against him, in Her passage.

Cazaril risked another breath. "What did you see?" he asked dy Cembuer.

"That man—was that dy Jironal?"

Cazaril nodded, a tiny careful nod.

"When he stabbed you, there was a hellish crack, and he burst into blue fire. He is . . . what did . . . did the gods strike him down?"

"Not exactly. It was . . . a little more complicated than that . . ." It seemed strangely quiet in the courtyard. Cazaril risked turning his head. About half of the bravos, and a few servants of Iselle's household, were laid flat on the ground. Some were mumbling rapidly under their breaths; others were crying like the Baocian captain. The rest had vanished.

Cazaril thought he could see now why a man had to lay down his life three times to do this. And here he'd imagined the gods were being arbitrary and difficult for the sake of some arcane punishment. He'd needed the first two deaths just for the *practice*. The first, to learn how to accept death in the body—his flogging on the galley, that had been. He had *not* miscounted—that death had not been for the House of Chalion at the time. But it had become so, with Iselle's marriage to Bergon and its consummation; the joining of two into one, that had shared the curse so horrifyingly between them, had apparently also portioned out this sacrifice. Bergon's secret dowry, eh. Cazaril hoped he might live long enough to tell him, and that the royse would be pleased. His second acceptance, of death of the soul, had been in the lonely company of crows in Fonsa's tower. So that when he came at last to this one, he could offer the goddess a smooth and steady partnering . . . humbling parallels involving the training of mules offered themselves to his mind.

Footsteps sounded. Cazaril glanced up to see dy Tagille, winded and disheveled but with his sword sheathed, running into the courtyard. He dashed up to them and stopped abruptly. "Bastard's hell." He glanced aside at his Ibran comrade. "Are you all right, dy Cembuer?"

"Sons of bitches broke my arm again. *He's* the scary one. What's happening out there?"

"Dy Baocia rallied his men, and has driven the invaders out of the palace. It's all very confused right now, but the rest of them seem to be running through town trying to get to the temple."

"To assail it?" dy Cembuer asked in alarm. He tried to struggle to his feet again.

"No. To surrender to armed men who will not try to tear them limb from limb. It seems every citizen of Taryoon has taken to the streets after them. The women are the worst. Bastard's hell," he repeated, staring at dy Jironal's smoking corpse, "some Chalionese soldier was screaming and babbling that he'd seen dy Jironal struck by lightning from a clear blue sky for the sacrilege of offering battle on the Daughter's Day. And I scarcely believed him."

"I saw it, too," said dy Cembuer. "There was a horrible noise. He didn't even have time to cry out."

Dy Tagille dragged the corpse a little way off and knelt in front of Cazaril, staring fearfully at his skewered stomach and then into his face. "Lord Cazaril, we must try to draw this sword from you. Best we do it at once."

"No . . . wait . . ." Cazaril had once seen a man plugged with a crossbow bolt live for half an hour, until the bolt was drawn out; his blood had gushed forth then, and he'd died. "I want to see Lady Betriz first."

"My lord, you cannot sit there with a sword stuck through you!"

"Well," said Cazaril reasonably, "I surely cannot *move* . . ." Trying to talk made him pant. Not good. He was shivering and very cold. But the throbbing pain was not as devastating as he'd expected, probably because he'd managed to hold so still. As long as he held *very* still, it wasn't much worse than Dondo's clawings.

Other men arrived in the courtyard. Babble and noise and cries from the wounded washed between the walls, and tales repeated over and over in rising voices. Cazaril ignored it all, taken up with his pebble again. He wondered where it had come from, how it had arrived there. What it had been before it was a pebble. A rock? A mountain? Where? For how many years? It filled his mind. And if a pebble could fill his mind, what might a mountain do? The gods held mountains in their minds, and all else besides, all at once. Everything, with the same attention he gave to one thing. He had seen that, through the Lady's eyes. If it had endured for longer than that infinitesimal blink, he thought his soul would have burst. As it was he felt strangely stretched. Had that glimpse been a gift, or just a careless chance?

"Cazaril?"

A trembling voice, the voice he had been waiting for. He looked up. If the pebble was amazing, Betriz's face was astounding. The structure of her nose alone could have held him entranced for hours. He abandoned the pebble at once for this better entertainment. But water welled up, shimmering, in her brown eyes, and her face was drained of color. That wasn't right. Worst of all, her dimples had gone into hiding.

"*There* you are," he said happily. His voice was a muzzy croak. "Kiss me now."

She gulped, knelt, shuffled up to him on her knees, and stretched her neck. Her lips were warm. The perfume of her mouth was nothing at all like a goddess's, but like a human woman's, and very good withal. His lips were cold, and he pressed them to hers as much to borrow her heat and youth as anything. So. He'd been swimming in miracle every day of his life, and hadn't even known it.

He eased his head back. "All right." He did not add, *That's enough*, because it wasn't. "You can draw the sword out now."

Men moved around him, mostly worried-looking strangers. Betriz rubbed her face, undid the frogs of his tunic, and stood and hovered. Someone gripped his shoulders. A page proffered a folded pad to clap to his wound, and someone else held lengths of bandages ready to wrap his torso.

Cazaril squinted in uncertainty. Betriz was here: therefore, Iselle must be, must be . . . "Iselle? Bergon?"

"I'm here, Lord Caz." Iselle's voice came off to his side.

She moved around in front of him, staring at him in extreme dismay. She had shed her heavily embroidered outer robes in her flight, and still seemed a trifle breathless. She had also shed the black cloak of the curse . . . had she not? Yes, he decided. His inner vision was darkening, but he did not mistake this.

"Bergon is with my uncle," she continued, "helping to clear dy Jironal's remaining men from the area." Her voice was firm in its disregard of the tears running down her face.

"The black shadow is lifted," he told her, "from you and Bergon. From everyone."

"*How?*"

"I'll tell you all about it, if I live."

"Cazaril!"

He grinned briefly at the familiar, exasperated cadences around his name.

"You live, then!" Her voice wavered. "I—I command you!"

Dy Tagille knelt in front of Cazaril.

Cazaril gave him a short nod. "Draw it."

"Very straight and smoothly, Lord dy Tagille," Iselle instructed tensely, "so as not to cut him any worse."

"Aye, my lady." Dy Tagille licked his lips in apprehension and grasped the sword's hilt.

"Carefully," gasped Cazaril, "but not *quite* so slowly, *please* . . ."

The blade left him; a warm gush of liquid spurted from the mouth of his wound after it. Cazaril had hoped to pass out, but he only swayed as pads were clapped to him and held hard fore and aft. He stared down expecting to see his lap awash in blood, but no flood of red met his sight; it was a clear liquid, merely tinged with pink. *Sword must have lanced my tumor.* Which was *not*, it appeared, and the Bastard fry Rojeras for inflicting that nightmare upon him, stuffed with some grotesque demon fetus after all. He tried not to think, *At least not anymore.* A murmur of astonishment passed among the ring of watchers as the scent of celestial flowers from this exudation filled the air.

He let himself fall, boneless and unresisting, into his eager helpers' arms. He did manage to surreptitiously scoop up his pebble before the willing hands bore him off up the stairs to his bedchamber. They were excited and frightened, but he was growing delightfully relaxed. It seemed he was to be fussed over, lovely. When Betriz held his hand, as he was eased into his bed, he gripped hers and did not let go.

28

A *tapping and low voices at his* chamber door drew Cazaril from his doze. The room was dim. A single candle flame pushing back a deep dark told him night was fallen. He heard the physician, who had been sitting with him, murmuring, "He is sleeping, Roy—Royina . . ."

"No, I'm not," Cazaril called eagerly. "Come in." He tensed his arms to push himself upright, then thought better of it. He added, "Make more light. A deal more light. I want to see you."

A great party of persons shuffled into his chamber, attempting to make themselves quiet and gentle, like a parade gone suddenly shy. Iselle and Bergon, with Betriz and Palli attendant upon them; the archdivine of Taryoon, with the little judge of the Father staring around in his wake. They quite filled the room. Cazaril smiled up amiably at them from his horizontal paradise of clean linens and stillness as candle was held to candle and the flames multiplied.

Bergon looked down at him in apprehension and whispered hoarsely to the physician, "How is he?"

"He passed a deal of blood in his water earlier, but less tonight. He has no fever yet. I daren't let him have more than a few sips of tea, till we know how his gut wound progresses. I don't know how much pain he bears."

Cazaril decided he preferred to speak for himself. "I hurt, no doubt of that." He made another feeble attempt to roll up, and winced. "I would sit up a little. I cannot talk looking up all your noses like this." Palli and Bergon rushed to help gently raise him, plumping pillows behind him.

"Thank you," said Iselle to the physician, who bowed and, taking the royal hint, stepped out of the way.

Cazaril eased back with a sigh, and said, "What has transpired? Is Taryoon under attack? And don't talk in those funereal whispers, either."

Iselle smiled from the foot of his bed. "Much has happened," she told him, her voice reverting to its normal firm timbre. "Dy Jironal had men advancing as fast as they could march from both his son-in-law in Thistan and from Valenda, to follow up in support of his spies and abductors got in at the festival. Late last night the column coming down the road from Valenda met the delegation carrying our letter to Orico in Cardegoss, and captured them."

"Alive, yes?" said Cazaril in alarm.

"There was some scuffle, but none killed, thank the gods. Much debate followed in their camp."

Well, he *had* sent the most sensible, persuasive men of weight and worth that Taryoon could muster for that embassy.

"Later in the afternoon, we sent out parties of parley. We included some of dy Jironal's men who had witnessed the fight in the courtyard, and . . . and whatever that miraculous blue fire was that killed him, to explain and to testify. They cried and gibbered a lot, but they were very convincing. Cazaril, what *really*—oh, and they say Orico is dead."

Cazaril sighed. *I knew that.* "When?"

The archdivine of Taryoon replied, "There's some confusion about that. A Temple courier rode through to us this afternoon with the news. She bore me a letter from Archdivine Mendenal in Cardegoss saying it was the night after the royesse's—the royina's—wedding. But dy Jironal's men all say he told them Orico had died the night before it, and so he was now rightful regent of Chalion. I suppose he was lying. I'm not sure it matters, now."

But it might have mattered, had events taken a different path . . . Cazaril frowned in curious speculation.

"In any case," put in Bergon, "between the news of dy Jironal's startling taking-off, and the failure and capture of their infiltrators, *and* the realization that they marched not against a rebellious

Heiress, but their rightful royina, the columns have broken up. The men are returning to their homes. I'm just back from overseeing that." Indeed, he was mud-splashed, bright-eyed with the exuberance of success—and relief.

"Do you think the truce will hold?" asked Cazaril. "Dy Jironal held the strings of a very considerable network of power and relations, all of whom still have their interests at risk."

Palli grunted, and shook his head. "They have not the backing of forces from the Order of the Son, now it's headless—worse, they've the near certainty that control of the order will pass out of their faction now. I think the Jironal clan will learn caution."

"The provincar of Thistan has already sent us a letter of submission," put in Iselle, "just arrived. It looks to have been hastily penned. We plan to wait one more day to be sure the roads are clear, and to give thanks to the gods in the temple of Taryoon. Then Bergon and I will ride for Cardegoss with a contingent of my uncle's cavalry, for Orico's funeral and my coronation." Her mouth turned down. "I fear we will have to leave you here for a time, Lord Caz."

He glanced at Betriz, watching him, her eyes dark with concern. Where Iselle rode, Betriz, her first courtier, must needs follow.

Iselle went on, "Don't speak if it pains you too much, but Cazaril . . . what *happened* in the courtyard? Did the Daughter *truly* strike dy Jironal dead with a bolt of lightning?"

"His body looked it, I must say," said Bergon. "All *cooked*. I've never seen anything like it."

"That is a good story," said Cazaril slowly, "and will do for most men. You here should know the truth, but . . . I think this truth should go no further, eh?"

Iselle quietly bade the physician excuse himself. She glanced curiously at the little judge. "And this gentleman, Cazaril?"

"The Honorable Paginine is . . . is in the way of being a colleague of mine. He should stay, and the archdivine as well."

Cazaril found his audience ranged around his bed, staring at him rather breathlessly. Neither Paginine nor the archdivine, nor Palli, knew the preamble about Dondo and the death demon, Cazaril realized, and so he found himself compelled to revert to that beginning, though in as few words as he could make come out sensibly. At least he hoped it sounded coherent, and not like the ravings of a madman.

"Archdivine Mendenal in Cardegoss knows all this tale," he assured the shocked-looking pair from Taryoon. Palli's mouth was twisted in something between astonishment and indignation; Cazaril evaded his eye a trifle guiltily. "But when dy Jironal bade his men hold me unarmed, and ran me through—when he murdered me, the death demon bore us all off in an unbalanced confusion of killers and victims. That is, the demon bore the pair of them, but somehow my soul was attached, and followed . . . what I saw then . . . the goddess . . ." his voice faltered. "I don't know how to open my mouth and push out the universe in words. It won't fit. If I had all the words in all the languages in the world that ever were or will be, and spoke till the end of time, it still couldn't . . ." He was shivering, suddenly, his eyes blurred with tears.

"But you weren't really dead, were you?" said Palli uneasily.

"Oh, yes. Just for a little while . . . for an odd angle of little that came out, um, very large. If I had not died in truth, I could not have ripped open the wall between the worlds, and the goddess could not have reached in to take back the curse. Which was a drop of the Father's blood, as nearly as I could tell, though how the Golden General came by such a gift I know not. That's a metaphor, by the way. I'm sorry. I have not . . . I have not the words for what I saw. Talking about it is like trying to weave a box of shadows in which to carry water." *And our souls are parched.* "The Lady of Spring let me look through Her eyes, and though my second sight is taken back—I think—my eyes do not seem to work quite the same as they did . . ."

The archdivine signed himself. Paginine cleared his throat, and said diffidently, "Indeed, my lord, you do not make that great roaring light about you anymore."

"Do I not? Oh, good." Cazaril added eagerly, "But the black cloak about Iselle and Bergon, it is gone as well, yes?"

"Yes, my lord. Royse, Royina, if it please you. The shadow seems to be lifted altogether."

"So all is well. Gods, demons, ghosts, the whole company, all gone. There's nothing odd left about me now," said Cazaril happily.

Paginine screwed up his face in an expression that was not quite appalled, not quite a laugh. "I would not go so far as to say that, my lord," he murmured.

The archdivine nudged Paginine, and whispered, "But he speaks the truth, yes? Wild as it seems . . ."

"Oh, yes, Your Reverence. I have no doubt of that." The bland stare he traded Cazaril bore rather more understanding than that of the archdivine's, who was looking astonished and overawed.

"Tomorrow," Iselle announced, "Bergon and I shall make a thanksgiving procession to the temple, walking barefoot to sign our gratitude to the gods."

Cazaril said in muzzy worry, "Oh. Oh, do be careful, then. Don't step on any broken glass or old nails, now."

"We shall watch out for each other's steps the whole way," Bergon promised him.

Cazaril added aside to Betriz, his hand creeping across the coverlet to touch hers, "You know, I am not haunted anymore. Quite a load off my mind, in more ways than one. Very liberating to a man, that sort of thing . . ." His voice was dropping in volume, raspy with fatigue. Her hand turned under his, and gave a secret squeeze.

"We should withdraw and let you rest," said Iselle, frowning in renewed worry. "Is there anything you desire, Cazaril? Anything at all?"

About to reply *No, nothing*, he said instead, "Oh. Yes. I want music."

"Music?"

"Perhaps some very quiet music," Betriz ventured. "To lull him to sleep."

Bergon smiled. "If it please you, then, see to it, Lady Betriz." The mob withdrew, tiptoeing loudly. The physician returned. He let Cazaril drink tea, in trade for making more blood-tinted piss for him to examine suspiciously by candlelight and growl at in an unsettling fashion.

At length, Betriz came back with a nervous-looking young lutenist who appeared to have been wakened out of a sound sleep for this command performance. But he worked his fingers, tuned up, and played seven short pieces. None of them was the right one; none evoked the Lady and Her soul-flowers, till he played an eighth, an interlaced counterpoint of surpassing sweetness. That one had a faint echo of heaven in it. Cazaril had him play it through twice more, and cried a little, upon which Betriz insisted that he was too tired and must sleep now, and bore the young man off again.

And Cazaril still hadn't had a chance to tell her about her nose. When he tried to explain this miracle to the physician, the man responded by giving him a large spoonful of syrup of poppies, after which they ceased to alarm each other for the rest of the night.

❦IN THREE DAYS' TIME HIS WOUNDS STOPPED LEAKING scented fluid, closing cleanly, and the physician permitted Cazaril thin gruel for breakfast. This revived him enough to insist on being allowed out to sit in the spring sun of the courtyard. The expedition seemed to require an inordinate number of servants and helpers, but at last he was guided carefully down the stairs and into a chair lined with wool-padded and feather-stuffed cushions, with his feet propped up on another cushioned chair. He shooed away his helpers and gave himself over to a most delicious idleness. The fountain burbled soothingly. The trees in the tubs unfurled more fragrant flowers. A pair of little orange-and-black birds stitched the air, bringing dry grass and twigs to build a nest tucked up in the carvings on one of the gallery's supporting posts. An ambitious litter of paper and pens lay forgotten on the small table at Cazaril's elbow as he watched them flit back and forth.

Dy Baocia's palace was very quiet, with its royal guests and its lord and lady all gone to Cardegoss. Cazaril therefore smiled with lazy delight when the wrought-iron gate under the end archway swung aside to admit Palli. The march had been assigned by his new royina the dull task of keeping watch over her convalescent secretary while everyone else went off to the grand events in the capital, which seemed to Cazaril rather an unfair reward for Palli's valiant service. Palli had attended upon him so faithfully, Cazaril felt quite guilty for wishing Iselle might have spared Lady Betriz instead.

Palli, grinning, gave him a mock salute and seated himself on the fountain's edge. "Well, Castillar! You look better. Very vertical indeed. But what's this"—he gestured to the table—"work? Before they left yesterday your ladies charged me to enforce a very long list of things you were not to do, most of which you will be glad to know I have forgotten, but I'm sure work was high on it."

"No such thing," said Cazaril. "I was going to attempt some poetry after the manner of Behar, but then there were these birds . . . there goes one now." He paused to mark the orange-and-black flash. "People compliment birds for being great builders, but really, these two seem terribly clumsy. Perhaps they are young birds, and this is their first try. Persistent, though. Although I suppose if I was to attempt to build a hut using only my mouth, I would do no better. I should write a poem in praise of birds. If matter that gets up and walks about, like you, is miraculous, how much more marvelous is matter that gets up and flies!"

Palli's mouth quirked in bemusement. "Is this poetry or fever, Caz?"

"Oh, it is a great infection of poetry, a contagion of hymns. The gods delight in poets, you know. Songs and poetry, being of the same stuff as souls, can cross into their world almost unimpeded. Stone carvers, now . . . even the gods are in awe of stone carvers." He squinted in the sun and grinned back at Palli.

"Nevertheless," murmured Palli dryly, "one feels that your quatrain yesterday morning to Lady Betriz's nose was a tactical mistake."

"I was *not* making fun of her!" Cazaril protested indignantly. "Was she still angry at me when she left?"

"No, no, she wasn't angry! She was persuaded it was fever, and was very worried withal. If I were you, I'd claim it for fever."

"I could not write a poem to all of her just yet. I tried. Too overwhelming."

"Well, if you must scribble paeans to her body parts, pick lips. Lips are more romantic than noses."

"Why?" asked Cazaril. "Isn't every part of her an amazement?"

"Yes, but we kiss lips. We don't kiss noses. Normally. Men write poems to the objects of our desire in order to lure them closer."

"How practical. In that case, you'd think men would write more poems to ladies' private parts."

"The ladies would hit us. Lips are a safe compromise, being as it were a stand-in or stepping-stone to the greater mysteries."

"Hah. Anyway, I desire all of her. Nose and lips and feet and all the parts between, and her soul, without which her mere body would be all still and cold and claylike, and start to rot, and be not an object of desire at *all*."

"Agh!" Palli ran his hand through his hair. "My friend, you do not understand romance."

"I promise you, I do not understand anything anymore. I am gloriously bewildered." He lay back in his cushions and laughed softly.

Palli snorted, and bent forward to pick up the paper from the top of the pile, the only one so far with writing on it. He glanced down it, and his brows rose. "What's this? This isn't about ladies' noses." His face sobered; his gaze traveled back to the top of the page, and down once more. "In fact, I'm not just sure what it's about. Although it makes the hairs stand up on the backs of my arms . . ."

"Oh, that. It's nothing, I fear. I was trying—but it wasn't"—Cazaril's hands waved helplessly, and came back to touch his brow—"it wasn't what I saw." He added in explanation, "I thought in poetry the words might bear more freight, exist on both sides of the wall between the worlds, as people do. So far I'm just creating waste paper, fit only for lighting a fire."

"Hm," said Palli. Unobtrusively, he folded up the paper and tucked it inside his vest-cloak.

"I'll try again," sighed Cazaril. "Maybe I can get it right some-day. I must write some hymns to matter, too. Birds. Stones. That would please the Lady, I think."

Palli blinked. "To lure Her closer?"

"Might."

"Dangerous stuff, this poetry. I think I'll stick to action, myself."

Cazaril grinned at him. "Watch out, my lord Dedicat. Action can be prayer, too."

Whispers and muffled giggles sounded from the end of the gallery. Cazaril looked up to see some servant women and boys crouched behind the carved railings, peeking through at him. Palli followed his glance. One girl popped up boldly and waved at them. Amiably, Cazaril waved back. The giggles rose to a crescendo, and the women scurried off. Palli scratched his ear and regarded Cazaril with wry inquiry.

Cazaril explained, "People have been sneaking in all morning to see the spot where poor dy Jironal was struck down. If he's not careful, Lord dy Baocia will lose his nice new courtyard to a shrine."

Palli cleared his throat. "Actually, Caz, they're sneaking in to peek at *you*. A couple of dy Baocia's servants are charging admission to conduct the curious in and out of the palace. I was of two minds whether to quash the enterprise, but if they're bothering you, I will . . ." He shifted, as if to rise.

"Oh. Oh, no, don't trouble them. I have made a great deal of extra work for the palace servants. Let them profit a bit."

Palli snorted, but shrugged acquiescence. "And you still have no fever?"

"I wasn't sure at first, but no. That physician finally let me eat, although not enough. I am healing, I think."

"That's a miracle in itself, worth a vaida to see."

"Yes. I'm not quite sure if putting me back into the world this way was a parting gift of the Lady, or just a chance benefit of Her need to have someone on this side to hold open the gate for Her. Ordol was right about the gods being parsimonious. Well, it's all right either way. We shall surely meet again someday." He leaned back, staring into the sky, the Lady's own blue. His lips curled up, unwilled.

"You were the soberest fellow I ever met, and now you grin all the time. Caz, are you sure She got your soul back in right way round?"

Cazaril laughed out loud. "Maybe not! You know how it is when you travel. You pack all your things in your saddlebags, and by the journey's end, they seem to have doubled in volume and are hanging out every which way, even though you'd swear you added nothing . . ." He patted his thigh. "Perhaps I am just not packed into this battered old case as neatly as I used to be."

Palli shook his head in wonder. "And so now you leak poetry. Huh."

👒TEN MORE DAYS OF HEALING LEFT CAZARIL NOT AT all bored with resting, if only his ease were not so empty of the people he desired. At last his longing for them overcame his revulsion at the prospect of getting on a horse again, and he set Palli to arranging their journey. Palli's protests at this premature exercise were perfunctory, easily overborne, as he was no less anxious than Cazaril to see how events in Cardegoss went on.

Cazaril and his escort, including the ever-faithful Ferda and

Foix, traveled up the road in the fine weather in gentle, easy stages, a world apart from winter's desperate ride. Each evening Cazaril was helped from his horse swearing that tomorrow they would go more slowly, and each morning he found himself even more eager to push on. At length the distant Zangre again rose before his eyes. Against the backdrop of puffy white clouds, blue sky, and green fields, it seemed a rich ornament to the landscape.

A few miles out of Cardegoss they encountered another procession on the road. Men in the livery of the provincar of Labran escorted three carts and a trailing tail of mules and servants. Two of the carts were piled with baggage. The third cart's canvas top, rolled up to open the sides to the spring scenery, shaded several ladies.

The ladies' cart pulled to the side of the road and a serving-woman leaned out to call to one of the outriders. The Labran sergeant bent his head to her, rode up in turn to Palli and Cazaril, and saluted.

"If it please you, sirs, if one of you is the Castillar dy Cazaril, my lady the Dowager Royina Sara bid—begs," he corrected himself, "you to wait upon her."

The present provincar of Labran, Cazaril was reminded, was Royina Sara's nephew. He gathered that he was witnessing her removal—or retreat—to her family estates there. He returned the salute. "I am entirely at the royina's service."

Foix helped Cazaril from his horse. Steps were let down from the back of the cart, and the ladies and maidservants descended to stroll together about the fallow field nearby and examine the spring wildflowers. Sara remained seated in the shadow of the canvas. "Please you, Castillar," she called softly, "I am glad for this chance crossing. Can you bide with me a moment?"

"I am honored, lady." He ducked his head and climbed into the cart, seating himself on the padded bench opposite hers. The baggage mules plodded on past them. A peaceful, distant murmur enveloped the scene, of birdsong, low voices, the bridle-jingle and champing of the horses let to graze by the roadside, and the occasional trill of laugher from the maidservants.

Sara was dressed now in a simply cut gown and vest-cloak of lavender and black, mourning for poor doomed Orico, presumably.

"My apologies," said Cazaril, with an acknowledging nod at her garb, "for not attending the roya's funeral. I was not yet recovered enough to travel."

She waved this away. "From what Iselle and Bergon and Lady Betriz have told me, it is a miracle you survived your wounds."

"Yes, well . . . precisely."

She gave him an oddly sympathetic look.

"Orico was taken up safely, then?" Cazaril asked.

"Yes, by the Bastard. As gods-rejected in death as he was in life. It stirred a bit of unpleasant speculation about his parentage, alas."

"Not so, lady. He was surely Ias's child. I think the Bastard has been special guardian of his House since Fonsa's reign. And so this time the god picked first, not last."

She shrugged her thin shoulders. "A sorry guardianship, if so. On the day before he died, Orico said to me that he wished he'd been born the son of a woodcutter, and not the son of the roya of Chalion. Of all the epitaphs on his death, his own seems the most apposite to me." Her voice grew a shade more sour. "Martou dy Jironal, they say, was taken up by the Father."

"So I had heard. They sent his body to his daughter in Thistan to take charge of. Well, he, too, had his part to play, and little enough joy it brought him in the end." He offered after a moment, "I can personally guarantee you, though, his brother Dondo was carried to the Bastard's hell."

A small, grim smile curved her lips. "Perchance he may learn better manners there."

There seemed nothing to add to this, as epitaphs went.

Cazaril was reminded of a curiosity, and diffidently cleared his throat. "The day before Orico died. And which day would that have been, my lady?"

Her eyes flew to his, and her dark brows went up. After a moment she said, "Why, the day after Iselle's wedding, of course."

"Not the day before? Martou dy Jironal seemed strangely misinformed, then. Not to mention premature in certain of his actions. And . . . it seems to me very like a certain cursed luck, to die just a day before one's rescue."

"I, and Orico's physician, and Archdivine Mendenal, who all attended on him together, will all swear that Orico yet lived to speak to us that afternoon and evening, and did not breathe his sad last until early the next morning." She met his gaze very directly indeed, her lips still set in that same grim curve. "And so Iselle's marriage to Royse Bergon is unassailably valid."

And thus a legal quibble was rendered unavailable to disaffected lords as a pretext for defiance. Cazaril imagined it, her daylong secret deathwatch beside the gelid bloated corpse of her husband. What had she thought about, what had she reflected upon, as the hours crept by in that sealed chamber? And yet she had made of that horror a pragmatic gift for Iselle and Bergon, for the House of Chalion that she was departing. He pictured her suddenly as a tidy housewife, sweeping out her old familiar rooms for the last time, and leaving a vase of flowers on the hearth for the new owners.

"I . . . think I see."

"I think you do. You always had very seeing eyes, Castillar." She added after a moment, "And a discreet tongue."

"A condition of my service, Royina."

"You have served the House of Chalion well. Better, perhaps, than it deserved."

"But not half so well as it needed."

She sighed agreement.

He made polite inquiry after her plans; she was indeed returning to her home province, to take residence at a country estate happily to be entirely under her own direction. She seemed not just resigned but eager to escape Cardegoss and leave it to her successors. Cazaril, rising, wished her well, and a safe journey, with all his heart. He kissed her hands; she in turn kissed his and, briefly, touched her fingertips to his forehead as he bent to her.

He watched her train of carts rumble away, wincing in sympathy as they jounced over the ruts. The roads of Chalion could use improvement, Cazaril decided, and he had ridden over enough of them to know. He'd seen roads in the Archipelago made wide and smooth for all weathers—perhaps Iselle and Bergon needed to import some Roknari masons. Better roads, with fewer bandits on them, would do a world of good for Chalion. Chalion-Ibra, he corrected this thought, and smiled as Foix gave him a leg up onto his horse.

29

Palli had sent Ferda galloping ahead while Cazaril lingered by the roadside to speak with Royina Sara. As a result, the Zangre's castle warder and an array of servants were waiting to greet the party from Taryoon when they rode at last into the castle courtyard. The castle warder bowed to Cazaril as the grooms helped him down from his horse. Cazaril stretched, carefully, and asked in an eager voice, "Are Royina Iselle and Royse Bergon within?"

"No, my lord. They are just this hour gone to the temple, for the ceremonies of investiture for Lord dy Yarrin and Royse Bergon."

The new royina had, as anticipated, selected dy Yarrin for the new holy general of the Daughter's Order. The appointment of Bergon to the Son's generalship was, in Cazaril's view, a brilliant stroke to recover direct control of that important military arm for the royacy, and remove it as a bone of contention among the high lords of Chalion. It had been Iselle's own idea, too, when they had discussed the matter before she and Bergon had left Taryoon. Cazaril had pointed out that while she could not in honor fail to reward dy Yarrin's loyalty with the appointment he'd so ardently desired, dy Yarrin was not a young man; in time, the generalship of the Daughter, too, must revert to the royacy.

"Ah!" cried Palli. "Today, is it? Is the ceremony still going forward, then?"

"I believe so, March."

"If I hurry, perhaps I can see some of it. Cazaril, may I leave you to the good care of this gentleman? My lord warder, see that he takes his rest. He is not nearly so recovered from his late wounds as he will try to make you believe."

Palli reined his horse around and gave Cazaril a cheery salute. "I shall return with all the tale for you when it's done." Followed by his little company, he trotted back out the gate.

Grooms and servants whisked away horses and baggage. Cazaril refused, in what he hoped was a dignified manner, the support of the castle warder's proffered arm, at least until they should have reached the stairs. The castle warder called him back as he started toward the main block.

"Your room has been moved by order of the royina to Ias's Tower," the castle warder explained, "that you may be near her and the royse."

"Oh." That had a pleasing sound to it. Agreeably, Cazaril followed the man up to the third floor, where Royse Bergon and his Ibran courtiers had taken their new residence, although Bergon had evidently chosen another official bedchamber for himself than the one Orico had lately died in. Not, Cazaril was given to understand, that the royse slept there. Iselle had just moved into the old royina's suite, above. The castle warder showed Cazaril to the room near Bergon's that was to be his. Someone had moved his trunk and few possessions over from his old chamber, and entirely new clothing for tonight's banquet was already laid out waiting. Cazaril let the servants bring him wash water, but then shooed them away and lay down obediently to rest.

This lasted about ten minutes. He rose again and prowled up one flight to examine his new office arrangements. A maidservant, recognizing him, curtsied him past. He poked his nose into the chamber Sara had kept for her secretary. As he expected, it was now filled with his records, books, and ledgers from the royesse's former household, with a great many more added. Unexpectedly, a neat dark-haired fellow, who looked to be about thirty years old, manned his broad desk. He wore the gray robe and carmine shoulder braid of a divine of the Father, and was scratching figures into one of Cazaril's own account books. Opened correspondence lay fanned out at his left hand, and a larger stack of finished letters rose at his right.

He glanced up at Cazaril in polite but cool inquiry. "May I help you, sir?"

"I—excuse me, I do not believe we have met. Who are you?"

"I am Learned Bonneret, Royina Iselle's private secretary."

Cazaril's mouth opened, and shut. *But I'm Royina Iselle's private secretary!* "A temporary appointment, is it?"

Bonneret's eyebrows went up. "Well, I trust it shall be permanent."

"How came you by the post?"

"Archdivine Mendenal was kind enough to recommend me to the royina."

"Lately?"

"Excuse me?"

"You are lately appointed?"

"These two weeks past, sir." Bonneret frowned in faint annoyance. "Ah—you have the advantage of me, I believe?"

Quite the reverse. "The royina . . . didn't tell me," said Cazaril. Was he discarded, shunted from his position of trust? Granted, the avalanche of tasks attendant upon Iselle's ascension to the royacy was hardly going to halt while Cazaril slowly recovered; someone had to attend to them. And, Cazaril noted by the outgoing inscriptions, Bonneret had beautiful handwriting. The divine was frowning more deeply at him. He supplied, "My name is Cazaril."

Bonneret's frown evaporated, to be replaced with an even more alarming awed smile; he dropped his quill, spattering ink, and scrambled abruptly to his feet. "My lord dy Cazaril! I am honored!" He bowed low. "What *may* I do to help you, my lord?" he repeated, in a very different tone.

This eager courtesy daunted Cazaril far more than Bonneret's former superciliousness. He mumbled some incoherent excuse for his intrusion, pleaded weariness from the road, and fled back downstairs.

He filled a little time inventorying his clothing and too-few books and arranging them in his new chamber. Amazingly, nothing seemed to be missing from his possessions. He wandered to his narrow window, which looked down over the town. He swung his casement wide and craned his neck out, but no sacred crows flew in to visit him. With the curse broken, the menagerie gone, did they still roost in Fonsa's Tower? He studied the temple domes, and made plans to seek out Umegat at his first opportunity. Then he sat in bewilderment.

He was shaken, and knew it partly for an effect of fatigue. His energy was still fragile, spasmodic. His healing gut wound ached from the morning's riding, although not as much as when Dondo had used to claw him from the inside. He was gloriously unoccupied, a fact that alone had been enough to keep him ecstatically happy for days. It didn't seem to be working this afternoon, though. All his urgent push to arrive here made this quiet rest that everybody thought he ought to be having feel rather a letdown.

His mood darkened. Maybe there was no use for him in this new Chalion-Ibra. Iselle would need more learned, smoother men now to help manage her vastly enlarged affairs than a battered and, well, strange ex-soldier with a weakness for poetry. Worse—to be culled from Iselle's service was to be exiled from Betriz's daily presence. No one would light his reading candles at dusk, or make him wear warm unfashionable hats, or notice if he fell ill and bring him frightening physicians, or pray for his safety when he was far from home. . . .

He heard the clatter and noise of what he presumed was Iselle and Bergon's party returning from the ceremonies at the temple, but even at an angle his window did not give a view onto the courtyard. He ought to rush out to greet them. *No. I'm resting.* That sounded mulish and petulant even to his own inward ear. *Don't be a fool.* But a dreary fatigue anchored him in his chair.

Before he could overcome his wash of melancholy, Bergon himself bustled into his chamber, and then it became impossible to stay down-at-the-mouth. The royse was still wearing the brown, orange, and yellow robes of the holy general of the Son's Order, with its broad sword belt ornamented with the symbols of autumn, all looking a lot better on him than they ever had on old gray dy Jironal. If Bergon was not a joy to the god, there was no pleasing Him at all. Cazaril rose, and Bergon embraced him, inquired after his trip from Taryoon and his healing, barely waited for the answer, tried to tell him in turn of eight things at once, then burst out laughing at himself.

"There will be time for all this shortly. Right now I am on a mission from my wife the royina of Chalion. But tell me first and privately, Lord Caz—do you love the Lady Betriz?"

Cazaril blinked. "I . . . she . . . very fond, Royse."

"Good. I mean, I was sure of it, but Iselle insisted I ask first. Now, and very important—are you willing to be shaved?"

"I—what?" Cazaril's hand went to his beard. It was not at all as scraggly as it had started out, it had filled in nicely, he thought, and besides, he kept it neatly trimmed. "Is there some reason you ask me this? Not that it matters greatly, beards grow back, I suppose . . ."

"But you're not madly attached to it or anything, right?"

"Not madly, no. My hand was shaky for a time after the galleys, and I did not care to carve myself bloody, but I could not afford a barber. Then I just became used to it."

"Good." Bergon returned to the doorway, and thrust his head through to the corridor. "All right, come in."

A barber and a servant holding a can of hot water trooped in at the royse's command. The barber made Cazaril sit, and whipped his cloth around him. Cazaril found himself soaped up before he could make remark. The servant held the basin beneath his chin as the barber, humming under his breath, went to work with his steel. Cazaril stared down cross-eyed over his nose as blobs of soapy gray and black hair splatted into the tin basin. The barber made unsettling little chirping noises, but at last smiled in satisfaction and grandly gestured the basin away. "There, my lord!" Some work with a hot towel and a cold lavender-scented tincture that stung completed his artistic effort. The royse dropped a coin into the barber's hand that made him bow low and, murmuring compliments, retreat backwards through the door again.

Feminine giggles sounded from the hallway. A voice, not quite low enough, whispered, "See, Iselle! He does *too* have a chin. Told you."

"Yes, you were right. Quite a nice one."

Iselle stalked in with her back straight, trying to be very royal in her elaborate gown from the investiture, but couldn't keep her gravity; she looked at Cazaril and burst into laughter. At her shoulder Betriz, almost as finely dressed, was all dimples and bright brown eyes and a complex hairstyle that seemed to involve a lot of black ringlets framing her face, bouncing in a fascinating manner as she moved. Iselle's hand went to her lips. "Five gods, Cazaril! Once you're fetched out from behind that gray hedge, you're not so old after all!"

"Not old *at* all," corrected Betriz sturdily.

He had risen at the royesse's entry, and swept them a courtly bow. His hand, unwilled, went to touch his unaccustomedly naked and cool chin. No one had offered him a mirror by which to examine the cause of all this female hilarity.

"All ready," reported Bergon mysteriously.

Iselle, smiling, took Betriz's hand. Bergon grasped Cazaril's. Iselle struck a pose and announced, in a voice suited to a throne room, "My best-beloved and most loyal lady Betriz dy Ferrej has begged a boon of me, which I grant with all the gladness of my heart. And as you have no father now, Lord Cazaril, Bergon and I shall take his place as your liege lords. She has asked for your hand. As it pleases Us greatly that Our two most beloved servants should also love each other, be you betrothed with Our goodwill."

Bergon turned up his hand with Cazaril's in it; Betriz's descended upon it, capped by Iselle's. The royse and royina pressed their hands together, and stood back, both grinning.

"But, but, but," stammered Cazaril. "But this is very wrong, Iselle—Bergon—to sacrifice this maiden to reward my gray hairs is a repugnant thing!" He did not let go of Betriz's hand.

"We just got rid of your gray hairs," pointed out Iselle. She looked him over judiciously. "It's a vast improvement, I have to agree."

Bergon observed, "And I must say, she doesn't look very repulsed."

Betriz's dimples were as deep as ever Cazaril had seen them, and her merry eyes gleamed up at him through her demurely sweeping lashes.

"But . . . but . . ."

"And anyway," Iselle continued briskly, "I'm not sacrificing her to you as a reward for your loyalty. I'm bestowing you on her as a reward for *her* loyalty. So there."

"Oh. Oh, well, that's better, then . . ." Cazaril squinted, trying to reorient his spinning mind. "But . . . surely there are greater lords . . . richer . . . younger, handsomer . . . more worthy . . ."

"Yes, well, she didn't ask for them. She asked for you. No accounting for taste, eh?" said Bergon, eyes alight.

"And I must quibble with at least part of your estimate, Cazaril," Betriz said breathlessly. "There *are* no more worthy lords than you in Chalion." Her grip, in his, tightened.

"Wait," said Cazaril, feeling he was sliding down a slope of snow, tractionless. Soft, warm snow. "I have no lands, no money. How can I support a wife?"

"I plan to make the chancellorship a salaried position," said Iselle.

"As the Fox has done in Ibra? Very wise, Royina, to have your principal servants' principal loyalties be to the royacy, and not divided between crown and clan as dy Jironal's was. Who shall you appoint to replace him? I have a few ideas—"

"Cazaril!" Her fond exasperation made familiar cadence with his name. "Of *course* it's you, who did you *think* I should appoint? Surely that went without saying! The duty must be yours."

Cazaril sat down heavily in his late barber chair, still not releasing his clutch on Betriz's hand. "Right now?" he said faintly.

Her chin came up. "No, no, of course not! Tonight we feast. Tomorrow will do."

"If you're feeling up to it by then," Bergon put in hastily.

"It's a vast task." Wish for bread, and be handed a banquet . . . between those who sought to overprotect him and those who sacrificed his comfort mercilessly to their aims without a second thought, Cazaril decided he rather preferred the latter. *Chancellor dy Cazaril. My lord Chancellor.* His lips moved, as he shaped the syllables, and crooked up.

"We shall do these announcements all over again publicly tonight after dinner," said Iselle, "so dress yourself suitably, Cazaril. Bergon and I shall present the chain of office to you then, before the court. Betriz, attend upon me"—her lips curved—"in a little while." She tucked her hand through Bergon's arm and drew the royse out after her. The door swung shut.

Cazaril snaked his arm around Betriz's waist and pulled her, ruthlessly and not at all shyly, down upon his lap. She squeaked in surprise.

"Lips, eh?" he murmured, and fastened his to hers.

Pausing for breath some time later, she pulled her head back and happily rubbed her chin, then his. "And now your kisses do not make me itch!"

❧IT WAS LATE THE FOLLOWING MORNING BEFORE Cazaril was at last able to seek out Umegat at the Bastard's house.

A respectful acolyte ushered him to a pair of rooms on the third floor; the tongueless groom, Daris, answered the knock and bowed Cazaril inside. Cazaril was not surprised to find him wearing the garb of a lay dedicat of the order, tidy and white. Daris rubbed his chin and gestured at Cazaril's bare face, uttering some smiling remark that Cazaril was just as glad he could not make out. The thumbless man beckoned him through the chamber, furnished up as a sitting room, and out to a little wooden balcony, festooned with twining vines and rose geraniums in pots, overlooking the Temple Square.

Umegat, also dressed in clean white, sat at a tiny table in the cool shade, and Cazaril was thrilled to see paper and quill and ink before him. Daris hastily brought a chair, that Cazaril might sit before Umegat could try to rise. Daris mouthed an inviting hum; Umegat interpreted an offer of hospitality, and Cazaril agreed to tea, which Daris bustled away to fetch.

"What's this?" Cazaril waved eagerly at the papers. "Have you your writing back?"

Umegat grimaced. "So far, I seem to be back to age five. Would that some of the rest of me was so rejuvenated." He tilted the page to show a labored exercise of crudely drawn letters. "I keep putting them back in my mind, and they keep falling out again. My hand has lost its cleverness for the quill—and yet I can still play the lute nearly as badly as ever! The physician insists that I am improving, and I suppose it is so, for I could not do so little as this a month ago. The words scuttle about on the page like crabs, but every so often I catch one." He glanced up, and shrugged away his struggles. "But you! Great doings in Taryoon, were they not? Mendenal says you had a sword stuck through you."

"Punctured front to back," admitted Cazaril. "But it carved out Lord Dondo and the demon, which made it altogether worth the pain. The Lady spared me from the killing fever, after."

Umegat glanced after Daris. "Then you got off lightly."

"Miraculously so."

Umegat leaned a little forward across the table and gazed closely into his face. "Hm. Hm. You've been keeping high company, I see."

"Have you your second sight back?" asked Cazaril, startled.

"No. It's just a look a man gets, that one learns to recognize."

Indeed. Umegat had it, too. It seemed that if a man was god-touched, and yet not pushed altogether off-balance, it left him mysteriously centered thereafter. "You have seen your god, too." It was not a question.

"Once or twice," Umegat admitted.

"How long does it take to recover?"

"I'm not sure yet." Umegat rubbed his lips thoughtfully, studying Cazaril. "Tell me—if you can—what you saw . . . ?"

It was not just the learned theologian talking shop; Cazaril saw the flash of fathomless god-hunger in the Roknari's gray eyes. *Do I look like that, when I speak of Her? No wonder men look at me strangely.*

Cazaril told the tale, starting from his precipitate departure from Cardegoss riding to the royesse's ordering. Tea arrived, was consumed, and the cups refilled before he came to the end of it. Daris hunkered in the doorway, listening; Cazaril supposed he need not ask after the ex-groom's discretion. When he tried to describe his gathering-in by the Lady, he became tongue-tangled. Umegat hung on his halting words, lips parted.

"Poetry—poetry might do it," said Cazaril. "I need words that mean more than they mean, words not just with height and width, but depth and weight and, and other dimensions that I cannot even name."

"Hm," said Umegat. "I tried to recapture the god with music, for a time, after my first . . . experience. I had not the gift, alas."

Cazaril nodded. He asked diffidently, "Is there anything you— either of you—need, that I can command? Iselle has yesterday made me chancellor of Chalion, so I suppose I can command, well, rather a lot."

Umegat's brows flicked up; he favored Cazaril with a little congratulatory bow, from his seat. "That was well done of the young royina."

Cazaril grimaced. "I keep thinking about dead men's boots, actually."

Umegat's smile glimmered. "I understand. As for us, the Temple cares for its ex-saints reasonably well, and supplies us all that we can presently use. I like these rooms, this city, this spring air, my company. I hope the god will yet grant me an interesting task or two, before I'm done. Although, by preference, not with animals. Or royalty."

Cazaril made a motion of sympathy. "I suppose you knew poor Orico as well as almost anyone, except perhaps Sara."

"I saw him nearly every day for six years. He spoke to me most frankly, toward the end. I hope I was a consolation to him."

Cazaril hesitated. "For what it's worth, I came to the conclusion that he was something of a hero."

Umegat nodded briefly. "So did I. In a frustrating sort of way. He was a sacrifice, surely." He sighed. "Well, it is a particular sin to permit grief for what is gone to poison the praise for what blessings remain to us."

The tongueless man rose from his silent spot to take away the tea things.

"Thank you, Daris," said Umegat, and patted the hand that touched him briefly on the shoulder; Daris gathered up the cups and plates and padded off.

Cazaril stared curiously after him. "Have you known him long?"

"About twenty years."

"Then he was not just your assistant in the menagerie . . ." Cazaril lowered his voice. "Was he martyred back then?"

"No. Not yet."

"Oh."

Umegat smiled. "Don't look so glum, Lord Cazaril. We get better. That was yesterday. This is today. I shall ask his permission to tell you the tale of it sometime."

"I should be honored with his confidence."

"All is well, and if it's not, then at least each day brings us closer to our god."

"I had noticed that. I had a little trouble tracking time, the first few days after . . . after I saw the Lady. Time, and scale, both altered out of reckoning."

A light knock sounded upon the chamber door. Daris emerged from the other room and went to admit a white-smocked young dedicat who held a book in her hand.

"Ah." Umegat brightened. "It is my reader. Make your bow to the Lord Chancellor, Dedicat." He added in explanation, "They send a delinquent dedicat to read to me for an hour a day, as a light punishment for small infractions of the house rules. Have you decided what rule you mean to break tomorrow, girl?"

The dedicat grinned sheepishly. "I'm thinking, Learned Umegat."

"Well if you run out of ideas, I will harken back to my youth and see if I can't remember a few more."

The dedicat tipped the book toward Cazaril. "I thought I would be sent to read dull theology to the divine, but instead he wanted this book of tales."

Cazaril glanced over the volume, an Ibran import judging by the printer's mark, with interest.

"It's a fine conceit, " said Umegat. "The author follows a group of travelers to a pilgrimage shrine, and has each one tell his or her tale in turn. Very, ah, holy."

"Actually, my lord," the dedicat whispered, "some of them are very lewd."

"I see I must dust off Ordol's sermon on the lessons of the flesh. I have promised the dedicat time off from the Bastard's penances for her blushes. I fear she believes me." Umegat smiled.

"I, ah . . . should be very pleased to borrow that book, when you're finished with it," Cazaril said hopefully.

"I'll have it sent up to you, my lord."

Cazaril made his farewells. He recrossed the five-sided Temple Square and headed uphill, but turned aside before the Zangre came in sight and made his way to Provincar dy Baocia's town palace. The blocky old stone building resembled Jironal Palace, though much smaller, with no windows on its lower floor, and its next floor's casements protected by wrought-iron grilles. It had been reopened not only for its lord and lady but also the old Provincara and Lady Ista, who had arrived from Valenda. Full to bursting, its former sullen empty silence was turned to bustle. Cazaril stated his rank and business to a bowing porter, and was whisked inside without question or delay.

The porter led him to a high sunny chamber at the back of the house. Here he found Dowager Royina Ista sitting out on a little iron-railed balcony overlooking the small herb garden and stable mews. She dismissed her attendant woman and gestured Cazaril to the vacated chair, almost knee to knee with her. Ista's dun hair was neatly braided today, wreathing her head; both her face and her dress seemed somehow crisper, more clearly defined than Cazaril had ever seen them before.

"This is a pleasant place," Cazaril observed, easing himself down in the chair.

"Yes, I like this room. It is the one I had when I was a girl, when my father brought us up to the capital with him, which was not often. Best of all, I cannot see the Zangre from it." She gazed down into the domestic square of garden, embroidered with green, protected and contained.

"You came to the banquet there last night." He had only been able to exchange a few formal words with her in that company, Ista merely congratulating him on his chancellorship and his betrothal, and departing early "You looked very well, too, I must say. I could see Iselle was gratified."

She inclined her head. "I eat there to please her. I do not care to sleep there."

"I suppose the ghosts are still about. I cannot see them now, to my great relief."

"Nor I, with sight or second sight, but I feel them as a chill in the walls. Or perhaps it's just the memory of them that chills me." She rubbed her arms as if to warm them. "I abhor the Zangre."

"I understand the poor ghosts much better now than when they first terrified me," said Cazaril diffidently. "I thought their exile and erosion was a rejection by the gods, at first, a damnation, but now I know it for a mercy. When the souls are taken up, they remember themselves . . . the minds possess their lives all whole, all at once, as the gods do, with nearly the terrible clarity that matter remembers itself. For some . . . for some that heaven would be as unbearable as any hell, and so the gods release them to forgetfulness."

"Forgetfulness. That smudged oblivion seems a very heaven to me now. I pray to be such a ghost, I think."

I fear it is a mercy you shall be denied. Cazaril cleared his throat. "You know the curse is lifted off of Iselle and Bergon, and all, and banished out of Chalion?"

"Yes. Iselle has told me of it, to the limit of her understanding, but I knew it when it happened. My ladies were dressing me to go down to the Daughter's Day morning prayers. There was nothing to see, nothing to hear or feel, but it was as though a fog had lifted from my mind. I did not realize how closely it had cloaked me round, like a clammy mist on the skin of my soul, till it was lifted. I was sorry then, for I thought it meant you had died."

"Died indeed, but the Lady put me back into the world. Well, into my body. My friend Palli would have it that She put me back in upside down." His smile flickered.

Ista looked away. "The curse's lifting made my pain more clear, and yet more distant. It felt very strange."

He cleared his throat. "You were right, Lady Ista, about the prophecy. The three deaths. I was wrong with my marriage scheme, wrong and determined to be so, because I was afraid. Your way seemed too hard. And yet it came right despite myself, in the end, by the Lady's grace."

She nodded. "I would have done it myself, if I could have. *My* sacrifice was evidently not deemed acceptable." Bitterness tinged her voice.

"It was not a matter of—that's not the reason," protested Cazaril. "Well, it is but it isn't. It has to do with the shape of your soul, not its worthiness. You have to make a cup of yourself, to receive that pouring out. You are a sword. You were always a sword. Like your mother and your daughter, too—steel spines run in the women of your family. I realize now why I never saw saints, before. The world does not crash upon their wills like waves upon a rock, or part around them like the wake of a ship. Instead they are supple, and swim through the world as silently as fishes."

Her brows rose at him, though whether in agreement, disagreement, or some polite irony he was not sure.

"Where will you go now?" he asked her. "Now that you are better, that is."

She shrugged. "My mother grows frail. I suppose we shall reverse chairs, and I shall attend upon her in the castle of Valenda as she attended upon me. I should prefer to go somewhere that I have never been before. Not Valenda, not Cardegoss. Someplace with no memories."

He could not argue with this. He thought on Umegat, not exactly her spiritual superior, but so experienced in loss and woe as to have recovery down to nearly a routine. Ista had yet another twenty years to find her way to a balance like that. At about the age Ista was now, retrieving the broken body of his friend from whatever episode of horrors had shattered him, perhaps Umegat had railed and wailed as heart-rendingly as she had, or cursed the gods as coldly as her frozen silences. "I shall have to have you meet my friend Umegat," he told Ista. "He was the saint given to preserve Orico. Ex-saint, now, as you and I are, too. I think . . . I think you and he could have some interesting conversations."

She opened her hand, warily, neither encouraging this idea nor denying its possibility. Cazaril resolved to pursue their introduction, later.

Attempting to turn her thoughts to happier matters, he asked after Iselle's coronation, which Ista and the proud and eager Provincara had arrived in Cardegoss just in time to attend. He'd so far asked some four or five people to describe it to him, but he hadn't grown tired of the accounts yet. She grew animated for a little, her delight in her daughter's victory softening her face and illuminating her eyes. The fate of Teidez lay between them untouched, as if by mutual assent. This was not the day to press those tender wounds, lest they break and bleed anew; some later, stronger hour would be time enough to speak of the lost boy.

At length, he bowed his head and made to bid her good day. Ista, suddenly urgent, leaned forward to touch him, for the first time, upon his hand.

"Bless me, Cazaril, before you go."

He was taken aback. "Lady, I am no more saint now than you are, and surely not a god, to call down blessings at my will." And yet . . . he wasn't a royesse, either, but he had borne the proxy for one to Ibra, and made binding contract in her name. *Lady of Spring, if ever I served You, redeem Your debt to me now.* He licked his lips. "But I will try."

He leaned forward, and placed his hand on Ista's white brow. He did not know where the words came from, but they rose to his lips nonetheless.

"This is a true prophecy, as true as yours ever were. When the souls rise up in glory, yours shall not be shunned nor sundered, but shall be the prize of the gods' gardens. Even your darkness shall be treasured then, and all your pain made holy."

He sat back and shut his mouth abruptly, as a surge of terror ran through him. *Is it well, is it ill, am I a fool?*

Ista's eyes filled with tears that did not fall. Her hand, cupped upward upon her knee, grew still. She ducked her head in clumsy acceptance, as awkwardly as a child taking its first step. In a shaken voice she said, "You do that very well, Cazaril, for a man who claims to be an amateur."

He swallowed, nodded back, smiled, took his leave, and fled into the street. As he turned up the hill, his stride lengthened despite the slope. His ladies would be waiting.